4/18

P9-CQO-203

CLOSER THAN YOU KNOW

CLOSER THAN YOU KNOW

BRAD PARKS

THORNDIKE PRESS
A part of Gale, a Cengage Company

GALE
A Cengage Company

Farmington Hills, Mich • San Francisco • New York • Waterville, Maine
Meriden, Conn • Mason, Ohio • Chicago

LIBRARY OF CONGRESS CIP DATA ON FILE.
CATALOGUING IN PUBLICATION FOR THIS BOOK
IS AVAILABLE FROM THE LIBRARY OF CONGRESS.

ISBN-13: 978-1-4328-4427-1 (hardcover)

Published in 2018 by arrangement with Dutton, an imprint of Penguin Publishing Group, a division of Penguin Random Publishing Group, LLC

Printed in the United States of America
1 2 3 4 5 6 7 22 21 20 19 18

To Alice Martell — with thanks
for her talent, devotion, wisdom,
and unending kindness

ONE

He was dressed in his best suit, the one he usually reserved for funerals.

She wore pearls. It made her feel more maternal.

Arm in arm, they walked up a concrete path toward Shenandoah Valley Social Services, whose offices filled a cheerless metal-sided building. There was no landscaping, no ornamentation, no attempt to make the environs more inviting. As an agency of county government, Social Services had neither the budget nor the inclination for such gilding. Its clientele was not there by choice.

The man paused at the front door.

"Remember: We're perfect," he said to his wife.

"The perfect couple," she replied.

He pushed through the door, and they traveled down a stark cinderblock hallway toward the main waiting area. A sign read

NOTICE: NO WEAPONS.

The room they soon entered was ringed with blue imitation-leather chairs and stern warnings against food-stamp fraud. A smattering of people, all of them luckless enough to be born into multigenerational poverty, looked up and stared. Men in suits and women in pearls were not a common sight here.

Ignoring them, the man and woman crossed the room and announced themselves to a receptionist who was bunkered behind a thick chunk of clear plastic. This could be a tough business: The administering of benefits; the denying of requests; the dispensing of abused and neglected children, taking them from one family and bestowing them on another. There had been incidents.

After a minute or so, the man and woman were greeted by the family services specialist who had been assigned to them, a woman with a tight ponytail and square-framed glasses who received them warmly, by name, with hugs and smiles.

It was all so different from when they had first met her, about three months earlier, when it had been nothing but dry handshakes and justifiable suspicion. Families like this didn't just stumble into Shenandoah Valley Social Services and volunteer to become foster parents. Families like this — who had resources, connections, and that air that suggested they weren't accustomed to waiting for the things they wanted — either went with private adoption agencies or traveled abroad to acquire their babies: eastern Europe if they wanted a white one; Africa, Asia, or South America if they didn't care.

Seriously? the family services specialist wanted to ask them. *What are* you *doing here?*

But then she started talking with them, and they won her over. They told her about the failed efforts to get pregnant, then about the tests that revealed they would never be able to have children of their own.

They still wanted a family, though, and they had decided to adopt locally. Why go overseas when there were children in need, right here in their own community? They were just looking for a vessel to receive their love.

The family services specialist tried to explain to them there were no guarantees with this route. It might be months or years before a baby became available. Even then, they might foster the infant for a time and then have to turn it back over to its birth

9

mother. Adoption was always a last resort. Social Services' goal — to say nothing of Virginia statutes — prioritized reunifying children with their biological families.

The woman chewed her fingernails when she heard this. The man seemed undeterred.

After that initial interview had come the parent orientation meeting, then the training sessions. They had taken notes, asked questions, and generally acted like they were trying to graduate at the top of the class.

Their home study, in which every aspect of their residence was inspected, had been flawless, from the child safety locks all the way up to the smoke detectors.

And the nursery? Immaculate. A crib that exceeded every standard. Diapers squared in neat piles. The walls freshly covered in blue paint.

"Blue?" the family services specialist had asked. "What if it's a girl?"

"I have a hunch," the man said.

They flew through the criminal background check. Their paystubs showed ample income. Their bank statements swelled with reserve funds.

Home insurance, check. Car insurance, check. Life insurance, check. Their physician had verified that both the would-be mother and father were in excellent health.

Their references gushed with praise.

In her thirteen years on the job, the family services specialist had interacted with hundreds of families. Even the best, most loving, most well meaning among them had issues.

This one didn't. She had never met two people more ready for a child.

They were the perfect couple.

Shenandoah Valley Social Services did not officially rank potential foster families, but was there any question about who would be number one on the list if a baby became available?

Even now here they were, turned out like they were attending an important public ceremony when really they were just going back to a shabby, windowless office to accept a piece of paper. It was their certificate, indicating they had completed the necessary steps to become approved foster-care providers.

They beamed as they received it. They were official.

More hugs. More smiles. The receptionist came out of the bunker to take pictures. It was that kind of occasion for this couple.

Then they departed.

"What if we did this all for nothing?" the

11

woman asked as she walked out of the building.

"We didn't," the man assured her.

"You really think it's going to happen?"

He leaned in close.

"Don't worry," he said. "We'll have a baby in no time."

TWO

If you are a working mother, as I am, you know this truth to be self-evident: Good childcare — safe, affordable, and reliable — is rarer than flawless diamonds and at least twice as valuable. It is the connective tissue, the breath in your lungs, the essential vitamin that makes all other movement possible.

The flip side is that losing your childcare, especially when you have an infant, is basically incapacitating.

That was the catastrophe I was trying to avert on a Tuesday evening in early March as I sped toward Ida Ferncliff's house with one eye on the road and the other on the clock, which was ticking ominously close to six p.m.

Mrs. Ferncliff had been watching our now three-month-old son, Alex, since he went into childcare at six weeks. With children and babies, she was as magical as Harry

13

Potter — patient and kind, caring and calm, unflappable in all situations.

With adults, she was more like Voldemort. My husband, Ben, referred to her as Der Kaiser, after Kaiser Wilhelm. And not just because of her mustache. She had her rules, which she followed with Teutonic precision, and she expected everyone else to as well.

One of them was that children should be picked up by five thirty, no later. She had a fifteen-minute grace period, though Mrs. Ferncliff's idea of grace was pursed lips and a nasty glare. After five forty-five, she fined you $20, plus a dollar for every minute thereafter.

Picking up after six was cause for termination. That was in the contract that I, Melanie A. Barrick, and my husband, Benjamin J. Barrick, had signed. And Mrs. Ferncliff had made it clear she would not hesitate to exercise the after-six clause the last three times my shift replacement, the contemptible Warren Plotz, had ambled in more than a half hour late, sending me on mad dashes against the clock that had me arriving at 5:52, 5:47, and 5:58, respectively.

My complaints about Warren's tardiness had gone exactly nowhere. Apparently, being the owner's son entitled him to act like a human rug burn. I might have simply

14

walked out, whether he showed up or not, except the first rule at Diamond Trucking was that the dispatch desk — the lifeline to forty-six rigs crisscrossing the country, carrying time-sensitive fresh produce — had to be staffed 24/7.

And I simply couldn't afford to lose this job. It paid $18 an hour and didn't make me contribute a dime for a no-deductible healthcare plan, a perk that was worth its weight in free well-baby checkups now that we had Alex.

Admittedly, being a trucking-company dispatcher at age thirty-one wasn't the career I anticipated having when I graduated from the University of Virginia with a summa cum laude seal on my diploma and plans to do meaningful work for a socially responsible organization.

But those high-minded goals had collided rather abruptly with the realities of my graduation year, 2009, which has the distinction of being the absolute worst moment in the history of modern America to have entered the job market. I compounded my horrific sense of timing with a degree in English Literature, which meant I was articulate, urbane, and virtually unhirable.

It took five years and a thousand failed cover letters — five years of either unemployment or slinging lattes at Starbucks — before I finally landed this gig. And I wasn't going to give it up, even if it meant Warren Plotz's chronic tardiness gave me angina every other week.

It was 5:54 as I neared the light for Statler Boulevard, which forms a semicircle around the eastern side of Staunton, a quaint city of about 25,000 in Virginia's Shenandoah valley. Most of the time I enjoyed Staunton's slower pace, except when it came in the form of people who were leaving six car lengths between them and the next vehicle, forcing me to dance between lanes to get around them.

I knew, from hard experience, that it was exactly six minutes to Mrs. Ferncliff's house from Statler. As long as I made it through that light with the clock still at 5:54, I would be fine. Barely.

Then, when I was still about a hundred yards away, the light went yellow. The wait for the signal at Statler was, for reasons known only to the light-timing gods, notoriously long. If I stopped, there was no way I'd make it in time. Mrs. Ferncliff would fire us, and we'd be stuck trying to find new childcare.

That, I already knew, was hopeless. Ben was a grad student who was given only a small stipend — and growing up poor and black in Alabama hadn't exactly endowed him with family money — so we couldn't afford any of the fancy day care centers that promised all children would master quantum theory by age three. That left us with in-home settings, most of which seemed to be run by chainsmokers, inattentive great-grandmothers, or people who thought there was nothing wrong with a baby inhaling the occasional lead paint chip.

I stomped down on the accelerator. The light turned red a few nanoseconds before I crossed over the solid white line.

No matter. I was through. I breathed out heavily.

Then I saw the blue lights of a Staunton City police car flashing in my rearview mirror.

One traffic ticket and twenty-three minutes later, I was in a frenzy as I pulled into Mrs. Ferncliff's short driveway. I grabbed the ticket in the hopes I could use it to convince Der Kaiser to show me some leniency, then hurried up her front steps and grasped the handle of the front door.

It was locked.

Which was strange. Ordinarily, Mrs. Ferncliff left her door open. She didn't like to leave children unattended to answer it.

I pressed the doorbell button and waited. Fifteen seconds. Thirty seconds. I pressed the button again.

"Mrs. Ferncliff, it's Melanie Barrick," I said in a loud voice, knowing she was somewhere inside, peeved at me. "I'm sorry I'm late. I got held up at work again and then on the way here I was in such a hurry I got pulled over. And . . . I would have called, but I can't find my phone."

Pathetic. I sounded utterly pathetic. I couldn't say I was the worst parent in history — my own parents, who gave me up for adoption when I was nine, cemented their claim on that title long ago — but I had to be close.

"I'm sorry, okay?" I continued. "I'm so, so sorry. Could you please open the door?"

There was still no answer. Maybe she was just gathering Alex's things, which she would shove through the door, along with the baby.

And our contract, with the six o'clock termination clause highlighted.

After another minute of standing on that front porch — had that cost me another dollar? — I was starting to get a little angry. How long was the silent treatment going to last? I pounded on the door with the butt of

18

my hand.

"Mrs. Ferncliff, *please,*" I said. "I'm sorry I'm late. Very late. I'm sorry I'm a terrible mother. I'm sorry for everything."

Still no response.

Finally, Mrs. Ferncliff's stern voice came through the door: "Go away. Go away or I'm calling the police."

"Okay, fine. Just let me have Alex and I'll be on my way."

And then Mrs. Ferncliff said something that shot a few gigawatts of electricity to my gut.

"Alex is gone."

I took a sharp, involuntary breath. "What?"

"Social Services has him."

The charge was now spiking from my toes to my brain. I knew Mrs. Ferncliff was strict, but this was pathological.

"You turned him over to Social Services because I was twenty minutes late?" I howled.

"I didn't do anything of the sort. They came and took him a few hours ago."

"What? Why? What the —"

"You can ask Social Services. Now go away. I don't want you on my property."

"Mrs. Ferncliff, why did Social Services take Alex? I have no idea what's going on."

19

"Good," she spat. "They told me all about you. I hope they get that child as far away from you as possible."

"*What* are you *talking* about?"

"I'm calling 911 now."

"Would you please just have a . . . a rational conversation with me?"

No answer.

"Please, Mrs. Ferncliff, *please.*"

But she had stopped answering. I could hear her on the other side of the door — because she wanted to be heard — loudly telling the Staunton Police she had an intruder banging on her door and was very afraid for her safety.

Feeling like I had no choice, and knowing the ever-unyielding Mrs. Ferncliff was unlikely to change her mind, I departed from her porch and returned to my car.

As I sat in the driver's seat, I knew I had to find Alex, but I was too dazed to order my thoughts as to how I'd do it.

They told me all about you. I hope they get that child as far away from you as possible.

What did that even mean? Alex wasn't malnourished. He didn't have bruises. He wasn't abused in any way.

The only thing I could think was that someone had called Social Services on me. When you grow up in foster care, as I did, you learn there is a certain type of person — a mean, nasty, vindictive subspecies of subhuman — who will use Social Services as a weapon, calling in anonymous tips out of spite against neighbors, coworkers, or anyone they truly hate.

I didn't think I had anyone like that in my life. Warren Plotz was too busy oversleeping for that kind of treachery. I didn't have a feud with any of my neighbors. I didn't have enemies.

At least not that I knew of.

I made myself back down the driveway and pull out on the street, just so Mrs. Ferncliff couldn't sic a police officer on me.

As I did so, a panic lashed into me.

Alex is gone.

Social Services has him.

For as much as I tried to tell myself this was a misunderstanding, I knew better. Social Services didn't just swoop in and tear someone's baby away because a childcare provider was angry about tardiness. It did so only when it had a reason, or at least when it thought it had a reason.

And it didn't turn the baby back over without a reason either.

That's one of the things I learned during my time as a ward of the state. But the bigger lesson of my childhood — one that was now bouncing back at me like some ancient echo — was something one of my foster sisters once told me. I had been fuming about being ripped away from a solid, comfortable placement so I could be sent, for no apparent reason, to a group home.

"This is a disaster," I moaned.

"Honey, this is the foster care system," she replied. "Disaster is always closer than you know."

THREE

As I drove away, a thin sweat had broken out on my body. I was relying on muscle memory to steer the car. I had no sensation of being in control of my own limbs.

I turned on the avenue outside Mrs. Ferncliff's street. The double yellow line appeared blurred, either by perspiration or tears. I wanted to call Ben. Desperately. But in addition to his research and the two classes where he worked as a teaching assistant, he also had a part-time job tutoring in the Learning Skills Center at James Madison University. He never picked up when he was with his students.

There was also the matter of my missing phone. No amount of rooting around in the usual spots — the table by the front door, the diaper bag, the couch cushions, and so on — had unearthed it.

The only other person I could bother at a time like this was Marcus Peterson. He had been my manager at Starbucks and was now just a dear friend, the kind of guy who would drop everything to help me. The only problem was, his contact info was stored in my phone. Really, who knew their friends' phone numbers off the top of their head anymore?

There was no one else. The rest of my friends were either too far away or I wasn't in touch with them on a regular basis. As for our parents, Ben's lived in Alabama, and mine were nonexistent. That's one of the harsh facts of growing up in foster care: When things go sideways, you don't have a family you can rely on to keep you upright.

With no real plan, I drove toward Social Services, desperately hoping Alex was still there, or that someone working late might know his whereabouts.

The nearest office was just up the road in Verona, at the government center complex. Shenandoah Valley Social Services was one of two agencies I had come to know during my youth. It was, as Social Services offices tended to be, an austere box of a building with no windows, sort of like a warehouse. Which fit. There are a lot of times when, as a child being shuttled around between placements, you really do feel like you're being warehoused.

At quarter to seven o'clock on a Tuesday night, the parking lot had just one vehicle in it, a small Chevy. Maybe its driver would still be inside and could tell me something.

The employee entrance was on the left side of the building. There was a small light, housed in a protective cage, above the door. It had no buzzer or intercom.

Not knowing what else to do, I pounded on the door with the side of my fist.

At first, this didn't accomplish much more than giving me a sore hand. I am five foot five and a twiggy 120 pounds, hardly a threat to a solid steel door. Still, I was giving it all I had, turning that boxy building into one big bass drum. That Chevy driver had to hear me.

I thumped the door in a steady rhythm: four hits, a rest, then four more hits.

Boom, boom, boom, boom. Wait. *Boom, boom, boom, boom.* Wait.

Finally: "Can I help you?"

It was a woman, just on the other side of the door.

"Yes, thank you, *thank you,*" I said, aware I sounded overwrought. "Someone from Social Services came and took my son out of day care today and . . . I just . . . I wanted to talk to someone and straighten this whole thing out."

I was trying to present myself as something other than a woman who was rapidly becoming unhinged.

There was a pause.

"No one called you or visited you?" she said.

She asked like this was unusual. Against protocol, even. And it *was* unusual, wasn't it? You couldn't just rip a child away from his mother without any kind of notice.

"No. No one did," I said, relieved, because even the question made me feel like this woman might be reasonable, or at least willing to talk with me.

"Okay, hang on. What's your name?"

"Melanie Barrick. My son's name is Alex. They took him from Ida Ferncliff's house on Churchville Avenue and I don't . . . I don't even know why."

"Okay. Let me make a call. I'll be right back."

"Thank you," I said. "Thank you so much."

I stood there, staring at the door. The temperature was probably in the low forties and I hadn't bothered grabbing my jacket before I left work. It didn't matter. My heart was working so hard, I couldn't feel the cold.

My hope was that, right now, they were

examining Alex, with his chubby knees, his ready smile, and his ever-alert blue-gray eyes. They were realizing he could not possibly have been abused.

They had probably tried to call me, but we don't have a landline; and my phone, missing and probably dead from lack of battery, had gone straight to voicemail.

Right now, this was all being straightened out. It would take a little time, yes — everything with Social Services took time — but Alex would be back home with us for the evening. He would sleep in his own crib, wake up for his middle-of-the-night feeding, the whole thing. Our normal routine.

From the other side of the door, I heard a tentative "Hello?"

"Yes. Hi. I'm here," I said, leaning toward the door like that was getting me closer to Alex.

"I spoke to my supervisor about your case. She says you'll have to come back in the morning."

Something in my head exploded.

"What?!" I said. And not because I hadn't heard her.

"I'm sorry, that's what she told me. She said they would be able to tell you about the procedure from there."

The *procedure*? We were now part of a procedure?

"But where is he?" I asked.

"I'm sorry, I can't tell you that."

"No, wait," I said desperately. "You can't just take my son and then not tell me *anything*. I'm . . . I'm his mother. I have rights. This is . . . this is crazy. Can't you at least open the door and talk to me?"

"I'm sorry, ma'am," she said, now more firm. "You'll have to come back in the morning."

"No, *no!*" I screamed. "This isn't right. You've made a mistake, a huge mistake. I know someone has made a complaint or something, but they're lying. They're lying to you. People do that, you know. They use you guys to get back at people. You have to know that."

I was no longer worried that I sounded like a lunatic.

"Come back in the morning, ma'am," the woman said. "I have to go now."

"Can I please talk to your supervisor myself? This is . . . I'm not a bad mother. I would never hurt my baby. Just look at him. He's fine. Can't you see that? Please!"

There was no answer. I pounded the door again.

"Please!" I said. "Please help me."

For the next five or ten minutes, I reiterated this plea and other versions of it, getting increasingly hysterical.

I knew too much about the child welfare system, having experienced its shortcomings firsthand. I had seen how its best intentions could be twisted by the intransigence and senselessness of what was basically a broken bureaucracy. I had met too many shifty adults who took advantage of the lack of oversight, whether it was the chronically lazy caseworker doing as little work as possible to keep her job, or the foster family who saw only dollar signs when it took in a new child.

And yes, they were the minority. But even the good people were being thrust into this thing that was too big, too clumsy, and too overstressed by having to deal with society's collective dysfunction. It was almost inevitable something that unwieldy would create as many problems as it solved.

People who were enmeshed in that world called it, simply, "the system." And it was really the perfect term for something so cold, complex, and ultimately impersonal. Once you were in it, you lost some part of your humanity. Your family became a file to be passed around from one harried, underpaid, overworked civil servant to another.

I had come too far from my own splintered childhood and worked too hard to be free of that madness to get caught up in it again.

This wasn't happening, couldn't be happening.

Not to Alex.

Because I knew how it worked from here. Once you were in the system, there was no easy way out. Its collective machinery acted like a giant steel maw, trapping you between its sharpened incisors, tearing another chunk out of you every time you jerked or squirmed.

No matter what the law said, every parent who got reported to Social Services was guilty until proven innocent. The caseworkers either came in thinking that way or they learned it in a hurry. I saw how it had been for my own parents. Every time someone from Social Services dealt with me, it would be with the quiet assumption I was basically scum.

They would pretend to seek my input. They would talk with me about partnering and collaborating. All the while, they would be calling the shots, dealing cards off a deck that was far too short.

Already, someone had made a decision about where Alex would spend the night. Someone else — some stranger, some foster parent or group-home administrator I had never met, someone who couldn't possibly care about my child as much as I did — was now holding Alex.

Or not. Maybe he was lying in a crib, screaming from hunger. Or stewing in a dirty diaper. Or worse.

And I could cry about it, or rage against the heavens, or throw myself to the ground in agony, and it wouldn't matter. I sagged against the door, bawling, then slumped down to the cold concrete beneath my feet.

The woman was gone.

And so was Alex.

FOUR

Everyone has a vice.

For some people, it was cigarettes. Or booze. Or porn.

For Amy Kaye, it was less destructive but also somehow more embarrassing.

Dancing with the Stars. The reality television show — which paired eye-candy celebrities with hard-bodied professional dancers in competitions of exhilarating meaninglessness — was her drug, her comfort food, her obsession. Well, one of her obsessions, anyway.

No one down at the Augusta County Courthouse would have guessed that the chief deputy commonwealth's attorney, whose knowledge of the law even intimidated some of the judges, loved to spend her evenings curled up on the couch under a blanket watching this drivel; or that she sometimes wept when people lost (and always when they won); or that her dog,

Butch, who was supposedly not allowed on the couch, could be reliably found tucked under the blanket with her.

Amy just didn't give up those kinds of details — or, really, any personal details — about herself. She had seen too many times when people used those kinds of things against a prosecutor.

The image she worked hard to present was all about competence and efficiency. She kept her dark hair short. She didn't wear makeup. She dressed conservatively. No one knew her exact age (forty-two), if she was married (she was, to a man), or if she had children (she didn't, and didn't particularly miss them). The most they knew about her was that she played a mean third base for the Sheriff's Office's team in the local co-ed softball rec league.

This, naturally, led to rumors she was a lesbian. She didn't care.

What happened at the courthouse wasn't supposed to be about personalities. It was about the law. And within the law, the individual who represented the People of the Commonwealth had a certain role to play. It was more than a job. It was a sworn duty. And she intended to execute it to her utmost ability.

At least until *Dancing with the Stars* came

on. Then the law could wait.

The newest season featured an Olympian who had been semi-tarnished by a tabloid scandal that had boosted his Q-rating higher than any gold medal ever could have. He was the de facto bad boy. Amy was rooting for him, mostly because he was constantly taking off his shirt. His abs were sensational.

He was now in the semifinals, and she was all set to cheer him to greater glory, with Butch at her side and a bowl of popcorn in her lap.

Then, just as the title sequence began, her phone rang.

She frowned at it, sitting on the coffee table in front of her. The caller ID showed the name Aaron Dansby.

Dansby was the duly elected commonwealth's attorney for Augusta County, which technically made him Amy's boss — even if the reality was more complicated. To be sure, Dansby had graduated law school and passed the bar exam, but he was an attorney only in the titular sense.

In every other way, he was a politician, from his carefully styled hair to his plastic grin, from his model-gorgeous wife — she was a former Estée Lauder saleswoman — to his distinguished pedigree. His father had been commonwealth's attorney, then state

34

senator, then gone back to being commonwealth's attorney until Aaron was old enough to take the job. His grandfather had been a congressman. His great-grandfather had been governor.

Aaron Dansby's sights were said to be set at least that high. Only thirty-three, he had been identified by party elders as having a great future. He was just marking time as commonwealth's attorney. The practice of law was little more than a means to an end.

The phone rang again.

She was tempted to ignore it. Part of the recruiting pitch that lured her down to Augusta County from Fairfax County, where she had been a lower-level deputy in a large office, was that Dansby was a newbie prosecutor who would need time to knock off his training wheels; and that, in the meantime, she would get a lot of say-so as second-in-command in a small office.

Three years later, she was still running the place on a day-to-day basis. Dansby was almost entirely indifferent to routine matters. Only the high-profile cases interested him. In those, he sat first chair — so he could get credit for the victory with the media, which heedlessly burnished his boy-wonder legend. Amy, sitting second chair, still did all the work.

Another ring.

The only issue with ignoring a call from Dansby is that he only phoned when a case had the potential to be a big one.

The title sequence was ending. The show was about to begin. The DVR was recording it — some dances just *had* to be enjoyed a second or third time — but she liked to watch live.

One more ring and Aaron Dansby would slip into the sweet vacuum of voicemail, which is exactly where he belonged. Except Amy had that sense of duty. And the knowledge that if she didn't answer, Aaron Dansby might make a mess she'd just have to clean up.

In one quick motion, she jabbed the Pause button on the DVR, then tapped her phone.

"Amy Kaye."

"Amy, it's Aaron."

"What's up?"

"Are you busy?" he asked.

"A little, actually."

"This will just take a second," he said, because he was congenitally incapable of taking a hint. "I wanted to give you a heads-up there was a big coke bust this afternoon out on Desper Hollow Road."

"Okay."

"Big, as in half a kilo."

"Wow," Amy said, sitting up a little. In Fairfax County, which had DC right next door, five hundred grams of cocaine wouldn't get as much notice. Here, in the sleepy Shenandoah valley, it was a startling number.

"I know. I already leaked it to *The News Leader.* They're putting it on the front page tomorrow. I'm going to leak it to TV next so they can get it on at eleven. Sheriff said he'll lay out the bags for me. It'll make for great visuals."

Dansby still didn't understand that it wasn't considered a leak when the media outlet was either quoting you by name or putting you on camera.

He also didn't realize that by diving in front of the cameras — consistently upstaging Sheriff Jason Powers and his deputies — Dansby was sowing discontent in the ranks that would be harvested someday. Amy had close working relationships with several of the deputies. They were all waiting for the day when the guy they derisively referred to as "Dapper Dansby" got his.

"That's not even the best part," Dansby continued, and Amy cringed, because there was no "best part" about a criminal conspiracy to distribute narcotics. "The woman who had all this stuff, she's a mom. The guys at *The News Leader* are already calling her 'Coke Mom.' I think this thing is going to have some legs. It's got viral potential on social media. And TV will love it."

"I'm sure," Amy said, eyeing her own TV, wondering what she had already missed. "But after you get your face time, don't you think we should give this thing to the feds? That's a lot of coke."

There was no specific amount of drugs that automatically made a case federal. It was up to the local commonwealth's attorney. But half a kilo was usually more than enough. Larger amounts of product indicated larger distribution networks, which almost always crossed state lines.

"I know," Dansby said. "But I want to keep this one. I think this is going to end up grabbing a lot of eyeballs, and I want us to get points for it."

Dansby was constantly referencing "points," as if the electorate kept a giant scoreboard somewhere. It made Amy want to hit him with a frying pan.

"Plus," he added, "she's white."

Amy felt her eyes bulge. "What does that matter?"

"Well, after Mookie Myers, you know."

Demetrius "Mookie" Myers was the biggest bust of Dansby's three-plus-year tenure, the largest cocaine dealer the Shenandoah valley had seen since the bad old days of the late '80s. The case was now in the early stages of the appeals process, but it had been a solid win for the prosecution and had clearly enhanced young Dansby's reputation.

"No, I don't know," Amy said.

"There's talk in the black community we only go hard after the black dealers," Dansby said. "I want to make an example out of this woman, show everyone we're equal-opportunity hard-asses. Grand jury meets on Friday, right? What do you think of going for direct indictment?"

Direct indictment was a kind of prosecutorial shortcut. If a suspect was arrested on a normal warrant, the case first went to General District Court for arraignment, counsel determination, and a bond hearing. Two months later, it got a preliminary hearing, where a judge certified it to a grand jury, which then handed down an indictment.

Direct indictment skipped all those steps. Often used in drug cases, it took the matter straight to the grand jury. The clerk of court then issued a capias, which resulted in the defendant's arrest.

The only risk was that until the grand jury

met, the defendant was not in custody. For that reason, Amy preferred to use direct indictment only when suspects didn't yet know the law was onto them — not after a search warrant had already been executed.

"You're sure you want to give this woman two days to take off?" Amy asked. "I've got to think anyone with that much cocaine lying around has enough cash stashed away to disappear for as long as she needs to."

"She's not going anywhere," Dansby said with his usual breezy certainty. "She's got a kid. Social Services grabbed him already. She'll stick around as long as we've got the kid."

"I hope you're right."

"Don't worry. We got this. Anyhow, I told Powers you were going to start working on this in the morning. If we're going to put this before grand jury on Friday, we've got to get cracking."

Amy felt her spine straighten. "I can't. I've got that interview with Daphne Hasper tomorrow morning."

"Daphne Hasper?"

"I sent you a memo about her," she said. "She's one of the whisper victims."

This was Amy's other obsession, the one that actually mattered: a series of unsolved sexual assaults in the valley over nearly two decades. The link between them was that the perpetrator only ever whispered at his victims. There were at least eight cases but perhaps as many as twenty-five or more. No one really knew because no one, besides Amy, had ever dug into the case that hard.

Dansby usually reacted to Amy's mentions of the case with anything from apathy to antipathy, depending on his mood. This time it was the former.

"Oh, that," Dansby said. "That can wait."

"No, it can't. Not until we get that bastard in prison."

"This is more important right now."

"You getting a quick scalp for the TV news and some more of those mythical 'points' that only you seem to be counting is more important than incarcerating a man who breaks into women's houses at night and rapes them?"

"Don't be overdramatic."

"Don't be an asshole."

He paused. He preferred conversations that stayed on script and speeches he could read off a teleprompter.

The force of Amy's words had caused Butch to lift his head, which was now tilted.

"I think," Dansby said in a measured tone, "Coke Mom is more of a priority."

"I'm glad you think so, but I'm not going

to cancel this interview."

"Except when you say 'interview,' you really mean 'reinterview,' yes? This is a woman who has already talked to the cops."

"When the incident happened, yes. But they didn't know about the other cases then. And no one has talked to her in years."

"If it's been years, then you can put it off a few days."

"No, I can't. This woman moved out of town a long time ago. She's only back for a few days visiting family. I have to get her while I can. You have no idea how hard it was to track her down and then convince her to meet with me."

"I'm sure you can put her on the shelf for a little while."

"For the twelfth time: I can't," Amy said. "And I won't."

"I told Jason you would be talking to one of his deputies in the morning."

"Great. Jason's deputy will still be available to me in the afternoon. This woman might not be. I'm not postponing the interview."

Amy was nearly yelling into the phone. Butch, who was a notorious conflict avoider, looked at her nervously.

Dansby finally started fighting back. "You know you work at the pleasure of the commonwealth's attorney, right? I could fire you anytime I wanted. I'm . . . I'm ordering you to work on Coke Mom tomorrow morning."

"You're *ordering* me, Aaron? Oh, that's rich. That's really rich. Let me ask you something: When's the last time you prosecuted a DUI?"

There was silence on the other end of the line.

"Oh, that's right! Never," Amy said. "So how about this: We've got a bumper crop of drunks scheduled for General District Court on Thursday. Three or four, as I recall. How about I let you prosecute them instead of doing your job for you? Because I think at least two of the defendants have private attorneys and you can be sure the moment they see you, they won't even think about pleading it out. They'll smell blood, and they will pick apart every morsel of evidence you try to put forward, if you even know how to present it properly. You'll lose your Breathalyzer test so fast it'll make your head spin. Would that pleasure you, Mr. Commonwealth's Attorney?"

"Stop . . . stop being —"

"Oh just wait, I haven't even told you what you might call 'the best part.' I'll make sure to tip off *The News Leader* — or, sorry, 'leak' it to *The News Leader* — so they know to have a reporter there. They usually get those things online pretty fast. By Thursday afternoon, everyone will know Aaron Dansby lets drunks walk free. How does that sound?"

"You wouldn't dare."

"I would. And I will. Try me."

Amy could practically hear Dansby's butt smacking the wall she had backed him up against.

"You'll call Jason tomorrow morning. If his deputy can't meet with you until tomorrow afternoon, well, whatever," he said, trying to save face. "And you better damn well be ready on Friday. This thing has to be airtight."

"Fine," she said.

Then she hung up.

Butch was still staring at her.

"I know, I know, I shouldn't let him get me that upset," she said. "But he's a jerk."

Butch licked his nose.

"I should really stop propping him up the way I do," she said.

Except they both knew she never would. She placed the sanctity of the law far above whatever satisfaction she would get from watching a show pony like Dansby get mud on his ribbons.

Butch put his head back down. He wanted to get back to snuggling. Amy glanced toward the television, where the title sequence was still frozen, beckoning her to cast off her worldly burdens.

"Sorry, boy," she said. "I'm just not feeling it."

She rose from the couch, eliciting a groan from Butch, and walked into her home office, where several drawers of a filing cabinet were now packed tight with material from this case.

It had started with an offhand comment from a young sheriff's deputy a few months after Amy had arrived in Augusta County. There had been a sexual assault in Weyers Cave. A young woman had been attacked by a masked, knife-wielding assailant. His entire monologue — which included a lot of "please," "thank you," and "I'm sorry" — had come out in a whisper.

"Huh, that's weird," the deputy had said. "There was another guy in Stuarts Draft a few months ago who whispered at a girl. You think it's the same guy?"

Amy checked on the Stuarts Draft case but hadn't been sure there was a connection. The assailant was described as being both older and larger.

Nevertheless, Amy filed it away. When a

45

whispering rapist struck again a few months later, she started asking around. One of the older detectives told her he could remember three or four such cases. When she asked why he had never looked into a connection between the cases, all he could say was, "Don't most rapists whisper?"

So Amy dove in. It was her good fortune that Jason Powers had been sheriff for seven years and that his father, Allen, had been sheriff for twenty-four years before that. The records were all there. So was the evidence.

Amy went through every unsolved sexual-assault case she could find, battling dust mites and brushing away cobwebs during long hours in the file room. She worked at night, when her husband, who was a chef at one of Staunton's many restaurants, was gone anyway. It was a long process. But slowly, methodically, she unearthed evidence of a serial rapist on the loose.

The first case she found involving a man who whispered to his victim was in 1987, but she dismissed that as an outlier, unconnected to the current-day cases. There was also one in 1997. She wasn't sure about that one. He was described as talking in a "low voice," which may or may not have been the same as a whisper.

There was nothing the next five years, but

then there were three hits during a nine-month span at the end of 2002 and early 2003. Then nothing until 2005. Then there was one in 2007 and another in 2008. Just when it seemed the man was picking up steam again, there was nothing until 2010.

Then he began to strike with more frequency. The cases were separated by a measure of months, not years. She had come up with twenty cases over the previous seven years, plus the seven that came before 2010, not counting the 1987 outlier. They fit roughly the same pattern.

A masked, glove-wearing white male who was described as being somewhere between five foot nine and six foot two and anywhere between his late teens and his mid-forties — the age had crept up through the years, but it still varied widely — had broken into the home of a woman who lived alone. His assaults mostly took place in the early morning. He threatened her with a knife or gun until she acquiesced to undress and let him penetrate her. Yet he was also unfailingly polite, speaking to his victims in a voice that was later described as a hush, a murmur, or a whisper; and he never actually used either weapon.

To the profilers, this made him a classic case. He was a power-reassurance rapist, sometimes known as the gentleman rapist, who operated under the delusion that these encounters were somehow romantic. For him, stalking a victim was a twisted kind of courtship, the beginnings of what he saw as a relationship. If the victim resisted or found a way to shatter that romantic spell — by vomiting, peeing on him, or screaming — the power-reassurance rapist often broke off the attack.

Some power-reassurance rapists were actually caught because they couldn't resist contacting their victim later. After all, in the bizarre worldview of the power-reassurance rapist, she was like a girlfriend.

This one was too cagey for that.

Amy had, so far, uncovered eight cases where the DNA matched one another. That had been a long, hard slog. Forget the television crime dramas, where DNA test results were as readily available — and as quickly produced — as items on the Mc-Donald's Dollar Menu. In the real world, DNA tests took time. The state lab in Roanoke, where Amy sent evidence, usually returned results in five or six months.

Many of the earlier cases did not have DNA associated with them, because DNA tests were even less readily available back then. Amy was slowly trying to correct that.

There were also cases where no DNA had been recovered. The rapist never used a condom but frequently ejaculated on — not inside of — his victims. He was then careful about cleaning up, often taking their bed-sheets and clothing with him. Other times, the victim had been unable to resist the urge to take a shower after the assault, or had waited a day or more to report the crime, at which point the physical evidence was gone.

The other chief obstacle was that if the DNA didn't match someone already in the system, there was no mechanism in place that automatically compared the DNA in otherwise disconnected unsolved cases. It had to be done by hand, case by case. That's how the perpetrator had been able to go undetected for so long.

Based on the scattered pattern of the as-saults, Amy's theory was that the assailant only occasionally visited Augusta County at first, then decided to move there. Perhaps he was a traveling salesman. Or a construc-tion worker. Or a long-haul trucker.

After she had gotten her third DNA match, Amy had presented the case to Dansby, saying they should take it to the media. If there was a rapist on the loose, the citizens of Augusta County had a right to know about it. Besides, the publicity could help them crack the case — someone might come forward with information or a better description of the assailant.

Dansby had calmly listened to Amy talk, until he finally realized she not only couldn't definitively ID the perp, she didn't even have a suspect. At that point, he had a toddler-like meltdown.

"Are you *trying* to ruin my career?" he asked. "We can't leak it to the media unless we already have the guy."

To Dansby, it was the sort of thing that reflected poorly on law enforcement generally, and him specifically: a major menace to public safety at large, mocking the authorities' inability to apprehend him.

This resulted in a huge fight, and eventually a compromise. Amy could keep working on the case as long as it didn't interfere with her other responsibilities, she kept it away from the press, and she didn't tell any of the victims that they were possibly part of something much larger. As far as the public was concerned, there was no serial rapist terrorizing the Shenandoah valley.

Amy hated the thought that, because of this, there were doors being left unlocked, or women leaving themselves unwittingly vulnerable to attack, or evidence going uncollected because she couldn't appeal to citizenry for help. All because of Aaron Dansby's political ambitions.

It was the sort of thing that could make even the most hardened addict forget about *Dancing with the Stars.*

FIVE

As I sat on the ground outside Shenandoah Valley Social Services, my mind was a forest thicket of thoughts, all of them from my tangled past.

My first contact with the system came when I was two years old. My father, in one of his drunken rages, had grabbed me by the arm and thrown me across the room, giving me a greenstick fracture.

I don't actually remember it. A caseworker told me about it, years later. It helped me understand why my arm sometimes hurt when it rained.

My mother once told me my father wasn't always a violent man, that being a father had "brought it out of him." They had met in the navy, when they were both stationed in Norfolk. She described her first interactions with Chief Warrant Officer William Theodore Curran — Billy to his friends — in fairy tale–like terms. They were Billy and

Betsy. They both came from small towns in Pennsylvania. He was tall and broad-shouldered, romantic and charming, and so on.

That seems to be at least somewhat at odds with his dishonorable discharge from the navy, which he earned via a series of infractions committed while drunk or hung-over. My mother was already struggling to balance working for the navy with raising my half sister, Charlotte, who came from a brief-and-failed marriage to another sea-man. When her enlistment was up, Dad packaged her departure from the navy with a marriage proposal. She eagerly said yes.

The new Mr. and Mrs. Curran moved to Northumberland County, which was tucked away in a rural part of Virginia known as the Northern Neck. They liked having a small house in the middle of the woods, without any neighbors nearby.

Maybe Dad liked that part more than Mom.

Dad became a commercial fisherman, and the pattern of their life was pretty simple. My father would go out on long trips at sea, sometimes for weeks at a time, then return to her, happy and flush with cash. Life would be good for a little while, until he started drinking.

Then, inevitably, he'd get pissed off about something (or nothing) and beat the hell out of her.

One time I recall, he went berserk on her because there were some ants crawling in the garbage — the result of her slack house-keeping, he claimed — and that she had allowed creeper vines to climb up the house while he was gone.

Other times it was money. Or because he imagined she had flirted with some guy. Or because of some transgression only he understood.

The next morning, he'd apologize, swearing to God he was never going to do it again. Then he'd go back out to sea. When he returned, the cycle would repeat itself, like some kind of brutal tide.

Why my mother — who had once been smart, and pretty, and surely had better options — stayed with a man like that is testimony to how abuse can alter a person's psyche. She not only stayed, she doubled down on the relationship, giving birth to me.

By then, I think Mom already knew what she was in for. My middle name was supposed to be Hope, after Dad's grandmother. But when the hospital asked her what to put on the birth certificate, Mom changed it to Anne without telling him.

Nine years after me, there was the surprise/accident/miracle that was my brother, Teddy.

I don't know why my mother thought having more children would change my father or tame him. It surely didn't. Some of my earliest memories are of an assortment of caseworkers, their brows creased with concern as they tried to pull details out of me about the latest episode.

My childhood became a revolving door of living situations. I never fully understood the logic of the caseworkers: why some of my father's tirades resulted in removal from the home, while others (which had seemed, to me, much worse) did not.

I came to fear the group homes, which could be savage tests of survival between hardened foster kids who had learned to battle for whatever meager scraps of love, food, or adult attention that might be available.

The foster placements were more hit or miss. Some were nice enough that I cried when I was ripped away from them to be sent back to my parents.

Others were rougher, particularly the ones that were so obviously only in it for the paycheck. The state chipped in about $500 a month for my housing, feeding, and clothing, and it was amazing how little of that some of them could spend on me.

One of my foster mothers had a biological kid, a girl, to go along with three foster kids — two boys and me. The girl had her own room. I shared a room with the two boys. When we weren't in school, the three foster kids were booted out every day and told we couldn't return to the house until dinner. We were given a small bagged lunch, which I usually finished by about ten thirty in the morning. I have these memories of long afternoons in the backyard, peering jealously through the windows at my foster sister as she ate snacks in front of the television.

At another home, I was one of eight foster kids crammed into two bedrooms. The foster mother enjoyed pitting us against one another, encouraging us to report minor transgressions and then devising punishments for whoever had committed them. One time, after one of my compatriots turned me in for having hoarded a small stash of food in the closet, she cut off my hair in uneven chunks. Then she marched me into the boys' bedroom in my underwear and forced me to tell them I was a sneak and a liar.

These placements were followed by returns home for stints that could last anywhere from a few months to a year or so, depending on how artful my father was at hiding the results of his angry hands and how much he could cow my mother into silence.

My mother loved me, in her own fashion. She called me "pumpkin" — a name that still makes my skin crawl a little — and brushed my long hair much more tenderly than any foster mother did. She always made sure I had access to books and let me read as much as I wanted, allowing me to disappear into imagined worlds that were so much less chaotic than my own.

But she didn't do the one thing she really ought to have done to protect me, which was leave Billy Curran for good.

The pattern — home, then foster care, then home — continued until I was nine. By that point, my mother was fully addicted to the pain pills that were prescribed to her every time my father gave her a fresh round of bruises. Eventually she started having sex with a doctor in exchange for a steady supply of Vicodin, Percocet, or whatever he could get his hands on.

She was in a stupor one day when Teddy was found crawling out near Route 360, the major thoroughfare in Northumberland County, wearing nothing but a dirty diaper. Social Services swooped in again, like usual. But that time, my half sister, Charlotte, dropped the bomb that my father had been sexually abusing her, pretty much from the moment she developed hips.

A caseworker delivered my drug-muddled mother an ultimatum: Get sober and leave her husband or lose her children for good.

She chose him over us, voluntarily signing over her parental rights. Only people who work with the chronically abused and chemically dependent could recognize her logic.

That was twenty-two years ago. I haven't had contact with either of my parents since.

Once I became a full-time ward of the state, my life only became more unanchored. I understood there was no going "home" anymore, because I didn't have one. But I could never anticipate when the next move was coming, nor was anyone especially concerned with explaining to me why it was happening.

Had I done something bad? Were my straight A's not good enough? If I were a better kid, would they have sent me to a nicer place? Who, exactly, should I be most angry with? My latest foster parent? My latest caseworker? Myself?

Then, sometime in college, I decided I was through with the overanalyzing, the recriminations, the attempts at truth and reconciliation. Being a foster kid had defined my childhood, yes. But it was only going to define me as an adult if I let it.

I had survived. That's what mattered. And I never had to go back.

So to now have Alex coming into contact with that world was a vicious kind of cruelty, like an aftershock from an earthquake that should have been too far gone to still move the ground.

Yet there I was, sitting outside Social Services, shaking and cowering from this fresh temblor.

Eventually, I picked myself off the ground and wobbled to my car. Ben would be home soon. I wanted to be there when he arrived.

Our house is a tidy, three-bedroom post-war ranch. It sits alongside the eerily monikered Desper Hollow Road, named decades ago after the Desper family, a few of whom still live there. It is just outside the Staunton city limits, in what is quite literally the other side of the tracks: As soon as you turn off Route 250, you cross under a railroad trestle.

We bought our place when we first learned

I was pregnant. I told Ben I couldn't bring the baby home to the ground-floor apartment where I had been living. Not after what had happened there.

I wanted a proper house, one with four walls and a white picket fence and cheerful little flower boxes hung under the windows out front. It must have been the pregnancy hormones, filling me with the urge to feather a nest.

Ben, who was in the final throes of earning a PhD in history, made a few noises about the enormity of his student-loan debts, which would begin crushing us not long after he finished his program. He also pointed out we had no idea where he would end up getting a job. There had been hints he could maybe/possibly hook on at James Madison, where it was looking like there might be a retirement in the history department around the time he defended his dissertation, but there were certainly no guarantees. We had to be ready to move anywhere.

Ultimately, though, he gave in. We took our entire rainy-day fund and sunk it into the down payment — then started hoping like hell it never rained.

We closed on it last October, when I was about seven months pregnant, then spent the next two months fixing it up as much as we could before Alex made his big arrival. We borrowed a power washer to clean the grunge off the exterior. My friend Marcus came over with hedge trimmers and hacked back the overgrown bushes, allowing light to pour through the windows. His wife, Kelly, helped us paint.

Then there was Ben's surprise house-warming present to me: a beautiful, brand-new white picket fence. He was coy about how he had come up with the money for it. He joked he had sold a kidney.

We also hung some flower boxes under the windows. It was too late to really put anything in them, but Ben found tulip bulbs on end-of-season clearance and, together, we stuck them in the dirt.

For someone with my peripatetic past, there was a wonderful optimism about being able to plant something that wouldn't show itself for many months. This was the first place I could ever really think of as permanent after thirty-one years of near-constant itinerancy. And it was both dizzying and dazzling to think that by the time those flowers blossomed, we'd have a baby.

The green shoots had started to come up not long ago. Being that we were deep in the grind of new parenthood — the sleepless nights, the early mornings, the tyranny of an infant's demands — it was a nice reminder of the excitement we once had.

I tried to reassure myself, as I made the turn onto Desper Hollow Road and crossed under the tracks, that nothing had really changed. I was still going to gape at those flowers with Alex, watching one tiny miracle discover another. This was going to end up okay.

Then I reached the mailbox at the end of our driveway and made the turn up toward our house. That's when I realized there was police tape stretched across our front door.

SIX

Once I was out of my car, I saw the yellow tape wasn't the only way in which the peace and tranquility of our home had been disturbed.

The flower boxes had been removed and emptied. The dirt was piled on the ground next to them. The bulbs were lying on their side, scattered haphazardly about. Some of the stalks had been bent or broken by the rough treatment.

My hand flew to my mouth. I felt my throat constricting again.

Had the police done this? They must have. But . . . why?

And did this have something to do with Alex?

They told me all about you. I hope they get that baby as far away from you as possible.

After a few halting steps, I stopped, almost afraid to enter my house. If this is what they had done to the flower boxes, what would the inside look like? I stood there, paralyzed by uncertainty and dread.

Soon my attention was diverted by a flashlight beam, bobbing my way from down the hill. I felt myself stiffen. For a lot of reasons, I'm uneasy about being approached by strangers in the dark. Or any other time, for that matter.

I relaxed — a little — when I heard a familiar voice say, "Hey. Saw you drivin' up."

It was my neighbor, Bobby Ray Walters, a large slab of a man whose ample body fat had curiously solid properties. Bobby Ray was one of the last remaining Desper descendants. He saw nothing wrong with flying the Confederate flag outside his trailer, eagerly seized on every conspiracy theory that floated across the Internet, and lived in this fantastical alternate reality where the government was coming to strip him of his guns any moment.

He often referred to his large stockpile of munitions in casual conversation; and, in case anyone missed the hint, there was a hand-painted sign that read WARNING: SECOND AMENDMENT ENTHUSIAST prominently displayed outside his trailer. He also protected his property with a series of cameras, which he advertised with another hand-painted (if grammatically impaired) sign that read SMILE! YOUR ON CAMERA!

Our differing attitudes about politics aside, he was the kind of guy who never met a stranger. If he was sitting in one of the beat-up couches he used for outdoor furniture when I drove by, he waved, usually with his non-Budweiser-holding hand. He even cut our grass for us after we moved in when he realized we didn't yet own a lawnmower.

Once or twice he said things that made me think he had spent time in prison. I didn't pry into the details. And now I found myself backing up a step or two as he crowded my personal space.

"Sheriff was here," he volunteered, in case I hadn't figured it out. "I saw 'em rolling up 'bout three o'clock. There were, like, five or six of 'em. They walked right into the place like they owned it. Didn't knock or nothing. Two of them started digging up your flowers, like they were looking for something in there. They were just throwing dirt everywhere, so I came over and said, 'Hey, you don't need to go doing that.' They told me to mind my own business and just kept doing it, the sumbitches."

He spoke with a kind of clannish affection for me that I hadn't heard before. I could guess why. To people who have no idea how

65

I grew up, I come off as having an air of privilege. They heard my Yankee accent, the words I used or the ideas I expressed — all of which came from books I got out of the library, for free — and assumed it was the result of having parents who lavished money on private schools or sent me to Europe for the summer. They didn't look carefully enough at my teeth to see that I never had braces.

They definitely didn't see me after I graduated college. Unemployed — but without parents to move back in with, like most of my classmates — I was three months behind on my rent when my landlord told me he was kicking me out unless I gave him a blow job. He further suggested he could pimp me out, and that I might have a nice income waiting for me if I would dye my dark hair blond and surgically enhance my B cups into D's.

That was how I ended up living in my car. When I finally landed that job at Starbucks, I was just grateful they didn't notice I was sneaking food off customers' trays until my first paycheck came in.

Now that I was back on my feet, I'd like to think I hid those scars well. So, to Bobby Ray, this was my rite of passage, having the Sheriff's Office run roughshod over my stuff, just like all the other poor white trash.

"They came over when they were done and I told 'em to get the hell off my property," he continued. "I guess they wanted to know if I had seen a lot of people coming and going from your place. Like, you know, was you selling drugs and stuff."

"Drugs!" I blurted.

"Well, that's what I said," Bobby Ray insisted. "I told 'em, 'No, no, you got it all wrong. It ain't like that. Her husband, he's a professor or something up at the university. They high class.' But they just looked at me like maybe I was hiding something, like I must have been in on it or whatever. You know how they look at you, like they already made up their minds you're a piece a crap."

He took in a sharp breath, then held it, stifling the hiccup that was trying to escape.

"Yeah, I know," I said.

He looked at me with renewed sympathy. "Don't go gettin' your panties in a twist. Sheriff's gonna do what the sheriff's gonna do. Long as they didn't find nothing, you got nothing to worry about."

Then he bobbed his head toward the bulbs. " 'Cept maybe getting yourself some new flowers."

"Uh-huh," I said, bringing my hand to my mouth again. Bobby Ray stuffed his hands in his pockets and shivered a little.

"All right. If you need something, just give a holler," he said.

"Thanks, Bobby Ray."

And then he was off, his flashlight beam pointing back down the hill, toward his trailer.

I turned to face my house.

Long as they didn't find nothing, you got nothing to worry about.

I took a deep breath. There were no drugs in my house that I knew of. I would never bring something like that near Alex.

I'm not sure I could say the same about his uncle Teddy.

The boy who was born William Theodore Curran Jr. got his name from my father. I can only assume his taste for medication came from my mother.

He was just a baby when we were taken from our parents' home for the final time. Our caseworker was an astute woman who understood that I had basically assumed the role of Teddy's mother, changing his diapers, feeding him, bathing him. If we remained together, I'd keep right on doing it — depriving me of a childhood, and Teddy of a more suitable mother.

So she split us up. She literally had to pry

68

him from my arms.

She promised he would stay close by, and that I could visit him whenever I wanted. But that was a lie. While I languished in foster care, Teddy was quickly adopted by a local couple.

Then his new parents moved to Staunton. For me, losing Teddy was far more devastating than having my parents terminate their rights. Charlotte had already vanished by that point, having fled from a group home. Teddy was my entire family.

I conned his new address out of my caseworker, saying I wanted to write him a letter. Then I ran away from my foster home, taking a bus to Staunton. After the third time I did this, my caseworker offered a deal: If she found a placement for me in Staunton, I'd behave. That's how I ended up in the Shenandoah valley.

To me, Teddy was a beam of pure sunshine, a creative, energetic little boy. To everyone else, his adopted mother included, he was a problem child: obviously dyslexic (though his mother resisted having him tested), acting out in school from a young age, a troublemaker. Before long, vandalism begat cigarettes, which begat marijuana, which begat harder drugs and the petty thefts required to support his burgeoning habit.

I kept up a relationship with him the whole time, but I couldn't stay on him the way I needed to. Being penniless and near starvation doesn't leave you with a lot of wherewithal to help others.

He started running around with a girl named Wendy Mataya, who was as beautiful as she was dangerous. They made quite a pair — Teddy was broad-shouldered and handsome, like my father — and they spent their high school years scoring drugs, partying, and racking up juvenile records.

When Teddy turned eighteen, I sat him down and staged my version of an intervention, convincing him that the consequences of stealing and dealing were about to become a lot more severe. I then convinced his parents — who were just about through with him by that point — to fund his tuition at a local vocational school, where he learned HVAC repair.

To his credit, Teddy buckled down and earned his certificate. He then found a job and moved into a large house he shared with three other guys, one of whom was a young sheriff's deputy, none of whom he knew from his drug days. I was thrilled.

Once Alex was born, Teddy made noises

about how he planned to be a devoted uncle. But after a spate of visits early on, I hadn't seen him as much recently. My friend Marcus had shown more interest in Alex than Teddy had. I thought maybe Teddy was just busy.

Now, as I cleared away the police tape, I wondered what he had really been up to. Teddy had a key to my house. Knowing he couldn't risk bringing drugs into his apartment — not with a sheriff's deputy for a roommate — had he stashed them at my place?

I entered through the front door into the scene of a catastrophe. My once-tidy home had been ransacked.

In the living room, all the furniture had either been knocked over or shoved out of place. Picture frames had been removed from the walls. The television was lying facedown. Ben's jazz records — a collection of hidden gems he had found at yard sales or used shops for fifty cents or a dollar, even though many of them were worth far more — had been toppled from their place of honor on the shelf in the entertainment center and left in loose piles. Books, my beloved books, had been pulled from the shelves and stacked haphazardly.

In the kitchen, all the drawers had been

yanked out of the counter and emptied, their contents strewn about. Plates, bowls, and glassware had been removed from the cabinets and dumped on the kitchen table. Pots and pans littered the floor.

In our bedroom, the mattress and box spring were leaning against the wall. My dresser drawers had been pulled out and left wherever it was they landed. Most of our clothes were tossed in a heap in the corner, except for my bras and underwear, which were in the middle of the room. Someone wanted me to know they had received particular attention.

The loving sanctuary we had worked so hard to make for ourselves had been defiled. Along with it came the destruction of the myths I had built for myself: that I was somehow safe here, that this place was different, that bad things couldn't reach me as long as I was inside these four walls.

Nothing was broken, at least not that I saw. But they had gone out of their way to make our home as much of a shambles as possible. Anything that didn't have an implicit value had been tossed about or trampled.

We can do this to you, they seemed to be saying. *And there's nothing you can do back.*

I ended my tour in the nursery, which

hadn't been spared the authorities' fury. Alex's crib was lying on its side. The contents of his changing table were everywhere. His little onesies had been unfolded and flung into a mound along with loose diapers, tubes of A+D Ointment, packages of wipes, and all the other bits of babydom that had once been organized so perfectly.

Up in the ceiling, there was a gaping hole where the air-conditioning exchange cover should have been. It had been removed and placed over near the closet, leaving the vent wide open.

In the corner, I spied the plush bear Marcus and Kelly had given Alex — a little guy named Mr. Snuggs, according to his tag. Poor Mr. Snuggs had been knocked off the shelf where he lived. I picked him up and put him on the changing table.

It was impossible, in all the destruction, to tell if they had discovered any drugs; or where they had found them. But they must have gotten something. That's why Alex was now with Social Services.

I slumped into the rocker-glider where I often nursed Alex. Like some Pavlovian reaction, my nipples sprung leaks. Ordinarily, I would have fed Alex hours ago. My breasts were now rock hard, so swollen they felt like they were going to rupture. I needed to do something to relieve the pressure. My electric breast pump, the one provided to me by my fabulous insurance plan, was stored at work. So was the hand pump I used as a backup. I didn't need those things here. I had Alex.

There was no choice. I staggered into the bathroom and unbuttoned my blouse. I lowered the now-sodden flap on my nursing bra.

Then, trying not to see myself in the mirror — because I didn't even want to know what I looked like at a moment like this — I lowered my breast toward the sink and began massaging around the nipple.

The milk came instantly, thick at first, then thinner once I got it going.

All the while, I watched as the precious fluid that should have been nourishing my baby disappeared down the drain.

SEVEN

After coffee, after a shower, after an omelet, and after a quick perusal of *The Washington Post* on her iPad, Amy Kaye figured she had dawdled enough.

Her bravado with Aaron Dansby aside, she actually did need to familiarize herself with the Coke Mom case if she was going to write up a bill of indictment for the grand jury. Her interview with Daphne Hasper wasn't until ten a.m., still two hours away. Amy thought she might as well get her call to Sheriff Jason Powers over with.

Powers was a tobacco-dipping, Reba McEntire–loving, huntin', fishin' country boy, through and through. In defiance of stereotypes, he never seemed to have a problem with Amy being a Northerner or a woman. Amy had always found him both easy to work with and competent.

Now well entrenched in the job, Sheriff Powers did not keep a predictable schedule.

He might be in the office, or he might be patrolling the fairways at a local golf course. He was a notorious night owl and seemed to enjoy roaming around the county during the small hours. Patrol officers knew not to spend too much time hanging out at Sheetz, because it was entirely possible the boss would show up unannounced, driving his personal vehicle, and catch them loafing. Amy sometimes got emails from Powers at five in the morning and sometimes ten at night.

She wasn't sure when he actually slept. She simply called him when she needed him, knowing she would either get him or not.

This was one of the times she got him.

" 'Lo," he said.

"Hey, Jason, it's Amy Kaye."

"What's going on?" he said in typically easygoing fashion. Unlike Dansby, who was constantly paranoid about reelection, Powers had faced the voters twice now — and his father six times before that. They had never lost.

"I wanted to check in with you about this bust on Desper Hollow Road."

"Oh. So now that Dapper Dansby is done with the cameras the real work can begin?"

"Something like that."

"What do you need to know?" Powers asked.

"How'd you get probable cause?"

"CI."

A confidential informant. The standard-issue infantry rifle in the war on drugs.

"He do a buy for you?"

"Yep."

"You pay him?"

"Yep. Hundred bucks."

Not that it mattered. But it had to be disclosed. The defense usually tried to make an issue out of it, painting it as the prosecution buying its information. The argument typically didn't get much traction. Juries didn't care.

"Have you used him before?

"Yeah. Coupla times."

That was good. The law made a distinction between confidential informants who had previously provided information and new ones. Veteran CIs were deemed "reliable" and didn't have to be named in a search warrant. It was one less avenue of attack for defense attorneys whose first and best play in cases like this was to attack the validity of the warrant.

"Who executed the warrant?" Amy asked.

"Kempe."

Another good break. Lieutenant Peter

"Skip" Kempe was as solid a detective as could be found at the Augusta County Sheriff's Office. He was authoritative, but not overbearing about it. He presented information in a straightforward fashion that came off as incontrovertible fact. Amy had put him on the stand during the Mookie Myers case and was pretty sure at least four of the jurors wanted to invite him over for dinner when he was done.

"He do it clean?"

"Yeah, as far as I know, no troubles."

"Aaron told me they got half a kilo of coke. Is that . . ."

"Dapper Dansby stretchin' the truth?" Powers said, laughing. "No, he got it just about right. Four hundred eighty-seven grams. Almost as much as Mookie Myers. Same brand as Myers too."

In a sign that drug dealers were every bit as cognizant of the importance of product differentiation as Madison Avenue advertising executives, illicit drugs in modern America often came with brand stamps. The idea was that certain brands were better quality, something that mattered to a discerning junkie.

"Dragon King, right?"

"Yep."

"So, what, you think this lady took over

Myers's operation?"

"Looks that way. We found scales and baggies and all that, but we also found a list of customer names and numbers. It's a lot of the same folks who bought from Mookie. Some of our favorite people."

"But how does a white woman with a kid end up having any connection to someone like Mookie Myers?"

"Don't know. Maybe she was a customer? Doesn't really matter, does it?"

Virginia's statute regarding possession with intent to distribute was written in a way that meant the Commonwealth didn't actually have to prove a dealer had made a sale. The law presumed that a person who possessed enough product was planning to sell it.

"No, I guess not," Amy said. "Where did you find it anyway?"

"Taped inside the air-conditioning duct in the nursery."

"The *nursery*?"

"Yeah, I guess this lady figured that'd be the last place we'd look. The supplies were in a closet. Oh, and you're gonna love this: In the same box where she kept the supplies, we also got her cell phone. Had pictures of her and her kid on it and everything."

"Oh, perfect," Amy said.

Merely finding drugs in a defendant's home might not be enough to establish possession. You had to prove the person knew the drugs were there and had what the law called "dominion and control" over the materials. Pairing drug paraphernalia with the defendant's cell phone — and not just some anonymous burner — accomplished that quite nicely. In the modern world, few things were more personal than someone's mobile phone.

"All right," Amy said. "Anything else I need to know?"

"Nothing that comes to mind. This should be pretty open-and-shut. You want me to have Skip call you?"

"Yeah. I've got a meeting shortly, but sometime this afternoon would be great. Will he be available for a grand jury on Friday? Dansby wants to direct indict."

"I'll make him available."

"Thanks," Amy said. "By the way, what's the defendant's name?"

"Melanie Barrick."

Amy nearly dropped her phone.

"What?" she said sharply.

"Melanie, common spelling. Barrick. B-A-R-R-I-C-K."

Amy couldn't talk. And from the other

side of the phone, Powers had no way of knowing just how dumbstruck she was.

"You got anything else?" he asked. "I'm about to tee off here."

"No, I'm good," she squeezed out.

"Okay. See ya."

Amy put down her phone then spent a minute staring at her kitchen table. She didn't know Melanie Barrick personally.

But she did professionally.

Melanie Barrick was one of the whispering rapist's most recent victims.

EIGHT

Call it a flashback or some kind of post-traumatic stress reaction.

There was just something about spending the evening in my ruined home — steeping in that feeling of violation — that took me back to where I had been almost exactly a year before, to a day, a place, and an episode that was suddenly revisiting itself on me even though I certainly hadn't invited it.

The day was March 8.

The place was that awful ground-floor apartment.

The episode began when I felt a gloved hand clamp over my mouth, jolting me out of a sound sleep.

"Please don't scream," a man said in a whisper that was, all at once, both ethereal and terrifying. "I don't want to have to hurt you."

In the scant glow of a nearby streetlight that snuck around my blinds, I could see a man in a ski mask hovering over me. The hint of skin that showed around the eyeholes told me he was white. The rest of him — arms, hands, legs, neck — was covered.

My first thought was that I should bite his hand, even if it would just give me a mouthful of glove. Then I would kick him, then claw his eyeballs, then . . .

Then, with his other hand, he brought a machete up to my face. It was a thick, heavy chunk of metal at least eighteen inches long. Its steel had turned dark, basically black. Only its sharp, cruel edge remained silver, and it glinted at me.

"I'll only use this if I have to," he whispered. "Do you understand?"

I nodded.

"Am I going to have to hurt you?"

I shook my head.

"I'm going to take my hand off your mouth now. Can you please stay quiet?" He removed his hand. "Are you going to be good? You can answer."

"Yes," I said meekly.

"Thank you. Now could you please remove your top?"

I complied, resorting to a survival technique I had learned in childhood. I pretended that I could take a piece of myself — the most important part — and lock it in my heart, where it would be safe from the rest of the world. It was a trick I sometimes told my fellow foster kids about. And it helped me again with that loathsome whispering man.

For as much as I wondered later about what would have happened if I resisted — Should I have tried to fight him off? Should I have screamed and hoped it scared him away? Should I have peed on him or found some other way to gross him out? Should I have run? — the mere fact that I was around to have those thoughts eventually made me decide I had done the right thing.

He took my bedsheets and the clothes I had been wearing when he was done, then disappeared out the same window he had jimmied open to let himself in.

When I was sure he was gone, I put on a sweatshirt and jeans, then called Ben and asked him if he would come over. He was just my boyfriend then, though we had been dating exclusively for some time. The irony was that he had kept trying to convince me to move in with him, but I didn't want to give up my independence.

He held me through the night, crying with me the whole time, reminding me he loved me, saying it wasn't my fault, telling me there was nothing I could (or should) have done differently.

In the morning, he convinced me I had to call the police. The professor in him cited all the statistics about the underreporting of rape, saying the crime was never going to get the attention it deserved until its true prevalence was better understood.

The boyfriend in him was just angry. He wanted to nail the bastard who had done this to me.

That led to a long day of reliving the attack, first with the Sheriff's Office, then with the prosecutor, a woman who asked a lot of detailed questions.

At one point during our interview, she made a reference to the rapist's black machete being held in my face.

"I didn't say anything to you about the machete being black," I said. "How did you know that?"

"Oh, I thought you said it was black," she said.

But she was a terrible liar.

"I'm not the only one, am I?" I asked.

She didn't reply to that. She didn't need to. I already knew, from the way he acted with me, that he had done it before.

The Sheriff's Office got my attacker's DNA off the rape kit, though naturally it wasn't a match for anyone in the system.

Between that and my totally worthless description, the authorities got very quiet and the case went unsolved, just as I somehow suspected it would.

And then? Well, then nothing. I went on with my life.

I don't want to make it sound like I just shrugged the thing off. Far from it. I couldn't get that awful whisper to leave my mind. It was in there all the time — all day and, worse, all night. It made me feel like my assailant was forever around the corner, waiting to pounce.

Logically, I knew I was just imagining it. But don't underestimate the power of human imagination. It's given us everything from world-changing religions to the atomic bomb. It's more than capable of keeping a one-hundred-twenty-pound girl chained to her mental demons.

For weeks, I was afraid to stay in my apartment, but I was also terrified to leave. I felt exposed and vulnerable wherever I went. Even worse than hearing the echoes of that whisper was the feeling when I saw a man whose proportions resembled my attacker — which was a lot of them, given how average the guy was. It made me wonder: Is *that* the guy? Is he right now envisioning me naked, scared, totally in his control?

And then it was like being right back in my bedroom, tasting that glove.

Even friends could trigger the reaction. The first time I saw Marcus, who had never been anything but chivalrous in all the years we had known each other, I freaked out and had a full-blown panic attack.

Ben suggested therapy, but I knew it wouldn't help. I had done therapy before, as a kid. I didn't need to talk the thing into submission. Within a lifetime of crappy things that had happened to me, this was just one more crappy thing.

Or, at least it was until I learned I was pregnant. That was an extra kick in the uterus I really wasn't ready for. In a life where there had already been so many things outside of my control, I couldn't even decide when I got to reproduce.

I seriously considered an abortion, if only because there was no chance — and I mean no chance at all — I was going to consider adoption. Not after my own experience in the system, to say nothing of Teddy's.

A few things stopped me from ending the pregnancy. One, I wasn't actually sure whose child it was. Ben and I had a condom break a few days before the rape. There was always the spermicide to act as backup. But we couldn't be sure.

Two — and this was probably the larger factor — I felt this overwhelming love for the thing growing inside me. I was seven or eight weeks along by the time I went to the OB/GYN. She did an ultrasound and then asked me if I wanted to hear the baby's heart.

The question caught me by surprise. I'm not sure I had even considered that it had a heartbeat yet. I nodded, and the OB/GYN reached for a knob on her machine and turned up the volume.

At that moment, any ambivalence I had about the pregnancy disappeared. That miraculous sound — *ca-chunk, ca-chunk, ca-chunk* doing a vigorous double-time — filled the examining room. I can honestly say I had never heard anything so remarkable, so beautiful.

It already didn't matter whether the pregnancy started with an act of love or an act of violence. That baby was mine, not my rapist's.

Just because he owned the episode didn't mean he got to own the result.

Ben asked me to marry him not long after. We still didn't know who the father was. He said he loved me *and* the baby so much already, it didn't really matter.

When the baby came out, blond and pale and quite apparently not his, Ben never acted like anything but an excited new father.

That was just Ben. Steady. Reliable. Ready to roll with whatever happened.

Ben had begun wooing me while I worked at Starbucks, not long after I had finally scraped up enough money to move out of my car. He was a good-looking guy, a little younger than me, with flawless dark skin and a wiry body that tapered to a V at the waist. Every time he came into the shop, he found a way to make me laugh, whether it was with a sly, offhand observation about how a customer had acted or a self-deprecating joke. He was obviously very bright.

But it was his empathy that most attracted me to him. In each comment he made, I could tell how good he was at seeing the world from other people's perspectives.

It was a rare trait in a guy. In anyone.

He later admitted he frequently drove by Starbucks, but only came into the store when he saw my car. It took him three months to gin up the courage to ask me out on a date. By then it felt easy to say yes.

Marcus, who had watched this slow courtship up close, gently asked me if I knew what I was getting myself into, dating a black guy. It wasn't because he had any personal objection to it. He just understood that while Staunton was a progressive town, it was still in the South, located roughly in the middle of a state that only surrendered its anti-miscegenation laws in 1967, and only after the US Supreme Court ordered it.

In truth, Ben got more resistance from his side than I got from mine. His friends back home teased him about how he was just another black guy who wanted to get with a white woman. Some of his older family members asked why he couldn't just stick with his own kind.

But really, it was pretty much a nonissue. I got used to the occasional stares — mostly from old white people — when we got close to each other on dates. I met his parents, who were lovely from the start and didn't seem to have any concern about the color of my skin. We certainly didn't have to worry about introducing him to my family.

As things progressed, Ben's devotion to me only got more flattering, something I wasn't sure I was even worthy of after so many years of having my self-esteem battered. I had stopped thinking of myself as intelligent — I mean, how smart could I be? I worked at Starbucks, right? — until Ben came along and reminded me of it. Because, make no mistake, he was brilliant; enough to overcome the not-inconsiderable obstacles of race, poverty, and growing up in a family where no one had gone to college. He had earned a full academic scholarship at Middlebury College, then graduated Phi Beta Kappa.

If someone that smart loved me, it must have meant I wasn't as dumb as I thought, right?

Ben's thesis adviser at James Madison, Richard Kremer, was one of the nation's foremost scholars in post–Reconstruction era US history. Ben was his star student. With Kremer's guidance, Benjamin J. Barrick had already published a few journal articles. Kremer even thought Ben might be able to get his dissertation published as a book, which would really put him in the stratosphere of young historians.

Every now and then, we'd permit ourselves to daydream about when he completed his PhD and slid into the job that would, we hoped, open up at JMU at just the right time. It was tenure-track, and Kremer had said he would throw around his weight for Ben to get it. We'd never have to worry about money again.

Beyond that, Ben was just exceptionally well grounded. He didn't have a lot growing up either — his parents worked jobs that paid low hourly wages, and every generation before that picked cotton — but his family was supersolid, churchgoing, pillar-of-the-community types.

Our dynamic, which somehow established itself pretty quickly, was that I had a troubled present and a screwed-up past. He didn't. So he helped me overcome mine.

The downside to this arrangement was that he wasn't always the best communicator when it came to his own issues. If anything, the bigger they were, the less likely he was to say anything at all.

But we were on familiar turf here: This was another time when my troubles became his troubles. After Ben got home, we spent the night talking things through. He concurred with me that whatever the Sheriff's Office found in our house must have belonged to my brother. I had called and texted Teddy but got no response. Ben went over to his place, but his roommates said they hadn't seen him.

Long-term, we had to get Teddy to admit the drugs were his. If that meant he got in trouble with the law, so be it. There was exactly one thing I wouldn't sacrifice to save Teddy, and that was Alex.

More immediately, we had to plead our case to Social Services, trying to make them realize we weren't drug addicts or child abusers.

Ben went online to figure out how we might do that. He soon found a handbook for parents in child dependency cases, which we began poring over. Within twenty-four hours of taking a child, Social Services had to file a petition with the Juvenile and Domestic Relations Court for an emergency removal order.

As far as I could tell, there wasn't a thing we could do to fight an emergency removal order in court. It was just an attorney for Social Services telling a judge what horrible parents we were.

If the judge agreed, we would have an attorney appointed to us. Within five business days, there would be a preliminary removal hearing, where the judge would make an initial finding of abuse and neglect. Thirty days later, there would be an adjudicatory hearing, where that initial finding would be confirmed. Then there would be a dispositional hearing, where the judge would approve Social Services' foster care plan.

And on. And on.

The document finished with an admonishment in bold type, framed in its own box.

"Unless you do what the Court requires, you could lose custody of your child forever," it read. "Start working now on the things you need to do."

I knew we had to stop the system from latching its teeth into us in the first place, and the only way to do that was to convince Social Services not to file that emergency removal order.

That was what had inspired us to spend three hours that morning feverishly putting the house together, shoving things back into place without bothering to organize them, just in case someone wanted to do a home visit.

All the while, I could practically hear the system's drumbeats. A tribe of cannibals was massing. And it was hungry.

NINE

We arrived at Shenandoah Valley Social Services a few minutes before its scheduled 8:30 a.m. opening time. It wasn't much more inviting in daytime than it had been the night before.

Though exhausted, we had made a game attempt to clean ourselves up. I had put on a dress with cap sleeves and a prim neckline. There wasn't much I could do with my hair, because I didn't have time for a shower. So I pulled it back and anchored it with a barrette. I only hoped a fresh dusting of makeup stopped me from looking like a total zombie.

Ben nailed the part of a young academic. He wore slacks and a blazer that was two elbow patches away from being promoted to full professor. His thick-framed glasses — he jokingly called them his Malcolm X glasses — gave him an even more studious air. His shirt was well ironed and neatly

tucked. He once explained his fastidious-
ness came from not wanting to give the
white world an excuse to tag him with any
of the labels it liked to pin to young African
American men.

Taken in sum, I thought we looked like
responsible parents.

"We ready to do this?" I asked.

He crossed his hand over mine and gave it
a reassuring pat. "We'll be fine," he said.
"All we have to do is tell the truth, right?"

He said this with the assuredness of
someone who had never been made to
understand that disaster was always closer
than you know. He believed he had some
control over the situation; that because we
were morally in the right, the system would
respond accordingly.

I knew better. The moment that emergency removal order was granted, our family would become another small pebble in a
rushing stream swollen by a spring flood.

But I smiled nervously. "Yeah, for sure.
Let's go."

We got out of the car and crossed the
parking lot. Once we reached the waiting
area inside the building, we slipped our
drivers' licenses under a thick piece of glass.
The woman barely looked at us before she

told us to have a seat in some blue pleather chairs.

What she didn't tell us is how long we'd be sitting there. I was not unfamiliar with this particular aspect of Social Services. It's one of the subtle ways in which the system makes you feel less human: with constant reminders of how little your time matters to anyone.

After a while, even Ben was knitting his brows and looking at the time on his phone, which was about as demonstrative a display of impatience as he ever made.

I was mostly just numb, reliving the dozens of times I had sat in this office — the furniture had changed, but I swear the toys in the corner were the same — utterly terrified about what awaited me once the bureaucrats were done consulting their Magic 8 Ball.

An hour and a half later, the door to the side of the glass windows opened. A woman with square-framed glasses, whose hair was pulled back into a severe ponytail, said, "Ms. Barrick?"

I leapt up, every nerve ending in my body jangling at once. "Yes?"

"I'm Tina Anderson. I'm the family services specialist assigned to your son's case. Come with me, please."

Tina Anderson's face was devoid of expression as she led us through a warren of hallways. I had expected her to turn into one of the tiny offices along the way. Instead, she led us all the way to the back of the building, to a door labeled DIRECTOR.

As she knocked, my stomach flopped about. The director? Why would the director need to be involved? I had never interacted with one in all my years of dealing with Social Services.

"Come in," a female voice said.

The woman sitting behind the desk inside the room was older, with permed, bottle-blond hair. She had a fleshy face with too much makeup. Loose skin hung off her neck, which was covered in skin tags. Her suit was many seasons out of date and ill fitting.

I immediately despised her. And not because she was ugly or had bad clothes. Throughout my childhood, I developed a sixth sense about social workers. I could always tell which ones still had some decency left in them and which ones had it completely beaten out of them. It usually took me about five seconds to make up my mind.

This lady flunked the five-second test after two. There was no humanity in her anywhere, as far as I could discern. She stood as we entered and pointed to a round table in the corner.

"Hello, Ms. Barrick," she said with this supercilious air and a voice that came from somewhere within her jowls. "Have a seat, please."

We sat. Ben remained composed and self-possessed. He still didn't fundamentally understand how much we were at someone else's mercy.

Both women joined us and slid business cards across the table. The director's name was Nancy Dement.

"I know you were here last night looking for your son," she said. "I'd like to begin by assuring you he's safe and being well cared for in an approved foster-care setting."

"Thank you," I said.

"I trust you've had contact with the Sheriff's Office?"

"No. Not yet."

She looked like this surprised her a little. "Well, the first thing you should understand is that while our agencies cooperate with each other, we are completely separate. What you have happening with your drug charges is up to them and the Commonwealth's Attorney's Office. We have no bearing on any of that. Here, our only concern is your child."

"I understand."

"I also want you to know that our first goal is always to get children reunited with their biological family. Everyone here wants that for you, but there's a lot that needs to happen before we reach that outcome. We have some reading material in here that will lay everything out for you."

She opened a plain folder with several printouts and some glossy pieces of paper. I immediately recognized the handbook Ben and I had already read. This gave me the perfect opening. Swallowing my nerves, I began a speech I had been rehearsing in the waiting room.

"I'm familiar with your process," I said. "That's actually why we're here. We'd like to convince you that there's no need to file an emergency removal order. Alex is not abused in any way. Ms. Anderson, or anyone else who has examined him, can confirm that for you. He's a healthy, happy baby boy who is well nourished and progressing along through all the appropriate developmental milestones. If you'd like, you can come out to our home and see it for yourself: Alex is in absolutely no danger there."

Nancy Dement looked like she was sucking rhubarb. She had obviously been at this for a number of years. She had probably never heard a mother talk about developmental milestones.

I pressed on: "I haven't heard from anyone in law enforcement yet, but when I do I'll tell them what I'm about to tell you. I'm assuming they found drugs in my house and . . . Unfortunately, my brother has had a problem with addiction for years. He has access to our house and we think he and his girlfriend used it to stash their stuff. As soon as I find him, I'm going to drag him in here and he's going to tell you that whatever the Sheriff's Office took from our house belonged to him. In the meantime, you're separating an infant from his mother for absolutely no reason. Please, I'm begging you, don't file that emergency removal order."

As I finished, I thought my speech had an impact on Tina Anderson. She had fared better on the five-second test. There was a part of her, buried under that hard helmet of a ponytail, that still cared.

Nancy Dement was another matter.

"It's not that simple," she said. "As I understand it, you are about to have some very serious charges pressed against you. Do you have a lawyer yet? I think once you do, you'll realize this a very serious matter.

101

Very serious."

She was lecturing me like I was some teenage mother who was flunking not only her civics class but life in general. I didn't need to be told losing my baby was "very serious," much less be told it three times.

"I understand what you're saying," I said slowly. "I fully get that you have a job to do and you have your procedures to follow. I'm asking you to please pull yourself out of your rulebook for a second and look at us. Look at our baby. We're not —"

She held up her hand. "That's not up to me."

"But it *is* up to you. Don't you see that? Don't just hide behind doing things the way you've always done them. You can decide not to file that order. You have that authority."

Nancy Dement was completely unmoved by my argument. I might as well have been talking to the table.

"If you can get those charges cleared up, we can begin to move toward reunification," she said. "But for right now, we have to let this play out."

I took in a deep breath, the kind that made it clear to all I was about to get too loud, but Ben reached out and squeezed my hand, silencing me with his eyes. Then he returned his gaze to the Social Services director.

"Ms. Dement," he said gently. "Are you a mother?"

The question seemed to startle her, as did the softness of Ben's voice. There was a quick glitch in her programming before she recovered with, "Yes, I have two sons."

"Then I'm sure you can understand why my wife is upset. She went to pick up our baby at day care yesterday only to learn he had been taken. She came back to our house to find the Sheriff's Office had turned it upside down. We're as legitimately confused by this as you would be if it happened to you. We're law-abiding people. It's been quite an ordeal. We barely slept last night."

Shockingly, Nancy Dement said, "I'm sorry."

I suddenly felt hopeful. Ben was working his way under this woman's bulletproof shell. He adjusted his Malcolm X glasses in a way that made him seem even more professorial than usual.

"And I appreciate that," he said. "But of course, none of that matters right now. What matters is Alex. We've read a lot of your materials and I've also read the applicable laws. The phrase I seem to keep seeing is 'best interest of the child.' What is in Alex's best interest? That's what we're all here for, aren't we?"

"Yes, of course," she said, falling further under his spell.

"In that case, I don't think there's any question. Alex is an infant. He's still breast-feeding. I'm sure you know the health benefits of that, just as you're familiar with the literature about attachment theory. This is an absolutely critical time for our family. I don't think there's any question that it's in Alex's best interest, both now and going forward, to be returned to his mother and father. We'll happily submit to whatever monitoring you'd like to put us under. We're very reasonable people, and I know you're a reasonable person too. I'm sure there has to be a way to make this happen that allows you to follow your rules but also returns the baby to us. Please. Make this a win-win."

Hope surged in me. Nancy Dement brought her hands up onto the table and folded them.

"Mr. . . . Barrick, is that right?" she said.

"Yes."

And then that hope was dashed.

"Are you the child's biological father?"

Ben and I exchanged wary glances.

It was as obvious as his mocha skin color that he wasn't. I had convinced myself it didn't matter, because he had convinced me it didn't matter. Until, suddenly, now, it did.

"Ah, I . . . I mean, no, not in the biological sense, obviously," Ben admitted. "But in every other —"

"Have you been appointed by a court as the child's legal guardian?"

"No," he said flatly.

We hadn't even thought to do it.

"Well, then, I'm afraid you don't get a lot of say in this situation. We can't consider you as a temporary guardian because there have been illegal drugs found in your residence. I'm glad you're here to support your wife and I'm sure she appreciates your presence. But legally you have no standing."

Whatever air there had been in the room seemed to have left. Nancy Dement's ruling was an insidious cruelty: I was essentially being punished for having been raped. As if the first victimization wasn't enough.

I felt my insides giving way.

"Where . . . where is Alex right now?" I asked.

"As I said, he's with an approved foster-care family," Nancy Dement said.

"When can I see him?"

"That's not possible right now."

"But I thought . . . I mean, you guys do

supervised visits, don't you?"

"I'm sorry. That's not going to be happen."

"Why not?"

"Ms. Barrick, I have to be candid with you. We've been made aware . . . ," she began, then stopped, like she was reconsidering her words.

When she resumed, she spoke deliberately: "There's an allegation that you have been making arrangements to sell your baby on the black market."

TEN

The house was midway up a large hill, which told Amy Kaye a little something right there.

In the Shenandoah valley, as in so many other parts of the world, elevation was a proxy for social status. Rich people lived up on the hill. Poor people populated the hollows.

The address Daphne Hasper had given Amy was somewhere in between, a nice — but not too nice — split-level not far from New Hope.

Hasper was one of the earliest victims, from 2005. She had been twenty-four at the time, a second-year teacher at New Hope Elementary. She was living just outside Staunton city limits, by herself, on the first floor of a garden-style apartment.

The report on her assault bore similarities to the others, but it also had its idiosyncrasies. She had been out at a concert in Gypsy

Hill Park with some friends earlier in the evening, then at a bar. Around midnight, she had been driven home by a male friend, a fellow teacher.

She went to sleep shortly after getting in. An hour later, she was awakened when a man in a ski mask peeled back her bedsheets. She described her attacker as a white male, approximately five foot ten, in his early to mid-twenties.

He was on top of her before she could react. He showed her the knife, then whispered to her that he didn't want to use it.

"The victim stated she closed her eyes and told him, 'Just get it over with,' " the deputy's report read. "The suspect proceeded to sexually assault the victim. The victim stated the assault lasted for approximately three minutes."

After he was through, he took her panties and the sheets. But he hadn't been very thorough about cleaning up his semen. Traces of it remained on Hasper, who called the authorities immediately after the attack and had a rape kit administered within the hour at a nearby hospital.

The investigation immediately centered on the man who drove her home. Other teachers said they thought he had a thing for Hasper. Her broad description of the attacker loosely fit him. But she couldn't say for sure whether it was him. It had been dark. She had kept her eyes closed. It had been over with so quickly.

The man had no alibi for the time of the assault. He claimed he went home and went to sleep, but his roommates, who were still out at the bar, couldn't confirm that.

Augusta County Sheriff's deputies extensively canvassed the neighborhood with the man's picture, looking for anyone who might be able to place him there after he dropped off Hasper — hanging around and waiting for her light to go off, hiding in the shrubbery, whatever. The canvass came up empty.

Then the DNA recovered from the rape kit came back. It didn't match the sample the lead suspect had voluntarily provided. With no other leads, the case went cold.

Hasper finished out the school year, then moved to Oregon. At first, there were notes in her file from when she had called the Augusta County Sheriff's Office, asking if there were any updates on the case, or to give them a change of address so they could contact her if something came up. The last call had been eight years ago.

She was now thirty-seven. When Amy tracked her down through her parents, she had been reluctant to speak. She explained how, after a few painful years and some therapy, she had decided to move on. She was married with three kids now. She couldn't see the point in rehashing it. They hadn't caught the guy, and as far as she was concerned, they never would.

Amy explained she was doing a routine review of unsolved cases — that was the line Aaron Dansby had insisted on — and would appreciate her cooperation. Hasper refused, but Amy wore her down with you-never-knows and a talk of the improvements to DNA testing that had occurred since 2005.

Hasper finally agreed to talk. But not over the phone. She had said she just booked a plane ticket home to surprise her mother for her sixtieth birthday. Maybe they could talk face-to-face then? Amy insisted on nailing down a date and a time.

That was two months ago. Amy had sent her emails since then. None of them had been returned. Now here was Amy, knocking on Hasper's parents' front door.

A woman answered the door with: "Hi. Can I help you?"

"Ms. Hasper?" she said.

"Yes?" she said, blank-faced.

"Hi, Amy Kaye from the Augusta County Commonwealth's Attorney's Office."

Recognition dawned on Hasper. But not in a good way.

"Oh my goodness, I'm so sorry. I . . . I completely forgot about our meeting."

"Not a problem. I'm glad I caught you. Can I come in?"

Hasper glanced behind herself, then walked out onto the porch, closing the door behind her.

"Look, I'm sorry, this isn't a good time," she said quietly.

"I understand. Do you need me to come back later? Or tomorrow or —"

Hasper was shaking her head. "I just don't . . . It turns out my dad is having surgery tomorrow. It's sort of unexpected and this . . . I don't want to put him through everything again. He's just finishing his breakfast right now, and I don't even want him to know you're out here. I'm sorry to make you come all the way out here for nothing. I'm sure you understand."

Amy Kaye smiled weakly in acknowledgment but wasn't deterred.

"I do understand. But I'd still really like to talk with you. We could take a walk or a drive so your dad doesn't hear. Tell him I'm an old high school friend."

Hasper made a face. She was a nice woman, a first-grade teacher who didn't like confrontation. "I'm sorry, I just . . . I just don't see the point. I mean, it's not like there's any new evidence or anything, is there?"

"No, but —"

"Then I can save us both the time and trouble," she said, getting a little more firm. "Because I told the police everything I could think to tell them thirteen years ago and I've spent a lot of time since then trying *not* to think about it."

"I understand, but —"

"And it's my mom's birthday this weekend and now my dad is sick and he's probably already wondering what I'm doing out here and, I'm sorry, it's just too much. Too much."

"Ms. Hasper, I'd really appreciate if you could spare just a few minutes here."

"I'm sure you would," she said, edging toward the front door. "But I'm going to go back inside now. You can check off that you talked to me and there was nothing new."

"No, please, wait."

But Hasper had already reopened the door. She was about to disappear inside.

Then Amy blurted, "You're not the only one."

She wasn't supposed to say anything like that. She knew the rules. Aaron Dansby

112

would regurgitate a voting booth if he found out.

Hasper's momentum toward the inside of her parents' house had momentarily stalled. "What do you mean?" she asked.

There was no stopping now.

"You're not the only woman this guy has attacked," Amy said. "There have been others. Lots of others."

"How many?"

"At least eight that I have confirmed through DNA evidence, but almost certainly more. More than twenty. Maybe more than thirty. I'm not really sure. These cases have been out there for a long time, but no one ever tried to tie them together. It's been a lot of work over the last three years just getting what I've gotten so far. I've worked nights and weekends trying to nail this bastard and I'd really appreciate your help. A case like this just needs one break. For all I know, something you say might be that break."

Hasper still looked unconvinced. Amy plowed ahead.

"He's still doing it. The most recent attack was four months ago. Based on his previous patterns, that means he's due for another one soon. I think he attacks someone, is satisfied for a little while, then starts stalking a new victim. He's very careful, so he takes his time. The attacks are usually anywhere from three to five months apart. And he's been doing it for years. You can't tell anyone, but I'm afraid you're one of many."

Hasper was absorbing this with relative stoicism. At least outwardly. Amy could only imagine what was boiling underneath.

"And why can't I tell anyone?" she asked.

"Because, to be perfectly honest, my asshole boss thinks it'll make him look bad in front of the electorate, and he's ordered me to keep it quiet until we have a suspect. But it's hard to get a suspect if I can't appeal to the public for tips and I can't get the victims to talk."

Hasper took one last glance behind herself, toward the interior of the house. Then she stepped out onto the porch and quietly closed the door behind her.

"Okay," she said, "let's take a walk."

As they climbed the hill, toward the rich people, Hasper recounted the details of the attack.

There was, true to her word, nothing she hadn't previously told the authorities. By the time Hasper was through with her account, they were a half-mile away.

"So it sounds like the entire investigation focused on the man who drove you home," Amy said. "Did they ever look at anyone else?"

"Not that I know of. They had zeroed in on him from the start. They quoted those statistics about how whatever-percent of sexual assaults are committed by acquaintances. And then when two of my girlfriends told them they thought the guy had a thing for me, it was pretty much over."

"Did you think it was him?"

"I didn't know what to think. But not . . . not really. I knew he was interested in me. He had made that pretty obvious. But he wasn't pushy about it like some guys, you know? Once I heard he volunteered a DNA sample, I sort of knew it wasn't him."

They were getting to a spot on the hill where they could start to make out the Blue Ridge Mountains, ringing them like a majestic purple bowl in the distance. Hasper, who had been talking almost non-stop and was getting a little winded, stopped to take in the view.

Amy thought it was a good time for a short break. She couldn't cite the science behind it, but there was something about being high up that put people in an expansive mood. Or maybe it had nothing to do with science.

After a little while, Hasper turned to Amy.

"All this time, I always wondered if there were others. I mean, just the way the guy went about things, I thought . . . Well, I wondered. It seemed like he had done it before. And I did enough research online. I know sexual predators don't usually stop at one. What were . . . I mean, if I can ask, what were the other victims like?"

"A lot like you, actually. They were young and either lived alone or were alone at the time of the attack. If you can promise you'll keep it to yourself, I can give you a look at the other names. I've been wanting to figure out if this guy went after women he knew or whether he picked random victims. If it turns out some of you know each other, you might have also overlapped with the attacker in some way."

While she was trying to maintain the facade of the dispassionate prosecutor, Amy was feeling tremendous excitement. This was the kind of investigating she had always wished she had been able to do — full contact, not hampered by the anchor that was Aaron Dansby's political calculations. She should have started going behind his back like this a long time ago.

"Yeah, like, maybe we all shopped at a

store where he worked or something?" Hasper asked.

"Something like that. Though, based on the distribution of the attacks, I don't think the guy was local at first. You were part of the early wave. Maybe number six on the list, though I'm not sure which one of the early ones I should count."

"When did he start?"

"Maybe 1997. It's tough to tell, because there's no DNA from that one. There were three during nine months that stretched from 2002 to 2003. I've confirmed DNA in one of those. Then came you in 2005. But they stayed pretty sporadic for a while after that. It didn't start picking up in frequency until the last seven or eight years. I always thought the guy was maybe a trucker who passed through now and then or a salesman who had Augusta County as a territory and then decided to move here. Something like that."

Hasper's face went slack.

"What's the matter?" Amy asked.

"A trucker," Hasper said, her voice thick.

"It's a possibility, yes. Why?"

Hasper didn't speak for a short while. She had returned her gaze to the mountains in the distance and seemed to be having a debate with herself. Amy wasn't going to rush her.

"I never said anything about this," Hasper finally said. "The investigators were so sure they had the right man and . . . all I had was this sense of who it might — just *might* — be. To call it a hunch would be too strong. It was really just this . . . this feeling I had.

"And the thing was, I saw the hell my friend was being put through. I mean, we waited four months for that DNA test, and the whole time everyone was treating him like a rapist. The school district made him take a leave of absence. He lost all his friends. To this day there are people who look at him like he did it, even after the DNA cleared him. And I didn't . . . I didn't want to ruin someone else's life with a false accusation."

"But you weren't really the one making the accusation," Amy pointed out. "It was the Sheriff's Office."

Hasper's eyes were still fixed on a faraway point.

"I know," she said. "But I also felt like, I don't know, like I already had my bite at the apple. Four months later, it was too late to start all over again. I just wanted to move on."

"It's never too late," Amy said. "This guy

118

is still doing to other women what he did to you. If there's someone you think it is, even if it's just a vague feeling. I can be discreet. There are enough other victims that if it's not him, I'll be able to rule him out pretty quickly. But if it *is* him . . ."

She let that thought dangle.

Hasper took in a deep breath and let it out unevenly. She brought her hand over her heart.

"Oh my God," she said. "I can't even believe I'm back here. I . . . You have no idea how hard I worked to bury this and . . . I just wanted it to stay buried."

"I know, I know," Amy said. "I can't imagine how hard this is."

Hasper wiped at the corners of her eyes.

"I seriously, seriously don't know, okay? But there was something about the way the guy moved that made me think it was this guy I went to high school with. He was always . . . He was just a bit of a creep, that's all. He went to work for his dad as a trucker after we graduated. That was another reason I didn't want to tell anyone about him. I didn't think he was even around. But I kind of kept track of him after the attack, because I always . . . I just had this feeling. And last I heard, he got off the road a few years ago and was now working for his dad in the front office."

"What's his name?"

Hasper took one last deep breath, then said, "Warren Plotz."

ELEVEN

Time seemed to suspend itself for a moment. My mouth just hung open.

The words floated out there — *sell your baby on the black market* — like they were encapsulated in a quote bubble that belonged in some ghastly comic book.

Ben whipped his head in my direction as if he actually believed it. Or at least, in that first fraction of a second, he considered it a possibility.

I finally understood why I was in the director's office, and why they weren't treating this as a routine case. It also explained why they hadn't visited me before taking Alex, why they wouldn't open the door last night, why we waited an hour and a half today. As far as they were concerned, they had to keep Alex as far away from me as possible. I was the mother they'd tell stories about long after they all retired: *You remember that woman who tried to sell her baby?*

"That's . . . that's completely . . . that's not true," I stammered. "I mean, that's preposterous. I would never . . ."

Words were failing me. I felt hot. My too-full breasts ached. Tears were leaking out of my eyes. Snot ran from my nose. It all made me look that much more guilty.

I wanted to deny this absurd accusation with full force and a steady gaze. But I couldn't compose myself, much less form a coherent sentence.

Tina Anderson was staring me down. Nancy Dement's face was a mask.

"Under the circumstances, I felt I had no choice but to order no contact between you and the child," the director said. "We also can't consider placing the child with a relative or putting him in any kind of setting where you might have access to the child.

"We will be presenting our emergency removal order to a judge at about one o'clock this afternoon. You have the right to attend, but I should warn you the emergency removal hearing is ex parte. That means the Department of Social Services is the only one allowed to present evidence. You'll have more of a chance to talk to the judge at the preliminary removal hearing on Tuesday."

Right. Sure. Come Tuesday, I'd talk to a

judge who would look at me like I had four heads and a forked tail. And then in thirty days, I'd talk to him again and nothing would have changed. And on. And on.

The whole time, someone else would have my baby. In the year since his conception, Alex had gone from being a part of my body to being a part of my soul. The connection between us was more than just flesh. I would sooner lose an arm than lose him.

Yet he was being torn away from me by these bloodless women.

"Wait, just wait," I said. "This . . . this allegation about selling the baby. I mean, that's . . . It's completely . . . Where did that even come from?"

"To be honest, Ms. Barrick, I'm not sure how much that even matters at the moment. If I were you, I'd start worrying about those drug charges. If you are convicted, you are looking at a lengthy prison sentence and your parental rights will be terminated. That's the larger issue here. Do you understand that?"

"No. No, I do *not* understand," I said, way too loudly. "Who told you I was selling my baby?"

"Ms. Barrick, keep your voice down or I'm going to have to ask you to leave."

I glared at her, hating her more with every

second. She was this robot of a bureaucrat who would forget about all of this unpleasantness and go home to her family at precisely four thirty this afternoon, at which point my life would still be shattered.

I gritted my teeth and repeated, "Who told you I was selling my baby?"

"That's not really something I can share with you right now."

"That's not something you can *share*?" I said, really losing it now. "Lady, this isn't playtime. We're not talking about *sharing* our blocks. We're talking about someone making the most horrible accusation I can imagine, and you're not letting me see my baby because of it, and I don't even get to know who said it or where it came from? That's —"

"I think it's time for you to go," Nancy Dement said, pushing away from the table and standing.

"I'm not going anywhere until I get some answers."

"Please lower your voice."

"I'm not lowering anything!" I yelled.

"Okay, you have to leave now."

Tina Anderson had retreated into a corner — as far as she could get from the mother who was losing her mind — and had pulled

124

out her cell phone and was talking softly into it.

Ben was still trying to be reasonable. "Ms. Dement," he began. "I think it's only fair if you —"

But I didn't have the patience for his levelheadedness.

"Who told you I was selling my baby?" I demanded.

"Ms. Barrick, this conversation is over," Nancy Dement said.

"It's not over until you answer me. Was it an anonymous phone call? Was it something the Sheriff's Office told you? How can I begin to convince you it's completely untrue when you won't even tell me where it's coming from?"

"You're going to have to talk to your lawyer."

"I don't *have* a lawyer. I have twelve cents in my bank account and a mortgage. I don't have money for a lawyer."

"Then one will be appointed for you this afternoon. You're going to have to leave now."

"Why? Because I'm a poor white trash drug dealer who wants to sell my baby? Is that what you think I am?"

"It doesn't matter what I think," Nancy

Dement said. "That's the part you don't get."

"Oh, I get it. Believe me, I get everything that's going on here. I've been dealing with people like you since I was two years old. The only thing you really care about is keeping your job until you get your pension. You'll talk about doing what's in the best interest of the child, and it's just your lips moving. You people don't have even the faintest idea of what those words mean. Because if you did —"

There was a quick knock, then the door to her office opened. Two beefy Augusta County Sheriff's deputies, their chests puffed to superhero proportions by Kevlar vests, their belts jangling with weaponry, crossed the room toward me with long strides. One was at least six foot four. The other was probably six two. They were both more than two hundred and fifty pounds.

The larger one briefly inclined his head toward Nancy Dement. The smaller one focused on me.

"Ma'am, why don't you step outside with us?" he said.

"I'm not going anywhere," I declared petulantly.

"Please just come with us, ma'am," he said.

"Officer, this really isn't necessary," Ben said, standing now, trying to put his body between the cop and me.

"*Sir,* this doesn't concern you," he snarled.

"I'm her husband. This most certainly *does* concern me."

With a forearm, the cop easily shunted aside Ben, who was giving up at least eighty pounds to the guy, and reached for my arm.

"Don't touch me," I said, shrugging away from him and ducking low.

He moved toward me more aggressively, seeming to fill all the space above me. "Come on, now," he said, trying to grab me by the shoulders.

I flailed upward at him, backhanded, just to stop him from manhandling me. My hand bounced off his arm and, purely by accident, connected with his cheek.

"Dammit," he said.

His hand flew to his face, and he staggered back a step or two. My engagement ring — a cheap, half carat, nothing little bit of occluded rock — had grazed his jaw, opening a small cut.

"Ma'am, that's assaulting an officer," the larger one said. "Now we're going to have to arrest you."

"That's not assault! That was . . . that was an accident."

"Officer, please, I've got this," Ben said, again trying to get himself between me and the smaller guy. "Honey, let's just —"

"Sir, I'm going to have to ask you to stand over there," the larger deputy said, agitated.

"Officer," Ben said, still moving forward, "it would really be better if —"

"Sir! Stand back! Now!" the larger one ordered, reaching menacingly toward his Taser.

Ben, who had suffered from some bad run-ins with law enforcement as a teenager, threw up his hands and stopped in his tracks. The smaller deputy pressed forward.

"Ma'am, are you on drugs?" he asked.

"I'm not . . . No, of course I'm not on drugs. Jesus, what's wrong with you people? I just want my baby. That's not an irrational thing."

They were backing me toward the corner. It was like a wall of uniforms, closing in on me.

"Ma'am, we've received a report about you disturbing the peace and now you've assaulted an officer. Do you really want to add resisting arrest?" the smaller one said. "You're going to have to come with us. Do you want to do this the easy way or the hard way?"

"I'm *not* coming with you. Not until I get

some answers out of this woman."

"All right. Let's do this," the smaller one said. But not to me.

They moved with precision, each locking down a side of my body. They seemed to have more than just four arms between them, and they were strong. Gorilla strong. I bucked and thrashed and growled at them like a wounded animal, with very little impact. I could hear Ben protesting, but the threat of the Taser was keeping him at a distance.

Nancy Dement's face had this look of smug triumph as I was hauled out of her office, one officer holding each arm, my toes dragging along the carpeted floor.

"Let go of me. *Let go of me.* You're hurting me!" I yelled repeatedly, to no avail, as they hauled me back through the waiting room, where other Social Services clients recoiled from me.

They hauled me out the door, into the main hallway. I kept trying to get my legs pointed forward so I could dig my heels in. I heard the seam of my dress tearing as I struggled.

The smaller one was tiring. It gave me more energy. As we reached the front door, I was still putting up a hell of a fight, making it as difficult on them as I could. I couldn't even say why. I was well beyond exercising that kind of logic.

Once we were outside the building, the smaller one — the one who had a small rivulet of blood dripping from his jawline — said, "All right, I've had enough of this. Put her over there."

His partner seemed to understand. They steered me to the rock bed that fronted the building, then dumped me down on the stones.

I didn't really understand why they had let me go. I was just kneeling there, breathing heavily. One of the cap sleeves on my dress had been mostly ripped off. A chunk of my hair had been pulled out of the barrette.

The smaller one reached toward his belt and pulled out a black canister. Without a wasted movement, he aimed it in my direction, then depressed a button on top, sending a small burst of whitish fluid hurtling at my face.

My eyes, nose, and mouth instantly felt like they were on fire. I howled and dropped, completely incapacitated, trying vainly to wipe away this terrible singeing hell.

Pepper spray. The small part of me still capable of corresponding with my senses understood I had been hit with pepper spray.

The rest of me — body and spirit — was in total agony. They let me writhe on the ground for a little while, choking on my own snot and spit, allowing the pepper spray to dissipate so they didn't have to taste it themselves.

Once they felt it was safe enough, they moved in, pinned my wrists behind my back, then fastened them together with handcuffs. I couldn't have resisted if I wanted to. I was incapacitated by the pain, not to mention blind from the torrent of tears that had flooded my eyes.

I was dimly aware Ben was lurking somewhere nearby, aiming his cell phone at them, recording their actions in silent protest. The deputies ignored him as they hauled me to their patrol car and locked me in the back.

At that point, I thought the sum total of what had happened to me — having my baby taken, having my house torn apart, being accused of wanting to sell my child, then being pepper-sprayed for wanting to know who had made that accusation — was punishment enough.

But there were more ignominies waiting

for me over the next few hours. The sheriff's deputies took me to their headquarters, a short drive away.

There, I was put in front of a magistrate. With my eyes stinging and my nose still running like a faucet, I can't imagine I made much of an impression on the man. He charged me with assault, disturbing the peace, and resisting arrest. To him, the fact that I caused the good people at Social Services to call the sheriff on me — then forced those nice hulking officers to use pepper spray on bad little me — indicated I was enough of a menace to society that I needed to have some prison bars around me.

His exact words, after he ordered for me to be held without bond, were: "I think we're going to give you a little time to cool off, Ms. Barrick."

He said I'd get a bail hearing in front of a judge the next day. In the meantime, I was permitted one phone call. I used it to inform Diamond Trucking I wasn't going to be at work the next day.

I was then processed, fingerprinted, and transported to the Middle River Regional Jail, where things only got worse. I've read stories about challenges to the constitutionality of the strip searches they do at jails to make sure new inmates aren't smuggling in drugs and whatnot. But until you actually experience one, there's no understanding the humiliation of stripping stark naked and being made to squat and cough, all the while having your anus and genitalia inspected by a stranger.

Eventually, I was outfitted in a loose-fitting orange jumper and deposited into the general population. It was not unlike entering a new group home for the first time: I was the new kid, and the other women were now appraising me for signs of weakness.

I felt myself trying to engage that survival technique I had long ago taught myself. Except it wasn't working anymore. I couldn't take the most important part of myself and lock it away when that part — Alex — was somewhere else.

And didn't I know that already? That being a mother had changed everything?

Not long ago, I read a story in the newspaper about how researchers at a university in the Netherlands performed a series of MRI scans on a group of women's brains. Some of the women went on to get pregnant, others didn't. Follow-up scans showed significant differences in the gray matter of the pregnant women as compared to the non-pregnant women. Becoming a mother had triggered physical alterations in their brain's structure in at least eleven different areas.

I could have told them that without all the fancy gadgetry. My twenties had felt like a kind of extended adolescence. I could make bad choices — go out and get drunk on a Friday night, eat nothing but ice cream for dinner, whatever — and it felt like the consequences were fairly limited. I wasn't hurting anyone but myself.

Even when I ended up living in my car, I had this sense that it wasn't *that* big a deal, because the only person suffering was me.

Pregnancy ended that, along with so much else. Even if I didn't know Alex yet, I felt a powerful sense of responsibility, a charge that went to the core of who I was. What happened to me was now happening to someone else. I wasn't merely Melanie Barrick anymore. I was someone's mother.

Except now, at least in the legal sense, I wasn't anymore.

While I was being poked and prodded and pushed from one station to the next, Alex was being formally removed from my care. A few miles away from the jail, at the courthouse in downtown Staunton, Social Services had submitted its emergency removal order.

Then a judge, who had been endowed by the Commonwealth of Virginia with the authority to take people's babies from them, had decided that Alexander Barrick, by dint of being in my care, had been subject to abuse and neglect.

Shenandoah Valley Social Services now had legal custody of my child. Just as it had once had legal custody of me.

A vicious circle that began long ago, when my mother first met my father, was now coming around for a second lap.

TWELVE

She couldn't believe it. The baby was crying. Again.

No, not just crying. She had always thought of a baby's calls as a pleasant sort of noise — the gentle yawl of neonate human life, announcing itself to the world.

This was something more than crying. This kid had a set of lungs on him that would shame an opera singer, and his protests came out not only at an earsplitting volume but at a frequency that seemed to have been perfectly tuned to make her lose her mind.

What's more, he had been doing it practically nonstop since he arrived the previous afternoon. If he wasn't sleeping or eating, he was making this . . . this cacophony.

The latest eruption began when he woke from his nap and quickly worked himself into a red-faced fury. She had been trying to sneak in a little shut-eye herself, after a long and mostly sleepless evening, and now was just praying someone else would deal with it.

Then she remembered there was no one else home.

"Okay, okay," she muttered, rising from her bed. "I'm coming."

She staggered into the nursery, which was already descending into disarray. The diaper pile, once so neatly aligned, had been knocked over. The box of baby wipes had been left open, turning the top wipe into sandpaper. There was a smudge of poop on the changing-pad cover, which she hadn't subbed out because the other changing-pad cover was in the wash, having previously been pooped on.

As she leaned over the crib, the baby was really ramping up.

"Would you *please* just . . . shut . . . up?" she moaned.

She bent down and took the baby out of his crib. For a moment, she had the child grasped in both hands and all she wanted to do was shake the damn thing until he quieted.

No, you can't do that, she reminded herself.

She still wanted to.

Finally, she brought him to her body and began patting his back, like you were supposed to do with a baby, like every baby in the known history of Homo sapiens wanted.

Except for this baby. Her efforts to snuggle him were, once again, futile.

It was stunning, really, how this little creature could be so demanding of her attention and yet so manifestly unsatisfied when he received it. And she didn't have any idea what to do about it.

The majority of their preparation had been focused on the things they needed to do to acquire a baby. They had crossed *t*'s and dotted *i*'s, trying not just to meet the standards but exceed them by a wide margin. It had almost become this game: How much can we impress Social Services? How perfect can we be?

She had really thought it would all be for nothing, or at least that there would be a long wait before anything happened.

And then, suddenly, mere days after they received their certificate, the family services specialist, Tina Anderson, had called. *You're not going to believe this, but a baby just became available. Would you like to begin your journey as a foster parent?* she asked.

Yes, the woman had said immediately. *Yes, yes, yes, of course we want the baby!*

That was less than twenty-four hours earlier. It already felt like years. Having failed, again, to soothe this unsootheable baby, she considered her other options. He wasn't hungry. Correction: He wouldn't eat. He kept refusing the formula she gave him.

Diaper change. Maybe she'd try that. She flopped him down on the changing-pad, unsnapped his onesie, took off the old diaper, balled it up, and tossed it in the diaper pail.

Except the moment fresh air hit the baby's penis, a stream of urine came jetting out. It arced high in the air, then landed on the baby's face and in his mouth — resulting in an even louder protest from the child.

"Oh God!" the woman yelped. "Stop that! Stop that!"

Grabbing a rag, she cleaned the baby, then the floor next to the changing table, where some of the pee had landed. She was just straightening herself when her husband walked into the room.

She immediately burst into tears.

"What's going on?" he asked, confronting a woman and a child who both appeared to be on the brink of apoplexy.

"I am *so* bad at this," the woman said in frustration. "I've been a mother for less than a day and I already want to give up."

He took her in his arms.

"You're a great mother," he said. "You two

just need time to get to know each other."

"You . . . you think?" she said between sniffles.

"Yes. And you're going to have all the time you need. This is our baby. And he's always going to be our baby."

THIRTEEN

A name. Amy Kaye finally had a name.

She could barely keep herself in her seat as she drove back from Daphne Hasper's house and let this new discovery flop around in her mind.

There had been so many times, sitting in a dusty file room, poring through cases that had been forgotten by all but the victim, when she daydreamed about having something other than a shifting description of a man who whispered.

A name changed everything. A name came with a face you could put in a lineup; a story you could check against existing facts; movements you could surreptitiously follow, especially early in the morning, which is when so many of the attacks occurred.

Best of all, a name corresponded to a human being brimming with DNA.

She couldn't get a court order to test Warren Plotz yet, of course. One victim,

141

thirteen years after the fact, saying she had a vague feeling it might be some creepy guy she went to high school with? She couldn't put something so half-baked in front of a judge.

Her greatest fear, of course, wasn't that a judge would laugh her out of his chambers. It's that she'd get the order and, shortly after Warren Plotz had the inside of his cheek scraped, he'd hop on the interstate and never again be seen in Augusta County.

She wanted to find a way to get him locked up first, *then* get her sample.

There was already a lot about Plotz that, at least circumstantially, seemed to fit. He graduated high school in 1999, the same year as Daphne Hasper, and was now thirty-seven.

That meant he was sixteen at the time of the 1997 rape. It was a little young, but Amy had never been sure about that case — it was the "low voice" perpetrator, which wasn't quite the same as a whisper. Maybe it wasn't him. Or maybe he was too young to think someone might recognize his voice and didn't start whispering until later.

Hasper said she believed Plotz had gone out on the road in one of his father's rigs not long after graduation. So it would have made sense there weren't many attacks locally during those years.

Amy wondered about the other jurisdictions, littered along the routes Plotz had traveled, with their own smattering of unsolved sexual assaults. Had he focused on certain areas or just looked for opportunities wherever he pulled off the road?

Maybe once they got Plotz's data in CODIS, the FBI's combined DNA index system, there would be a slow, steady trickle of cold cases being solved in cities and towns all along America's interstates. How many young women were there out there, wondering if their personal demon would ever be brought to justice? How many more women had suffered Plotz's malevolence and never reported it?

Whatever the number, the women of Augusta County eventually got it the worst. That run of attacks in 2002–03 would have been when Plotz was twenty-one or twenty-two. That fit solidly within the profile Amy was already developing. Power-reassurance rapists get their name for their need to reassure themselves of their own sexual dominance. Plotz, at twenty-two, would have been growing into his own physically and sexually, and would have been particularly attuned to that need.

Amy wondered if she could subpoena his

company's records and match attacks to when he was at home, in between hauls. That would also have to wait until she had more solid evidence against Plotz.

And then — and this was the part that really had Amy thinking Plotz was her guy — there was Hasper's belief Plotz had returned to work an office job.

No more roaming. No more interstates. Just his home county and his twisted carnal urges. That's why the attacks had been nonstop since then.

As soon as Amy returned to her office, she went onto her computer to see what it could tell her about the suspect she had been waiting three years to meet.

He had no criminal record. Or at least if he did, it wasn't in the Commonwealth of Virginia. His name didn't pop up on any cases in LexisNexis, which covered other states. He had also never been a federal inmate.

Which made sense. That's why his DNA wasn't on file.

From there, Amy began doing other searches. It's a common misconception that prosecutors and other law enforcement officers have access to a host of comprehensive, all-knowing, Big Brother–style databases far beyond the reach of the general public.

Maybe the NSA did. As for Chief Deputy Commonwealth's Attorney Amy Kaye? Her best sources for penetrating the privacy of everyday citizens was a little less exotic.

Facebook. LinkedIn. Instagram. Amy had learned to stalk subjects on social media platforms with the best of them.

It turned out she and Warren Plotz had a mutual Facebook friend — a man Amy had played softball with — which gave her access to some of Plotz's profile.

His photos revealed an unremarkable man in his mid- to late thirties. He was a little bit on the heavy side, but more solid than overweight. He had short brown hair, which he parted to the side. He favored aviator-style sunglasses that Amy thought made him look like a douchebag. He wore a chunky watch on his left arm that appeared to be expensive.

Judging from his vacation pictures, he was doing just fine financially — certainly better than your average trucker. But that made sense, given that his father owned the company.

It was difficult to tell his exact height. But from looking at a few group photos, he appeared to be in the average range. There were a lot of pictures of him with friends at bars. He didn't appear to have children.

According to his "About," he was married to a Deirdre Plotz. That was slightly unexpected. Power-reassurance rapists tended to be the live-in-the-basement-with-Mother types; or, if not that, at least unassuming. Their failure in other areas of life — with their families, on the job, and particularly in relationships — fed their feelings of sexual inadequacy.

But that was not what leapt out most in that section. It was his employer. Diamond Trucking. The name was familiar. Amy just couldn't place it.

She was in the midst of pondering this when there was a knock on her office door.

"Come in," she said.

She soon saw the dark brown hair and small blue eyes of Aaron Dansby. In truth, he was not unattractive, in a strictly physical sense. He looked a bit like a poor man's Matthew McConaughey. And like McConaughey, he played the role of the scion of Southern aristocracy quite well.

He was looking particularly foppish on this day, with a new light-blue suit, a subtly checked shirt, and a bow tie. She had told him never to wear bow ties in front of a jury because they made him look smug and pretentious. He told her she was wrong, because his wife liked them — as if the entire jury pool was made up of former Estée Lauder girls.

This was a somewhat rare appearance for Dansby. He usually asked her to come into his office.

"Hey," he said.

"Hi."

"How'd it go with your interview?"

"Fine," she said tersely. She hadn't forgotten his threat from the previous night.

"Great, great," he said. "Did the victim remember anything useful?"

Amy could feel him trying too hard, forcing the conversation in an effort to project normalcy. This was classic Aaron Dansby. He had attempted to bully her the night before. She had fought back. Like most bullies, he immediately backed down. And now he was going to play nice while pretending the confrontation had never happened.

"She actually gave me the name of a potential suspect," Amy said. "She admitted it was just a hunch, but she said she never told investigators about it at the time."

"Oh, really? Who?" Dansby said, continuing to feign interest.

"Warren Plotz. His family owns a trucking company. Don't get too excited, because it might not turn into anything. But it's at least someone to check into a little."

"Plotz, huh? That's a good lead. You should definitely chase that," he said absently. And then he made his awkward pivot to what he really wanted to talk about: "Did you see the news last night?" he asked.

"No," she said.

She knew he wanted her to ask how it went. She wasn't going to give him that pleasure.

"Oh, well, Claire said it looked great."

Claire Dansby was his wife. She was usually kind in her assessments.

"That's . . . good," Amy said.

"Definitely. So, no problems for Friday? You'll be able to get an indictment?"

"Sure. I talked to Jason this morning. I don't think we have anything to worry about. The bust was clean. Possession is clear. The defendant left her cell phone with the paraphernalia. It's a slam dunk."

"Good, good," he said with a nod. "Keep the pedal down. I want us to send this one away for a good long time. Maybe even longer than Mookie Myers."

"That's probably not going to happen. Myers had a record. This woman doesn't."

Dansby crossed his arms. "I don't want people saying we went soft on Coke Mom because she's white."

"She'll still get at least five years," Amy

assured him. "The sentencing guidelines are what they are."

This seemed to satisfy Dansby. "Okay. Okay, I guess we can spin that with the media when the time comes."

He knocked on the doorframe twice for emphasis, then walked back to do whatever it was he did instead of his job.

Amy returned her eyes and her thoughts to the screen. Diamond Trucking. Warren Plotz worked at Diamond Trucking. And then . . .

Of course. It was also where Melanie Barrick worked.

Amy's arm hair stood at attention as a chill passed through her. She had always hypothesized that as soon as she had a name, she would start finding connections — between the perpetrator and the victims, and between the victims themselves.

It was an unexpected twist that this particular victim was about to be indicted on drug charges. It complicated matters, because it meant Amy couldn't immediately march off and reinterview Barrick.

But that would come in time. What mattered for now is that she was making actual headway on Warren Plotz. Three years after she started her investigation, it finally had momentum.

FOURTEEN

My first night in jail reminded me of being back in a group home: the thin mattress, the smell of human exhaust, the night noises from too many people in too small a space.

There would have been a time in my life when I actually would have been soothed by this soundtrack — the coughs and snores, the groaning of cheap bedsprings, the occasional nonsensical somniloquy from one of my bunkmates. Now it was just a reminder of times I had worked hard to forget.

If I slept, it was only intermittently — more like dozing. My heart wouldn't stop pounding. I kept thinking about Alex: Where was he? Was he okay? How was I going to get him back?

I yearned to run my hand over his soft head, to smell his sweet baby smell, to hear his lovely laugh. That was something he had only started busting out in the past week or two. It came from deep in his belly, and it was the most perfect, joyous sound in the world. Ben was so enamored of it, he sampled it so he could turn it into a ringtone.

Would I ever hear that laugh in person again?

Then there was the darker, even more perplexing question: Who told Social Services I was trying to sell my baby? Who would invent such a fiction? Who despised me that much? And why? I couldn't assemble it into a narrative that made any kind of sense.

In the morning, I was awakened from my not-quite-sleep at five a.m. I was soon seated in front of a representative from Blue Ridge Court Services, who had to make a bail recommendation for the judge I would face later in the day. After grilling me for a little while — Did I have a criminal background? How long had I lived in the area? Did I have family here? Did I have a job? — he returned me to the general population.

By that point, it was after six, and my fellow inmates were shuffling around, going to the bathroom, cackling at one another, bickering over this or that.

No one told me what I was supposed to do or where I was supposed to go, but the rhythms of institutional living were familiar to me. I slipped into the flow easily and succeeded in not making eye contact or otherwise engaging with my fellow inmates all the way until breakfast. Then, just after I had parked myself alone at a table in the dining hall, placing my tray of watery oatmeal and rubbery eggs in front of me, I was approached by three young black women.

"Yeah, I told you that's her," one of them said, like she was proud of herself.

"We saw you on the news this morning," another said. "You, like, famous."

"They calling you Coke Mom," the third said. "They say you had a lot of coke. They put your picture on the TV and everything."

I tried not to show any reaction as I absorbed this information. If it was true — and I couldn't imagine they were making it up — it was another ignominy to add to the ones I had already suffered. Right now, everyone in Staunton I had met since I was thirteen, everyone from my teachers to my former employers to my current one, were clucking their tongues and wondering whatever happened to Melanie Barrick.

The second one's face brightened. "Hey," she said, "if you Coke Mom, you think maybe I could be Coke Daughter? You can hook me up when I get out."

The other two laughed at this, elbowing each other in a good-natured fashion.

"Yeah, yeah, I'll be Coke Cousin," the third said. "You be Coke Aunt. We be, like, one big happy Coke Family."

More laughter. I still hadn't said anything.

"Aww, come on, now," the third one said. "We just messing with you."

I returned my attention to my eggs, which had chunks of powder in them from where they hadn't been well stirred. I lifted my fork to my mouth. I just wanted them to go away.

"What? You too good for us, is that it?" one of them said, then shoved my tray toward me.

I caught it just before it tumbled into my lap. Some of the oatmeal sloshed out of its shallow plastic bowl and onto the table.

"Is that it? You think you all hot because you been on TV?" she said.

Since silence didn't seem to be accomplishing much, I looked up at the woman and glared.

"I have nothing to say to you," I said quietly. "Now please leave me alone."

"Ohh, Coke Mom wants to be left alone," she taunted. "You think I take orders from you, bitch?"

"No. But I think I have a right to be left alone."

The woman was about to come up with a rejoinder when a corrections officer strode up toward us. She was an African American woman, close to six feet tall, with large breasts and a rounded butt. Her hair was in long braids — extensions, probably — that she had wrapped into a tight bun for work purposes. She had a set to her jaw that made her disapproval of this situation plain.

"All right, Dudley, that's enough," she said. "Go sit down somewhere. Not here."

"I'm just talking to —"

"You want me to write you up? You want some time in seg? Keep talking."

"Damn, yo, we just having some fun," Dudley said. But then she sulked off, taking her friends with her.

Once they were out of earshot, the officer said, "Sorry about that."

"That's okay. Thanks for helping me out, Officer. I'm just trying to mind my own business here."

I gave her a quick smile, thinking that was the end of our exchange. But she stayed where she was, looking down at me with this strange countenance.

"You don't remember me, do you," she said quietly.

Startled, I studied her face, which I was reasonably certain I had never seen before.

"Ah . . . sorry, I . . ."

I glanced at her name tag, which read BROWN. Had we been coworkers at Starbucks? Gone to school together? I'm reasonably certain I would have remembered a woman of her stature. Nothing was coming to me.

"Don't worry about it," she said.

I wanted to ask her the whens, hows, and whats of any relationship we might have had. I could surely use a friend in here.

But I already had the sense this wasn't the time. It certainly wasn't the place. Officer Brown wouldn't want to risk other inmates overhearing.

"Thanks again for helping me out," I said, nodding in the direction of the women who had already sat down.

"Oh, don't worry about them. They're harmless," she said. "Some of the other women aren't, though. Best to stay out of their way."

"Got it."

"You take care of yourself," she said. "I'll see you around."

I kept my head down for the rest of the morning. Knowing I would soon be appearing before a judge, I attempted to make myself look less like a bedraggled inmate and more like a woman who didn't really belong in her current circumstance.

But the orange jumper doesn't exactly help in that regard. And it's hard to do much to your hair without a comb.

Not long after lunch, I was led to a room with six other inmates — two women, one of them pregnant; four men — and told to sit quietly on a bench and wait. It was time for our bond hearings.

It seemed strange to me they had a judge come out to the jail. Didn't inmates go to judges, not the other way around?

Either way, my nerves had really started kicking in. I felt like I was waiting to go into the principal's office, only the consequences were considerably higher.

One by one, my fellow inmates were summoned. When they were finished, they exited quietly. Well, except for the pregnant woman. She was crying.

When it was my turn, I was escorted into a spare concrete room. There was no judge, just an older-model flat-screen television. On top of the TV, there was a camera. It pointed down at a chair that was backed up against the wall.

It was justice via teleconference. So much

for the human element.

I settled into the chair. On the television screen, the judge sat in what appeared to be a drab, cramped courtroom. Through reading glasses, he studied something on his desk.

In the upper right-hand corner of the screen, there was a small picture-in-picture cutout of me, looking small in my orange jumper, backed up against that concrete wall. I assumed that was the image of me being beamed back to the courthouse.

I couldn't see much besides the judge and the few feet in front of his desk, so I couldn't tell if there was anyone in the gallery. I wondered if Ben was there, offering silent support. He had a section of a large intro class that he TAed for Professor Kremer, his thesis adviser, on Thursday afternoons. But his wife's court appearance took precedence over that, right? Or could he not bring himself to tell Professor Kremer he was married to a cop batterer?

The judge looked up, taking off his glasses.

"Melanie Anne Barrick?"

"Yes."

"Ms. Barrick, you are charged with misdemeanor disturbing the peace and resisting arrest, and with assaulting an officer, which is a Class Six felony, punishable by one to five years in prison. Do you understand the charges against you?"

One to five years? For a scratch? Was he kidding?

"No . . . not, not really."

"What don't you understand?"

"I . . . I barely touched him. And it was only because he was —"

"Ms. Barrick," he said, holding up a hand like he was already out of patience with me. "We're not here to argue your case today. I just need to know that the words I'm using make sense to you and that you don't need a translator. Do you understand the charges against you? It's a pretty simple yes or no question."

To him, I was just another rumple-haired woman in an orange jumpsuit who apparently lacked the intelligence to comprehend his big, fancy words.

"Yes," I said, with what little dignity I could muster.

"Thank you. This is an offense that, if you are convicted, could result in your incarceration. You are therefore entitled to be represented by an attorney. If you cannot afford one, the court will appoint one for you without charge. Would you like me to appoint an attorney?"

"Yes, please."

"Raise your right hand."

I did.

"Do you swear or affirm the evidence you're about to give is the truth?"

"Yes."

"Ms. Barrick, do you have a job?"

"Yes, sir."

"What's your rate of pay?"

"Eighteen dollars an hour."

"And how many hours a week do you work?"

"Forty."

"Are there people living in your residence who rely on you for support?"

"Yes, sir," I said. "I have a son. And my husband is still a student."

The judge looked at the clerk for a moment. She nodded at him.

"Okay, Ms. Barrick. As I understand it, Mr. Honeywell is representing you on your Social Services case, is that right?"

"Uh, actually, I don't know anything about that."

The judge didn't seem fazed by this. "Then let me be the first to tell you. Ordinarily, I'd appoint someone from the Public Defender's Office to represent you. But since Mr. Honeywell is already going to be working with you on this other matter, I'm going to appoint him to represent you here as well. Is that acceptable?"

It wasn't. I knew about the kind of lawyers who were appointed in Social Services cases. With a few exceptions, they were the bottom feeders of the legal swamp. I can remember one of them telling my mother the reason he hadn't returned her phone calls was that the court was only paying him $100 to represent her and that didn't buy such personalized service. "You're lucky I even get out of bed for a hundred dollars," he said.

That was twenty years ago. I couldn't imagine the pay rate for court-appointed attorneys had improved much. I would get exactly what I paid for with this Honeywell guy: nothing. But at the moment, he was my only option.

"Okay," I said.

The lower-left side of the screen was now filled with a short, round, gray-haired man in a rumpled gray suit. His tie was too long for him. There were heavy bags under his eyes, which protruded out unnaturally far.

He looked like he already understood I was disappointed this was the best representation I could get.

"Ms. Barrick, can you see me all right?" he asked in a lugubrious, marble-mouthed Southern accent.

"Yes, sir."

"I have a report here from Blue Ridge," he said, waving it in his right hand, and then proceeded to make me repeat most of the things I had already told the court services officer that morning.

He finished by saying, "Your Honor, Blue Ridge has recommended a two-thousand-dollar unsecured bond. But under the circumstances, I think we can give Ms. Barrick a PR bond. She doesn't have a record, so she's never had to appear in court before. But if she's been working at the same place for four years, we know she's pretty good at showing up for things."

The judge turned to his left and asked, "Does the Commonwealth have any thoughts on the matter?"

And then, in the lower-right corner, the prosecutor appeared. I recognized her as the woman who had interviewed me after my assault. I couldn't recall her name and I wondered if she remembered me. I couldn't imagine there were *that* many rapes in Augusta County.

If she did, there was no sign of it. She was staring straight ahead at the judge.

"We do, Your Honor. Ms. Barrick seems to have recently developed a talent for getting in trouble with the law. In addition to these charges, the Sheriff's Office recently executed a warrant on her home, where they found a significant amount of cocaine."

This was the first time anyone in an official capacity had said it was cocaine they had found. Teddy's tastes must have shifted. He used to be a heroin user.

The judge's head swiveled toward me.

I couldn't believe the prosecutor was going to be able to use those damn drugs — the same drugs that had been the justification for taking my child from me — to make it even more difficult to get my child back. I could scarcely make the argument to Social Services that I was a fit mother when I was rotting in jail.

Desperate, I leaned toward the camera. "That wasn't mine, Your Honor. It belonged to my brother."

"Ms. Barrick," the judge said sharply, "you'll know when I want to hear from you, because I will have asked you a question. Otherwise, I need you to keep your mouth closed. Do we understand each other?"

"Yes, Your Honor," I said.

"Good. Now, this cocaine, how much are we talking about here?"

"Nearly half a kilo," the prosecutor said. "And I'm sure I don't need to tell you this, but the sentencing guideline for that amount is more than five years, Your Honor. That's a factor that would make her a flight risk."

I didn't know which to be more stunned by: the length of the potential prison sentences I was facing or the amount of drugs they had dragged out of my home.

Five years.

Half a kilo.

Holy hell. I had been around Teddy long enough to know that was a huge amount, enough to keep a small army of addicts high for a month. Where had he possibly come across that much coke? He must have been dealing again, and at a volume way beyond what he had ever done before.

"And has she been arrested on those charges?"

"Not yet, Your Honor. In the meantime, her violent behavior toward Officer Martin shows she's dangerous. And such a large amount of drugs is clearly a threat to the community. We feel like the sooner that threat is removed, the better.

"In addition, we know that people who deal drugs in such large quantities often have resources and contacts outside the community. Those are other factors that make her a flight risk. The Sheriff's Office found close to four thousand dollars in cash when they executed their search warrant, but she certainly could have more hidden somewhere else. The Commonwealth would like to see that taken into consideration."

"So what's your recommendation, Counselor?

"I honestly think you should deny bail, Your Honor. It'll save us the time of going through this again after she's indicted on the drug charges."

It was all I could do to keep from screaming. If the judge hadn't already admonished me, I would have.

The judge leaned back, picked up his reading glasses, and twirled them by the stem.

"Mr. Honeywell, do you have anything to say on your client's behalf?"

Mr. Honeywell had been standing there like a lump the whole time. I tried to mind control my good-for-nothing lawyer into saying something that might stop this ridiculousness.

"Well," he said as he thought it over. His Southern accent made it sound like he was saying "whale." Then he came up with: "Your Honor, my client and I haven't really had a chance to talk yet, as you know, so I haven't heard the facts of the assault case from her perspective. But she hasn't been convicted of anything yet. I'd just ask you to keep that in mind."

Pathetic. The man was absolutely pathetic.

"Okay, Mr. Honeywell, I hear you on that," the judge said, then gave his glasses another twirl. "I have to say, I understand the Commonwealth's concerns, but I think denying bail outright seems a little extreme at this juncture. Let's just take things one step at a time here and see what the grand jury has to say. In the meantime, I'm going to come up with a nice, meaningful amount. Let's call it twenty thousand dollars, secured. Ms. Barrick, if you choose to work with a bail bondsman, you'll have to come up with ten percent of that."

I slumped, shrinking further into my orange jumpsuit. Two thousand dollars might as well have been two million. I hadn't seen that kind of number in my checking account since we bought the house.

"Thank you, Judge," Mr. Honeywell said, as if I had somehow been done a massive favor.

He turned to me. "Ms. Barrick, do you have someone who might be able to bail you out? A family member? Your husband, perhaps?"

"I don't . . . I don't think so. We don't really have that kind of money."

"I'm sorry to hear that," he said, then turned back to the judge. "Your Honor, under the circumstances, we'll waive the preliminary hearing and go straight for trial. I don't think Ms. Barrick wants to be at Middle River any longer than is absolutely necessary."

The judge was again looking at something on his desk.

"Okay. How is May eighteenth for trial?"

May 18? So I was going to be in jail until May 18? Mr. Honeywell disappeared from the screen for a moment. When he came back, he said, "That's fine, Your Honor."

"Okay, then I think we're set," the judge said. "Ms. Barrick, you'll be in Circuit Court on May eighteenth. You'll have to talk with your attorney to prepare for trial. He'll be able to advise you on that. In the meantime, do you have any questions?"

Tons. But none he was likely to answer for me.

"No, Your Honor," I said.

"All right. Good luck to you, ma'am. Mr. Honeywell, do you have anything else for your client?"

"I'll pay you a visit sometime next week so we can talk things over," he said. "It's likely I'll be appointed to represent you on the drug charges too, so we'll probably have

166

lots to talk about."

"Can you . . . can you stop them from indicting me on the drug charges?"

"Not really, Ms. Barrick. I'm sorry. It doesn't work that way."

"But those drugs *aren't mine*," I said, again.

But this fact — which seemed rather significant to me — seemed to have no impact on him.

He had heard it all before.

FIFTEEN

As I shuffled back to the general population, the reality of my situation started to settle over me like a dense, demoralizing fog.

May 18 was more than two months away. By then, Alex would be five months old — and so, so different from what he was now. I had seen it with my friends' children. Babies undergo a metamorphosis during the fourth and fifth months, shedding the last bits of that newborn strangeness and transforming into the little people they are fast becoming.

Two months from now, I would have missed out on nearly half his life. And that was assuming I'd be able to clear up the assault charges, the drug charges, and this absurdity about wanting to sell my child — all of which would be very difficult to do from a jail cell.

I was barely keeping my composure as I

rejoined the other inmates. To deflect attention from myself, I found a book, a Nora Roberts paperback, and buried myself in a corner, shoving my face into it like it was the second coming of *To Kill a Mockingbird.*

Maybe an hour later, I was still hiding there, lost in my own misery. I didn't even understand what was happening when one of the guards approached me.

"Barrick?" he said.

"Yes."

"Come with me."

"What . . . where are we going?" I asked, braced for more bad news — that I had been put in segregation, that I had been randomly selected for another strip search, that I was being sent to a prison far away.

"You got bailed out," he said, opening a door for me and letting me shuffle past him. "Come on."

In short order, I signed a property form that said I had received all my possessions — which, in this case, consisted only of a ripped dress and the shoes I had been wearing. I changed in a bathroom, eagerly peeling off the dreaded orange jumper.

Soon, I was led into the visitors' waiting room — a free woman, apparently — where Teddy, of all people, was waiting for me. He stood up and came over toward me, looking

169

broad-shouldered and handsome, as usual.

I didn't know whether to be furious or perplexed.

"What . . . what are you doing here?" I asked. "Where's Ben?"

"He had class. I told him I could handle this."

Any gratitude I felt toward him for bailing me out was swamped by the fact that I wanted to pummel the life out of him. I wouldn't have been in there in the first place if it weren't for him.

"Besides, after all the times you did this for me? I wouldn't want to miss my one chance to spring my big sis from jail," he added, his handsome grin a little crooked.

"But where did you get two thousand dollars?"

"Don't worry about it," he said, casting his eyes about at an elderly couple that was waiting for its own newly freed criminal. "Let's go. This place sucks."

"No, Teddy, I'm serious. Where did you get that money?"

"I've been saving up," he said. "It's no big deal. Come on."

He crossed the waiting room toward the front door, then disappeared through it. I stayed rooted where I was, my fists jammed in my hips. I didn't want to follow him. I was too furious at him.

There was a pay phone in the corner. I could call Ben — wherever he was — and wait there until he could give me a ride. The only thing that made me chase after Teddy was that I wanted answers. Also, he needed to understand he was going to have to do everything in his power to get Alex back, even if it meant he would go to jail himself.

I was out in the parking lot, three-quarters of the way to his ancient rust bucket of a pickup truck, when I caught up with him.

"Hey," I said, slapping at his shoulder to get his attention. "I'm not an idiot. I know you've been dealing again. The Sheriff's Office pulled half a kilo of coke out of my house. Where the hell did you get that? Are you working for a cartel or something?"

He turned. "Seriously? Jesus, I come here to do you a favor and you're going to start accusing me of stuff? Can't you just be happy you're out?"

"Happy? Alex has been taken away by Social Services and I might have to serve five years in prison for barely hitting a cop — to say nothing of what will happen with those drug charges — and you think I should be *happy*?"

"Okay. Bad word choice. Look, just get in

the truck. I haven't been dealing drugs or doing drugs or anything like that. I've been working and saving, okay? It's surprising how fast your bank account grows when you're not injecting all your money."

I crossed my arms and stared at him. There was a long time during his teenage years when Teddy was little more than one heartbreak after another. But if there was one thing that kept me from giving up on him — beyond the tug of sororal bonds — it was that he was seldom untruthful with me. Even when he stole from me to support his habit, or suffered a relapse, or broke one of his many promises to turn over a new leaf, he always came clean about it later, once he was sober and feeling sheepish about his latest transgression. It had really helped salvage our relationship during some tough times. He once told me he respected me too much to lie to me.

"Are you really going to swear to me you haven't relapsed?" I demanded.

He looked straight into my eyes and said, "I swear to you I am totally and one hundred percent clean. I'll pee in a cup right now if you want me to."

"And those drugs weren't yours. You weren't selling them or holding them for Wendy or anything like that."

"Sis, I know we've been through a lot of crap together. But I'm telling you, I had nothing to do with that stuff."

"Are you seeing Wendy again?"

"No! I swear!" he said.

I studied him as if I were a human lie detector. But he just stood there and returned my gaze.

"You know Ben already grilled me about all of this, right?" he continued. "I thought he was going to take a swing at me. But then I convinced him it wasn't me."

"How?" I asked.

Teddy shrugged. "Because it's the truth? I don't know. Think about it. I never did coke. It's too damn expensive. For me it was always pills or H. You know that."

"So where did those drugs come from?" I asked. "Half a kilo of cocaine doesn't just show up out of nowhere."

Teddy took a few steps toward me. "Sis, this is going to sound a little nuts, but . . . Ben told me all that stuff about them thinking you want to sell Alex, which is . . . I mean, this is all crazy, but . . . Have you ever thought that someone is messing with you?"

"What do you mean?"

He sighed. "You know, for such a smart girl, you're kind of dumb sometimes. I think it's pretty obvious. Someone planted those drugs in your house and then told the Sheriff's Office they were there. Then they told Social Services you wanted to sell your kid. Someone is *totally* messing with you."

It was startling to hear him lay it out like that, so straightforward, so certain, so . . . correct?

"Who would do something like that?"

"I don't know," he said. "But you better figure it out. Because if you don't, they're just going to keep doing it."

I felt my brow crinkling. I didn't know what to think about any of this.

"Come on," he said. "Get in the truck."

We rode away in silence. On the way home, I made Teddy detour to the Walmart, then borrowed money for a handheld breast pump. I wanted to be able to leave the electric one at work.

As we completed the trip to Desper Hollow Road, I realized I was gripping the door handle on his truck extra hard.

Despite the surface-level plausibility of what Teddy had said, I was having a hard time convincing myself anyone was out to get me. I just didn't see how I was worth the trouble. For whatever people say about millennials and our everyone-gets-a-trophy upbringings, I didn't view myself as some special snowflake. I had long ago shed whatever delusions of grandeur I might have harbored as a teenager.

The very real truth of my life was that I was a thirty-one-year-old trucking-company dispatcher, living an until-now ordinary life with my baby and my husband.

Beyond that, I had generally come to believe most people in this world were too consumed with their own dramas to spend much time concerning themselves with anyone else's. Even when I was a child, in the throes of the system, I came to recognize that what could feel like people out to get me was mostly just a hodgepodge of tenuously connected human beings, each of them bumbling along in narrow-minded self-interest — with the occasional act of altruism thrown in just to keep you from losing hope in the species altogether.

To think that there was a mastermind orchestrating a well-coordinated attack against me strained credulity. It was the stuff of one of Bobby Ray Walters's conspiracy theories.

And yet there was no doubt that what Teddy said made sense. That drug stash hadn't just appeared in our house on its own. And it hadn't been there when we bought the place. The last owner had been an elderly churchgoing widow, pretty far from fitting the profile of a coke addict.

So, yes, those drugs had to have gotten into our house somehow. Likewise, this wild allegation that I wanted to sell Alex hadn't just materialized on its own. That Social Services director, for as much as I disliked her, was acting on what she felt was solid information.

Where had that lie originated from?

I remained every bit as baffled as I had been the day before in her office.

We made the turn onto Desper Hollow Road, then drove past Bobby Ray's property — with his couch, his Confederate flag, and his SMILE! YOUR ON CAMERA! sign.

Teddy turned up our driveway, then brought his truck to a stop. He turned to me with an earnest look.

"What?" I said.

"Nothing, it's just . . . I didn't want to bring this up, because . . . I don't know, I mean, I don't want to freak you out more. But don't you think it's kind of weird they haven't arrested you on those drug charges yet?"

"I don't know, is it? The prosecutor alluded to something about how she might be doing something about that soon, but it didn't make sense. I don't really have a lot of experience with this sort of thing."

"I do. They don't usually raid your house, find drugs, and then let you keep hanging out like nothing happened. They arrest you, and then you either get bail or you don't," he said. "This is just weird. I have a friend whose mom works down at the courthouse. I'm going to ask her about it, because I don't think . . ."

He stopped himself there. He didn't want to tell his big sister she really ought to be back in jail.

"Thanks," I said. "And thanks . . . thanks for bailing me out. I'm not sure if I said that yet. It's really —"

And suddenly I couldn't get the words out. The benevolence of what he had done crashed into me. Teddy hadn't grown up as poor as I had, but he certainly had his own tribulations to battle, self-made and otherwise. And yet he had battled through them and was just now coming out the other side.

This was probably the first time in his whole life that he had a sum like $2,000 saved up. He obviously had plans for that money. And yet he had not hesitated to use it on me — his big sister, who was supposed to be the responsible one; the quasi–mother figure; the one who should have been saving him, not the other way around.

"Hey, no big deal," he said, leaning over and hugging me. "I still owe you, like, a thousand times over."

"You don't, but thanks," I said.

I pulled myself down from his truck before I wept all over him. I got halfway to the front door and was reaching for my keys when I realized I didn't have any. The last time I left home, I had been with Ben, and I had assumed I was going to be returning with Ben. I jogged back to Teddy's truck just as he was starting to back down the driveway and waved to get his attention. He cranked down his window.

"Hey," I said. "Can I borrow your key? I don't have mine."

"Yeah, sorry, neither do I, actually. I have no idea where my key is. That was part of what made Ben realize that it wasn't my coke. I couldn't even get into your house if I wanted to. You want to come back to my place?"

"No, no," I said. "I'll just wait for Ben. No big deal. Seriously."

"All right."

"Thanks," I said, tapping the side of his truck. "Love you."

"Love you too, sis."

■ ■ ■ ■

I walked back to the front stoop, looking at the upended bulbs, which we hadn't yet had time to stick back in the dirt.

It was a warm afternoon for early March. I could have very easily curled up on our porch and napped there until Ben got home.

I sat instead. My gaze again fell on Bobby Ray's trailer. I had never given much consideration to his camera fetish. It was just one more strange thing about a strange guy. I had certainly never inquired as to what was — and wasn't — being captured by his lenses. Sometimes the less you know the better.

But now I was wondering if I might be able to use Bobby Ray's paranoia to my benefit. My driveway passed right by his trailer. If someone had gone to my place and planted drugs there, it's possible his cameras might have recorded some part of the act.

I had never been inside Bobby Ray's trailer. All of our interactions had occurred on his front lawn or mine — in open places, safe places. And I probably should have waited to approach him. Until Ben got home. Until my brain felt sharper. Until I didn't have a torn dress.

If I went down there and something happened to me, I could already hear those victim-blaming voices. *She went into his trailer alone. Shouldn't she, of all people, have known better? What did she* think *was going to happen?*

But no. I couldn't let that kind of groundless fear run my life. If there was something telling on those cameras, it might help me get Alex back. That mattered more than whatever theoretical threat Bobby Ray might pose.

The thought propelled me — first on my feet, then down the hill. This was a new frontier for Bobby Ray and me, nothing more. Just because there were men out there who were predators, it didn't make all of them that way.

I passed his couch, then tapped on his rickety screen door.

"Hang on a sec!" he yelled.

From inside, I heard his weight making the floor creak. Bobby Ray appeared at the door in white tube socks, camouflage cargo shorts, and a T-shirt that read BASKET OF DEPLORABLES. In the silk-screened image that appeared beneath that lettering, the basket had been wrapped in the Confederate flag and contained a bunch of guys who

180

looked as though they were extras from *Duck Dynasty.* A variety of long-barreled rifles were arrayed behind the basket.

It struck me, and not for the first time, just how big Bobby Ray was — well over six feet and approaching three hundred pounds. He was in no kind of cardiovascular shape, but there was a thickness to his neck, arms, and shoulders that suggested he wouldn't have much trouble lifting his end of a piece of furniture.

He goes three bills and she weighs, what, a buck twenty? Of course he was going to overpower her.

"Hey," he said. "Saw you on the news. Didn't think you'd be around for a while."

"My brother bailed me out."

"Decent of him."

"Yeah, he's a good kid."

"So what's . . . I mean, you got a trial, or . . ."

He let the question trail off. How much of my legal troubles did I share with Bobby Ray Walters? How much did he actually care?

"Yeah, something like that," I said. "I was actually wondering if you could help me out with something that sort of relates to all that."

"Sure. Shoot."

"So you know how the Sheriff's Office found all this cocaine in our place?"

"Yeah."

"It's not mine. And it wasn't Ben's. And my brother swears it wasn't his either. We actually don't know how it got there."

Bobby Ray sniffed up a wad of phlegm, then swallowed it. "Shoot. Sheriff probably brought it in with them. They have one of the deputies sneak it in and then toss it where they know one of the other investigators'll look. That way the guy who finds it can go on the stand later and say, 'Yes, Your Honor, I swear on a big ol' stack a Bibles that I ain't never seen those drugs before.' But it's all bull."

I had never considered that possibility. "They really do that?" I asked.

"Oh, yeah. All the time. I had a buddy they did it to. He went to work one day and when he got back: Surprise, surprise, they had raided his place and found a bunch of drugs. Then they throw in some bags and scales and say you were planning to distribute. It's what they do."

Is it what they had done to me? I couldn't think of anyone with a badge who had it out for me.

"Okay, so I guess that's one possibility. But I was also wondering if it was possibly

182

someone else."

"Like who?"

"I don't know. That's why I'm here. I was wondering . . . ," I started, then paused. I didn't know how to form my request, and my sleep-deprived brain wasn't giving me much help. "You have a bunch of cameras around here, right?"

"Some you can see, some you can't," he said proudly.

"Is it possible one of them might capture some part of my driveway or my house?"

He looked to his right, in the direction of my driveway. "Maybe. Why?"

"What if someone else, not the Sheriff's Office, planted those drugs in my place? And then they tipped off the Sheriff's Office that I was dealing, knowing it would trigger a raid?"

If there was one person who didn't need much convincing there was a nefarious plot afoot, it was Bobby Ray.

"Yeah," he said. "Yeah, I guess it could have been that. You want to have a look?"

"That'd be great."

"Come on in," he said, backing away from the door.

I took a few tentative steps inside. All the shades were drawn. There were no lights on. The small kitchen table was covered with the detritus of a slovenly bachelor life — a pizza box, the remainder of a TV dinner, a pile of junk mail, crushed beer cans.

"Sorry about the mess," Bobby Ray said. "Maid's off this week."

"No problem," I said, though it only fed my unease.

It was this dingy little trailer, her dress was ripped, and he had all those guns . . . What was she, too stupid to live?

I followed Bobby Ray through a small sitting area into his bedroom, where the shades were drawn. I thought maybe I'd see a gun rack or a shotgun on a wall or some sign of his enthusiasm for weaponry, but there was nothing visible.

He sat down heavily in front of his computer. My discomfort was only amplified when I saw his screensaver was a naked woman with a come-hither look on her face. In case the gentleman's imagination needed more prodding, her legs were spread wide and she was squeezing her voluptuous breasts between her arms.

She should have run out the moment she saw that porn. She was practically begging for it.

"Sorry about that. That's my girlfriend right there," he joked, swiping at his mouse until the screen went away.

184

"You might want to buy her some clothes," I said, trying to be jocular about the whole thing.

He had already moved on. "All right, so I set this up myself. It all gets saved to the hard drive and it stays there for two months before it gets wiped out. Any deputy who tries to plant something in here is gonna wind up on *Candid Camera,* you know what I'm sayin'?"

Bobby Ray brought up a program that showed a split screen of six different camera views and continued his narration. "I got two inside, four outside and . . . Oh yeah, this one gets some of your driveway."

He centered the mouse over one of the camera views and clicked on it, enlarging it so it filled the entire screen. I was now looking at a real-time view of his side yard, which included my driveway in the top portion.

"Yep," he said. "Camera three. Hang on."

He clicked off the live feed and was soon opening a folder, where the archived footage must have been stored.

Over the next twenty minutes, we rewound through Thursday, Wednesday, then Tuesday, the day of the Sheriff's Office raid. Then we kept going backward.

There was nothing suspicious the remainder of the day on Tuesday. It was just Ben leaving for school, and me leaving for work that morning. I felt a little hitch in my breathing as I saw my car. Those would have been among the last moments I got to be with Alex before dropping him off at Mrs. Ferncliff's. Little did I know how much I should have savored that time.

Bobby Ray scrolled further back. Monday night was uneventful. Ben returned from JMU, then I came home from Diamond Trucking — two creatures of habit, acting in their customary ways.

Then, at 1:17 p.m. on Monday, there was something that flashed before my eyes, a quick blur that didn't fit the pattern. It was a vehicle of some sort. But it wasn't one we owned.

"Wait, wait, stop it there," I said. "Can you go back?"

"Yeah, hang on."

Bobby Ray monkeyed with the footage until he got it to the right spot, then set it at normal speed. The blur had been a van with a decal on the side, backing down my driveway.

"What did it say on the side?" I asked.

"Dunno. Let me see if I can get it when it came in."

He kept rolling the footage back until he

reached 1:01 p.m., which was when the truck had arrived.

"Here we go," he said. "Let me pause it."

He brought the van back on the screen, then froze it there, allowing me to make out the words.

A1 VALLEY PLUMBING
BONDED * LICENSED * FREE ESTIMATES
"WHEN YOU HAVE A DRIP, WE DROP
EVERYTHING."
(800) GET VALLEY

It looked like a perfectly legitimate service van, except for one small detail.

I hadn't called a plumber.

Sixteen

Amy Kaye had been playing this out in her head ever since the idea first occurred to her during that restless time after two a.m.

It had been rattling around in there during General District Court, through the arraignments, the speeders, and the drunks. It had even been somewhere in her mind when she got the surprise that was seeing Melanie Barrick's name on the docket for a bond hearing relating to assault charges.

Now here was the conversation she had been mentally preparing for all day.

"All right, Amy," a sheriff's deputy said. "We've got Warren Plotz waiting for you in the conference room."

"Great," Amy said, already walking away from the detective's bullpen at the Augusta County Sheriff's Office, where she had been bantering with one of the investigators. "Did he give you any trouble?"

"Not a bit. We told him it was voluntary

and he practically leapt in the car. He seemed pretty excited about it, actually."

"Perfect," she said.

This was her middle-of-the-night brainstorm: She wasn't about to approach Warren Plotz head-on about the two-decade string of unsolved sexual assaults in which he was now the primary suspect. There was too great a chance he'd spook and run.

But she still wanted to size the guy up, to look him in the eye and see what she was dealing with. Maybe she'd catch him in a lie or two she could use against him later. Maybe she'd even get more than that, if he fell into the trap she had planned for him.

And Melanie Barrick, of all people, had given her the perfect excuse to be able to come at him — not head-on, but from the side.

"Mr. Plotz," she said as she entered the conference room. "Thank you so much for coming in. I'm Amy Kaye with the Commonwealth's Attorney's Office."

In person, he was the same slightly stocky guy she had seen on Facebook. The douchebag aviator glasses were perched atop his brown hair. He wore the chunky watch on his left wrist.

Otherwise, she was seeing how he could have eluded so many women's description.

He had no scars, no tattoos, nothing unusual about his size or shape that stood out.
It was almost like he went out of his way to
be average.

She gave him what she felt was a professionally appropriate smile and a firm hand-
shake.

"Nice to meet you," he said easily.

"Pick a seat, any seat," she said casually.
She wanted this whole thing to feel as
informal as possible. He sat at the end of
the table. She sat across from him and
placed a blank legal pad in front of her.
Then she tilted back in the chair.

Again, casual. According to Virginia statute, he didn't need to know about the
digital recorder she had just started.

"So, I'm sure you've heard about the raid
on Melanie Barrick and what was found in
her house?"

"Everyone in the valley's heard, I think,"
he confirmed.

"Right. So, as you've probably already
guessed, we're investigating Ms. Barrick's
role in what appears to be a major drug
distribution conspiracy. At this point, we're
trying to get a full picture of her activities. I
really appreciate your cooperation."

"Sure."

And then Amy coughed. Just once. She

wanted to start slow.

"Anyhow, how long has Ms. Barrick been employed with Diamond Trucking?"

"Uhh, it's prolly been, like, three, four years now? I'd have to check with my bookkeeper."

Amy jotted this down on the legal pad. What she didn't write down — but certainly noted in her mind — was that he hadn't said "the" bookkeeper or "our" bookkeeper. It was "my" bookkeeper.

He was insecure but trying to make himself seem more important. Just like a power-reassurance rapist would.

"And what is her position there?" she asked.

"She's a dispatcher."

"So . . . she tells the trucks where to go, where to pick up their next load, that sort of thing?"

"Yeah. That sort of thing."

"That means she has a lot of interaction with all your drivers. She knows all of them, talks to them all regularly?"

"Definitely."

"Right," Amy said, nodding. Then she added, as if it were an afterthought: "Oh, I should also probably ask you, what's your position at the company?"

"Uh, I guess you'd call me vice president."

Amy was sure no one called him anything of the sort. But again, it was worth noting.

"And how long have you been employed with Diamond?"

"It's my family's company, so I basically grew up there."

"A long time, then," she said.

"Yeah."

"You've always worked on the administrative side?"

"Naw, I was on the road for a lot of years. I felt like it'd be good experience to learn the business from the ground up, you know?"

"Oh, that's smart," Amy said. "So when did you shift to the office?"

"Uhh, I'd say twenty eleven, twenty twelve, something like that," he said.

Bingo. It was just as Daphne Hasper said: Warren Plotz got off the road right around the time the whispering rapist stepped up the frequency of his attacks. And now she had him saying it on a recording.

Amy coughed again. Twice, this time. She didn't want to oversell it. "Excuse me," she said.

Then she resumed: "Would you say Ms. Barrick has been a good employee? Punctual? Reliable?"

"Yeah, I guess."

"You guess?"

"I don't know. I mean, don't get me wrong, she always did the job. She just always acted like she was better than everyone else; like, you know, she was just lowering herself to work there. My dad, he was all into her, because she went to UVA. . . . I guess you could say he had an old-man crush on her."

"I can understand that," Amy said, trying to sound objective. Then she tossed out some bait, to see if he would rise to it: "She's a pretty girl, isn't she?"

Plotz didn't bite. "Not my type. I like 'em with a little more meat on their bones."

He grinned at her. His eyes darted up and down Amy's body, which was full-figured. She had to suppress a shudder.

She should have known he'd be too cagey to indicate he was attracted to one of his victims. He was so relaxed, sitting there in the sheriff's conference room, gabbing easily with the chief deputy commonwealth's attorney.

"So your dad liked her," Amy said. "But you didn't."

"Yeah. To be honest, none of this surprises me. I always thought she was hiding something."

"Like what?"

"I don't know. I mean, I guess it was drugs, obviously."

With that, Amy launched into a coughing fit, this time going at it until she was sure she was a bit red in the face.

"You know what? I'm sorry, I think I need a soda or something," she said, then tossed in: "You want one?"

"No, I'm good."

Crap.

"You sure? My treat. Come on, it's not every day I offer to buy a guy a drink," she said, adding a wink.

Amy, the woman with a little meat on her bones, couldn't believe she was flirting with a suspected rapist. Anything to get the job done.

And it worked.

"Uh, all right," he said.

"What do you want?"

"They got Sprite?"

"Sure. I'll be right back."

Amy rose from her seat and left the room. She found herself breathing a little hard as she went to the vending machine. This was the part she had been thinking about since the small hours of the morning. And it was working out the way she hoped.

She got Sprite for him, Coke Zero for herself. Then she returned to the conference room and slid the can in front of him. Like, you know, no big deal.

Then she sat, cracked open her soda, and took a long drink.

"Ahh," she said. "That hit the spot."

Plotz didn't touch his.

Damn. She put her Coke Zero down next to her legal pad, then continued.

"So you thought Ms. Barrick was hiding something."

"Right."

"Did she ever attempt to sell you drugs?"

"No, nothing like that."

"Did she ever try to sell drugs to any of your other employees?"

"Not that I know of. But I'll definitely ask."

"Thank you," she said. "Now, this next question is . . . I know it might be a little difficult for you, given that this is a family business. But as you know, an eighteen-wheeler is a pretty big piece of real estate. There have been many documented cases of truckers using them to smuggle drugs around the country. We're looking into the theory that's what was happening here. Do you think it's possible Ms. Barrick's supplier is one of your drivers?"

This actually wasn't a theory at all. She just wanted to make Plotz feel thirsty.

He grimaced. "I don't know. Our guys, they're pretty clean. They're family men, for the most part. And a lot of them have been with us for ten, twenty, thirty years. They're not the sort to go around doing something like that."

"Still, think hard. You have a lot of drivers, do you not?"

"Yeah."

"There's not one that might try to make a little something extra on the side? Maybe someone who didn't come from around here, who might have connections elsewhere — especially in Texas or Florida. A lot of cocaine enters the country in those two places."

He stared off at the wall for a moment. Then, finally, Amy got what she was waiting for. He reached for the Sprite, popped the top, and took a long sip.

As he took it away from his mouth, Amy could see a small strand of saliva — brimming with DNA — stretching from his lips to the can.

Seventeen

After he loaded the pertinent computer file onto a thumb drive for me, Bobby Ray asked if I wanted to stay for a beer.

I politely declined, making noises about how I still needed to tidy up after the deputies' rampage through our house.

What I really wanted to do was figure out who was behind A1 Valley Plumbing and what prompted that person to bring poison up my driveway and into my life.

He persisted, but my references to government overreach eventually triggered his sympathy. He led me out with assurances that if I required his services again, all I needed to do was ask.

I now felt silly for having built Bobby Ray into a menace. Yes, he was a crackpot who shunned basic housekeeping, liked pornography, and kept a large cache of weapons — all choices I wouldn't necessarily condone or make for myself. But he was also a friendly man who was willing to help a neighbor in need. It turned out the basket of deplorables wasn't as irredeemable as some might make it seem.

Walking back toward my place, I remembered I was still locked out. It would be a few hours before Ben got home. But this now struck me as an excellent opportunity to simulate the first obstacle that would have faced the A1 Valley plumber after he reached the top of my driveway.

How hard was it to break into our house? It had been constructed in the 1950s, a more guileless time when doors and windows were not made as impregnable as they are now. We also didn't have a security system.

Still, the front door handle was locked. That was pickable for someone with the right tools. But we also had a deadbolt. I didn't think the A1 Valley plumber could have overcome that without leaving major damage to the door.

Then I moved on to the window to the left of the front door and was immediately stunned.

It wasn't locked. How was that possible? Had we really been that careless? Or had the mystery plumber jimmied it open and then left it that way in case he felt like coming back?

There was no way to tell. I slid it open and climbed into the house, just as anyone else with a mild amount of dexterity could have done. I closed it and locked it behind myself.

As much out of frightened curiosity as anything, I then went around to look at all the other windows. They were all locked. But obviously it only took one.

Once I completed my sweep, I sat down on the couch with my aging laptop and plugged "A1 Valley Plumbing" into Google.

The first hit was a plumber out in Ohio, though it had a different name. There was also an "A1 Plumbing" in California that might or might not still have been in operation.

Next I tried "A1 Valley Plumbing Staunton, VA." This led to a variety of pages offering to connect me with plumbing services, most of them weird aggregating sites that were clearly run by algorithms and just missed in their attempts to seem like they had been written by humans.

Then I tried Angie's List. And Yelp. And a domain registry search. And the State Corporation Commission. I went with different combinations of words, even different spellings. In every instance, none of what returned to me remotely matched.

As far as the combined knowledge of the world wide web was concerned, an enterprise known as A1 Valley Plumbing did not do business anywhere, and certainly not within the state of Virginia.

It was clearly a fraud, a company that existed on a decal and nowhere else.

Confirming my suspicion, I dialed the 800-number listed on the side. I was soon connected to an adult entertainment line.

That made it official. To borrow Teddy's phrasing, someone was messing with me.

Merely allowing the thought to take root made me feel like I must have been suffering from some paranoid fantasy. I took enough psychology at UVA to know that people with persecution complexes are usually suffering from either schizophrenia or extreme narcissism.

And yet there it was, bizarre but true, as plain as the video I had just seen.

Thinking about that footage made me want to watch it again. I plugged Bobby Ray's thumb drive into my laptop and saved the file onto my desktop. I clicked it, and before long the van was driving up my driveway. Then, sixteen minutes later — most of which I fast-forwarded through — the van was backing down my driveway.

Up, then down. Up, then down. I played it backward and forward. I played it in real time and slo-mo. I freeze-framed it so I could study it more carefully. Bobby Ray's home-cooked system wasn't very high resolution. When I zoomed in on it for a closer look, all I got were big, blobby pixels that quickly became indistinguishable as discrete lines or objects.

The angle wasn't helping me either. Bobby Ray hadn't been trying to capture my driveway, just his own side lawn. I couldn't see the top of the van, nor the front, nor the back.

So no license plate. And the only look at the driver was a fleeting glimpse from the side. He appeared to be an angular white man with a buzz cut.

But he did have one distinguishing feature: a scar running along the side of his head. You couldn't really tell where it started, but once it crossed into his scalp, it stood out as this thin, vivid white line where the hair refused to grow.

Who was he? Why had he felt the need to obliterate my life?

And how could I find him? Surely, a man with a scar that distinctive would be memorable. But what if he wasn't from around here and had already gone back to wherever he came from?

I ran the footage back and forth until I got the best picture of him I could, then grabbed a screenshot and emailed it to Teddy. If this plumber was someone involved in the drug world — and he had to be if he had access to a half kilo of cocaine, right? — then there was a chance Teddy, with his checkered youth, might have bumped across the guy.

Who knows? If he turned out to be a real lowlife, maybe my deficient lawyer, Mr. Honeysickle — or whatever his name was — would actually start trying to defend me.

"Do you know this man?" I wrote in my message to Teddy. "I think this is who broke into my house and planted the drugs there."

I watched the video a few more times until I decided I had seen it enough to know I hadn't missed anything. I needed to get a grip on myself. I also, after three long days of accumulating sweat and grime, needed a shower.

Like a lot of people, I think well in the shower. There's something about it — the soothing feeling of water striking skin, the warm haze of the air, the ritual of cleansing — that helps eliminate the noise of the world to focus instead on the signals that are trying to break through.

It was in that calming environment that I again asked myself the question: Why? Why had this nefarious, scar-headed faux plumber come up my driveway? What was so important or significant about me that made me worth this much effort?

I was stumped. I wasn't a threat to anyone. Framing me as a drug dealer and getting me tossed in jail didn't make anyone's life better. Who needed me out of the picture that badly? What did I have that was even worth taking?

The shower poured down on me. The lather carried the dirt away. The steam did its work, taking away some of the wrinkles of the world.

And then the answer crushed me.

Alex.

The people messing with me were trying to get my baby removed from me. They had already succeeded, temporarily. And they were going to persist until they made it permanent.

It was starting to make sense. Alex was the only valuable I could claim as my own. And as a healthy white male baby, he clearly had tremendous value to someone else too. What was he worth? Twenty thousand dollars? Forty? A hundred? Had there been an auction?

Whatever the amount, I'm sure there was enough money involved that whoever was doing this could bribe Social Services. Or perhaps they had found another way to control the system. The how of it only mattered so much now that I understood the why.

I had thought of myself as the target in this attack and Alex as the collateral damage. What if it was the other way around? What if taking Alex was the prime objective all along?

And what if I was just the woman in the way?

EIGHTEEN

I barely recalled getting myself under the covers that night. I also didn't stir when Ben got home and climbed into bed.

My sleep was deep and unbroken, which was in itself a novel phenomenon. Between pregnancy and nursing, I hadn't experienced a solid night's sleep since sometime in my second trimester.

At morning light, I was still groggy. My first thought came to me when I was still in half-dreaming mode, before my central processor really kicked in. And it was a panic: I had slept too hard, straight through Alex's cries. He must have been starving by now.

I bolted upright. Then I remembered reality, which hit me with a sharp stab to the heart.

For a moment or two, I laid back down. But there was no getting back to sleep. I looked over at Ben, curled on his side, still in slumber. Wanting to feel closer to Alex, I rolled out of bed and padded softly into the nursery.

It was exactly as I had left it two mornings earlier, when I had hastily straightened it. The hole in the ceiling remained. I had yet to put the air-conditioning exchange cover back into place.

I picked up Mr. Snuggs from the changing table, just to have something to hold. Then I wandered over to where Alex should have been and stared down at the sheet cover, which was stretched out drum tight and snapped down, to prevent suffocation. There was a thin dusting of baby powder on the cover. I hadn't noticed it before, though Ben was sometimes a little more liberal with the powder than I was. A blanket was laid out, waiting to swaddle a child who wasn't there.

What I should have been doing right then was bending down, scooping Alex up, unbundling him so he could move his little arms around, then taking him over to the chair where I nursed him.

He was always so snuggly and soft and warm first thing in the morning. His absence made me feel all that much colder by comparison.

What sprang into my mind was the famous

six-word memoir usually attributed to Hemingway: "For sale: baby shoes, never worn." Mine probably would have read something like, "My morning: throbbing breasts, empty crib."

I used my hand pump, then sat down on the carpet that filled the middle of the room. After a feeding, I often plopped Alex down on his stomach so he could have some tummy time. He had this mat with a flexible plastic mirror built into it. He loved staring at himself and slobbering on it while he struggled to lift his head, which was so big compared to the rest of him. I always cheered him on.

So what was I supposed to do with myself now? Alex's arrival had not only given me purpose, it had filled every crevice of my days and nights. When I wasn't at work or asleep, I was with him. What *did* I do with my time before Alex?

I stared dumbly at the wall, waiting to get some idea. Nothing came to me.

Somewhere in the midst of this pathetic reverie, Ben entered the doorframe. The first thing I saw was his dark, skinny legs, jutting out from his boxer shorts. My eyes worked up from there to his face, which looked puffy behind his glasses.

"Good morning," he said.

"Hey," I replied.

"What are you doing?"

"I don't know," I said quite honestly. My voice sounded hollow to me.

"You want some company?"

"Sure," I said.

He entered the room and sat down next to me, close but not quite touching.

"You were out cold when I came home last night," he said.

"Yeah, I just passed out."

He accepted this without comment. "I tried to call you yesterday. A couple of times."

"I still don't know where my phone is."

"We should really just get you a new one," he said. "You've got to be eligible for an upgrade by now. You haven't gotten one in a while. They have a bunch you can get for free if you sign up for a new contract. I'll stop by the wireless store today and see if I can do that for you if you want."

I craned my neck and stared at him for a moment. With everything going on, it struck me as preposterous my brilliant, perceptive, empathetic husband was talking to me about cell-phone plans.

"Whatever," I said, and returned to staring at the wall.

Then, without looking at him, I asked

what I really wanted to know.

"Where were you yesterday?"

It came out as an accusation as much as it did a question.

"Yeah, I'm sorry about that. I couldn't find anyone to take my section. You know what Kremer is like if someone tries to cancel anything. Teddy convinced me he could handle it. He said they'd probably just give you a court date and let you go. He said it was really no big deal. I . . . I mean, I figured he'd know better than I would."

And I figured my husband would want to be there.

"How did it go, anyway?" he asked.

"It turns out assaulting an officer is a felony, punishable by up to five years in prison."

"Oh my God. You didn't even mean to hit him."

"I don't think that's considered a defense."

"But what are you . . . what are you going to do?"

Maybe my English background made me too sensitive to pronouns, but I was annoyed by his use of the second-person singular. An ugly thought sprang from my head: If I was the mother of his biological child, would he have used the first-person plural? Would he have showed up in court yesterday?

"The trial is scheduled for May eighteenth. They assigned me a lawyer. Mr. Honeysomethingorother."

"Is he any good?"

"I can't say I've been terribly impressed so far."

Ben adjusted his glasses.

"I talked to Teddy for a while yesterday," he said. "I really don't think those drugs were his."

"Me neither."

"So . . . I'm sure you're been thinking about this too, but . . . A half a kilo of cocaine doesn't just magically show up in your house."

"I know."

"Where did it come from?"

I just shook my head.

"Do you think there's a way we could, I don't know, track it back to the source?" he asked. "Maybe if we can find who the original dealer was, we can figure out who bought it and therefore who planted it?"

"How would we do that?"

"I don't know," he admitted. "But whenever you're trying to understand something historically, you usually have to go all the way back to the beginning. It seems to me the same concept applies here."

We sat in silence, still not touching.

"And what's the deal with the drugs charges?" he asked. "It seems weird you haven't heard from anyone about that."

"The prosecutor mentioned something about indicting me, but . . ."

"Yeah, but don't they have to arrest you first? Or charge you? Or something?"

"I don't know," I snapped.

I knew Ben was just trying to be helpful, but his questions were irritating me. I didn't feel like rehashing any of this with him. Whether I had to beat the drug charges first or the assault charges first, the fact remained I couldn't convince Social Services I was a fit mother from the wrong side of a jail cell. I needed a legal strategy.

And neither Ben nor Mr. Honeywhatever was going to help me with that. I had to find a real lawyer. I wondered if I could eke out the money to afford one who wasn't appointed by the court. Could I talk to the bank about reducing our mortgage payments for a few months? Could we sell the house I loved in the hopes our small improvements would allow us to make some money on it?

Ben finally tuned into the testy edge to

my voice, because he placed his hand over mine.

"I'm sorry I wasn't there yesterday, okay? That was obviously a mistake. I shouldn't have listened to Teddy and . . . That's not even the point. It's not Teddy's fault. It's my fault. I should have been there. And I want to help, okay? Don't freeze me out here."

I stood up. "I have to get ready for work. Can we just talk about it later?"

"Yeah, sure."

"What's your schedule like today?"

"Same as usual. I was going to do some dissertation stuff in the morning. I have a section this afternoon. Then I'm tutoring till eight."

"Okay," I said. "I guess I'll see you at home after that."

He was still sitting on the floor when I left the room.

NINETEEN

My morning routine — which usually involved spending 90 percent of my time getting Alex ready and about 10 percent on myself — was now significantly streamlined, as was my commute. There was no trip out to Mrs. Ferncliff's to worry about.

I was fifteen minutes early when I pulled into the parking lot of Diamond Trucking. Which was fine. I was actually eager to get to work. At the moment, eight hours of playing eighteen-wheel Sudoku — which was dispatching at its essence — sounded like a vacation.

Once inside, I was greeted warmly by the guy who pulled the graveyard shift, a former trucker everyone called Willie, because he looked like Willie Nelson.

Willie was just finishing up his rundown on everything I needed to know when the front door opened. A nervous-looking woman in a teal sweater set, gripping a matching purse, peered around the door for a tentative moment, then entered.

"Hi? I'm Amanda? I'm here for the training?" she said in a squeaky voice that had the habit of turning up at the end of every sentence.

Willie and I swapped empty looks.

"Training for what?" I asked.

"The . . . the logistics manager job?" she said, now even more uncertain.

"Oh," I said. "Then, yes, I guess you're in the right place. I'm Melanie. This is Willie."

In the past four years, I had trained several dispatchers, including Willie. Normally I got an email saying I should expect a new trainee coming in. But I would forgive the lapse if it meant I was preparing Amanda to replace deadbeat Warren Plotz on the swing shift.

"On the phone, I spoke to a Warren?" Amanda said.

Warren? Since when did Warren hire dispatchers?

"Warren is the owner's son," I said. "He's not . . . Well, whatever. First thing you're going to need is a headset. You'll be spending your whole shift on the phone, and you'll need your hands free to type. Let me see if there's a fresh one in the supply closet. We sort of have a rule among dispatchers that you don't use someone else's headset."

"Yep," Willie chimed in. "Believe me, you don't want mine. I spend my whole shift spittin' on it."

Welcome to Diamond Trucking, Amanda.

I went into the supply closet in the next room and rooted around in it until I found a headset. When I returned, I felt a scowl reflexively spreading across my face.

Warren Plotz had just walked in. He was wearing his $250 aviator sunglasses, the ones he thought made him look like Justin Timberlake and I thought made him look like a jerk.

"What are you doing here?" he demanded.

"Uhh, my job. Why?"

"Shouldn't you be in jail or something?"

I felt my face flush. Amanda's eyes widened. She clutched her purse a little tighter.

"No," I said. "I got bailed out."

"Well, we don't need you here anymore."

"What are you talking about?"

"You've been fired."

The earth shifted a little under my feet. "What?" I demanded.

"Fired. As in not working here anymore. This girl here is your replacement. You can just get along now. I'll have your last check mailed to you."

Trying to stay calm, I placed the headset

box on the table next to the phone. Warren's animosity for me dated back to an incident that happened in the office maybe a week or two after I started working there. He made a clumsy pass at me, and I firmly swatted it away. Maybe too firmly. He had been looking for a chance to get his revenge ever since.

I narrowed my eyes at him. "I have been a dedicated employee of Diamond Trucking for four years now. You have absolutely no cause to fire me."

"Yeah, I do. You didn't show up for work yesterday."

"You don't show up for work all the time!" I burst out. "And unlike you, I actually called to say I wasn't going to be here so I didn't leave anyone hanging."

"Yeah, that doesn't matter now. I had the Sheriff's Office come to my house yesterday, asking about you. I ended up going down to headquarters. They told me all about you. They were saying you might have been getting your drugs from one of our drivers. Next thing you know they're going to be sniffing around here, wanting to talk to everyone. I can't have that."

"Those. Drugs. Weren't. Mine," I said fiercely.

"Sure they weren't. Look, this is my

family's business. We got a reputation to uphold. I can't have people at church going around thinking we employ drug dealers."

"Would you stop? For the love of God, Warren, you've known me for four years. You really, seriously think I'm a drug dealer?"

"I think the Sheriff's Office pulled a whole bunch of coke out of your house and they say you've been dealing. That's good enough for me."

"This is absurd," I said. "This is . . . I mean, this is just an accusation at this point. I'm innocent until proven guilty. And besides, you can't fire me. I don't work for you. I work for your father."

At this point, Warren got a wicked grin on his face.

"Oh yeah? You think I didn't talk to him about this? Go ahead. Call him if you want to. He'll tell you the same thing."

This stopped me cold. I could handle Warren Plotz being as nasty to me as he wanted to be. His father was supposed to be different. He had been unfailingly kind, a man who always looked out for me, a man I thought cared for me as more than just an employee.

To have him assuming the worst about me, thinking I could have possibly done what I was accused of — and essentially giving up on me — was crushing.

"Oh," I choked out.

"That's right. So you just get along now," Warren said, sneering at me, knowing he already had me beaten. Virginia employment law was a joke. A private employer like this one could fire you for virtually any reason, or no reason at all.

There was no fighting this. I had too many other fights on my hands already.

I had to get out of there. Any moment, I was going to cry. Warren was enjoying my distress too much already. I stumbled into the women's bathroom, where I stored my breast pumps, and grabbed both of them.

Then I went back out into the office and looked around to see if there was anything I needed to take with me. There wasn't.

I had poured four years of my life into Diamond Trucking, but I would be leaving it without a trace.

Not knowing what else to do, I drove home. My hope was that Ben would still be there when I arrived. For as bitchy and standoffish as I had been to him earlier in the morning, I was now aching to collapse into his arms.

But he had already left. The house was

empty — way, way too empty.

I couldn't stay there. That home had been meant for a family, not a morose, childless, jobless woman.

Sparing myself any internal debate about whether I should bother him, I got back in my car and pointed it north, toward Harrisonburg, and James Madison University, and Ben. Selfish as it may have been, I was on the brink of a breakdown. I needed my husband.

As I drove, I tried not to think about the implications of what had just happened to me. But it was impossible. I felt like the Little Dutch Boy, trying to stick my finger in the dike and hold back the sea. The problem was, I had more leaks than fingers. The deluge was coming.

What was I going to do without an income? My $18 an hour might not have been princely, compared to what some of my UVA classmates were now pulling in, but I was still our primary breadwinner by a large margin.

I needed to find another job. And quickly. There were other trucking companies in the area, but they'd all want to know why I left my old job. Diamond Trucking was known to have the best benefits package in the area. Most people left other companies to go to it, not the other way around. There would be no hiding that I had been fired.

Who was I kidding? There would be no hiding anything about my circumstances. If the entire Shenandoah valley didn't know about me already, one quick Google search of my name would bring up media reports where I had been christened Coke Mom. Who would hire me with felony charges hanging over my head?

Even my fallback, or what used to be my fallback, was gone: Marcus had left Starbucks two years ago and was now working at some kind of benefits management company.

It was pure catastrophe. We had no financial cushion. We had spent most of it on the down payment for the house, and the rest of it on whatever small renovations we could afford. My checking account currently had about $900 in it. My savings account had $50, the minimum amount needed to keep it open.

Ben might have had a little more. He and I still had separate accounts. Everything leading up to Alex's arrival had happened so quickly — my rape, my pregnancy, our shotgun wedding, buying the house, having the baby — consolidating our finances had not been a priority.

But he also might have had even less. We certainly didn't have any kind of invest-ments we could liquidate. Nor did we have any true valuables to sell, other than maybe Ben's vinyl record collection. That would buy us, what, a few weeks' worth of grocer-ies? Maybe a mortgage payment?

There wasn't even anyone we could ap-peal to for help. Ben's father was a high school janitor. His mother worked at a grocery store. They didn't have anything to loan us. They were counting the minutes until they could collect Social Security and get a little breathing room.

And my parents? Ha. I couldn't imagine what kind of sad shape they were in by now. If they were even still alive. It wasn't hard to imagine one of them killing the other, or themselves.

We were on our own in every way.

One thing was for sure: There was now no chance of being able to shuffle around our finances to pay for a private lawyer. We'd be lucky if we could keep the house.

Then there was our family's health insur-ance, which I had also just lost. Diamond Trucking would have to offer me COBRA coverage, but I doubted we could afford it.

Or there was the biggest issue of all: How would I convince a judge to give me Alex back when I might not even be able to provide for his basic needs?

I suddenly understood what it was like to live in one of those wartorn countries salted with land mines. Everywhere I even thought about stepping, there was something blowing up on me.

By the time I reached the JMU campus, I was desperate to find Ben. I was glad he didn't have a class. It meant I would have him to myself for a little while.

I would have called to find out where he was, but I still didn't have a phone. Maybe Ben was right to focus on that this morning, after all. I was tired of being in the Dark Ages of communications.

No matter. I would just have to find him the old-fashioned way. I parked and headed into the library, where he had a small study carrel assigned to him.

Except he wasn't there. The tiny room was dark and locked.

I knocked just in case. No Ben.

The only other place he could have been was the history department. He and the other PhD candidates had desks in a windowless interior room they referred to as the broom closet.

The history department was on the second floor of Jackson Hall, just across the quad from the library. I walked as quickly as I could, passing knots of oblivious undergraduates, all of them blissful in their little college cocoon.

I took the stairs, passing through the department's small reception area, then down a long hallway of professors' offices, one of which would hopefully belong to my husband someday.

When I reached the broom closet, I was disappointed again. Still no Ben. The small desks were crowded with books and papers, as they always were, but there were no people sitting at them.

I reversed track to the reception area, where there was an older woman, sitting by herself, staring at her computer screen — the department secretary, I presumed.

"Excuse me," I said, and she looked up from the screen. "I'm trying to find Ben Barrick. Have you seen him?"

Her head tilted. "Ben Barrick?"

The woman must have been new. "He's a grad student. He has a desk just down the hall."

"I know who you're talking about," she said. "But he's not here. Ben's not with the program anymore."

I shook my head, refusing to believe the words I was hearing. "Are you sure we're talking about the same person? My Ben Barrick is about five-nine, glasses, dark skin. He's . . . he's TAing a class for Professor Kremer this semester."

"Yes, that's the same Ben Barrick," she said. "And I can assure you he's not TAing anything for Professor Kremer. Professor Kremer left last spring. He's at Temple University in Philadelphia now. Didn't you hear?"

TWENTY

There were two ways Amy Kaye could go about handling the Sprite can that was, she hoped, teeming with Warren Plotz's genetic material.

She could do it the conventional way, which was to slip it in a padded evidence envelope and mail it to the Virginia Department of Forensic Science's Western Laboratory, a state-run facility located in Roanoke.

There, it would be placed in line behind the enormous mountain of evidence that came in from all over the western half of Virginia. Murder cases got priority. Everything else was handled in the order it was received. The average wait time, according to the Department of Forensic Science's most recent report, was 156 days.

Or she could do it the unconventional way, which involved driving and begging.

She opted for the drive. With the Sprite can sealed in an evidence bag next to her on the front seat, she got on Interstate 81. Then she began tracing her way south through the Blue Ridge Mountains, enjoying the scenery as she fought past slow-moving trucks.

She was about halfway there, just south of Lexington, when her phone rang. She practically groaned when she saw the caller was Aaron Dansby.

"Amy Kaye."

"Amy, it's Aaron."

"Hey."

"Where are you?"

The commonwealth's attorney seldom expressed interest in where she was or what she was doing at a given moment. It was one of the nice things about working for Aaron Dansby. He wasn't the type of boss who breathed down anyone's neck — mostly because he couldn't be bothered, but whatever. When she wasn't in court, Amy set her own schedule free from his harassment.

"Uhh, I'm driving some evidence down to Roanoke. Why?"

"I thought you were presenting Coke Mom to the grand jury today."

"I am," she said.

"Okay. I want to do it with you."

Amy's face formed a question mark. "I'm not sure I understand."

"No offense, but I think it would make a real impression on the grand jury if they get to see the commonwealth's attorney, the guy they actually elected, and not the chief deputy. I'll talk to them a little, give them a rah-rah speech, let them know how it important this case is. Then you can take it from there."

Amy wished she had a recording of this to play for the next meeting of the Commonwealth's Attorneys' Executive Conference. No one would believe it otherwise.

"Aaron," she said carefully, slowly, "the grand jury meets in secret."

"Yeah, I know."

"It's secret from us too."

For a moment, Amy heard nothing but dead air on the line. More than three years into his four-year term, Aaron Dansby still didn't know how some of the basics worked.

"Oh," he said at last.

"They get to ask questions of the investigator or whatever other witnesses they want to hear from, but it's actually illegal for us to be in there with them, unless we're appearing as witnesses or they tell the clerk they need advice on a legal question."

"Oh," he said again.

Because she was actually enjoying herself, she added, "If you or I even stepped foot in the room and spoke to them without being invited, it would invalidate whatever indictment we were seeking."

"Right. Got it," Dansby said.

"I'll let you know when the clerk has issued a capias. I know you're an eager beaver on this one."

"That's good, then. Thank you," he said, suddenly using his politician voice, the one that was a little more commanding — and a little more fake — than his normal voice, which was already pretty fake. "I'll look forward to hearing about the . . . the capias. I'd like to leak this —"

Then, amazingly, he actually corrected himself: "I'd like to report this to the media as soon as we have an indictment."

"Sure thing, Aaron."

"Talk to you later."

"You got it."

She hung up. And then, for the first time in days, she laughed.

The Western Laboratory was not an old building to begin with but had recently gone through a multimillion-dollar renovation that made it even more modern, from its array of cutting-edge gadgetry to its LEED certification.

Amy was soon entering the office of its

director, a man with bushy white eyebrows named Chap Burleson.

She was holding her evidence bag in her left hand. She thrust her right hand across the desk as Burleson stood up.

"Dr. Burleson, I'm Amy Kaye with the Augusta County Commonwealth's Attorney's Office," she said.

"Augusta County," he said. "That's quite a haul."

"A little more than an hour," Amy said. "Not so bad."

"Have a seat, have a seat," he said in a friendly manner, waving toward the chairs in front of his desk. Amy selected the one on the left. "So what can I do for you, Ms. Kaye?"

"You can help me catch a rapist," she replied evenly.

"Happy to. That's what we do here."

"Great," she said, bringing the evidence bag up and placing it gently on his desk. "Then you can put a rush on this for me?"

The eyebrows rose for a moment before falling. "Well, Ms. Kaye. That's always the issue, isn't it? Let me explain how things work here at Western. You may not be aware, but we have —"

Amy cut him off with a torrent of words: "A backlog of twelve-hundred cases, all of which are very important to someone some- where in the state; an obligation to treat every case like it's of the greatest concern; a need to be fair to the many jurisdictions that rely on you for forensic services. Yes, sir. I'm very aware of all of this."

Burleson cracked a quick grin before his face settled back to its original state of indifference. "You're stealing my speech, Ms. Kaye."

"I know. And I want to convince you this case is more important. It's term day in Augusta County. I skipped out on babysitting a grand jury so I could drive down here and convince you of it."

"Okay. So what's the case?"

In brief, broad strokes, Amy told him about the man who had been terrorizing her county for two decades and how he had eluded detection for so long. Then she described how she had painstakingly assembled his brutal history, one case at a time — and one long wait for DNA results at a time.

"Why haven't I heard about this?" Burleson asked, his eyebrows mashing together into a long white line across his forehead.

"Because my boss is afraid of the negative publicity associated with an unsolved case and ordered me to keep it quiet."

"I see."

"And to be honest, I haven't bothered you with any of my other requests, because I knew it was a cold case, and I couldn't really make the argument that this had to take precedence over the many, many other important investigations you have," Amy said, letting that very reasonable statement hang out there for a second before she brought home her demand. "But things are different now. I actually have a name to go with all these vague descriptions. And I have this soda can with his DNA on it. We have the key to catching this bastard right here."

She shoved the bagged Sprite can a little closer to him.

"His pattern has been pretty clear," she said. "He attacks every three to five months. It's been four months since his last one. I'm playing with fire right now."

"And if you have to wait five or six months for results, he might attack two more women before you can bring him in," Burleson said.

"Now you're stealing my speech. But yes, every day that goes by —"

"I get it," he said, dragging the Sprite can over to his side of the desk. "I'll see what I can do."

Twenty-One

I drove away from JMU feeling some combination of a blind rage and an all-seeing depression.

To state the obvious: Ben had been lying to me. For months now. About nearly everything.

I thought of all the seemingly benign conversations we had, about all the deception he had shoveled at me in his attempts to keep me believing he was still a grad student, about how hard he had worked to sustain this elaborate fabrication.

It was the level of detail that really shocked me. Because when I asked him, *How was your section today?* he didn't just dismiss it with a simple, junior varsity lie like *Good.* No, no, he went straight for Olympic-level prevarication.

Kremer gave me a good group this term. They're really making some thoughtful connections between the readings we picked for them and the lectures.

And then he'd prattle on for a while about some esoteric aspect of historiography they had mistakenly stumbled upon.

Or he'd discuss how woefully unprepared his tutoring students were to do anything resembling real research, how their local high schools had spent four years teaching them to take tests but hadn't prepared them to perform any scholarly interrogation that went beyond a Google search.

There were now hundreds of conversations coming back to me, all of them apparently exercises in fiction. Had all of that really been invented for my benefit? To keep me believing I was married to a young academic? If he wanted to drop out, why didn't he just tell me? Did he think I wouldn't understand? Or that I'd try to talk him out of it?

And then there was the other question:

If Ben hadn't been at JMU, what the hell had he been doing?

All I knew for sure was that he left sometime after me each morning, was still gone when I came back after work with Alex, and returned around eight thirty or nine each night. Was he just out there somewhere, wandering around, dreaming up all the nonsense he was going to spout at me later on? Did he have some bizarre second life he felt he couldn't tell me about?

It was just stupefying. And infuriating.

And what made my head hurt most — and this, let's be clear, was purely selfish — was that this meant my life had been a lie too. Throughout our relationship, but especially in the anguished aftermath of my attack, Ben had been my rock, the one human being I could always rely on.

And now my rock turned out to be nothing more than painted dust.

When I returned to Staunton, I went straight to our wireless provider's storefront, where they outfitted me with a two-generations-old knockoff iPhone for free, which still somehow felt like more than I could afford.

Once I got out in the parking lot, I sat in my car and wrestled with my next dilemma, which was what I ought to do with this awful newfound knowledge. Did I confront him immediately? Send him a text? Call him and catch him in one last lie?

Or did I wait until he came home that evening, so I could do it in person?

And *then* what? Would he have some explanation? Would I even care what it was? Were there some wrongs that couldn't be forgiven?

Part of me thought this was too great a breach of trust to possibly allow our relationship to continue. A marriage could perhaps survive an isolated, unpremeditated lie; like, say, a onetime infidelity born of lust or alcohol or stupidity.

This deceit felt so much larger than that, because it had been so carefully constructed and sustained over such a long period, with such a high degree of continuing duplicity. How could I ever again trust a single sentence that came out of his mouth?

And yet another part of me thought I had much bigger problems to deal with. I was currently facing felony charges stemming from two different causes. I had no job, virtually no money, and very little prospect of improving either situation until I got this cleared up. Without Ben, I would not be able to keep the house. I might not even be able to keep eating.

And — paramount above all those things — my baby was currently in the control of the Department of Social Services, which was a lot more likely to return custody to a stable two-parent household than to a single mom in the throes of a divorce.

But could I really forgive him just because it was the expedient thing to do? Did the human heart work that way?

There were no answers. And so I sat in the parking lot, staring down at my new phone. It was an implement of immediate marital destruction, but only if I had the fortitude to use it.

I didn't make the call. I was too afraid of setting that chain of events into motion.

Defeated and overwhelmed, I eventually forced myself to drive out of the parking lot and back toward Desper Hollow Road.

When I returned home, I resisted the urge to pull the covers over my head and die — which is what I felt like doing — and instead took the breast pumps inside with me.

I'm sure I was imagining it, but I already felt like my milk was faltering. Or at least it wasn't as plentiful as it had been.

When I finished pumping, I went through several days' worth of text messages. There were a few from Marcus, which grew increasingly anxious in their level of concern. I fired off a quick reply to him, saying I had lost my phone and that, yes, things were a mess. He was the kind of friend who could handle the truth.

The rest? I couldn't even deal. They were from friends I hadn't seen in a while — from my Starbucks days, from college, even from high school — who had obviously seen the media coverage of me and were checking in to see how I was doing. Some expressed wary support. Most were of the timid "Hey, you okay?" variety.

And how was I supposed to answer that?

There was also a voicemail message from my lawyer.

"Ms. Barrick, this is Bill Honeywell," he said in his thick, slow voice. "I hear you got bailed out after all, and that's . . . that's real nice. Why don't you call me as soon as you have a chance?"

He slowly left his number, repeated it, then hung up. When I called back, I spent three minutes on hold, then heard Mr. Honeywell, breathing a bit heavily, get on the line. He said my Social Services case was proceeding and he wanted to walk me through next steps.

Now that the emergency removal order had been granted, we moved onto the preliminary removal hearing, most often referred to as the five-day hearing — because the law required it to occur within five business days of when a child was removed from the home.

There, we would formally object to the finding of abuse and neglect, essentially pleading not guilty, though they didn't call it that in child protective cases. Then a

lawyer for Social Services would put on witnesses, most likely just the social worker
who had been assigned to the case.

We weren't allowed to put on witnesses.
Not until the adjudicatory hearing, which
would happen in another thirty days. But at
the very least, I would get to tell the judge
my side of the story.

Mr. Honeywell left a little air on the line
when he said that part, which I took as my
opportunity to discuss that side.

"So, basically, it's like I said in court the
other day. Those drugs the Sheriff's Office
found in my house, they weren't mine," I
said. "I swear to you, I have no idea where
they came from."

He grunted noncommittally. "Do you
have anyone living in your house besides
your husband?"

"No, sir."

"Well," he said — it came out "whale"
again — "then, as your lawyer, I have to be
honest with you: You're going to have a
tough time convincing people those drugs
weren't yours. Unless you're saying they
belonged to your husband?"

"No. They're not his either."

"Is there someone else who has access to
your home?"

"That's not what I'm trying to say. Look,

238

this is going to sound crazy, but I think someone is trying to frame me so they can take away my baby."

"I see," he said.

I could hear his skepticism, and it was hard to blame him. I sounded crazy to me too.

"I have this video from a security camera," I continued. "The day before the Sheriff's Office raided my house, a man in a fake plumber's van came up my driveway and spent about fifteen minutes at my house, then drove away. I didn't call a plumber. I'm pretty sure that's the man who planted the drugs."

"Have you been able to identify this mystery man?"

"No."

I heard him sucking air through his teeth. "Well, if you can figure out who this fella is, I can subpoena him, and then he'd have to show up in court and explain what it was he was doing in your driveway. Problem is, if he has a criminal record with drug involvement, the other side can try to argue he was there to buy drugs."

I felt my exasperation growing.

"So it's hopeless."

"Now, now, it's not hopeless, Ms. Barrick. And you won't help yourself much with that attitude. It's just a long process. You may or may not believe what I'm about to tell you, but the judge really wants to give you your child back. You just have to listen to him and show you're willing to do whatever it is he orders. Do you think you can do that?"

"Yes, of course I can," I said. "But what if . . . I mean, what if I'm convicted on those drug charges against me? The prosecutor said something about the sentencing guideline being five years. Would they . . . would they wait until I've gotten out of jail and then deal with me?"

My lawyer's voice got quieter. "Well, now, no. That's . . . that doesn't happen. It takes a minimum of a year to terminate parental rights. But most judges don't like to let cases go on much longer than that. They might wait a few months if they knew you were about to get out. But not five years. I'm sorry."

He let that hang out there like a massive, gut-spinning, heart-eating lump. My accompanying gasp was, apparently, audible to Mr. Honeywell on the other end.

"Let's just take this one step at a time, Ms. Barrick," he said in a lame attempt to now sound upbeat. "The first step is Tuesday. That's when your five-day hearing has been scheduled. It's on the docket for ten thirty. It's important to get off to a good start with the judge. You show up early, you wear a nice dress, you do your hair up real pretty, like you're going to a dinner or something. Can you do that?"

"Sure."

"Good. That's the right attitude to have. Now, I have to run off to court for another matter, but I'll see you on Tuesday, okay?"

I assured him he would, then mumbled my thanks.

In some ways, I didn't really need him to tell me more about this process. The contours of my future were already becoming clear to me. I couldn't convince a judge I was a worthy mother to Alex if I was incarcerated.

The assault case was mostly a nuisance. I couldn't imagine they'd really lock me up for more than a year for scratching an officer.

The drug case was another matter. That sentencing guideline was this towering monolith I couldn't go around or tunnel under. I had to go over it, but I didn't even know where to start the climb.

I had already seen how ineffectual my protests were. I could squeal out "but those drugs weren't mine" as many times as I wanted.

No one — not even my own lawyer — would believe me.

I needed to find real proof, not just of my non-guilt but of my actual innocence.

If I didn't, I would lose my son.

It really was that simple.

TWENTY-TWO

I was still pondering the impossibility of my task a few hours later when Teddy's rust-bucket truck came roaring up the driveway.

He leapt out, then beat me to the front door, bursting into the house a little out of breath.

"Hey, this is going to sound weird, but go get a bunch of underwear on," he said. "Four, five, six pairs. Whatever you can fit."

"What are you talking about?"

"Remember that friend whose mom works at the courthouse? He just called me. The grand jury met this morning. You got indicted on possession with intent to distribute. That's big-time. She just had to issue a warrant for your arrest. The sheriff is going to be coming here to take you in. Probably real soon."

"Okay, but . . . why the underwear?"

"Because Middle River takes your clothes but lets you keep your underwear. If you bring your own, you don't have to use jail underwear. And trust me: Jail underwear blows."

I was still just standing there, a little dazed, staring at him. He must have seen that I didn't get it yet, because he gently grabbed my shoulders.

"Sorry, sis. Even if they give you a bond, I can't help you this time. I'm tapped out. You're going to be in there for a while."

"O-okay," I said, and, at my brother's behest, went into my bedroom and donned as many pairs of bras and underwear as I could make fit over each other. Then I put on some baggy old jeans and a sweatshirt. More room for the underwear.

I returned to my living room and kept a wary lookout with Teddy. My new phone was still sitting on the coffee table, where I had left it. I was now even less sure what to text Ben, and I was running out of time to think of something.

"You'll tell Ben I was arrested, right?" I asked.

"Yeah, sure."

The next sentence sort of just fell from my mouth. "Can you also tell him I went by JMU to look for him today?"

"Uh, yeah. Why?"

"Just tell him," I said. I felt like that would

be enough to signal to Ben that I knew what was going on without involving Teddy too much. I didn't know how to explain to my kid brother that my husband had been living a blatant lie for months.

"I can't believe this is my life," I said.

"Me either," he said.

After thirty seconds he said, "You'll be okay."

He patted my hand.

"Don't do that," I said. "You're going to make me cry."

We waited in silence for a moment. Then I said, "Did you get my email, by the way?"

"Did you send it to my Gmail or my work email?"

"Gmail."

"Oh. I haven't checked that account in a while."

"Would you mind checking it?"

"Yeah, what's up?" he asked.

"I sent you a picture of someone who got caught on one of Bobby Ray's cameras, coming up my driveway. It was the day before the drug bust."

Teddy understood immediately. "You think it's the person who planted that cocaine?"

"Yes. But just give it a look. If you know who it is, great. If not, don't go doing

245

anything else with it, okay?"

"Okay."

We lapsed into silence as we stared down the driveway.

It didn't take much longer. They sent three cars, which struck me as overkill. But I guess, according to that prosecutor, I was a danger to the community.

Not wanting to make this any more difficult than this needed to be, I went out on my porch with my hands up. I know the Sheriff's Office doesn't make a habit of roughing up white girls, but I didn't need them breaking down the door on me. I wanted them to know I was going peacefully.

In truth, I didn't have the energy to resist.

They let me keep my underwear, just like Teddy said.

Otherwise, it was the same pushing and prodding, the same strip search, the same series of humiliations. The magistrate again denied me a bond — I was a violent offender, after all — meaning I'd have to wait until Monday for a judge to assign a bail amount that I couldn't afford anyway. Knowing I was now in for the long haul, until May 18 or longer, made everything that much more dispiriting.

My lone act of optimism was that, every few hours, I went into the bathroom, knelt in front of the toilet, and milked myself. I was determined to keep my supply up. That this qualified as a hopeful gesture perhaps speaks to how desperate my situation had become.

After a night of still-strange noises and a barely edible breakfast, I was just settling into life in the dormitory, trying to find something to read, when Officer Brown — who I still wasn't able to place — approached me. Without giving any acknowledgment of our past interaction, she told me to line up against a wall with some other inmates.

"What's going on?" I asked.

"Saturday morning is visiting hours," she said. "Someone is here to see you."

"Who?" I asked.

But she had already moved on to another inmate, leaving me to wonder. We were soon led into a hallway, where we stood in line some more. I was already starting to learn that jail was all about waiting. We all had the time.

When it finally became my turn to be allowed into the visitors' room, one of the guards — not Officer Brown — said, "Melanie Barrick?"

"Yes?"

"You got thirty minutes. Go ahead."

Then he opened the door for me. Sitting at a table against the wall was Ben.

He stood when I came through the door. For a moment, that was as far as I got. I was unsure whether to run to him or flee back to the dorm. I could see from his face he had accurately parsed the message I had Teddy relay for me. His shame was that obvious.

Even after a night in jail — time I had to myself, with nothing else to do but think — I didn't know what to do with him. I hated that the first clear emotion I was experiencing was this flood of relief at seeing him: Ben, my comfort blanket, was there to rescue me, just as he had so many times before.

And yet, at the same time, I also hated that he had lied, hated even more that I had caught him at it. What had possibly made him think he could get away with it? Didn't he know something like that would eventually come out, one way or another?

I don't know what it was that made me decide to walk over to him. Maybe it was curiosity: I had so many questions that only he could answer. Maybe I wanted to punish him, to inflict on him some fraction of the hurt he had made me feel. Maybe it was simple loneliness, which would have been the most pathetic possibility of all.

Whatever it was, my legs eventually started moving. As I neared him, he approached like he was going to hug me. There was nothing more I wanted, of course. I just didn't want him to know it.

He was maybe five feet away when I gave him a small, almost imperceptible head shake. He immediately backed off. And damn him if that wasn't one of the things I loved about him. He almost always knew how to read me.

I sat at the table.

He lowered himself across from me.

"There's a lot I need to say," he said softly, earnestly. "Do you mind if I go first?"

"I guess not."

"The first thing I want to say is, I'm sorry. I've been lying to you and I feel . . . I can't tell you how awful I feel about it. This is going to sound like a lot of rationalization, but it really did start as something I was doing because I thought it was best for you. That was . . . I mean, that was a mistake. But then once I made that mistake . . . I don't know, it became a lot bigger than I ever thought it would. And somehow that made it even harder to tell you the truth."

"You're not making any sense right now," I said.

"I know, I know. I'm sorry."

"Why don't you, just for a real change of pace, start by honestly telling me what's going on and what you've been doing?" I asked. I didn't like that I was hiding behind sarcasm, but sometimes you don't get to choose your defense mechanisms.

"Okay, that's . . . that's fair."

He took in a deep breath, then he sighed.

"I guess it started when Kremer announced he was leaving last spring," he said.

"For Temple. Yeah, I heard about that."

"Just to put it in context, he told me . . . Gosh, end of April? With what you were going through, I didn't . . . I don't know, I felt like it would be selfish to even say anything to you about it. I mean, for me it was this total academic and professional crisis, yeah, but it felt . . . I guess it felt pretty small compared to . . ."

The end of April was when I learned I was pregnant.

"You could have told me," I insisted. "You should have told me. I'm not some fragile piece of china."

"I know, I just . . . I didn't want to bring everything down when you . . . you needed me to lift you up. It was this big, steaming pile of bad news I thought I needed to swallow myself. Kremer was . . . To state the obvious, he was my guy. You know the politics in that department, and without Kremer around to advocate for me . . . I already knew we could kiss that tenure-track position goodbye."

"So you just quit?"

"No. Kremer actually wanted me to come with him, but I told him that wasn't possible. I went into the summer, still plugging away on my dissertation, thinking I'd just keep my head down and finish it off. The first domino to fall was when Portman" — the department chair — "assigned Scott Eaton as my new thesis adviser. He had been on sabbatical and didn't come back until the fall, and then he took his sweet time reading what I had sent him. When I finally did meet with him, it was . . . I mean, it was awful. He wanted me to add some new chapters, blow up most of the ones I had already done. He was pushing this document analysis that . . . I mean, I don't even know if it was possible. Like, the documents might not exist. He was basically talking about starting over. I was looking at another two years, minimum, to do it his way. And I . . . I couldn't deal. It was so depressing to even think about it.

"I went to Portman and asked if I could switch advisers, and he flipped out on me, going on about how Kremer had always coddled me and this was life in the real world and if I didn't like it I could just leave. He said it was Eaton or nothing."

Ben shook his head. "So we're now up to, what, October? I had been in touch with Kremer the whole time, and he suddenly had a slot open up for a PhD candidate to start in January. But I had to tell him quickly. Like, in a week. And at that point, you were seven months pregnant and we had just closed on the house and Temple is . . . I mean, it's fine for Kremer, because they gave him a bunch of money. But it's not like it's Penn, you know? I told him what was going on with you and he gave me this big lecture about how I had a lot of potential but I needed to see the bigger picture and be willing to make sacrifices for my career. He said if I didn't take this opportunity he wasn't going to be able to help me anymore and . . . I don't know, it was pretty bad. It was like every arrow was pointing to the same conclusion: that I wasn't meant to get this doctorate."

"Jesus, Ben. I can't believe you didn't tell me any of this."

But I also could believe it. This was so

typical: both of my husband, who was more likely to swallow a problem as it grew in size, and of our relationship, which was always about my issues, not his.

"I know," he said. "But I just felt like so much had happened, and I couldn't dump it on you at that point. We had this baby coming, and the new house, and —"

"And you thought it was your kid," I said matter-of-factly.

Ben had been looking down at the table. When I said that, he jerked up.

"No," he insisted. "No, that wasn't part of the calculus at all. I was thinking about you. About us. Whether Alex was mine or not, I mean . . . He *is* mine. He's my son."

I didn't know if I believed him. What man wouldn't let a child's biological paternity enter his mind, at least a little bit?

He continued: "In any event, JMU was just this big dead end. And I thought about starting over somewhere else but . . . to make you move and find a new job, all while we had a new baby? It just felt too formidable. There aren't a lot of good programs looking to take some other school's dropout anyway. Plus, if not all of my classwork transferred, that would be . . . three, four, five more years of this? No way. So, in mid-October, I quit. I told Portman I was done, and he said some nasty things, and that was that."

He placed his hands on the table, like the story was over. But, of course, it wasn't. That was when his fabrications morphed from mere lies of omission into something much more.

"So what *have* you been doing with yourself?" I asked.

"I got a job."

"Where?"

"Mattress Marketplace. I work noon to closing."

"You've been selling mattresses," I said, in disbelief. "Oh, Ben."

There was nothing wrong with selling mattresses. For someone else. Not for Ben. It was such a waste of his talent.

"Seven twenty-five an hour, plus seven percent commission on whatever I sell," he said, forcing a smile for half a second before he went back to staring at the table.

"So that quote-unquote 'tutoring' job was really mattress sales. Same with the picket fence. That's why you had that extra money."

"Yeah, I had some good weeks early on. The guy who hired me insisted he had salesmen making forty, fifty grand a year on commissions alone. And maybe at other locations he does. There? Not so much. I think that's another reason I kept not telling you. My whole idea was that once I had saved up a nice little nest egg, I'd tell you, but by then I'd have ten or twenty thousand dollars in the bank, and that would sort of cushion the blow."

He made a noise in his throat. "Truth is, I'm selling about one mattress a week. If that. I make four hundred in a good week. Sometimes less. I've been looking for another job. But it seems a degree from a liberal arts college in Vermont and three-quarters of a PhD doesn't mean much to people down here. I know we scoff about what you make, but it's damn tough out there to do any better. I mean, I never thought I'd say this, but thank God for Diamond Trucking."

I didn't bother blunting the news: "I got fired yesterday."

He looked at me for a moment, then brought his eyes back down.

"Sorry," he said.

"Not your fault."

"And I'm sorry I lied. I'm sorry for letting you down. I'm sorry I've failed you in just about every way possible."

My anger, my righteous indignation at having been lied to, had already given way to something else. Pity for him. Sadness over what he had lost.

Over what we had both lost. Ben's dream had really been my dream too. How many times — before things got so complicated — had we split a box of wine on empty stomachs and allowed ourselves to get giddy about the thought of life as Mr. and Mrs. Professor Benjamin J. Barrick?

And now that was over. Or at least it was for me.

But maybe not for him. Looking at him, I was struck by how damaging it was for him to stay with me any longer. Ben was this beautiful bird, but he would have another feather plucked from him every day we were together. Soon he would lose the ability to take flight.

I couldn't let that happen. I grabbed both his hands and lowered my head in an attempt to meet his gaze, which was still cast downward.

"Ben, why don't you just go to Temple? Call Kremer. Beg and plead. Tell him you made an awful mistake and that you've had a big epiphany and you're ready to make whatever sacrifices you need to make. He'll take you back. He loves you. He'll let you pick up right where you left off with your dissertation and you'll be done in no time.

From there, who knows? You'll be right back to having your bright future again."

He still wasn't looking at me, so I kept going: "It's what you want. It's what I want for you. I'm in a huge mess here and . . . Look, I don't have the time or the energy to be a wife right now. I'm going to be doing everything I can to beat this drug charge and get Alex back, and we've already heard about how little standing you have with Social Services. There's nothing you can do to help me anyway. Don't stick around and ruin your life trying. You can file for divorce on Monday. I won't contest it. God knows we don't really have any assets to split. Just take whatever you want from the house and get as far away from here as possible, okay? I can't live with myself knowing I'm this anchor on your potential. Just go. Go and write me a letter someday and tell me how well it worked out for you. Maybe when you make tenure somewhere. That's really the best thing you can do for me right now."

And then, because I truly meant it, I added, "I'll always love you. Goodbye."

With that, I stood from the table and started fleeing toward the exit, before he could see the tears in my eyes.

"Mel, wait —"

But I was already through the door, heading back down the hallway toward the dormitory, going to a place where I couldn't hear him calling for me; where I could be alone with my own torment; and where at least, no matter how bad things got, I wasn't taking anyone else down with me.

Well, except for Alex.

But maybe it was too late for us anyway.

TWENTY-THREE

Amy Kaye felt the weight of time all through the weekend.

It had been four months since Warren Plotz had attacked a woman. By this point, he had to be a bundle of pent-up sexual energy, waiting to explode. Amy could practically hear the fuse sizzling.

And knowing she was so, *so* close to having the evidence she needed to bring him in — and bring him down — made waiting a special kind of torture. The slow-drip kind.

She actually thought about trying to tail him, to possibly catch him in the act and/or thwart another attack before it could happen. Then she dismissed that idea as some combination of foolish and reckless. She was a lawyer, not a police officer. She fought crime from the courtroom, not in the streets.

But still. He was out there. Surely already stalking his next victim.

Could she have him arrested? It was tempting. A long-ago victim sharing a hunch many years later . . . the fact that Plotz worked with another one of the victims . . . the way Plotz's personal timeline seemed to match the pattern of the assaults . . .

It would all be great at trial. But Amy had to be honest with herself that it didn't really add up to probable cause. The danger was that if she arrested him and a judge later ruled she didn't have probable cause, she could blow the whole conviction. People bemoaned when criminals got off on a technicality, ignoring the simple truth that the law was nothing *but* technicalities.

She would just have to be patient.

It made for a nervous weekend. Ordinarily, Amy didn't have much contact with the Sheriff's Office on Saturday or Sunday. Jason Powers called her if something big happened. Otherwise, they had the understanding that things could wait until Monday.

This weekend, she called in to the dispatcher four times, just to ask if any major crimes had occurred. In between, she was so keyed up, she kept taking Butch on long walks, trying to calm herself down. The dog was now exhausted.

Her first check-in of the new week came

just after she woke up Monday morning.

Nothing doing, she was told each time.

It was slow going to work that morning. A fog had rolled into the Shenandoah valley overnight, thick and low, and it was looking like one of those days when it might take a while to clear up. If ever.

Normally, Amy loved mornings like this. It was the kind of weather that made life in the valley interesting, unpredictable. And it heightened her appreciation of the mountains, whenever it was they came back out of hiding.

Now it just felt ominous.

If there was any reprieve from the worry, it was that daytime was safe. Plotz preferred the darkness of early morning.

With that thought, Amy looked forward to a day of trying to bury herself in the other work she had to do. Instead, when she arrived at her office inside the commonwealth's attorney's, she was surprised to find a handwritten note waiting for her, from Aaron Dansby.

Amy —

Would you please come see me ASAP? It's important.

Thanks,

AHD

It was unusual for Dansby to be in the of-

261

fice first thing Monday morning. Dansby often commemorated Monday morning on Wednesday afternoon.

Wanting to get it over with, she set her things down and went to his nicely appointed corner office, which his wife, Claire, had decorated for him, making it look like something out of *Southern Living* magazine.

"Hey," she said, sticking her head through his open door. "You were looking for me?"

"Yeah, come on in."

He had dark smudges under his eyes. He still had that slight resemblance to Matthew McConaughey, except now it was more like Matthew McConaughey coming off a bender.

"You okay?" Amy asked, showing atypical concern for her boss's well-being. "You look tired."

"Yeah, yeah, I'm fine," he said, waving it away as Amy walked to the front of his desk. "I need to talk with you about Coke Mom."

"She has a name, you know. Melanie Barrick."

"Whatever."

Amy frowned. "Anyway, what about her?"

"You saw it made the paper on Saturday."

"Yes. And?"

"The party saw it too."

When Aaron talked about "the party," he

meant the local political party to which he belonged. It was always a little unclear to Amy who, exactly, this party consisted of; whether it was a large group of upstanding citizens, or just a boss and a few sniveling sycophants in a proverbial smoke-filled room. Whatever the case, there was no questioning the importance of party support. She understood that without it, Dansby would never have won the election in the first place. He was just as dependent on it for his impending reelection effort.

"Okaaaay," Amy said. "And?"

"And they mentioned it early on at the meeting last night. Then they went on to talk about the slate for November. It was mostly the statehouse offices, but they did discuss commonwealth's attorney a little. To be honest, they were sort of vague about it."

"Vague about . . . what?"

"The line!" Dansby burst. "No one said for sure I'd get it."

Amy suddenly understood why Dansby looked so tired. He had been up all night worrying. Augusta County politics had been a one-party system for generations now. If someone else got the party line, chances were good Dansby would be out of a job. And that wouldn't exactly do much for the career narrative he was trying to build. Wunderkinds didn't lose their first bids for re-election.

"Sorry, you're going to have to connect some dots for me here," Amy said. "What does the party's endorsement have to do with Melanie Barrick?"

"Nothing *directly*. But it's clearly on their radar screen. I had thought that after Mookie Myers, I had showed them I could do this job. But you should have heard them going on about the Coke Mom thing. I mean, a woman and a mother, dealing drugs like that? It represents a . . . a moral degradation . . . a breakdown of law and order."

Save it for the jury, Amy thought.

"What kind of commonwealth's attorney allows that to happen on his watch?" Dansby continued. "When we nailed Mookie, we got him good" — Myers was spending at least the next ten years as a guest of the Commonwealth of Virginia, and it was unlikely his recent appeal would change that — "and I think it's real important we nail Coke Mom good too. It'll show the party I'm for real. When's the trial? Can we move up the date?"

"She doesn't have a date yet. She hasn't even been arraigned."

"Let's make sure it happens sooner rather than later. The party usually finalizes the slate by mid-April. I'd like to have Coke Mom convicted by then."

"Aaron, today is March" — she paused to look at her phone — "twelfth. I doubt we'll even be able to find a judge with an open date on his calendar for a trial like this by mid-April."

"Oh, come on," he said breezily. "I thought the Fourth Amendment guarantees her the right to a speedy trial."

"That's the Sixth Amendment, Aaron."

"Whatever. You get the point."

"She's already got a trial set for May eighteenth for assaulting a police officer. There's no way the drug charges would be scheduled before that."

"Assaulting an officer?" he said. "When did she do that?"

"There was an incident in Social Services last week. It got a little out of hand."

He peered at her thoughtfully. "How long could we put her away for that?"

"It's a Class Six felony. But she doesn't have a record, and from what I understand the cop wasn't really hurt. To be honest, it's overcharged at the moment. I'd never take it to a jury, because they could decide we overplayed our hand. I was going to plead it down and then let her do PTI. Even if we kept it at this level, the judge would probably order her to take an anger management class, then give her six months suspended and tell her to behave herself. Something like that. Whatever she did end up getting, she'd probably be allowed to serve it concurrently with whatever she got for the drug charges."

Dansby didn't hesitate: "Nolle pros it."

"Really? Are you sure?"

A nolle prosequi is an entry into the legal record signifying the prosecution does not intend to proceed any further with a charge. It was something Amy did all the time, but usually as part of a deal — she agreed to nolle pros one charge in exchange for a guilty plea on another.

"Yeah. I don't want anything slowing up these drug charges. That's all the party is interested in anyway," he said. "As a matter of fact . . . She has the same attorney for both charges, right?"

"She hasn't had counsel determination for the drug thing yet. But yeah, that's usually how it happens."

"Who is it for the assault charge?"

"Bill Honeywell."

"That's the guy with the buggy eyes, right?"

"Yeah, that's him."

"He's basically a hack, right?"

He's more of a lawyer than you'll ever be, Amy thought. "I wouldn't underestimate him."

"Still, he'll deal, right?"

"If it's the right deal, I assume."

"Okay, then here's what we're going to do. Why don't you offer to nolle pros the assault charges in exchange for going to trial really quickly on the drug thing. Think that would work?"

Amy's mouth twisted. "I don't know. Maybe. First, we have to find a judge who has an open date."

"You'll make it work," Dansby said, bobbing his head emphatically. "I mean, just think of how lost you'd be around here without me."

He threw her a winsome smile. Amy did her best not to roll her eyes at him. "You're ridiculous," she said.

He grinned wider. For as lousy a lawyer as he may have been, he was not without skills as a politician.

"Thanks for helping me out," he said. "Let me know, okay?"

"Sure," she said.

In truth, for all of Dansby's shortcomings and annoyances, Amy didn't really want a new boss. Right now, she had the perfect job. She got to be commonwealth's attorney in the ways that mattered to her, trying cases and administering justice the way she saw fit, without having to put up with the political nonsense.

Dansby's replacement might be some micromanaging control freak who had very differing ideas about how she should go about things. She'd wind up having to ask permission to go to the bathroom.

Better the devil you know.

Twenty-Four

In what felt like a bad spin cycle on repeat, I was awakened early Monday morning and made to answer the same questions from Blue Ridge Court Services about how likely I was to run away from all my problems.

If only it were that easy.

By Monday afternoon, I was back on that hard bench, wearing the orange jumpsuit that eliminated any doubt about my criminality, waiting along with other inmates to appear in front of the camera that would beam my image to the judge.

When it was finally my turn, the judge looked even more bored than he had been the previous week. In the time it took me to enter the room and get settled into my chair, he yawned twice.

He told me I had been charged with possession with intent to distribute a Schedule II drug, then ran me through the same questions about whether I understood the charges, and whether I had an attorney. He then told me that since Mr. Honeywell was representing me on my other charges, he was going to represent me in this case as well.

Do I have a choice? I wanted to ask. Instead I just said, "Thank you, Your Honor."

Mr. Honeywell shambled into the bottom of the screen, wearing what appeared to be the same rumpled gray suit he had worn last time — or a reasonable facsimile thereof.

"Your Honor, if I may, I'd like to consult with my client for a moment or two before we begin our bond hearing?"

"Go ahead."

"Good morning, Ms. Barrick," he said, turning toward me. "We've had something of an unusual offer from Ms. Kaye, the prosecutor, and I'd like to discuss it with you before I accept it on your behalf."

"Okay," I said, sitting up a little.

"The Commonwealth has agreed to drop your assault charges. But in exchange, they've asked to go to trial on the drug issue much sooner than I otherwise might be comfortable with."

"How soon?"

"We've checked with Judge Robbins's

chambers in Circuit Court, and he has an opening for a one-day trial on April ninth."

I didn't need to consult lunar charts to know April 9 was before May 18. The possibility of getting Alex more than a month sooner overwhelmed any other rational thought I might have had. I was now practically leaping out of my chair.

"I'll do it," I said quickly.

"Now, now, hang on a moment," my ever-slow-talking lawyer said. "I want us to think this through. I know it's nice not having to worry about those assault charges, but the drug charges are much more serious. We'd be looking at four weeks to prepare your defense. That's not much time. My granddaddy always said it's better to do things right than to do them right away."

He was a man with all the time in the world. April or May or June made no difference to him. He couldn't understand there was a clock ticking inside of me, and that each second was another explosion. I would never get these months of Alex's life back. They were so precious. I had read the baby books. They all stressed how critical every phase of development was, especially during that first year. Every month mattered. Every day mattered.

And maybe it was stupid of me to rush to

trial. But unlike Mr. Honeywell — and the prosecutor, and the judge, and everyone else — I still believed in my own innocence. Which is what motivated my next utterances.

"It'll be fine," I said. "I'll take the deal."

Mr. Honeywell looked at me for an extra-long beat.

"Okay. April ninth it is," he said, then nodded in the direction of the prosecutor's desk.

What followed was a lengthy discussion about the appropriate bond for my drug charges. In the end, Mr. Honeywell got the Commonwealth to agree to $40,000. I'd get credit for the $20,000 that had already been secured, but someone would still have to come up with ten percent of the other $20,000.

I knew Teddy didn't have that much. Neither did Ben — assuming he hadn't already fled north, taking me up on my Get Out of Marriage Free card.

After that was settled, the judge announced the end of General District Court's broadcast day. As soon as he stood up, the camera at the courthouse began panning to the right, taking the judge out of the frame. I kept watching the screen as the view became the clerk's desk, then the wall, then the prosecutor's desk.

By the time the camera came to a rest, it was pointed back at the gallery, which was empty for all but one man.

It was Marcus Peterson. I felt this immediate — and strong — rush of gratitude toward him and this unexpected kindness. Just a glimpse of him was like spying a rose bush growing in a weedy vacant lot.

"Marcus!" I called out. "Thank you! Thank you for coming! You're the best!"

Marcus gave no indication he had heard me. It was possible the feed going to the courthouse had already been cut off.

"All right, Barrick, come on," a guard said. "Let's go."

"But it's Marcus," I said, as if the man cared.

"Uh-huh," he said. "Let's go."

By then, the screen was already blank.

I was still warmed at the memory of seeing my friend two hours later when that same guard approached me in the dormitory.

"Come on, Barrick," he said. "Get your stuff."

"I made bail?" I asked.

He nodded.

Marcus. It had to be. Marcus never flaunted it, but there was a modest amount

of money running through his family —
enough that he wasn't scraping along like
the rest of us.

I hurriedly collected my bras and underwear, rolling them into a ball, then signed
for my jeans and sweatshirt. After changing
quickly and trying to make my hair look
presentable, I went out into the waiting
room.

And sure enough, there he was. When we
first met five years earlier, I was twenty-six
and Marcus was thirty-four, which made
me think of him as being maybe half a
generation older. But once we became
friends I had never felt like we were different ages. Whether I was a little bit of an old
soul or he was young at heart, we just
clicked. I don't think we've ever had a bad
conversation or an awkward moment.

Once Ben came into the picture, he swore
Marcus's generosity toward me was motivated by feelings for me that were considerably stronger than friendship. Ben pointed
out that Marcus always seemed to be magically available anytime I expressed a desire
to hang out.

I swore, with equal conviction, that was
nonsense. Marcus put me on a little bit of a
pedestal, yes. But he was just a sweetheart
of a guy and nothing more. And here he

was, proving it again.

"Hey, you," Marcus said softly.

Marcus was medium height and build, with dirty-blond hair and blue eyes. He was now thirty-nine but had a boyishness about him that made him look a decade younger.

"I can't tell you how good it is to see you," I said, crossing the room toward him.

We hugged. He was a good hugger, the kind who didn't hold back. Ben always took our hugs as yet another sign of Marcus's feelings toward me, but I think I had finally convinced my husband how ridiculous that was. Marcus had never indicated the slightest unhappiness about his marriage; and, unlike Warren Plotz, Marcus had never hit on me, not even when we went out drinking together.

He was so asexual toward me that when I first met him, I wondered if he was gay. I mean, sure, he wore a wedding ring, but that's no longer a sure sign of heterosexuality. And when he referred to "Kelly," I knew that could sometimes be a man's name. It wasn't until I met Kelly that I stopped wondering.

"I have been *so* worried about you," he said, still hugging me.

"Thanks," I said. I let go. He clung for an extra moment or two, then released me.

I took in a deep breath and let it go sharply. "Marcus, this is really amazing of you, but I don't . . . I don't know when I'll be able to repay you."

"You don't have to. I didn't work with a bail bondsman. I posted the whole twenty thousand, so I get it back as soon as you show up in court."

"Oh my God, Marcus, that's . . . that's amazing."

"It's no big deal," he said, shaking his head slightly, like he had done nothing more consequential than lending me a pen. "You've just got to do me one favor: You can't breathe a word about this to Kelly, okay?"

"Uhh, okay."

I didn't want to make an issue out of it — not after he had so gallantly saved me from six weeks of bad sleep and worse food — but he had never asked me to keep anything from his wife before. They were the kind of couple who shared a Facebook account and knew each other's email passwords. As far as I knew, they didn't have secrets.

"It's just that, I sold some stock my grandparents left me and —"

"Oh my God, Marcus, you can't —"

"Take it easy. It's not a big deal, really. I think the stock is about to take a dive. It's safer sitting in a bond at the courthouse than it is in the market. After this is over, I'll tell Kelly I decided to sell. It'll be fine. This is really just a brief, no-interest loan."

"Okay," I said warily. It was selfish of me, but I had bigger things to worry about than a white lie to Marcus's wife. Then I added: "Thank you."

"Let's go," he said.

We left the building, walking out into a fog-socked day that felt metaphorically appropriate for someone whose future was as hazy as mine.

Sensing I needed some small talk, Marcus yammered at me during the short drive back to Desper Hollow Road.

When we arrived, Ben's car wasn't in the driveway. Was he at the mattress store? Or was he already in Philadelphia?

Marcus came to a stop.

"You want to get takeout or something?" he asked. "Kelly's working late tonight, so I don't really need to be anywhere."

"Thanks, but no. I've got" — I eyed the place where Ben usually parked his car — "some stuff to take care of."

"Okay," he said.

I grabbed my grubby little ball of underwear from where I had left it on the floor and looked him in the eye. "Thanks again for doing this."

"Don't mention it," he said, then cracked a little bit of a grin. "Like, seriously, don't mention it."

"Okay, okay, got it," I said.

We hugged one last time, then I got out, giving him a little wave before I hurried up the steps and to my front door.

Once inside, it didn't take more than three seconds before I knew something was off.

This wasn't like a few days earlier, when the entire place had been tossed. It was much more subtle. There was a small extra amount of negative space in my house. Something was missing, even if I couldn't tell immediately what was gone.

The furniture was where it should have been. The TV was in the same spot. The entertainment center was . . .

That was it. The entertainment center.

There was a hole in the place where Ben's vinyl records should have been.

TWENTY-FIVE

For a moment, or two, or three, I didn't move.

Our entertainment center was made of black laminate over particleboard, an IKEA special that was already beginning to sag under the weight of time. Those records were ordinarily a nice distraction from the shoddiness of the piece, a splash of polychromatic cheer, all those spines creating a bright mosaic of vertical lines.

Now it was just a black hole, like someone had punched out a tooth.

I quickly inventoried the rest of the house. In the kitchen, the first thing I noticed was that the Vitamix was gone. The super-strength juicer had been our Christmas present to each other, part of our promise to eat healthier now that we had a baby. Even though we went for one that had been reconditioned, and was therefore cheaper than a new one, it was still expensive.

Really? I thought, indignantly. *You're going to leave me and take one of the only nice things we own?*

I went upstairs next. Sure enough, his half of our closet was emptier than it used to be. Though, strangely, his nicer clothes — his professor duds — were still there. Only his casual clothing was absent.

His dresser was also a curiosity. Most of the socks and underwear were gone. So were his older jeans, the ones that I always joked came from his hip-hop phase, along with most of his T-shirts. Only the ones he wore while mowing the lawn or painting remained.

It was like he had packed for a long trip. But it was a trip whose destination made no sense. If he was running off to join Professor Kremer at Temple, why didn't he take his blazers, his slacks?

Had he fled or not?

Oddly, the thing that made me think he might still be around was that he hadn't bothered to leave a note. Surely, he would have done that — some last words for the woman he had shared five mostly good years with — if only to be polite.

But he hadn't written me, because he wasn't really gone. Not knowing I had been bailed out, he had probably spent time

280

before his shift at the mattress store going around to consignment shops and selling everything we had of value — the records, the Vitamix — in an attempt to get me out of jail. That's why he hadn't taken his professor clothes. The hip-hop jeans must have had extra value as collector's items that a white girl like me wasn't aware of.

Ben was right now at work, desperately trying to wrap up one or two more sales, counting his pennies on his way to the bail amount he needed to raise.

Or he had sold everything for gas money and taken off.

Either way, I had to know. The store was only a few minutes away. Before long, I was pulling into the narrow parking lot that fronted the strip mall containing Mattress Marketplace.

I walked through the glass doors into a large showroom, then approached a skinny young man, a few years younger than me, sitting alone at a desk. He stood when he saw me.

"Welcome to Mattress Marketplace," he said. "Do you want to just have a look around or can I —"

"Hi. I'm actually looking for Ben Barrick."

"He's not here right now. But I'd be happy to help you. Are you hoping for something on the firm side or —"

"I'm not a customer," I said. "I'm his wife."

The kid did a poor job hiding his surprise. He wasn't expecting a white woman.

"Uhh," he hummed.

"Is he in back?" I asked, walking in that direction, like I knew where I was going.

"He's . . . he's not here," he said.

"Is he on break or something?"

The kid was just staring at me. His Adam's apple bobbed up and down. "Didn't he . . . didn't he tell you?"

"Tell me what?"

"Ben quit on Saturday morning. He just came in, said he was done, and took off."

I forget how I replied, or if I said anything at all. I just know my exit from the store was probably less than graceful.

The hundred-foot wave of emotions crashing on top of me — embarrassment, shame, fury — made it difficult to remember more basic functions, like walking and breathing.

I tottered out to my car, barely able to get the keys in the ignition. I just had to get out of that parking lot, away from that skinny kid and his perplexed stare.

Ben really was gone.

For as much as I tried to trick myself into

believing I was a confident woman who had managed to survive her rotten childhood, there was always, lurking somewhere inside me, a little girl who had been abandoned by the two people who were supposed to love her most.

That little girl had always expected this day to come. That little girl knew there was nothing permanent about love, or the people who claimed to have it for her. It lasted only as long as it was convenient for them. It had been true for my parents, and for all the foster parents who had come and gone.

And now it was true for Ben too.

My soon-to-be ex-husband hadn't even bothered sleeping on the decision to leave me, nor had he taken more than perhaps an hour to come to it. He left the jail at, what, ten o'clock on Saturday morning? Ten thirty? He then either went straight to the mattress place and quit, or he had made it his last stop on the way out of town after hastily collecting his stuff. It's a wonder I hadn't seen tire marks as he laid rubber to get out of the driveway.

Except, of course, this wasn't some kind of rushed choice. He had probably been looking for an escape hatch since the sheriff's raid. Or maybe longer — like from when he first saw the pale-skinned baby he had obviously not fathered.

The moment I offered him a way out, he hadn't just walked through it. He had sprinted.

I had to put him out of my mind. Mourning his departure or letting it incapacitate me wouldn't do me any good. Shocking as it was, Ben was now a person in my past, another wound that would slowly heal over. I was returning to my natural state: on my own, with no one else I could depend on.

But I wasn't alone. For whatever the Commonwealth of Virginia might soon have to say about it, there was Alex. I was still his mother.

Alex needed me to stay strong for him, to spare him from the same kind of childhood I had, from the system. I wasn't going to abandon him the way my parents abandoned me.

April 9 was coming. Forget Ben. Forget Warren Plotz and Diamond Trucking. Alex — and the trial that would allow me to win him back — had to be my focus.

I wondered if Teddy had been able to make any headway over the weekend on that picture I had sent him.

He would just be coming home from work. I called him. No answer.

The turn for Desper Hollow was coming

up, but I already knew I wasn't taking it. I was going to Teddy's place. Maybe together we could figure out who that scar-headed man from the video really was.

Teddy's rental was a large, gruesomely asymmetrical Victorian on the wrong side of town that loomed over the street below it, looking like the Crazy Man's house in a B-grade horror flick.

I parked on the street and climbed the concrete steps next to the sidewalk, then the wooden steps that led to the porch. Teddy always told me I could just walk right in, that the other guys knew I was his sister and wouldn't care. But I always felt weird doing that, so I rang the bell.

After a short wait, one of his roommates, the one who worked at the Sheriff's Office, came to the door, looking a lot less official in jeans and bare feet than he did in his deputy's uniform.

"Hey," he said, opening the door wide so I could come in.

"Hey, thanks," I said, giving him a quick smile before I went up the stairs toward Teddy's room on the third floor.

But he stopped me before I could get that far. "If you're looking for Teddy, he's not here," he said. "You just missed him."

"Oh," I said. "Did he tell you where he

was going by any chance?"

"No. He was with that chick."

"What chick?" I asked. My twenty-three-year-old brother clearly didn't need to clear his dating life with me, but I wasn't aware he had a new girlfriend.

"You know, the one he used to date."

I immediately felt sick.

"Wendy?" I said, the name bringing a curl to my lips.

"I think that's her name, yeah. Dark hair, about yea high," he said, holding up his hand to roughly my height. "Hot as hell, but also a hot mess?"

"Yeah, that's her."

"She's been staying here the last few days," he said. "They left here maybe fifteen, twenty minutes ago."

He must have seen my shoulders drop, because he added: "It's none of my business, but . . . she's bad news, isn't she?"

"The worst."

"I just . . . well, whatever. Like I said, none of my business," he said. "If he comes back, you want me to tell him you were here?"

"No," I said firmly. "Don't bother."

I retreated back down the steps and sat in my car. I flashed back to the conversation we had in the parking lot, when he had bailed me out, when I thought I — his all-knowing older sister — could stare the truth out of him.

Are you seeing Wendy again? I had asked.

No! he insisted.

And I actually believed him. Now I found myself asking the question I least wanted to consider.

What else had he lied about?

TWENTY-SIX

The hand was on her hip, pressing just a little bit.

In those moments of incoherence between sleep and wakefulness, Amy Kaye wasn't sure if this was part of a dream, or whether her husband really was sitting on the edge of the bed.

"Ame . . . Ame . . . ," he said.

She stared at him with incomprehension, then it finally clicked in: Yes, her husband was there. He was no longer dressed in chef's clothing, but he still smelled like onions. Could you smell in dreams? No. So she must have been awake.

"Your phone was ringing, and I saw it was Jason Powers, so I answered it," he said softly.

He had been covering the mouthpiece with his finger but was now holding the phone out for her. Amy grabbed it, sitting up, now at least semifunctioning. The clock by her bed read 2:58.

Had she been a little more awake, she would have already known what this was about.

"Hey, it's Amy."

"Yeah, hey. Sorry to wake you," he said. The sheriff's voice sounded funereal, bearing none of its usual cordiality.

"No problem. What's going on?"

"We got a sexual assault on our hands. I think it's your guy."

Amy swore, then blindly pounded the pillow next to her.

"I was out driving around when the call came in," he said. "We haven't gotten the full story yet, but the victim told us the attacker was a guy wearing a mask who whispered the whole time. We're about to take her to the hospital to get checked out, but I wanted to give you a chance to talk to her first."

"Where are you?"

Powers recited an address in Mount Solon. It was in the northern reaches of Augusta County, at least a thirty-minute drive from Staunton. Amy didn't want to wait that long for the rape kit to be administered. Speed mattered.

"You think there's physical evidence?" she asked. She didn't need to get graphic with

Powers about what she meant.

"Might be."

"Then let's get her to the hospital. You taking her to Augusta Health?"

"That was the plan."

"All right. Why don't you send her on down, then? I'll talk to her after the kit is done."

"You got it," he said. Then he added: "I think you're really going to like talking to this one."

"What do you mean?" Amy asked.

"You'll see when you meet her," he said, then ended the call.

Augusta Health, the regional hospital, was only fifteen minutes away from where Amy lived. It had staff members who had been trained as sexual-assault forensic examiners. Amy could visit the scene in Mount Solon later in the day on Tuesday if she needed to. Right now, harvesting evidence mattered more.

As she pulled on a pantsuit, then hurriedly ran a brush through her hair, Amy felt physically ill. This was what she had dreaded all weekend, really from the moment she got Warren Plotz to kiss that Sprite can.

Plotz was so clearly due — overdue, actually. Sitting across from him, she had been able to feel the evil in him filling to the bursting point.

She was already second-guessing everything about the past few days of her life. Had she really pressed on the lab director, Chap Burleson, as hard as she could have? She should have camped out at the lab and refused to leave until he gave her a result.

For that matter, she could have had Plotz arrested. Yeah, so she didn't have rock-solid probable cause. Once she got a DNA match, no sane judge — and certainly no judge in conservative-leaning Augusta County, Virginia — would have gotten overly picky with her.

There was so much she could have done, should have done. She already knew it was one of those mistakes that would embed itself in her brain forever. It would sit there and slowly snack on her conscience, regurgitating its memory anytime Amy felt like berating herself for past failures.

As she rushed toward the door, she made a promise to this victim, to future victims, and to herself: She wouldn't rest until Warren Plotz was in custody, locked away in a place where he could never hurt another woman.

Her last words to her husband were: "Don't wait up for me."

■ ■ ■ ■

Lilly Pritchett. That was the name of the young woman Amy would never forget.

She was twenty-one, a student at nearby Bridgewater College. She had been living in a small rented cottage out in the country. It sat on the property of an elderly couple, who naturally hadn't heard or seen anything from the main house. The rest of the property was in such a rural area, there were unlikely to be any other witnesses.

That was the total of what Amy learned from a deputy while they waited for Lilly's rape kit to be administered. No one had gotten the full story of the attack yet. At the scene, Sheriff Powers had decided he wanted to make the victim go through the incident only once, and Amy was the right person to hear it.

Powers was still up in Mount Solon, collecting evidence, as Amy and the deputy waited outside the victim's hospital room. The smells of the hallway were so sterile, so antiseptic, so at odds with the vileness of the attack.

By the time the nurses had finished, it was after six o'clock. As the medical people cleared out, Amy went in.

Lilly was sitting up in bed, a sheet pulled up to her belly. She wore clean pajamas, not a hospital gown, which showed someone at Augusta Health knew what they were doing. Her yellow hair was sleep-matted. But there was something in her green eyes that encouraged Amy — a light that remained, even though it could have easily been extinguished.

"Hi, Lilly, I'm Amy Kaye. I'm with the Commonwealth's Attorney's Office."

"Lilly Pritchett."

Amy grabbed her extended hand. Her grip was still strong.

"How are you?" Amy asked.

"Tired."

"I'll bet. I wanted to ask you a few questions. Would you rather I come back after you've had a chance to rest?"

"No. Let's get this over with."

"All right. Why don't you just start at the beginning?"

"Okay," Lilly said, pulling the sheet up a little higher. "I probably went to bed around eleven or so. I was out cold when the guy came in my room."

"Do you have any idea how he got in?"

"The front door was locked, if that's what you're asking. There's a back door that you can kind of force open if you really lean on it, but . . . to answer the question: No, I don't know how he got in."

"Okay, go on," she said.

"The door to my room was closed, but it's an old house. It makes this *urrrr* noise when you open it, and I'm kind of a light sleeper. That's what woke me up. And then he started with this . . . this whisper. It was so scary."

"What was he saying?"

"He started by going, 'Shh . . . shh . . . don't scream . . . don't yell . . . I'm not here to hurt you.' And then he held up this, like, sword. And he goes, 'I'll only use this if I have to.' By then I could see that he was wearing gloves and dark clothes and this black ski mask and . . . I guess that's when I freaked out."

I'll only use this if I have to was a phrase more than a dozen victims had reported hearing. Any question about whether there was a connection between this attack and the others had now vanished.

"So he was wearing a mask," Amy said. "How else would you describe him? Did you get a sense of his height or weight or anything else about him?"

"I tried. I sort of went into this mode where I knew I was going to have to eventually be a witness about this guy. I . . . I watched a lot of *Law & Order SVU* reruns when I was in high school, and I actually used to think about how if Mariska Hargitay ever came to interview me, I wanted to be able to give her a lot of stuff to go on. Does that sound ridiculous?"

"Not at all," Amy reassured her. "It's quite helpful, actually. It means you kept your head about you. You'll be really good at testifying when we catch this guy."

Lilly smiled a little. "You think you will?"

"I feel good about our chances. But let's not get ahead of ourselves. Keep going. We were just getting to height and weight."

"Yeah, so . . . I'd say about five-ten or five-eleven, pretty average. And weight . . . I'm not very good at guessing guys' weights. It's not like he was fat or anything. Maybe one seventy-five? Is that normal for a guy?"

Amy knew Plotz was probably closer to two hundred. But twenty or twenty-five pounds certainly put it within an acceptable margin of error.

"Could you tell what race he was?"

"White."

"Anything else?"

"Not . . . not really. I'm sorry. I mean, it was dark, and . . ."

"I understand. Don't worry, you're doing great," Amy said. "We've gotten up to him coming into the room. What next?"

"Like I said, he started whispering at me and telling me not to be scared and that he wasn't going to hurt me as long as I co-operated. And he kept saying, 'please' and 'thank you' and he was . . . I mean, for a rapist, he was really *polite,* you know?"

Amy nodded.

"Anyway, I started crying, because I was so scared, and . . . And he actually tried to calm me down. He was like, 'Shh, don't cry, don't cry.' He said he was sorry he was do-ing this to me. And I was like, 'If you're sorry, why are you doing it? Why don't you just stop? Don't do this.' And then he said, 'Because I have to.' And then he said he was sorry again and told me to take my clothes off. I told him I wouldn't and then he brought the sword up and said something like, 'It would be a shame if I had to cut that pretty face of yours.' "

To Amy, this was evidence a power-reassurance rapist was progressing toward becoming what the profilers called a power-assertive. He still wanted the illusion of romance — because that was what excited him — but he was perhaps willing to use force to get it. It made him all that much more dangerous.

"What did you do?" Amy asked.

"I guess I . . . I knew he was going to do what he was going to do. And I mean, I've had sex with guys before when I didn't really want to, so I told myself to think of this as just one more time I was having bad sex. And that sort of helped calm me down.

"And then . . . I don't know, I really got thinking about how I was going to get raped no matter what, and I wanted to be able to catch this loser when this was all over. And I thought, 'Well, how am I going to take a better look at this guy so I can ID him later?' Because he had that mask on and all that . . . Anyway, I told him I felt embarrassed being the only one naked, and I would only take off my clothes if he took off his."

"Wow," Amy said, impressed by her quick thinking. "Did he do it?"

"He told me it didn't work that way. He told me I was the one who had to take off my clothes. But I was still thinking about *Law & Order* and what Mariska Hargitay would want me to do. And I was thinking about how she would want DNA or fingerprints. So I said, 'Okay,' and I took off my clothes and I let him . . . you know, get inside me. And then . . . You're going to think I'm a total slut, but —"

"You are *not* a slut," Amy said immediately. "Stop that right now. You are a survivor, and a damn smart one."

"Well, anyway, I started acting like I was really into it, you know? Just to get him distracted. I went full-on porn star, with the whole, 'Oh, yeah, baby, yeah, that feels so good.' And the whole time I was like, 'barf,' but I was just waiting for the right moment."

"For what?"

"To rip his gloves off," she said. "He had his hands on the bed at first, so I couldn't really get a grip on them. But then he put one of his hands on my boob and I just tore the glove off. He was like, 'What the?' But I was still in porn-star mode, so I was like, 'I want to feel your hand on my skin.' And he was like, 'Give me the glove.' And I was acting like I was in the heat of passion, so I was all, 'Don't stop. Come on, big boy. Harder! Harder!' And then I sort of knocked him into some stuff. He definitely touched my bedpost. And I had some books on my bed that I had been studying before I fell asleep. He touched those too."

In nearly thirty previous attacks, they had never gotten fingerprints. It was a remarkable bit of cunning from a scared twenty-one-year-old college student.

"You are incredibly, incredibly brave,"

Amy said. "And you may well have given us what we need to catch this guy. I want to call the sheriff to make sure he knows about this. Would you mind if I made a quick phone call?"

"Go ahead."

Amy went out into the hallway and dialed Powers's number.

As soon as he answered, Amy began the conversation with: "You are *never* going to believe this, but I think this asshole left prints."

Powers answered: "Well, you're never going to believe this, but on her way out the door, your victim told us to dust like hell for prints. And I think we already got some."

TWENTY-SEVEN

I slept in the middle of the bed that night.

This was my effort — pitiful, though it may have been — to assert control over my situation; over the husband who had left me, the brother who was back together with his drug-addict girlfriend, and the people who were trying to steal my baby.

My attempts at self-empowerment (and self-delusion) continued into the morning. My five-day hearing wasn't scheduled until 10:30, so I pumped, then showered and donned the most court-appropriate dress I had, a long-sleeved, belted maxi dress. I found it in a thrift store but had been told it made me look like Kate Middleton. Then I splurged and went into a coffee shop in downtown Staunton, where I sat with tea and a scone, busy with my phone, as if I were any other young woman with her act together.

I did all of this because I knew where I

was heading. Juvenile & Domestic Relations Court played a featured role in a number of my childhood memories. None of them were pleasant.

Mostly, I remembered the women. There was such sadness about them. It wasn't just that they had lost their pride, their self-esteem, or their looks; or that some of them had bruises or scars; or that they were overwhelmed by one aspect of the system or another.

It was that, in every one of them, there was still this sense of surprise, like they didn't belong there with all the other damaged women. They understood the choices that led them to this spot: the guy they never should have married, the drugs they never should have taken, the poverty they should have been clever enough to escape. But this still wasn't who they *really* were. Or at least it wasn't who they were supposed to have been.

I can remember being angry with my father that he had turned my mother into one of these women.

And now I was sitting in a coffee shop, nibbling at a scone, pretending I wasn't one of them myself.

Looking for a happier thought, I searched for some recollection of Alex that would restore some of the good mojo I was so desperately groping for. What I found, fairly quickly, was one from when Alex was about seven weeks old.

It was toward the end of my first week back at work, and we were all struggling with the transition. Long days were being followed by long nights. The excitement of having a baby had definitely worn off. What replaced it was the reality that no one really tells you about ahead of time: New parenting was mostly just drudgery.

I had picked Alex up from Mrs. Ferncliff's and given him his evening feeding. It was about time for him to drop off for a slumber that, if I was lucky, would last until at least one or two in the morning.

Alex hadn't really been looking at anything — just doing that thousand-yard newborn stare — and then suddenly his eyes locked onto mine. The color of Alex's eyes was still settling in, as happens with newborns, but they were showing signs of turning into this enchanting shade of blue-gray. They were the kind of eyes you could just get lost in.

And that's what I was doing, just staring into his eyes, when it happened: Like a fabulous new idea was slowly occurring to him, this huge smile spread across his face.

There had been times when I thought maybe he was smiling before that. But it was already hard to tell if it was that, or if he was just passing gas. This was the first time it felt totally intentional.

It was one of those moments that made his grip on my heart — which I had already thought was total — just a little bit stronger.

And now here I was in a coffee shop, needing to see those eyes and that smile again almost as much as I needed to keep breathing.

I made myself wait until twenty after ten to enter the courthouse building, if only because I didn't want to get myself too worked up about my first appearance before the judge who would have such an enormous say over my fate.

After passing through security, I made the familiar march toward Juvenile & Domestic Relations Court, which hadn't changed much since I was a teenager. It was a narrow, low-ceilinged room with seven rows of benches that were a bit like church pews, except it had always struck me this was about as far from God as you could get.

Up front, bantering with a woman who appeared to be another attorney, was Mr. Honeywell.

This was my first time seeing him in person. He was older than he looked on camera — at least sixty-five, though he was so droopy he easily could have passed for seventy-five. His nose had the fine spider veining of a man who often found his escape in a bottle. He had ditched his wrinkled suit in favor of a blue blazer and gray slacks. His tie hugged the top of his rounded belly, then dangled off the cliff at the bottom by at least a foot.

When he saw me, he actually did a double-take, like he was surprised I was there. He quickly excused himself from his conversation, then came my way. He had a limp that caused him to favor his left leg, something I hadn't been able to see on camera.

He was staring at me strangely, like maybe I had some food stuck on my cheek and he was debating whether to tell me. Then he mustered a weary smile.

"Ms. Barrick, if I may say, you look lovely this morning," he said in a way that managed to come off as kind, not old-man sleazy. I think it was the warmth of the smile. And the eye contact.

I realized he hadn't seen me in person before either. The other times I was on a television screen, dressed in jailhouse orange.

"Thank you," I said.

He looked at me for about three beats longer than he probably needed to, then sat next to me so we could talk in voices that couldn't be heard up front.

"The other matters scheduled for this morning have all wrapped up, so Judge Stone is just taking a break," he said.

He then ran through the people in the courtroom: Donna Fell, the attorney who would represent Social Services, an attractive dark-haired woman who looked to be in her mid-forties; Tina Anderson, the family services specialist, whom I had already met; the guardian ad litem, who would speak on Alex's behalf; the representative from Court Appointed Special Advocates; and so on.

Then Mr. Honeywell's eyes bugged out even further than usual. I followed his line of sight back to the front of the room, where Shenandoah Valley Social Services director Nancy Dement was now entering. She wore a jacket with a loud pattern and epaulettes on the shoulders. Her face seemed to have an extra caking of makeup.

"What's *she* doing here?" he muttered, mostly to himself. Then, not taking his attention from the front of the room, he began, "That's —"

"Nancy Dement. I know. Does she not normally show up at these things?"

"Not for years. Not since she went up to management," he said. His already lined face got a deeper set to it.

"Then what's she doing here?"

"No idea," he said. "But let's go to the table up front. I think we're about to get under way."

We had just gotten settled there when a sheriff's deputy strode purposefully into the courtroom and announced, "All rise!"

As I stood, Judge Stone entered the room. He was a tall African American man with just the right amount of gray in his otherwise black hair.

"Have a seat, everyone," he said in a deep voice that could have easily anchored the bass section in a church choir. "This is the preliminary removal hearing for *DSS versus Barrick*. Mr. Honeywell, I assume this is Ms. Barrick?"

"Yes, Your Honor."

"Is everyone else here that we need?"

Heads around the room bobbed.

"Okay, then let's get started. Ms. Fell, why don't you go ahead?"

"Thank you, Your Honor," Donna Fell said. "I'd like to start by calling Tina Anderson, family services specialist from

306

Shenandoah Valley Social Services."

Over the next twenty minutes, Fell led Anderson through her testimony. Some of it was perfunctory — how long she had worked at Social Services, what her qualifications were, that sort of thing. Then they moved on to the meat of the matter. She described how the Sheriff's Office notified Social Services it was executing a warrant on my house, how there was believed to be a child at the residence, and how she was on the premises when the raid occurred.

"You were standing outside on the lawn, is that right?" Fell asked.

"Yes, ma'am."

"And what did you then observe?"

"The deputies started coming out with drug paraphernalia that they said was consistent with a large distribution ring. They showed me a box with scales, baggies for packaging drugs, a list of phone numbers of what they said were known drug users in the area, and Ms. Barrick's mobile phone."

Ms. Barrick's mobile phone? Was that why I hadn't been able to find the thing? But how had it possibly gotten into that box along with all sorts of items I had never seen before?

And then, just as quickly, I understood. The people who were framing me must have

stolen it off the table by the front door —
where I made it all too easy for them to find
— then planted it with the other evidence,
knowing it would likely seal my guilt. I
couldn't very well claim I had never seen
the stuff in the box when my phone was
with it.

"And where did the deputies say they
found this box?" Fell asked.

"In a closet in the nursery."

Good God.

"You're calling it 'the nursery.' This is the
room where the child slept?" Fell asked, not
wanting the judge to miss the point.

"Yes."

"Did the deputies bring out anything
else?"

"Yes. After they found the drug paraphernalia, they discovered the drugs themselves.
They showed me several bags of white
powder that they said was cocaine."

"And where did they tell you they had
found that?"

"Also in the nursery, though they had
been taped inside the air duct."

Which told me why the air-conditioning
exchange cover had been removed. It also
meant Alex spent a night sleeping a few feet
from a half kilo of cocaine.

Anderson then testified how she "developed" knowledge that Alex was cared for by Ida Ferncliff, who was licensed with Shenandoah Valley Social Services as an at-home childcare provider; and how she went to remove Alex from there.

"And could you describe the condition of Alex at that time?" Fell asked.

I braced myself.

"He was in excellent condition," Anderson said. "He appeared to be healthy in all ways, very alert. He had just been changed. He was clearly well cared for."

"Did you ask the childcare provider for her observations about the child?"

"Yes. She told me that in her opinion the child's mother was very loving and was doing an excellent job caring for the boy. She was reluctant to surrender the child at first, because she didn't feel it was possible there had been any abuse."

I felt such a flood of gratitude toward Mrs. Ferncliff, I nearly started to cry.

Then Fell asked, "And what did you do to convince her that this was the necessary course of action?"

"I told her about what the Sheriff's Office had found in Ms. Barrick's house."

"About the cocaine?"

"Yes."

Which explained why Mrs. Ferncliff had

turned on me.

"What did you do next?"

"I took the child to our office in Verona, where we performed a more thorough examination."

"And what did you find?"

"The child appeared to be very healthy. There were no bruises or other signs of physical abuse. But given that there was cocaine found in the home, it's standard procedure for us to test the child for drugs."

"What kind of tests did you administer?"

"We performed a blood test, a hair-follicle test, and a skin test."

I was actually relieved to hear this: Finally, there would be some hard science here, not just anonymous accusations and easily misled sheriff's deputies. The people doing this to me could plant drugs in my home, but there's no way they could pump drugs inside my baby.

This would be a crucial first step toward proving my innocence. I leaned forward on the desk as the testimony continued.

"You've been trained in how to perform these tests?" Fell asked.

"Yes, ma'am. Multiple times."

"Have you gotten the results back yet?"

"Not for the blood test and the hair-follicle test. Those take a little while. We only have results for the skin test."

"Then let's talk about the skin test. Can you please describe for the court how this test is done?"

"It's pretty simple. You run a swab over the child's skin, paying particular attention to the hands, because that's the most likely way a child will ingest drugs — if there are, in fact, drugs present in the home. You then seal the swab in a tube and sign your name on the seal, so there's no dispute later about someone else in the chain of custody tampering with it. Then you send the tube to a laboratory here in Staunton."

"Have you gotten the results back yet?"

"Yes, ma'am. The child's skin and hands tested positive for cocaine."

Before I even knew what I was doing, I was on my feet. This was just too bizarre, and I couldn't take it sitting down for one second longer.

"No," I said. "No, that is *not* possible. She did the test wrong."

"Ms. Barrick, that's enough," Judge Stone said, scowling at me.

"She either did the test wrong, or she faked the results."

"Ms. Barrick, you're going to contain yourself or I'll have you removed from the courtroom."

"But, Judge, you don't understand, there has to have been a mistake of some kind. There is *no way* Alex could possibly have —"

And then I stopped myself. A recent memory came to me. It was from the morning after I had been bailed out for the first time.

I had gone into the nursery, marveling at its emptiness, thinking about Hemingway as I stared down into the crib. There, I had seen that fine white dust on the sheet cover.

It hadn't been baby powder.

TWENTY-EIGHT

The computer the Augusta County Sheriff's Office used to scan in fingerprints was a desktop model that was absolutely cutting-edge. For 2003.

A decade and a half later, it was cranky, interfaced poorly with every other piece of electronics brought within a dozen feet of it, and was so slow, Amy swore it was being powered by a hamster running on a wheel somewhere.

The man whose unfortunate job it was to massage results out of this imperfect system was Deputy Justin Herzog, a powerfully built former kickboxing champion whose close-cropped hair looked like it came straight out of a police equipment catalogue. Whatever aggressions he built up while battling the computer during his shift, he worked them out later on a heavy bag.

His hideaway at work was a small room that was nearly overpowered by the smell of chemicals. With Amy looking on, he slowly scanned the prints into the computer and digitally cleaned them so there would be a better chance of finding a match. Eventually, he got annoyed with Amy's shoulder-hovering and said, "How 'bout I just call you when I'm done?"

It was nearing noontime when that phone call came. Amy, who had been killing time in the detectives' bullpen, stopped just short of running down the hall to rejoin him.

"Okay, so what do you got?" she asked, not feeling any fatigue from having been up since three.

"Not enough, I'm afraid," Herzog said. "The detectives came back with a lot of prints and I haven't processed all of them, of course. But we're looking at prints from two individuals."

"The victim and the perpetrator," Amy said.

"I've referred to them as Person A and Person B. The set of prints the victim gave us is Person A, and of course hers are all over the place. With Person B, I'm mostly working off a few partials — it's not like he was nice enough to press his fingers down on our scanner or anything."

"I understand."

"I picked the best two and ran them

through our system and got three likely matches" — which wasn't unusual, though Amy didn't need to be told that. "But as soon as I looked at them, sorry, no dice."

"Are you sure?"

"I can talk you through all the arches, whorls, and loops if you want, or you can take my word for it. They're not a hit for anything we got. Person B is not known to us."

"Okay," Amy said. "So what now?"

"That's up to you," Herzog said. "We can send them down to Roanoke, if you want."

She didn't. The backlog for fingerprints at the state crime lab wasn't as long as it was for DNA. But it would still take months.

"Can you check for me if you have someone named Warren Plotz in the system?"

"Yeah, sure. Spell it for me."

She did, then watched him manipulate the tired, grubby mouse, filling in the appropriate fields. He clicked Search, the hamster went for a jog, and Amy waited.

"Sorry," Herzog said at last. "No Warren Plotz."

Amy crossed her arms and stared at the screen, taking in a deep whiff of chemically tinged air. She had been here before with Warren Plotz. Close. Achingly close. But not close enough.

It was possible that DNA result would come back from the state lab any day, making all this fingerprint stuff unnecessary. For that matter, the Sprite can might have Plotz's prints on it. She hadn't bothered checking, because the rapist had never before been duped into leaving prints.

But in either case, that would involve waiting. What if begging the lab director for an expedited result only knocked thirty or sixty days off the 156-day backlog?

In the past, she hadn't pressed the issue with Plotz. She had been patient, measured, careful . . .

All the things she was not going to be anymore. She was thinking of Lilly Pritchett, whom she hadn't been able to protect from this scourge; of Daphne Hasper and the other victims; even of Melanie Barrick, who deserved to have her attacker sent to prison whether she was a drug dealer or not.

But Amy was also thinking of a woman she hoped she'd never have to meet: the woman who wouldn't become a victim if she acted decisively.

"When does your shift end?" she asked Deputy Herzog.

"Not till six."

"Good. Don't go far. I'm going to get you a match for Person B this afternoon."

She marched out of the room and into the detectives' bullpen, where she prevailed on one of the deputies to let her borrow a computer that had printer access. She went to Warren Plotz's Facebook page, selected one of the photos without the douchebag aviator glasses, and hit Print.

Then she stared at the screen for a moment. She knew a legally viable witness ID of a perpetrator had to involve a properly arranged photo lineup. There needed to be a minimum of six pictures, all of people similar in size, appearance, and coloring. Even the setting had to be the same: you couldn't show, say, five portraits and one candid.

The case law governing the subject had generated enough paperwork to fell entire forests. The Supreme Court typically revisited the topic every few years for one reason or another, killing off another few hundred trees in the process. The Attorney General's advisory on the subject ran for many pages and was constantly being updated.

It would take time to create a proper mug book.

Time Amy could no longer tolerate wasting.

Without giving it further thought, she printed out five more Warren Plotz Facebook photos. She tucked them in a folder with the first one, then made the short drive back to Augusta Health. She paused at the door to Lilly's room in case she was sleeping, but the young woman was sitting up, almost like she was expecting company.

"Hello," she said.

"Hi, Lilly. How are you?"

"Still tired."

"I've got a photo ID book for you to look at. You think you can handle that?"

Lilly nodded.

"I'm going to show these to you one by one," Amy said. "Take as much time as you need. The man might not be in here. If he's not, no big deal, okay? Just do your best."

Amy handed the first photo to Lilly, who looked at it for ten seconds or so, then placed it facedown on the bed in front of her and gestured for the next one.

After the third, she said, "These are . . . these are all the same guy, aren't they?"

"No," Amy said firmly. "They're not."

Three years of law school. Fourteen years of prosecuting hundreds of cases in Fairfax. Three years and hundreds more in Staunton. Never once had she knowingly broken the law.

And now she was doing it without so much as a hitch in her voice.

Lilly returned her attention to the photos. She made it all the way through, then went back to two of the ones in the middle. She studied them a little more, then selected the fourth one.

"This could be him," she said. "It looks more like him than any of the other ones do."

"Okay, thanks," Amy said.

The witness positively identified the suspect from a sequential photo lineup. Amy was already writing the charging documents in her mind. She would get the warrant issued within two hours.

She could fix the mug book later. By the time it went to Warren Plotz's lawyer, it would little resemble what Lilly Pritchett had just thumbed through.

To hell with the Supreme Court.

TWENTY-NINE

It's difficult to describe what it's like to sit there in a court of law and have respectable, rational, upstanding people scrutinizing you like you're the kind of mother who lets her three-month-old baby roll around in cocaine.

The clerk's face had this dour downward cast, like she was offended to be breathing the same air as me.

The bailiff was staring at me with open contempt. He couldn't wait to get home and tell his wife about the human cockroach who crawled into his courtroom.

Judge Stone, who stopped just short of kicking me out of his courtroom after my outburst, kept giving me sideways glances. I wasn't merely one of Those Women who couldn't control their impulses anymore. I was maleficence personified.

Beyond that, there were my concerns for Alex's health. Were those trace amounts of

cocaine on him, or had he really gotten enough on him to ingest it? If he did, what kind of long-term consequences would that have?

Most of all: What kind of cretin would knowingly endanger an infant like that? And what else would a person like that be willing to do?

With those thoughts occupying me, I passed through the remainder of Tina Anderson's testimony in a haze.

I only refocused when Nancy Dement and her epaulettes came to the witness stand. In that jowly voice of hers, she went through the same routine of establishing herself and her credentials for the court.

Then Donna Fell began solving the riddle of Dement's presence.

"Ms. Dement, can you please tell the court how Ms. Barrick and her child first came to your attention?" Fell asked.

"Ms. Anderson asked me to consult on the case," Dement said. "She told me she had received a call from Lieutenant Peter Kempe of the Augusta County Sheriff's Office, and she wanted me to talk to Lieutenant Kempe about a certain aspect of the case."

"And what did you and Lieutenant Kempe discuss?" Fell asked, in that way that made

it clear she already knew the answer.

"He told me he had been working with a confidential informant relating to the criminal case against Ms. Barrick, and that the confidential informant had shared information with the Sheriff's Office that might be of interest to us."

"And what was that information?"

"The confidential informant told Lieutenant Kempe that Ms. Barrick wanted to sell her baby."

"Sell her baby!" Judge Stone boomed.

The charge, the mere suggestion of it, affronted him so greatly he leaned away from Dement. Then he rotated his whole body toward me. He could scarcely make his disgust more plain.

At least for the moment, I didn't care. I was more focused on the revelation itself. This was what Dement refused to tell me in her office the previous week. I now at least had some inkling as to where this horrible accusation had come from, even if all it did was open up yet another mystery: Who was this confidential informant?

As much as I wanted to think it was an invention of Nancy Dement's imagination, that couldn't be the case. She wouldn't rope a sheriff's lieutenant into a fiction like that.

It had to be a real person saying made-up things.

I began talking to Mr. Honeywell in a low, urgent voice: "That's not true. It's not true. I don't know who this confidential informant is, but he's lying. I never told *anyone* I wanted to sell my baby."

Donna Fell had waited a beat for the judge to contain his shock, then continued: "And how did you respond to that?"

"I was taken aback, just like anyone would be," Dement said. "As I said, I have been working at this agency for thirty-three years, and I have never been confronted with a situation like this."

"What did you do next?"

"I asked Lieutenant Kempe for more details, and he couldn't really give me any. I think Lieutenant Kempe was more concerned with Ms. Barrick selling drugs and was going to leave the selling of the baby to us. I told Lieutenant Kempe I needed more information and I asked if I could talk to the confidential informant myself."

"How did Lieutenant Kempe respond?"

"He was hesitant. He told me about how the Sheriff's Office has to protect the identity of its informants, and of course I understand that. He asked if perhaps he could relay some of my questions to the confidential informant and then get back to me with answers. I told him that given the nature of the issue, I really needed to talk with the informant myself. We went back and forth on this subject until we decided Lieutenant Kempe would bring the informant into his office and have the informant make the call from there."

At this point, Mr. Honeywell stood up with more force than I knew him to be capable of. And for the first time since he had come into my life, he started acting like he was defending an innocent woman.

"Your Honor, I have to object. It sounds like Ms. Fell is about to have Ms. Dement recall the details of a conversation this confidential informant is alleging he had with Ms. Barrick. I realize Ms. Barrick is a party opponent, so her utterances are a hearsay exception. But what Ms. Fell is asking you to accept is clearly hearsay within hearsay. If Social Services wants you to consider what this confidential informant has to say about a conversation with Ms. Barrick, let's bring him in and get him under oath. Otherwise, I don't see how the court can allow Ms. Dement to bring this conversation into evidence."

I didn't know what had gotten into him. But when he was through, I felt like standing up and applauding him, or maybe like kissing his pudgy, wrinkled cheek.

Someone — someone who actually mattered — was finally sticking up for me.

Better yet, Judge Stone seemed to be pondering my lawyer's argument.

"Ms. Fell?" he said. "What do you have to say about this?"

The plaintiff's lawyer straightened, making herself even taller. "Your Honor, I'd love nothing more than to bring this confidential informant in and have him testify. That's just not possible under the circumstances. But I think what this informant has to add to this case can't be ignored, and there's no other way to get it on the record.

"I'd ask that you remember the courts have long recognized the role of confidential informants in enforcing our laws, particularly our drug laws. We trust sworn law enforcement officers to make sound judgments about the reliability of their informants, and it seems reasonable the court have that kind of trust in Lieutenant Kempe. This isn't just someone Lieutenant Kempe picked up off the street. This is someone Lieutenant Kempe had used in other cases and considered to be solid."

The judge turned back our way. "Mr. Honeywell?"

"Judge, the courts have recognized the importance of confidential informants in *criminal* matters. This isn't criminal. It's civil. And in any court, it's still hearsay within hearsay. I'd ask you to disregard Ms. Dement's testimony entirely. We're talking about basic due process here."

Judge Stone tented his fingers, a gesture that made him look very judicial, indeed. The courtroom fell silent.

I can't say I comprehended the legal underpinnings of the verbal melee that had just occurred. Hearsay rules weren't something they taught in my literature classes. But I certainly understood the consequences of what the judge was about to say.

It would essentially decide whether or not I'd get to see my son while this case dragged out. If Nancy Dement's testimony was tossed — taking the absurdist fiction this confidential informant was spouting along with it — Social Services would have no basis to deny me supervised visits.

I had this brief fantasy about being able to hold Alex again; about his soft little head resting against my cheek; about his warm, chunky body pressing against mine. I felt that loss like a phantom pain.

Judge Stone shifted his weight in his seat, then crossed his arms as he gazed toward the back of the room. Then he looked at Mr. Honeywell and uttered a sentence that broke my heart.

"I'm sorry, Mr. Honeywell, but I'm going to have to overrule your objection," he said. "If this were a jury trial, I'd side with you all the way. But as you know, the law recognizes that a judge can assess evidence like this in a more nuanced way and assign it the proper weight. At the end of the day, I have to decide what's in the best interest of this child. And I need to use all evidence at my disposal to make that determination. You have my assurances that I'll take the hearsay factor into consideration. With that caveat, I'll allow it."

Mr. Honeywell sat back down. He didn't look at me. Maybe he didn't realize how devastated I was.

Or maybe he knew precisely.

Fell just picked up where she left off: "So, Ms. Dement, you accepted Lieutenant Kempe's offer to talk with the confidential informant?"

"Yes."

"And when did this phone call occur?"

"Later that same day. The informant called and confirmed that Ms. Barrick had asked him whether he knew someone who might be interested in buying a baby. The informant was mindful that he had to keep up the facade of having criminal contacts, so he told her he could look into it. Ms. Barrick told him she wanted a minimum of fifty thousand dollars."

When she uttered the amount, Judge Stone's eyes darted toward me and narrowed. In that moment, I knew I could completely disregard all his judge double-talk about what weight he would give certain evidence.

As Nancy Dement finished, the judge clearly had decided which way he fell on the subject of Melanie Anne Barrick. My own testimony — during which time Mr. Honeywell attempted to rehabilitate the tattered remains of my credibility — only did so much good.

Judge Stone spoke like a man with bile on his tongue as he rattled off his various proclamations and decisions. He started with a preliminary removal order, confirming the emergency removal order he had given the previous week. He told me I needed to get a job and stay out of prison if I wanted to have any hope of convincing him I could provide a fit home for Alex.

He finished by issuing a protective order against me, saying I couldn't knowingly come within five hundred feet of Alex, wasn't allowed to make attempts to find him, and couldn't communicate with the foster family that had custody of him.

My jaw was as unhinged as the rest of me, and I'm pretty sure it hung down the entire time. Because, sure, I could tell myself that I was being framed, that this was the work of hidden hands masterfully manipulating the levers of justice for their own purpose, and that therefore none of this reflected objective reality.

But the fact was, the law — very real, and very enforceable, with all the king's horses and all the king's men behind it — had just spoken.

And it said I was the kind of mother whose child needed to be protected from her.

THIRTY

I was so defeated and dazed by the time I left the courtroom, I felt like someone had spent the past two hours beating on me with a bagful of padlocks.

Needing to put some distance between myself and that awful courtroom, with its stale air and its preposterous accusations, I emptied out onto the street, setting a furious pace toward my car.

For a moment, I thought I heard someone saying my name. But then I dismissed it. No one out here was looking for me.

Then it came again: "Ms. Barrick! Ms. Barrick!"

I turned to see Mr. Honeywell. He had followed me out of the courtroom.

"Slow down," he said.

"I . . . I don't want to talk," I said in his direction, then quickened my pace.

"You left your purse," he said.

He was waving it in the air as he came

toward me in the speediest limp he could manage.

"Hold up," he said. "I'm an old man. My days of running around after young women are long gone."

I walked back in his direction, feeling churlish for having made him chase me.

"Thank you," I said when he handed me my purse. "I really appreciate it."

I turned to continue toward my car, but Mr. Honeywell wasn't having it.

"Now, hang on a second. Just hang on," he said, out of breath. "I want to talk for a moment."

"What's there to talk about?" I said petulantly, then pointed toward the courthouse. "That man hates me, and he's clearly never going to let me have my son back."

"Now, now. Judge Stone is just . . . Well, this is your first time in front of him, so he wants to set a certain tone. Some women, they don't take this as seriously as they need to, so he goes a little rough on them at first."

"A *little* rough," I said.

"Ms. Barrick," he said, still panting a little.

Then he surprised me: "Would you sit with me, please?"

He pointed to a stone bench that was under a tree in front of the courthouse.

"Uh, sure," I said.

I almost took his arm as he hobbled toward the bench. I would have, if I hadn't thought he'd be offended by my offer to help.

"There. That's better," he said after lowering himself.

He patted the spot on the other side of the bench. As I sat, he pulled out a handkerchief and dabbed his face with it.

"Now, look, I'm going to be honest with you: That was a heck of thing in there," he said. "I'm not sure I've ever had a five-day hearing that was so . . . combative is the word that comes to mind. If you're feeling a little woozy, I don't blame you. I do too."

"Thank you," I said. And I meant it.

"I'm sorry I couldn't keep that nonsense about the confidential informant out of evidence," he said, shaking his head as he returned his handkerchief to his pocket.

"I appreciate that you tried," I said. "Who *is* that confidential informant, anyway? Do we have any way of figuring that out?"

"We might," he said.

"How?"

"Well, I've been thinking about that, and some fancy lawyering from yours truly just might be in order. The search warrant is a public record, so that's not the issue. The problem is, in the warrant, they list the confidential informant by number, not name. The only way we can unmask him, so to speak, is to challenge the warrant itself."

"You can do that?"

"Oh, sure. This would be connected to your criminal case, so it happens over in Circuit Court. I can make a motion to have the warrant suppressed on the grounds that the confidential informant was lying to the Sheriff's Office. The judge'll eventually tell them to produce their CI. At that point, we'll have what's known as a motion hearing. Depending on how it goes, that might be your whole case right there."

"What do you mean?"

"Once I get that fella up on the stand, I'm hoping I can trip him up and catch him in a lie. Maybe more than one. Once the judge sees that the confidential informant isn't on the up and up, he'll have no choice but to toss the warrant. If the government loses the warrant, all the evidence found as a result of that warrant is known as 'fruit from a poisoned tree.' It's inadmissible."

"Inadmissible, as in . . ."

"Gone," he said. "And without any evidence, they don't have any case. The prosecutor would have to drop the charges."

I took in a deep breath. It was tempting to listen to Mr. Honeywell's strategy — simple, straightforward, and seemingly so possible — and get hopeful.

But hadn't I already learned how dangerous that emotion could be?

I looked up at the tree hanging over us. Its buds were just about to burst, heavy enough that they were bending the branches. It was one of those portents of spring, of rebirth. It made me think of the tulips in front of my house.

They had once filled me with optimism too; and look how that turned out.

"You really think that's going to work?" I asked.

"We won't know until we try."

We. There I was, overvaluing pronouns again, but to hear the first-person plural come out of his mouth was heartening. And as I looked at him — my wrinkled champion — I wondered what it was that had come over him. Until recently, he had been as skeptical of me as everyone else. Something had clearly changed his thinking.

"Mr. Honeywell, thank you, but . . . I guess I'm curious: Why are you helping me like this?"

The question seemed to amuse him. "Ms. Barrick, I know I might not look like much, but I am your lawyer."

"No . . . I know that, but . . . I'm not

naïve. The court barely pays you anything for this. And you've probably had a million clients singing the same song as me about how innocent they are. And you . . . You can't possibly believe them. I know you probably didn't believe me at first. But in court just now, you were acting, I don't know, differently."

He chuckled softly. "That's . . . that's hard to answer."

"Please try."

We sat in silence for a little while as he composed an answer. When he finally began, it was in a voice that was as slow and marble-mouthed as ever, but also somehow deeper and sadder.

"Ms. Barrick, I've been doing this a long time. Maybe not always well, and certainly not lucratively; but a long time nevertheless. When you sit where I've sat for forty years, you realize no one is purely bad and no one is purely good. We're all somewhere in the middle, and sometimes it's just a question of . . . of what position the world puts us in that determines which side of the courtroom we sit on. Do you follow me so far?"

"Sure."

"I don't kid myself about who my clients are. They've probably done bad things, you're right. But they're not really bad people, much as some folks in the legal system might like to view them that way. It's my job to represent them all the same. I've got to make sure the courts treat them fairly, of course. And maybe, if I'm having a good day, I can even get the courts to see my clients the way I do — as that mix of good and bad that we all are. That's probably the best I can do for most of them, and I can sleep okay at night knowing I've tried my best."

He paused and sighed heavily. "But then, every once in a while, a client comes along . . ."

Mr. Honeywell was now the one looking up at the tree. "When I saw you in court this morning, I was really struck by . . ."

He was struggling with the words, almost choking on them. "Well, you remind me of someone, put it that way. Seeing you in that dress, maybe I understood who you really were for the first time."

"What do you mean?" I asked.

"I see you, Ms. Barrick," he said cryptically. "I see you."

"I don't understand."

"And I don't think I can explain it," he said. "It doesn't matter anyway."

He lifted himself slowly from the bench. To my astonishment, he had tears in his eyes. He pulled out his handkerchief again and blotted his face.

"I see you, Ms. Barrick," he said one last time. "And to be perfectly honest, it scares me to death."

"What do you mean?" I asked. "Mr. Honeywell, wait."

But he was already limping away.

THIRTY-ONE

There were four vehicles in the convoy pointed toward Warren Plotz's residence: three Fords bearing the mustard-yellow-and-brown insignia of the Augusta County Sheriff's Office; and a Subaru that was unmarked, save for the Coexist sticker on the back bumper.

They made for a strange quartet, though that was fitting. This was not a normal occasion for Amy Kaye, the driver of the Subaru. Arrests were something she usually only experienced on paper.

But she wasn't going to miss this one. This was three years and an enormous pile of personal hours in the making.

The deputies, who might normally have balked at having a lawyer watching over them while they did their jobs, didn't protest when Amy said she wanted to join them.

This was her bust. Even if she wasn't going to be the one laying the cuffs on Plotz, they all knew she had earned this.

Beyond the self-satisfaction she was savoring as they turned into Plotz's neighborhood, there was also a heaping measure of retribution she felt on behalf of the victims. She had met with nearly every one of them, many of them more than once. She had seen the pain in their eyes as they recounted the most harrowing experience of their lives.

She wanted to be able to share this moment with all of them: What, exactly, their tormentor had looked like when he realized that he had been caught; that he was never going to spend another moment of his life as a free man; that one of his victims had bested him.

Amy hoped he cried or blubbered or begged for forgiveness. After all the tears the women had spilled because of him, that would be poetic justice.

Plotz's house was in a new subdivision, a place where the landscaping was twiggy and the driveways weren't yet cracked. People there weren't used to seeing a phalanx of sheriff's cars making quick time through the quiet streets. The deputies pulled into Plotz's driveway, blocking in a Dodge Ram 2500 whose presence suggested the owner was at home, perhaps even watching from inside.

It was no matter. They weren't going for stealth here. They wanted a show of force.

There were six deputies, each wearing a bulletproof vest. Records indicated Plotz had a concealed-carry permit. They weren't taking chances.

Two deputies went around back, in case Plotz tried to run. The other four came up the front steps. Amy wasn't very far behind. She felt like she carried the emotional authority of the victims with her.

The deputies did not bother knocking. Plotz had certainly never extended such courtesy to his victims. They took down his front door with a small battering ram.

A sergeant led the way inside. "Police! Warren Plotz, this is the Augusta County Sheriff's Office, and we have a warrant for your arrest!" he shouted. "Do not try to resist. We have you surrounded."

With their service weapons raised, the other deputies poured in behind him, then fanned out across the first floor, going room by room with smooth efficiency.

He wasn't there. The deputies reassembled at the bottom of the carpeted steps and moved quietly up them. The sergeant again led the way.

Pausing at the door to the master bedroom, he made eye contact with each of his subordinates, making sure they were ready. It was possible Plotz, now aware of their presence, was holed up in his bedroom, ready to make his last stand.

All four deputies now had their guns unholstered. It wouldn't last long if Plotz tried to resist. But was this how Plotz wanted to go out? Suicide by cop?

Amy retreated down the stairs by two treads, but was still peering around the corner. The sergeant mouthed a *"one . . . two . . ."* then opened the door on three.

The room was tomb dark, unnaturally so for three o'clock on a sunny March afternoon. From what little light made it in from the hallway, Amy could see a shade that entirely wrapped the window it enclosed, blocking any attempt by the sun to penetrate the room. The deputies had seemingly disappeared into the gloom.

Then: "Warren Plotz, do not move, you are under arrest."

It was the sergeant. One of the deputies flipped on a light switch.

Amy could now see one of the deputies had a gun aimed at Plotz, who was sitting up on a king-size bed in the middle of the room, appropriately astonished at having been woken up by four armed men. His upper half was bare. His lower half was still wrapped in a tangle of blankets.

"What the — ?" Plotz began, then finished the phrase with a vulgar intransitive verb.

Amy walked into the room as Plotz clawed at his ears and removed two hunks of wax from them. Earplugs. He had been wearing earplugs. That's why he hadn't heard the officers breaking down the front door or coming in. He was a man who slept most of the day, exhausted as he was from his nocturnal activities.

The moment Plotz saw Amy, he recoiled a little.

"Oh, what the — ?" he said again, ending with the same curse. "Is this because of that bitch Melanie Barrick? What did that cunt say about me? Whatever she said, it was a lie. She's a lying bitch."

"Mr. Plotz, turn around and lie on your stomach," the sergeant ordered.

But Plotz wasn't hearing it. He was pointing at Amy, his sleep-lined face red with rage.

"Melanie Barrick is a lying bitch. She's a lying bitch. She's had it out for me for a long time. I fired her last week for being a scumbag drug dealer. She's nothing more than a disgruntled ex-employee. Anything she says about me is a lie. If you arrest me, I'll sue you. I'll sue the crap out of all of you."

"Shut up, Plotz," the sergeant said. "Turn over and lie on your stomach *now,* or we're going to do this the hard way."

Plotz offered a few more choice opinions about Melanie Barrick before complying with the order. The sergeant brought Plotz's wrists together, then clamped on a set of black handcuffs.

"There we go," the sergeant said. "Let's get this asshole out of here."

If the wait for fingerprint results was slow before, it was now interminable.

This time, the delay was more human than technical. Plotz had to be brought before the magistrate, then processed. The bureaucracy would not be rushed.

At some point, Plotz must have been allowed to use a phone. His wife, father, and lawyer were now down at the Sheriff's Office, filling the reception area with their anxious energy.

Maybe they knew, or suspected. Especially the woman. Plotz was a patient hunter who scoped out his victims thoroughly before he pounced. It was no accident the women he attacked had been alone. How could the wife not at least wonder where her husband disappeared to night after night?

Still, Amy felt sympathy for them. They were about to become two more of Warren Plotz's victims, their lives inalterably changed by their association with the worst serial rapist the Shenandoah valley had ever known. They would forever be known as the wife of, the father of.

Once she retreated from the dispatcher's area, Amy was mostly making a conscious effort not to pester Deputy Justin Herzog for the fingerprint results. Everything would happen in due time.

Amy hoped to have a confession by dinner. She wondered if he'd start with Lilly Pritchett and then slowly admit to the rest of them after they confronted him with DNA matches, or if he'd give up the whole thing right away.

One thing was for sure: She planned to start notifying the victims that night. Lilly first, then Daphne Hasper. Then maybe Melanie Barrick. It would be a shorter conversation, perhaps. But drug charges or no, Barrick deserved the same care and concern as the other women.

Amy hoped to reach all of them, if possible. She was only going to be able to stall Aaron Dansby's incredible urge to "leak" this to the media for so long. She wanted each victim to hear it from her first, not read about it in the paper.

That was about as far as her thinking had advanced when she finally got the call from Herzog. The kickboxing maestro of the fingerprint matching system was ready for her.

Her calves felt turbocharged as she churned down the hallway toward that noxious-smelling room. Her nerves jangled.

"Hey," she said as she entered.

Herzog looked up from the screen. She walked around behind him. He had positioned the two prints side by side on the screen.

"Okay, so this is the partial for Person B," the deputy said, pointing to the one on the right. Then he shifted his finger left. "And this is the guy you just brought in."

Amy narrowed her eyes at the images. There was something off about them, but she couldn't quite place it. While she had seen a lot of fingerprint results in her time, she couldn't read them quickly.

Herzog could.

And he already had.

"These are two different people," he said. "Sorry."

Amy could practically feel the blood

draining from her face. It took a moment for her to even summon words.

"Are you . . . are you sure you didn't . . . I don't know, mix them up, or —"

"Sorry," he said again.

She stared at them a little harder and, sure enough, there was a distinctive whorl in Person B that simply wasn't present in Warren Plotz.

They weren't a match.

Warren Plotz wasn't the whispering rapist. Amy had to acknowledge two painful truths.

One, she had arrested the wrong man.

And two, she was back to where she had been two weeks ago.

Nowhere.

THIRTY-TWO

The baby liked to face out.

That's all there was to it. That was the whole trick. That, by God, was *everything.*

Try to cuddle the little guy against your chest or shoulder, and you might as well have been thrusting him against hot coals. He'd wail himself crimson, squirming and bucking the whole time.

But then turn him around, and it was like flipping a switch. Instant calm.

Happy baby.

Happy foster mother.

And yes, it took her about five days to discover this — five hellishly long days, during which time she seriously considered suicide, gouging her eardrums with a screwdriver, and myriad other solutions that felt like they would be less painful than listening to the kid cry any more.

Now? He was as contented as any baby could be. Sure, he had needs. He cried some. He fussed when he was tired.

But for the most part, all she had to do was feed him, change him, and give him a nice view until he fell asleep again.

"You just want to see the world, that's all," she told him. "I bet you're going to be a traveler when you grow up."

They took walks around the neighborhood, because she discovered facing him outward *and* being outside made the baby even happier.

At one point, one of the neighbors had asked to hold him. And of course, the moment he was turned inward — like people did when they held a baby — he started howling. It was almost comical. Or at least it was now that she knew the secret.

"Oh," she explained, "he's an outward-facing baby."

After that simple epiphany, order was restored to the household. She was able to get some basic cleaning done — as long as she did it with one hand, and held the baby in a way that allowed him to see what was going on.

She could even vacuum. The boy seemed fascinated by the machine.

So it was a relatively calm, relatively clean, relatively stable household when her husband returned from work one night.

He walked in to find his wife dancing around the room with the baby, whose back was against her front in a BabyBjörn, allowing him to enjoy the scenery as she spun slowly around.

"You two certainly seem to be getting along well," he said, smiling warmly.

She stopped in mid-twirl. "You know, I've been thinking. Should we change his name?"

"To what?"

"I don't know. I just . . . I think he should be named after his daddy, don't you think?"

The man smiled even more broadly.

"Let's do it tomorrow," she said. "I downloaded some boilerplate name-change documents online while he was napping. We can go down to the courthouse and file the papers."

"Slow down," the man said. "We need the adoption to go through first."

"I know, but . . . you said that was just a matter of time."

"It is. It is."

"You keep saying that. But what if . . . what if Melanie's rights aren't terminated?"

Melanie. Always, that's how the baby's mother was referred to in the household. Melanie. As if they knew her. As if they were the best of friends.

"I just . . . ," the woman continued, then her voice faltered. "I mean, I can't even bear the thought of losing him."

She wrapped her arms around the baby and kissed him protectively on top of the head.

"That's not going to happen," the man said firmly. "I keep telling you: I'm on it."

THIRTY-THREE

Mindful of Judge Stone's order to get a job — and of my fast-emptying bank account — I started looking for employment first thing Wednesday morning.

I set my expectations low, aware of my obvious liabilities. I didn't bother with anything white collar. The people who hired at those kind of places read newspapers and did Google searches.

My first stop was Starbucks. Had Marcus still been the manager, becoming reemployed there would have been as easy as asking him to fill my name in on the schedule. But it turned out Marcus was now two managers removed from the current one and had basically been erased from the institutional memory of the Staunton Starbucks. I didn't know any of the people who were working the counter when I went in.

The new manager curtly told me they weren't hiring at the moment. He took my number in case things changed, but we both knew he'd lose it as soon as I was out the door.

This set me off on a long and frustrating tour through Staunton. The manager at Chili's stared at me hard enough that I could tell she recognized me from the newspaper. Firehouse Subs was adding to its management team but required a background check.

Walmart wasn't hiring. Neither was Staples. Nor anything at the down-on-its-luck Staunton Mall. Lowe's wanted to know if I had any home-improvement experience and didn't seem to act as if painting my living room qualified. The rest of the big-box stores I drove past were, likewise, busts.

Martin's, one of the local grocery stores, was looking for a produce manager and the woman there seemed interested when I described my experience on the other end of the supply chain and my detailed knowledge about spoilage rates. Then she asked if she could call Diamond Trucking for a reference.

And on it went. There were at least ten different places that had me fill out applications, but I received only vague promises about whether or when I'd hear back.

My second-to-last stop was Mattress

Marketplace. Maybe they'd be trying to fill Ben's position. As I drove there, I tried to fend off the strong sense of loss gripping me by thinking how this could be a sign the universe had some sense of fairness: Ben had run out at the lowest point in my life, and it hurt like hell, but at least he would also be leaving me his job.

The manager smiled at me nicely, then said he was sorry, but they had already found someone.

It was getting late in the workday at that point, and I might have broken down on him a little bit. In his attempts to console me, he told me he heard Waffle House was hiring.

I slid into the place around four o'clock in the afternoon, well after the lunch rush but before dinner got going. The woman at the counter directed me to the back, where I discovered a harried-looking manager in a dreary, grease-stained office. She looked at me like she had given up on pretty much everything long ago, and that she was surprised to still be here — "here" being not just the restaurant but the planet.

Her first question was whether I had any service experience. I told her about my two years at Starbucks. She asked if I was okay not having a regular shift — they had holes in the schedule all over the place. I said that was fine. Until I got Alex back, I could work whenever she needed me.

The job paid $2.13 an hour, plus tips, which I had to report down to the penny. If, at the end of a pay cycle, my tips didn't add up to at least $7.25 an hour (Virginia's sad concept of a minimum wage), Waffle House would make up the difference.

I asked the manager how often that would happen. "I guess you'll find out, honey," was her answer. "You want to work or not?"

Judge Stone said I had to get a job. He didn't say it had to be a good one.

THIRTY-FOUR

Amy Kaye had two headaches that Thursday morning.

The first could be attributed to Warren Plotz.

She had spent most of the day Wednesday cleaning up that mess. The heir of the Diamond Trucking empire wasn't some scared kid who was just grateful to be cut loose. He had his indignation, and he wielded it with a heavy hand, taking the minor flesh wound that was being wrongly accused of a crime for a few hours and turning it into a gaping psychological hemorrhage.

He eventually agreed to be placated by a letter of apology from the commonwealth's attorney. But even that turned into a fecal tempest, with the election-minded commonwealth's attorney refusing to sign anything that might be "leaked" to the media.

In the end, Plotz grudgingly accepted a

letter signed by Chief Deputy Commonwealth's Attorney Amy Kaye, accompanied
by an in-person apology.

Somewhere in the midst of that back-and-
forth, Amy got the additional punch in the
mouth that was the phone call from Chap
Burleson, the lab director in Roanoke.

Unsurprisingly, the DNA sample on the
soda can did not match the DNA from the
other sexual assaults. Burleson was civil
about it, but there was a why-did-you-
waste-my-time undertone to his words.

All the while, Amy stewed in her chief
mistake: She had allowed herself to become
overly emotional and therefore overzealous.
That had led her to ignore policies and
procedures that had been put in place for
just this reason, to prevent one person's passion from having undue influence on what
was supposed to be a dispassionate process.

By Wednesday night, at which point Amy
had felt like a puppy whose nose had been
rubbed in her mistakes altogether too much,
she finally went and did what she should
have done all along: Go to the restaurant
where her husband worked, get slowly and
thoroughly inebriated on whiskey, and then
let him take her home and tuck her into
bed.

Which had all seemed like a fine, wonderful idea — until she had to wake up Thursday morning.

So that was the first headache.

The second came shortly after she was alerted that an appeal had been filed on behalf of one Demetrius "Mookie" Myers. The appeal itself was no surprise — Myers had a new lawyer who had filed notice a month earlier.

She hadn't been expecting trouble. Maybe a claim for ineffective assistance of counsel or some kind of quibble with the jury instructions, neither of which would really involve her. Most criminal appeals were basically legal spaghetti, flung against the walls of the Court of Appeals in Richmond in the hopes they might stick.

But to Amy's surprise, this particular appeal was gooey enough to do just that. One of the witnesses against Myers had been an elderly neighbor who bravely testified she had repeatedly seen Myers selling cocaine in a small alley behind their apartment building. She had come forward against Myers because she was tired of all the undesirables Myers's activities were attracting to her home.

According to the petition, the witness, who was afraid of Myers's remaining foot soldiers, had been paid $5,000 out of a victim/witness fund to relocate out of the county. There was nothing illegal about that, of course. The Sheriff's Office did it all the time.

Except this small fact had never been introduced at trial. And Myers's new lawyer was pointing out — rightly, unfortunately — that the jury should have heard about it, the argument being that the payment might have helped motivate her testimony. Depending on how profound a slip the appellate judge deemed it to be, it could result in a new trial for Myers.

If it was true. And there was one way to quickly find out.

Amy pulled out her phone, hoping this was one of the times Sheriff Jason Powers could be quickly found.

Two rings later, she heard, " 'Lo?"

"Hey, Jason, it's Amy Kaye."

"How's it going?"

"Not good. I'm looking at the appeal in the Mookie Myers case."

"Yeah? And?"

"You remember that nice little old lady who brought the case to you guys?"

"Yeah."

"Did you pay her five grand to help her move out of that apartment building and into a new place?"

"Uh-huh. She was doing that whole 'I'm on a fixed income' thing. She said she wouldn't testify until we got her out of there. Why?"

"Don't you think you could have, I don't know, told me about that?"

"We didn't?" Powers asked.

Amy let out a long sigh and shook her throbbing head.

Two hours later, having swallowed some aspirin and drank as much water as she could force down her throat, Amy was walking through the glass front doors at the Augusta County Sheriff's Office.

She was already thinking about her evidence and how she'd have to present it all over again. Lieutenant Kempe had been the lead investigator, and obviously he wouldn't give her trouble about testifying a second time — he had only himself to blame for not telling Amy about the payout.

Then there was the old lady. Amy wanted Kempe to contact her to make sure she hadn't moved again.

That left the drugs and the guns.

The latter were still in existence. They had been confiscated and were waiting to be melted down, something the Sheriff's Office did once a year, in December.

The former should have been handled already. After the trial, it's the duty of the Sheriff's Office investigator to destroy the drugs, then certify to a judge he has done so. But Amy couldn't find the certification in the file.

That meant the drugs were still in the evidence lockup, which was a small break in Amy's favor. In larger drug cases like this one, she liked to put the product in front of the jury, to make the crime more concrete. *Look here, see this? This is what the menace looks like. This is the sickness this man was spreading throughout our community.*

Now she just needed to make sure the drugs weren't scheduled to be destroyed, say, today.

Amy could have done all this with a phone call. But it was a delicate thing, telling the lead investigator he had botched a detail like this, and she valued her relationship with Lieutenant Kempe enough to do it in person.

She found the lieutenant in his small office just off the detective's bullpen. Skip Kempe had always reminded her of an introverted high school English teacher in some way she couldn't quite place. Maybe it was his unassuming air. Or that she had once caught him reading an Aldous Huxley novel over lunch.

As soon as Kempe saw Amy, he slumped his shoulders and hung his head.

"I am so, so sorry," he said. "Sheriff just reamed me out pretty good, but if you want to take a turn, I fully deserve it."

"It's okay," Amy said. "No one bats a thousand."

"No, it's really *not* okay. As soon as Sheriff told me, I . . . I mean, I just couldn't believe I bungled something so basic."

"Seriously, don't beat yourself up too much," Amy said. "It's possible the judge will let us off the hook and decide this disclosure wouldn't have changed the outcome. And look, if there is a new trial, our case will be every bit as solid the second time as it was the first, okay?"

"Yeah, I know, I know. It's just . . . I feel like we spent too much time landing this fish to throw it back like this."

"We'll land him again, don't worry," Amy said. "Speaking of which, I noticed there wasn't anything in the file about the drugs being destroyed. Have you not done that yet?"

If it was at all possible, Kempe shrunk even further.

"You're not going to like this," he said.

Amy just cocked her head.

"A few weeks after the trial, I was collecting all my notes and everything, getting ready to put them in the morgue. That's usually when I get rid of the drugs, right? Then I do that little write-up for the judge and sign my name in blood that I've done it and all that. But when I went back to evidence and started looking for them, they were . . . they were sort of gone."

"Gone?" Amy said. "What do you mean, *gone*?"

"I don't know what to tell you. The sergeant and I literally emptied the entire lockup and went through every item piece by piece. The drugs weren't there."

"So where are they?"

Kempe just spread his hands wide. "I wish I could tell you, but I can't even make something up. According to the chain-of-custody sheet, they're still in there."

"When were you planning on telling me about this?"

"To be perfectly honest, I was hoping they'd either turn up or we'd figure out which one of our guys stole them so we could flay him alive and then put the stuff back before anyone outside the department knew it was gone."

Amy's headache, which had only recently abated, was returning with a terrible vengeance. If this came out at the second trial, they would look like fools.

Depending on how good Myers's new attorney was and how much he exploited this blunder, they might even lose the conviction.

THIRTY-FIVE

My first shift began Thursday morning and stretched into Thursday afternoon, encompassing both the breakfast and lunch rushes. The manager believed in leadership by beratement, so most of my time was spent being chastised for one minor transgression or another, like how I didn't properly orient the bills in the cash register.

For eight hours of hard labor and censure, my tips totaled $51.74, the most generous of which came when a trucker told me to keep the change after handing me a ten for a $5.79 tab. To be fair, I earned it: he had stayed there two hours, insisted on nine coffee refills, and ogled my ass every time I walked away.

As I trudged back out toward my car, wearing my blue button-down Waffle House shirt and cheap black pants, the urge to quit was overwhelming. My feet and ankles throbbed. My hair felt and smelled like it had been infused with bacon grease. The rest of me reeked like burnt coffee.

The only thing that stopped me from turning back around and telling the manager where she could shove her cash register was Alex. I thought of Judge Stone, staring at me haughtily from on high, asking me if I had gotten a job like he asked. I needed to be able to answer in the affirmative.

I flopped in my car and, feeling too tired to even turn the ignition right away, checked my phone. It had two messages waiting.

The first was a voicemail from Mr. Honeywell. He had filed a motion to suppress the search warrant in my criminal case. He said the clerk would schedule us for a motion hearing, and that it would likely be soon. The matter needed to be adjudicated before the April 9 trial date.

Then he hung up. He did not acknowledge or attempt to explain the strange end to our conversation on the bench. Maybe he never would.

The second message was a text from Teddy.

Hey, I have some good news that might lead to better news. Where ru?

I don't want to say I had forgotten about

365

Teddy since Monday, when I had learned he was once again gallivanting with Wendy. But his newest dalliance with danger simply hadn't been a priority. As had been the case in the past with Teddy, I had enough problems without adding in his issues.

Where am I? I thought. *Where are* you, *Teddy? And what the hell have you been up to?*

But I didn't text that. I was too tired for the drama. So I just tapped out

Heading home. Where ru?

Then I got back on my way toward Desper Hollow. Halfway there, Teddy texted back.

I'll be right there. I have a surprise. A good one.

Great, I thought. *I can't wait.*

When I got home, it seemed to take the breast pump longer than ever to draw milk out of me. It was one more thing that was making me feel grim as I changed out of my Waffle House finery. I had just finished when I heard a truck rumbling up the driveway. I opened a slit in the blinds to have a look. Sure enough, it was Teddy.

But that wasn't the reason I was cursing and fuming as I ran back down the steps toward the front door. It was who he had in the passenger seat.

Wendy Mataya. The succubus herself.

The first time I met Wendy, she was maybe sixteen, and she was already beautiful to the point of distraction, this human concoction that I thought only existed in romance novels: hair so dark brown it was practically black; flawless pale skin; huge green eyes that brought to mind emeralds; and, what the guys liked best, an hourglass figure so curvy, and yet so impossibly slim in the waist, that you'd swear she was wearing a corset.

But let's be clear, I didn't hate her because she was gorgeous or had a great body. I hated her because, in all the time I had known her, she had done nothing but lie to me, steal from me, and lead my baby brother to the gates of hell and back.

I was on my front porch as they got out of the truck.

"What is *she* doing here?" I demanded.

"She's been helping me," Teddy said, innocently and a bit goofily, the way he always talked when he was around Wendy. He looked like he hadn't shaved in two days. Wendy liked scruff.

"Are you sober?"

"Yes," he insisted. "You can stop with the Spanish Inquisition. We're both sober."

He had joined her at the hood of the truck and they were now coming up the walk, hand in hand. Wendy wore tight jeans, a T-shirt that barely contained her oversize bosom, and a hoodie that was unzipped so as not to obscure her best feature.

"She can't come in," I said, because while I could always tell whether Teddy was stoned, I was never sure with Wendy. Her looks had this way of hiding everything.

"Would you take it easy? She's finally trying to get right."

"Yeah? How long have you been clean, Wendy?"

"Three weeks," she said.

"Oh Jesus," I said, rolling my eyes. How many times had I heard earnest professions of new leaves being turned over that lasted a week or two or four before they reverted back? A junkie claiming sobriety after three weeks was really just someone whose resolve had yet to be adequately tested.

Wendy was now directly beneath me, still clutching Teddy's hand, looking up at me with those witchy emerald eyes.

"Melanie, I know I've . . . I've wronged you. I've wronged a lot of people, actually.

But when I think of you, I . . . I know I've done a lot of bad stuff to you. I mean, there was the bracelet . . . and the thing with your credit card . . . and that time with your car . . . and I guess there have been a bunch of times, and I'm sorry, okay? I really am sorry. And I'm going to try to do everything I can to make it up to you."

"Nice speech," I spat. "Where'd you get it, the Narcotics Anonymous website?"

"Come on, sis. She's trying. Would you give her a chance?"

"I did. Seven years ago. Then again six years ago. Do you really need me to rehash everything? I can if you want."

Teddy took a step boldly forward. "Okay, okay, I get it. You're still pissed. But we don't have time for that right now."

And then, with his free hand, he reached into his back pocket, unfolded a piece of photo paper he had extracted, then held it out so I could see it. I recognized the side view of my A1 plumber mystery man, blown up to an eight-by-ten.

"She knows who this guy is," Teddy said. "And he might be meeting with us in a little bit. You want to hear more or not?"

They followed me inside and sat stiffly on the couch, like they were meeting someone's mother for the first time.

I remained standing in front of them with my arms crossed, still too distrustful of Wendy to let my guard down.

"Let's hear it," I said.

"As soon as I saw the picture, I recognized the guy," Teddy said. "I didn't know his name or anything, but he's one of those guys who kind of hangs around downtown or out at the mission."

Valley Mission was a homeless shelter in a storefront on West Beverley Street, on the other side of Thornrose Cemetery. I had tried it once or twice after I got kicked out of my apartment but decided I preferred my car. The mission itself was clean and well run. It was the clientele that proved a bit much for me.

The area around the mission served as ground zero for Staunton drug culture. There had been at least a dozen times, during Teddy's wild years, when his mother called me in a panic and told me he had disappeared again. Probably half the time, I found him hanging out on the well-worn path between the bars downtown and the mission, stoned out of his mind.

Teddy continued: "So I know you said I was just supposed to look at the picture and not do anything with it, but I kind of assumed you didn't really mean it — especially since you were in jail and couldn't do anything about it. And well, anyway, on Saturday, I kind of went out to the mission, just to scope things out."

"Oh, Teddy," I said, burying my face in my hands. The scenario he was describing — putting himself among the people and places that had so often led to his drug use — was a recipe for relapse.

"Relax, relax, I was just looking, not talking to anyone or anything. Anyway, that's when I saw Wendy."

Naturally.

"The people at the mission are trying to hook me up with a real job," she said. "In the meantime, I've been volunteering, serving lunches and that sort of thing."

Of course she had been. Because now that she was three weeks sober, she was practically a candidate for sainthood.

"I didn't actually talk to her at first," Teddy said. "Because, you know, she's a trigger and all that."

"Wait, I thought *you* were a trigger for *me,*" she teased, patting him on the knee.

They were being so nauseatingly sweet with each other, I didn't have to ask if they were sleeping together again. My plight had become their romantic quest. And yes, it had started with noble intentions. I feared its end all the same. In truth, it wasn't alcohol, marijuana, or heroin that was the common theme in my brother's battle with addiction. Wendy Mataya had always been his drug of choice.

"Anyway, I kind of hung back, not wanting to talk to her or anyone, really," Teddy said. "I was just there to look for the guy from the picture. And then she finally came up to me."

Wendy picked up the story: "And I was like, 'I see you, you big dummy. It's kind of hard to miss a guy who's six-four and gorgeous, you know.'"

Teddy: "Anyway, we started talking, and she was telling me about how things were different this time."

Wendy: "They had to be different after what happened to me. I woke up in the back of an ambulance and, like, three days of my life were gone. The EMTs said when they found me, my heart was stopped. They had to give me Narcan and everything."

She shuddered.

"Anyhow, I'm done this time," Wendy continued. "Seriously. No more drugs. No more booze. Not even weed. I get that if I don't quit, I'm going to wind up being a statistic."

Teddy resumed the narrative. "So after we got talking, I showed her the picture."

"And I was immediately like, 'Oh my God, that's Slash!' " Wendy exclaimed.

"Slash?" I said.

"Yeah," Wendy said. "I mean, that's what people call him because of the scar and all. He's this, I don't know, drifter, I guess you'd say. He claims he paints houses for a living, but I've never seen him with a truck, or paintbrushes, or anything like that. He's just another one of those guys you see around. When he's not at the mission, he's at the Hardee's, or the bus stop near the Howard Johnson. So I asked Teddy if he had checked there."

"And I hadn't," Teddy said. "But that's where we went next. We started asking around a little bit. We kind of kept it on the down-low. . . . I mean, I think people just thought we were looking for him to buy drugs, but whatever. Anyhow, this is where it gets kind of interesting, because apparently everyone down at the bus stop said Slash had some kind of big score recently. He doesn't take the bus anymore."

"As of when?" I asked.

"Well, that's exactly the point. The word is he dropped out of sight about two weeks ago. He went from being normal old Slash, taking a bus out to this job he had, staying at the mission or at a boardinghouse when he had the money for it. And then all of a sudden, he was flush."

"Because someone paid him a bunch of money to plant drugs in my house," I said.

"That's what we think," Wendy said.

"But you said you had a meeting with him?" I asked. "How'd you set up that?"

"We kind of put the word out that we wanted to talk to him," Teddy said. "We found a few people who knew him, and we said we were looking for him, that it was a business thing, and that we would be hanging out at Hardee's around dinnertime if he wanted to find us."

"And that worked?" I asked.

"Not the first few days," Teddy said. "Monday and Tuesday we went there, and . . . nothing."

I thought back to Monday. I had shown up at Teddy's place at maybe 5:15 or 5:20. That's why I had just missed them. They were heading out to what they hoped was a rendezvous with Slash.

"But then yesterday," Wendy said, "one of his buddies came by and was like, 'You looking for Slash?' And we were like, 'Yeah.' And he was all, 'What do you want with him?' And we played it pretty cool and were

like, 'I guess he'll have to come by and see.'
So this guy texted Slash and Slash texted
back and said he'd meet us around five
today."

I looked at the clock on the wall. It was
quarter to five.

THIRTY-SIX

We piled into Teddy's truck, the three of us sharing the front bench.

On the way, we decided that since Slash was expecting only two people, not three, I needed to keep my distance. Also, compared to Teddy and Wendy — with their tattoos and piercings — I looked like a den mother, with my untorn jeans and uninked skin. Just the sight of me might cause him to spook and run.

So it would be up to Teddy and Wendy to coax Slash's real name out of him. They said they had some ideas how they might go about that.

Once armed with a name, Mr. Honeywell could subpoena the man. Maybe he wouldn't show up in court, and maybe if he did he'd lie under oath, sure. But merely being able to show a jury that the guy with the scar was a real person — likely one with a long criminal history — would be some-thing.

If Slash was too cagey to give us his name, which seemed likely, I could at least get some better pictures of him. I was going under the assumption Slash was known to local law enforcement. Maybe a friendly cop would help us out with a name.

That was about as far as our planning got. As we neared the end of the short ride, I turned to Wendy and said, "Thank you, by the way. I really do appreciate your help."

"You're welcome," she said.

We left it at that. When we were two blocks from the restaurant, I had Teddy drop me off so we wouldn't be seen getting out of the same vehicle. By the time I got to Hardee's, Wendy and Teddy were already seated at a booth across the way from the counter.

The establishment was otherwise empty, except for one elderly couple chewing their dinners in silence. I ordered a Thickburger, even though I was far too nervous to be hungry, then sat two booths away from my brother and sank my eyes into my phone.

My burger was brought out to me a few minutes later. I nibbled at it. Five o'clock came and went. No one else entered the restaurant.

Ten minutes went by. Then fifteen. Teddy's legs were bouncing up and down. Another elderly couple came in. Then two kids with their father, who wandered by and leered at Wendy even as he pretended to be concerned with his children's meal orders. He sat a few tables away, turned so he had a nice view of her.

Nothing else of even minor consequence happened. I rechecked the same email I had already read three times, then perused headlines whose words I couldn't even parse.

The time slipped from 5:25 to 5:35. I couldn't imagine men who went by the nickname "Slash" were especially worried about punctuality, but I was starting to think we had been stood up.

Then, at 5:37, I felt a slight change in air pressure as the door behind me opened. I didn't turn, because a woman lost in her phone wouldn't notice someone walking in. But Teddy's eyes had locked in on whoever had walked in.

Then a man walked by me. Without moving my head or seeming to remove my attention from my screen, I shoved my eyes hard left. Slash was even more angular in real life than he was on camera. His face and arms were almost entirely devoid of fat.

He was white, racially anyway. But his skin had the rawhide coloring of a man who spent most of his time outside. The only thing truly white on him was that scar, which looped over the top of his head from one ear to the other, like a set of very thin headphones worn too far forward. He stopped in front of Teddy and Wendy's table.

"Y'all looking for me?" he said, his Southern accent thick.

" 'Sup," my brother said casually.

"Wendy, right?" he said to her.

"Yeah."

"We were at that thing at Cooch's one time."

I had no idea who or what "Cooch's" was. But I'm guessing Slash remembered Wendy a lot more than the other way around.

"Oh, yeah," she said. "That was epic."

"Have a seat," Teddy said, cleverly switching over to Wendy's side of the table. It meant Slash would have to sit facing me.

Slash slid into the booth. With my camera app already loaded, I brought my phone up — while still acting like I was reading headlines — and tried to get a clean picture of him.

It was impossible. Slash was too strung out. His movements were rapid, almost birdlike. In the span of a few seconds, he wiped his running nose with the back of his hand, cracked his neck, and brought his elbows up to the table. That last act hunched him far enough forward that his face was mostly blocked from my view by Teddy's back. I lowered my phone so I wouldn't seem suspicious.

"So, I might have something I need done," my brother said, sounding older than his twenty-three years, semi-muffling his voice in his hands.

"Yeah? What's that?" Slash asked, looking everywhere but at my brother.

"I hear you're good at getting people in trouble."

Slash's head quick jerked left then right. "Don't know what you're talking about. I paint houses."

"That woman on the news, I hear that was you, planting that stuff in her house."

Slash's denial of this was laced with curse words.

"Yeah, yeah, I know," Teddy said, playing it cool. "But let's just say I wanted you to do the same thing to someone else."

Slash was now even more animated and agitated. He wiped his nose again. I still wasn't trying to take his picture. It was too big a risk for too little chance at success.

"You working for the cops or something?"

he demanded. "You a snitch?"

"Are you serious?" Teddy said.

"Come on, Slash, you think I'd really be hanging out with someone like that?" Wendy said.

"I think he could be, and you wouldn't even know it," Slash fumed. "They got snitches all over, you know."

Said the guy who would know.

"I'm not working for the cops," Teddy insisted. "I just got someone I need to eff up, that's all."

"Then why don't you do it yourself?" Slash asked.

"Because I hear you do it right. Where'd you get that plumber's van, anyway?"

Slash got a little smile on his face and, for the first time, stopped moving quite so much. I quickly brought my phone back up like I was taking a selfie and tapped off five quick pictures.

Then I brought my phone back down to look at the results. All of them missed. I got Teddy's wide shoulders, the back of Wendy's head. None had Slash's face.

"How you know about that?" Slash asked.

"Doesn't matter. I just know people."

"Lift up your shirt," Slash said.

"Huh?" Teddy said, confused.

"I want to see if you're wearing a wire."

"Whatever, man," Teddy said and, without standing, brought the hem of his T-shirt up to his chin for a moment.

"Let's see your phone. You could be recording this."

Teddy fished it out of his pocket, tapped in his PIN, then handed it to Slash for inspection. While Slash was distracted, I brought my phone up, more brazenly this time, and took a few more pictures of him. But I worried all I was getting was the top of his head. It shouldn't have been so difficult, getting a picture of someone who didn't know they were being photographed, but I was starting to panic I wouldn't be able to pull it off.

"Slash, he's not working for the cops," Wendy said.

Slash ignored her. He sniffed loudly. "Yeah, well, I still don't know what you're talking about, but you couldn't afford it anyway."

"How do you know?" Teddy asked.

"Because if I did that sort of thing, and I don't, I'd need at least five."

"Five?" Teddy said. "As in five thousand?"

"You said it, not me. It's that, and you supply the stuff. But I take ten percent of it as a thank-you."

"Okay, I hear you, I hear you. Damn,"

Teddy said, looking at Wendy. "You think our friend will be able to make that happen?"

"Maybe," Wendy said, playing along. "He can get the product, but he's going to want to do the Western Union thing. Send the money straight to Slash. No way he's going to trust us with that much cash."

The Western Union thing? Where was Wendy going with that? I wasn't going to be able to wire anyone money I didn't have. Meanwhile, my angle for a picture had gotten worse. Teddy was blocking me again.

"Yeah, you're probably right," Teddy said.

"Western Union?" Slash said. "I don't know about that, man. I —"

"No, no, it's really easy," Teddy said. "Our guy pays us this way all the time. He wires the money to Western Union. You can cash it out at the grocery store. You give them your name and your ID, they give you the money. What is your real name, anyway? I could have that money waiting for you there tomorrow."

Ah. Now I got it. Genius.

Except Slash was now bouncing around again. "Naw, man. It's cash or nothing."

"Our guy won't do cash," Teddy said.

"This is some bull right here," Slash said. "You're just trying to mess me up. I paint houses. That's it."

He slid out of the booth and stood. Now desperate, I brought my phone up, squared him in the camera's frame, and started furiously jabbing at my screen. I was going to get as many shots as I could and hope one of them was decent.

"Come on, man," Teddy said. "Don't be like that."

Slash wasn't hearing it. He swore at my brother one more time, then started heading for the door.

That put him on a path directly for my booth. This was my chance, my only one. He took one step toward me, then another.

I had dropped any pretense at subtlety. I was firing as fast as I could, my finger a blur.

As he passed directly by me, he looked down for a moment and I could almost see the curiosity crossing through his drugged brain.

What's she doing? Why is she aiming that thing at me?

But ultimately, he couldn't reach any solid conclusions about the random woman on her phone. His neurons were too jammed up with other stuff — with anger and suspicion at my brother, with the cocaine he had just taken and the cocaine he had done in the past.

All he did was walk on by.

As soon as he was out the door, Teddy and Wendy came over.

"Nice try with the Western Union thing," I said.

"It was worth a shot," Teddy said. "Did you get any good pictures?"

I switched over to the photo gallery and started scrolling through them.

And yes. Yes, I did. The ones as he got up and left the restaurant captured him perfectly — in focus, in the middle of the screen, and square-on.

I handed the phone to Teddy. He smiled. "Good stuff," he said, then showed it to Wendy.

"Bingo," she said.

"I'm going to email these to my lawyer right now," I said.

I selected the best photo, then included a short narrative about our Hardee's rendezvous. If a cop wouldn't help Mr. Honeywell with an ID, someone would. Maybe another defense lawyer who had represented Slash in the past. Maybe a bail bondsman. Someone had to know Slash's real name.

Once I sent the best photo on its way, we squeezed ourselves back into Teddy's truck.

On our way home, we discussed what we

had just heard. Slash's employer had procured a half kilo of cocaine (plus fifty grams as an added bonus to an addict), created a fake decal for a van, then paid Slash $5,000 to break into my house and plant the drugs there.

That employer — the person who wanted to separate Alex from me — had obviously gone through a lot of trouble and planning. And it was now clear, if it hadn't been reasonable to conclude already, that it was a person with some financial resources.

The first question was: Who?

It was, obviously, someone who wanted a baby. But there had to be easier ways to go about getting one. Which led me to the question that really bewildered me: Why Alex?

Had someone just randomly selected a healthy white baby boy and gone after him? Or was it because his mother was both well educated (and thus likely to pass her smarts on to her offspring) and poor (and thus unlikely to be able to put up much of a fight when she was framed)? Or was there something in particular about Alex this person prized?

I didn't have any answers, and neither did Teddy or Wendy.

It was getting dark by the time we pulled

back into my driveway, but I was surprised to see the lights of his truck glinting off a vehicle that was now parked there, a sedan I didn't recognize.

"Who's that?" Teddy asked.

"Beats me," I said.

We came to a stop. I hopped out of the truck.

As I did, two people emerged from the car: a man from the driver's side, a woman from the passenger's side. They walked toward us.

As soon as their faces became clear, I felt myself rock backward. I had to lean against the truck for support.

They looked like the doppelgängers of two people I knew long ago, in another life. They were now older, their features thinned out and wrinkled, their movements creakier.

But of course I recognized them. There are some faces you never forget, for however much you might like to.

They just stood there for a moment, grinning awkwardly. I didn't know whether to run away screaming, demand that they leave immediately, or have Teddy ram them with his truck.

And then my mother said, "Hello, pumpkin. We've missed you so much."

THIRTY-SEVEN

It's difficult for a man to get his thoughts straight when he's just done two lines of cocaine and he's already itching for a third.

What the hell was that all about? Slash wondered as he walked, head down, away from the Hardee's.

Then he asked himself: What if they really could come up with five grand? Should I go back?

It was tempting, to be honest. The job he had done on that woman, the one who was now all over the paper, was pretty easy. There was the one night, when he stole her phone. And the man hiring him had told him exactly where he could find it. And then there was that next afternoon, breaking back into the place to plant the drugs.

A few hours here and there for five grand and all that coke.

What if it was that easy again? What if these people — smoking-hot Wendy and whoever that guy was — could really deliver?

But no. Slash didn't like the vibe. Why did they need his name? Why didn't they just deal in cash like everyone else?

He could practically smell the trap, and he wanted no part of it. He had been in jail before and he was not eager to go back. With all the time he had hanging over his head — suspended sentences and whatnot — all it would take was one slip-up.

He wanted more money, yeah. He knew he was going quickly through what had once been a nice stack of hundred-dollar bills. But this payday wasn't worth the risk.

Worrying that Wendy and that guy might be watching him or trying to follow him, Slash got the brilliant-seeming idea to walk past the Howard Johnson, where he was staying, until he was out of sight. Then he doubled back around, entering from around the other side, and took the stairs up to Room 307.

He had been there for more than a week, watching HBO, doing lines, having a one-man party with the PRIVACY PLEASE sign hanging on the door, going out to celebrate, then coming back to the room and celebrating some more. This was the biggest score of Slash's life and he had been enjoying the hell out of it.

Because, man, when you compared it to the mission — or to sleeping in the woods — life was pretty damn good at Howard Johnson. Nice roof over your head. Soft bed to sleep on. No one to say you couldn't be high or you had to wake up and get your ass out at a certain time. No one to throw Jesus in your face.

After he reentered the room, he put the chain on the door, suddenly curious as to how his supplies were holding out. He removed his stash from its hiding spot.

At first, he had tried to be judicious in how much he used, rationing himself. No more than, say, eight lines a day. Well, okay, maybe twelve. Or sixteen, but that was *it*.

Lately, he maybe hadn't been paying as much attention. And there was a woman or two he had partied with, and . . .

Wait. Was that all he had left? Where was the rest of it?

The money situation was even more startling. Out of the original $5,000, he was down to fourteen hundred-dollar bills. Yeah, Howard Johnson was expensive — and the manager had insisted on a $500 deposit against damage, because Slash didn't have a credit card. And yeah, he had gone out a lot. And yeah, there had been those women.

But had he really gone through that much

cash already?

He needed another line. Now. That would help him think straight. He got out his razor blade, mirror, and the rolled-up hundred he had been using — because it made him feel like a tough-ass gangsta.

Except the coke didn't settle him. It only made him more anxious.

Where had all the money gone? Had someone stolen from him?

And who *was* that guy with Wendy? How had they known about him in the first place?

He looked at the coke. He did another line.

The thoughts in his head were a real jumble now. But eventually one kept coming back to him.

He should call the man, the one who hired him. That would fix everything.

Slash fumbled with his phone until he finally got it to make the call.

"What do you want?" the man answered.

"Hey, it's Slash."

"Yeah, I know," the man said. "What do you want?"

"I just had some dude asking me if I could plant coke in someone else's house. He acted like he knew about that woman I did it on."

"What? Who?"

"I don't know," Slash said. "Just this dude. I don't know him. He had this chick with him. I think her name is Wendy."

"*Wendy?* Describe Wendy for me."

"She's . . . damn, I mean, she's a piece of ass like you wouldn't believe. Superhot."

"What color is her hair?"

"Brown. Black. Whatever."

"What color are her eyes?"

"I don't know. I was too busy looking at her jugs."

"What else? Does she have any tattoos?"

"Yeah. Couple of 'em."

"Okay," the man whispered. "Then it's nothing to worry about."

"Hell it's not. How did they know about me?"

"I don't know. Did you tell anyone? Brag to one of your drug friends?"

"Naw, man. I didn't say nothing to no one."

"Well, I sure didn't tell anyone."

"Then how do they know about me?" Slash asked.

"I don't know."

And then Slash came out with it: "I want more money. And more coke."

"What? No. Forget it."

"There's more risk now. These people

know about me. That's risk I hadn't planned on."

"That's your problem, not mine."

"If this gets out, it'll be worse for you than for me. I'm not the one who pretends to live this straight life."

That was true. They both knew it.

"No way," the man said. "I don't have it anyway."

"Which? The money or the coke?"

"Either. Don't call me again."

The man hung up. Slash did another line.

THIRTY-EIGHT

My first instinct — as it always had been around my parents — was to protect Teddy.

I had no idea why they were suddenly showing up in my driveway, or how they found me, or what they hoped to achieve there. Whatever it was, I didn't want Teddy to be anywhere near it. His recovery was teetering on a precarious ledge, which crumbled just a little more every time he looked at Wendy. I feared if he understood who these two strangers were, it would be the small shove needed to send him toppling into the abyss.

"Stay right there," I snarled at my parents. "Don't move."

Still using the truck for balance, I forced myself back to the door and yanked it open.

"You have to leave. Now," I said, a little too breathlessly.

"Who are those people?" Teddy asked.

"No one," I said.

"O . . . Okay," Teddy stammered. "Are you sure you —"

"You have to leave *now,* goddammit," I said through gritted teeth.

My parents were walking toward the truck. I slammed Teddy's door.

"Stop right there!" I yelled at my parents.

I couldn't allow them to see Teddy through the windshield. There was probably little chance they would recognize the baby they had last seen at nine months now that he was a twenty-three-year-old man. But I didn't want to risk it.

They stopped. I could feel Teddy's indecision from inside the truck, so I banged twice on the hood and again yelled, "Get out of here."

As he finally began backing down the driveway, I squared to face my parents for the first time since they abandoned me twenty-two years earlier.

My mother's hair, which had been dark brown like mine the last time I had seen it, was now almost completely gray. Her face was weathered. But she was far more clear-eyed than in most of my memories of her; and, all things considered, she definitely looked better than I assumed she would.

Then again, I thought she was dead.

My father was still broad-shouldered,

though more hunched, and not nearly as tall. His hair, which had been bushy and sand-colored, was now gray and mostly gone. He had grown a mustache, which was closer to the color his hair used to be.

They stood there at the bumper of their car with nervously hopeful expressions.

I couldn't count the number of times during my teenage years I had imagined this moment — my parents showing up unexpectedly, announcing they were ready to resume their roles in my life. Most of the time, the scene involved me reciting a long list of the horrors and indignities I had been subjected to because of them, because before there was any talk of absolution there had to be punishment. In those waking daydreams, I tried out a great variety of emotions, typically beginning with fury over what they had done before moving on to gratitude at being rescued.

But now that they were actually here, I was mostly just stuck on fury.

"How did you find me?" I demanded.

My mother started with, "Pumpkin, I'm sorry, I just —"

"Stop calling me pumpkin. I'm a grown woman. My name is Melanie."

"Yes, Mel . . . Melanie, of course."

"We wanted to call first," my father said.

"But all we could find for you was an address, not a phone number. I'm sorry we —"

"Answer my question: How did you find me?"

My mother started shaking and crying. I would have felt sympathy for any other woman in that situation. Not her. She had been the cause of too many of my own tears.

"Your mother read about you on the Internet," my father volunteered. "She's been looking for you for years."

"I prayed and prayed I'd find you," she said. "The social workers would never tell us where you and Teddy had gone. We knew the family that adopted Teddy had left the area, but we had no idea where they moved. The people at Social Services said if you wanted to reach out to us, that would be one thing, but they couldn't give us any information about you."

"Privacy laws," my father volunteered.

My mother continued. "Your father was out long-lining when I saw an article about your . . . your problem. We came here as soon as he got back. I didn't realize you had changed your name. Are you . . . Are you married now?"

"What do you care?" I snapped.

"Melanie, honey, I'm so, so sorry. I've

done . . . so many terrible things in my life, so many things I . . . I can't tell you how much I regret them," she said, her voice trembling. "After we lost you —"

"You didn't lose me; you abandoned me."

"I know, I know," she said. "I can't expect you to understand what a dark, dark place I was in. I just . . . I hated everything about myself. There was this hole in the middle of me and I . . . I know you might not believe this, but I really thought that terminating our rights was the best thing we could do for you."

"Great. Congratulations on that," I said.

"Melanie, please. We don't deserve your forgiveness and we're not even asking for it. But . . . We got cleaned up. It took some years and a whole lot of pain, but we both came to realize how sick and destructive we were, and how substance abuse was at the root of all of it. We gave our lives over to Jesus Christ and with his love we don't use drugs or alcohol anymore. We go to a wonderful church —"

"Fabulous," I said. "Why don't you go back there now?"

My mother brought her hand to her mouth in a failed effort to stanch a sob. I was being cruel and juvenile — like I was reverting back to the nine-year-old I was when they left me — and I didn't care. They deserved so much worse.

"Melanie," my father began, "we know you're angry, but —"

"Stop talking," I growled at him. "You don't even have a right to talk. Forget about what you did to me and this poor woman. How are you not in jail after what you did to Charlotte?"

His head immediately went down.

"Oh, what? You think I didn't know about that?" I said, yelling now. "Or did you think I would forget? What kind of man has sex with any fourteen-year-old girl, much less his wife's daughter? You're a disgusting, disgusting human being."

It was strangely exhilarating to have this confrontation, to say the things in real life I had said in my head so many times.

"We didn't have sex. When I was drunk, I would just —"

"Shut up!" I shrieked. "Just shut up. There's no excuse for what you did. None."

"Your father spent five years in jail because of that," my mother said quietly. "That's when he stopped drinking and was born again. He's been sober since he came out. It wasn't him, doing those things to Charlotte. It was the alcohol. He never would have —"

"Is that what you tell yourself so you can sleep at night?" I railed at her. "Well, I'm glad that works for you. It doesn't quite cut it for me."

"I know, I know," my father said. "I don't blame you one bit. I'm . . . I'm ashamed of what I've done and . . . One day I'm going to be judged for it, I know. All I can do for the rest of my time here is try to live in the word of Jesus and ask for his forgiveness. I —"

"Why don't you start by asking Charlotte?" I sneered.

This brought a lurching halt to their attempts at explanation and apology. My mother and father bounced glances off each other. They shifted their weight. My father exhaled noisily.

"Didn't anyone tell you?" my mother asked.

"Tell me what?"

"Charlotte, she . . . Oh, honey, this was so long ago. Charlotte . . . died of a drug overdose when she was nineteen. She had run off to New York City and had gotten into . . . into some bad things. And . . . Oh, Melanie."

The news of my half sister's death, delivered however many years too late, was one more piece of information I couldn't put in proper perspective. Not standing in my driveway. Not while facing the parents I hadn't seen since I was nine years old.

I always assumed Charlotte had been like me: off with a new life somewhere; surviving, even if she wasn't fully healed from the scars inflicted by Mr. and Mrs. William Theodore Curran.

Instead, it turned out she was their most profoundly affected victim. All this time I should have been mourning her. If only I had known. Yet when she succumbed to her sadness, she had already aged out of the system and I was halfway across the state. There was no one who would have even thought to tell me. There was no one who cared.

"Well, that's just great. Thanks for letting me know seventeen years too late," I said, using my sarcasm as a shield. "If you don't mind, I'm going to go into my house now and enjoy that news. Good night."

I stomped off quickly toward my front porch and those overturned bulbs, which were still exactly where I had left them — but now browner and frostbitten.

"Melanie, we're here because we want to help," my mother said plaintively, taking a few steps toward me. "We've hired a lawyer. We're asking the court to consider placing your son with us permanently. We're his grandparents, you know. We can take care of him while you sort through your issues."

I whirled to face them again. This was beyond any nightmare the darkest reaches of my subconscious could have whipped up for me.

"Oh. My. *God!*" I screeched. "You think that's helping? You think you did such a bang-up job raising me and Teddy and Charlotte that you really deserve a shot at screwing up the next generation too? Are you really serious? You people are unbeliev-able."

My father put his arm around my mother. "I know this is a shock, seeing us," he said. "And I know you're upset and you have every right to be. But our lawyer says —"

"I don't want to hear —"

"This is the best way for you to be able to keep your child. We can adopt your son and he can live with us while you serve your jail time. Then, when you get out, we can all be together as a family."

I brought my hands to the sides of my head, clutching two fistfuls of hair. "A fam-ily? Is that a joke? You're really talking to me about *family?* We were a family. And you, sir, threw it into a big drunken meat grinder until there was nothing left of it."

"I know, I know," my father said. "And I can see you're too upset to talk right now. We're staying at the Econo Lodge not far from here. Can I at least leave our phone numbers with you so you can call us if you want to talk?"

"You know what I want?" I said. "I want you to get out of my driveway and get out of my life. You were doing the best parenting you could do by staying away from me. You should have kept it that way."

I opened my front door, then slammed it behind me with all the strength I could muster.

At first, I was too angry to even have distinct thoughts. I ran upstairs to the nursery, if only to put that much more distance between myself and them.

From the relative safety of the second floor, I watched them. They leaned against each other in a sort of hug and seemed to be talking things over. Then they walked slowly back to their car.

For a minute or so, they just sat there with the engine running and the lights on. It was hard to tell what they were doing from my angle. I worried they were just regrouping, trying to decide on a new line of attack.

Finally, they backed down the driveway.

At the end of it, they stopped. My father got out, opened my mailbox, and put something inside of it — A note? A piece of paper with their phone numbers on it?

Then they drove away.

The first identifiable emotion I felt after they were finally gone was that I was furious with myself for being furious. I wanted to be the grown woman who had moved on, not the petulant teenager flailing at them, landing cheap shots wherever I could. They shouldn't have been able to reach me like that anymore.

But I couldn't stop the anger. With my entire life in turmoil, with forces unknown conspiring to separate me from my child and send me to prison, Mommy and Daddy Dearest chose this time, of all times, to reenter my life. And they did it not with a letter, or with some noninvasive approach that put the interaction on my terms and allowed me to decide whether I wanted it. They did it on their terms.

Which was nothing unusual, really. It had always been all about Billy and Betsy. Even now, when they were coming with this offer of so-called help, I felt like they were really just trying to use me as another piece of the testimony they would offer their congregation: *Jesus is so good, he even gave us back*

404

our daughter after all these years. Hallelujah! Praise him!

Not knowing what else to do with myself, I took Mr. Snuggs into the crook of my arm and sat in the nursing chair. I thought about what my father had said, about them adopting Alex, or fostering him, or whatever absurdity they were proposing.

Unbelievably, I was actually considering it. Was it, in fact, the best of my nonexistent options? My father was right: If the courts would give Alex to his grandparents, he would remain in my life even if I did end up incarcerated.

There was a state women's prison in Goochland, less than two hours from Northumberland. If I were sent there, they could visit every weekend. I wouldn't miss him growing up. More important, he would know that he still had a mother, that his mother loved him more than anything, and that all she wanted was to be with him.

Then, when I got out, we could be together again. Alex would be, what, six? It would be strange for him at first, sure. But there was still a whole lot of parenting left to be done from age six until whenever he left the nest. Six-year-olds were just losing their first teeth. They hadn't read Roald Dahl or learned to play complex board games or been introduced to multiplication or done any of the things I imagined myself doing with Alex.

And yes, my parents were pretty far from ideal. It would be taking a great leap of faith on my part that they really had changed and that they could keep him safe and loved until I got out.

The alternative was that Alex would be ripped away from me forever, to be raised by the top bidder in the white-baby auction.

But would that actually be worse or better? It was possible they were some nice couple, totally unaware they were on the receiving end of a criminal enterprise. They had been told the tens of thousands they had paid was for medical care, or some legitimate expense. I could spin a thousand scenarios in which they were actually loving parents.

I could spin just as many that ended a lot less nicely.

As I wrestled with the issue, a memory came to me. I was maybe seven and my father had just come back from Nova Scotia or someplace like that. I was still at an age where I mindlessly aped my mother's reactions to most things, so I was excited he had returned — because she was excited.

After all, it was going to be different this time. She had done up her hair and was wearing a new dress. We had a nice family dinner, and I went to bed feeling warmth and love and optimism.

I woke to the sound of breaking glass.

My father was chasing my mother around the house, throwing beer bottles at her, yelling at her about how she was a goddamn cock-tease. It seemed (and this is my adult interpretation of the memory coming in) my mother didn't want to have sex with him because she was on her period. And this had sent my father into a rage.

I came out of my room in my little bare feet, ready to protect my mother — how, I don't know. What I got for my bravery was a nasty gash on my heel that required eleven stitches to close up. But that, in retrospect, wasn't nearly as bad as the four months of foster care that followed when my social worker discovered what happened.

Those were the parents I knew, the childhood I experienced. And sure, they said they were reborn — clean and right with Jesus and all that — but how many times had I heard variations of that? They ran out of second chances with me several decades ago.

There was no way I could trust the people

who couldn't be bothered to give me a real childhood to have any role in Alex's upbringing.

In the morning, I called Mr. Honeywell to tell him I wanted to oppose my parents' petition to be given custody of Alex.

He listened without much comment. At the end I asked, "Do you think my opinion will even matter?"

"Well, grandparents don't have any specific rights over anyone else in this process," he said. "The judge'll listen to whatever we have to say. It'll probably depend on how well your boy is doing in his current placement. He's going to do what he thinks is best for your son."

"Okay, well, thanks. I appreciate —"

"Hang on, hang on. Don't run off just yet. I've got some news."

"What's that?"

"Well, a few things actually. We've scheduled your adjudicatory hearing with Social Services for April the tenth. That's the day after your criminal case, of course. But maybe we'll have something positive to share with Judge Stone at that point."

"Let's hope so. What else?"

"I showed that picture you emailed me of that fellow with the scar to a Staunton city detective I'm friendly with."

"Oh, great," I said. That was fast.

"The detective knew him immediately. Does the name Richard Coduri mean anything to you?"

It didn't. Whether he was the mystery plumber, Slash, or Richard Coduri, I had never met the man before.

"No. Sorry."

"Can't say I'm surprised. My detective friend had some more colorful terms for this, but Mr. Coduri is what you might call a known commodity to the local police. They've pick him up for vagrancy, public intoxication, public urination, you name it."

"Oh, lovely," I said.

"Well, it might be. The detective says he's got a rap sheet that practically goes back to kindergarten. Most of it is drug-related, but there's also a breaking-and-entering and a malicious wounding. He's on probation right now. He's got five years hanging over his head for this, that, and the other thing. We can use that at the motion hearing. Plus, there are the visuals of the thing."

"What do you mean, 'the visuals'?" I asked.

He didn't immediately answer. Then he came up with: "Well, first I should tell you I think it's wise for us to ask for a bench trial.

That's where we waive the right to a jury and let the judge decide your innocence or guilt. There's been so much publicity surrounding your case, I just worry the jury pool is a little too poisoned. Besides, this judge . . ."

I waited for more, but it didn't come. I finally said, "What about him?"

"Ms. Barrick, I have to be careful not to sound like a dirty old man here. But you know how I asked you to wear a dress the other day?"

"Yes."

"It's because in a court of law, appearance matters. That's why I'm going to keep asking you to wear a dress. You're a fine-looking young woman, Ms. Barrick. And that will make an impression on this particular judge. I want him to have to consider you sitting there in your nice dress versus this Coduri fellow, with his tattoos and his big scar. If we have Coduri saying one thing and you saying another, and we can force the judge to decide which one of you is more likely to be telling the truth, it's possible we win. Do you follow me?"

"I do," I said.

I was already thinking of Coduri/Slash/Whatever on the witness stand, sniffling and twitching.

"That's good. Okay then, we'll talk soon."

"Wait. Mr. Honeywell?"

"Yes, Ms. Barrick?"

"Would it be okay if I asked an impertinent question?"

"You can ask me anything, Ms. Barrick."

"If appearance is so important, why do you dress the way you do?"

He just chuckled softly.

"Have a good day, Ms. Barrick," he said.

THIRTY-NINE

Amy Kaye couldn't remember the last time she had looked forward to Saturday morning this much.

The end of her week had been like medieval torture, only the headsman was wearing wingtips. She had to insist on a formal inquiry into the missing Mookie Myers drugs, to be conducted by the state police, with oversight from the Attorney General's Office.

She ordered it knowing it was both fundamentally necessary and a complete waste of everyone's time. Kempe had already done an informal inquiry weeks earlier, when he first realized the drugs were gone. Augusta County's best investigator had talked to everyone with a reason to go near the evidence lockup and scoured the security camera footage.

His questioning had come up empty. So had the camera, whose hard drive only had room for thirty days' worth of data.

Then he had told Sheriff Powers, who tore through the department, pressuring his guys to turn in any fellow deputy they suspected might be responsible. Powers assumed whoever took the drugs was using them recreationally, and he was going to make sure that deputy would find his number had randomly come up for drug testing.

But even the sheriff's aggressions accomplished nothing. So, in addition to the state police, Amy had also called for a thorough review of policies and procedures related to the evidence lockup. This was the quintessential closing of the barn door after the horses were already gone. It had to be done all the same.

Still, it was a grind. And now that Saturday morning was here, she was ready to put it all behind her. The weatherman said the late-winter day would feel like mid-spring, with sunshine, a light breeze, and temperatures in the seventies.

A perfect day for a hike. Amy's plan for herself and Butch involved a battered old map, entitled "Trails of Augusta County," she had found for $5 in one of Staunton's myriad antique stores. It had been produced by the Civilian Conservation Corps in 1936.

The young men who carved those trails

and made that map — young men who had been put to work by FDR in the depths of the Great Depression — were now very old men, or gone altogether. But had their work outlived them? Were the trails still in use?

Finding out would be Amy's adventure. After fortifying herself with a breakfast of waffles drenched in real maple syrup, she went into her office and spread out the map in front of her. She was ready to pick out the trail she and Butch would try first.

And then the words "Mount Solon" caught her eye.

Mount Solon was where Lilly Pritchett had been attacked.

Then she saw Weyers Cave. That was where one of the first victims she learned about had lived.

Desper Hollow Road. That made her think of Melanie Barrick.

Before she knew what she was even trying to accomplish, Amy found a box of pins. She hung the map on the corkboard near her desk, then placed pins in the places where she could remember assaults had taken place. There were a few where she wasn't sure of the exact address, so she looked them up in the dog-eared case files she kept in her home office.

Once she was into the files, she decided

she might as well do it systematically and correctly. She started over again, removing pins and putting them in a more precise place when she decided her memory of an address had faltered. She went through each file, making educated guesses at the location when it was on a modern road that did not yet exist when the map had been made.

Fishersville. Pin. Stuarts Draft. Pin. Middlebrook. Pin.

She used blue pins, green pins, yellow pins, whatever she pulled out of the box. She wasn't trying to make art here. And it's not like she'd ever put something like this — an eighty-odd-year-old trail map that didn't even have, say, Interstate 81 on it — in front of a jury. But it felt like a good way to informally reboot her investigation.

When she was done, she walked across the room and looked at the map from that vantage point. There was no discernible pattern. Spottswood in the south. Mount Sidney in the north. Buffalo Gap out west. Sherando in the east. All points on the compass were represented.

But that wasn't what really caught Amy's eye now that she was looking at the geography for the first time.

It was the big, heart-shaped hole in the middle, representing the City of Staunton.

There were pins on the outskirts of it, like the one just north of city limits that signified Daphne Hasper's attack. There just wasn't a single pin inside it.

Staunton wasn't Amy's jurisdiction, of course. Only Augusta County was. Staunton had its own police force, its own commonwealth's attorney.

But seeing the distribution of the attacks, Amy was struck by how strange it was the rapist had never — to the best of her knowledge — struck within city limits. It was surely a target-rich environment: apartment buildings, old houses that would be easy to break into, even a women's college.

She had never reached out to any of her colleagues in Staunton to learn if they were also investigating a serial rapist. Dansby wouldn't allow it.

Were there other cases she wasn't aware of? Perhaps with other evidence she could now use? Or had the rapist really never found anyone to his liking inside city limits? Amy had been so focused on where this menace *had* attacked, she had never thought to learn from where he *hadn't*.

Amy looked down at Butch, napping on the floor. Then she looked out the window. It was as warm and sunny as the forecast had promised.

416

But she already knew she wasn't going on any hike.

She pulled out her phone and dialed the cell phone number for Staunton City Police Chief Jim Williams. Amy had always liked the man, who paired an easygoing manner with a quick sense of humor. He also readily admitted his mistakes and taught his officers that apologizing for small transgressions often prevented them from becoming big ones. Few things were more endearing on a police chief than humility.

Once they had dispensed with a small amount of banter, Williams asked, "Anyhow, what can I do for Augusta County today?"

Mindful of Dansby's standing order not to divulge her investigation, she kept it vague. "I'm doing some research into a defendant," she said, which was not untrue. "I was hoping I could get into your file room."

"Wait, I'm not the defendant, am I?" he joked.

"Not yet," she teased back.

"Okay," he said. "Meet me at the station in fifteen minutes."

Fifteen minutes later, she was in. Fifteen minutes after that, she was situated at a small desk in their archive room.

As the day grew old, she plowed through

every unsolved sexual-assault file she could find, going as quickly as possible. Staunton had roughly one-third the population of Augusta County, so there were fewer cases. Most of them were easy to rule out: The attacker was the wrong size, shape, or color. In only a few files did she have to delve deeper into the police report to learn a detail that disqualified the case as being a possibility.

Still, it was nearing midnight before she emerged.

In all that time, she didn't find a single instance of a rapist who whispered.

FORTY

My parents made three more attempts to contact me, leaving notes on my doorstep on Friday, Saturday, and Sunday.

The first note was asking me to reconsider supporting their petition to take custody of Alex. The second suggested maybe we could share a meal, just to talk. It also offered money for a lawyer. The third said they were praying for me and hoped they might hear from me soon.

They weren't going to. My anger at their sudden reappearance had abated somewhat over the weekend, but that didn't mean I was ready to resume a relationship with them.

By Monday, they had perhaps gotten the hint I needed some time, because there was no note that day. Nor was there one on Tuesday.

My life had slowly settled into this odd new routine. I had been slotted into the 11-

to-7 shift at Waffle House — plus whatever stray shifts I could tack on — hoping that if I could please enough customers and get enough tips, I might be able to keep my house.

I would then come home bone-weary, ankles pulsing, smelling like grease and burned coffee. I would settle into the nursing chair with Mr. Snuggs the teddy bear on my lap and let thoughts of Alex fill my head while I pumped.

Marcus came over a few times. Ever since Ben left, he had been checking in on me daily. We ordered takeout (that he paid for), watched movies, played board games, whatever. Kelly was working late seemingly all the time — it felt like forever since I had seen her — so we both needed the company.

I also hung out with Teddy some. He and Wendy were supposedly trying to take it slow with their rekindling, making a conscious effort not to spend all their time together. I was happy to help with that.

Then there were nights, when I just didn't feel like I was fit to be around people, I stayed home by myself and tried to make my mind as empty as possible. That way, I didn't have to think about the missing baby and absent husband who until recently had filled my life. I would lose myself in brain-rotting television and attempt to drift off to sleep in front of whatever cooking show, HGTV special, or *Castle* rerun my restless remote control had settled on.

It didn't always work. The misery simply overwhelmed me, and I couldn't even see the images on the screen. I'd find myself crying uncontrollably or screaming into a pillow, unable to fend off the tsunami of sadness that threatened to wash me away.

At times like that, I was confronting the very real possibility of being convicted of a crime I didn't commit. It was an offense that came with essentially two punishments. One was serving five years in prison. The other — the far harsher of the two — was losing my child. And the term was life.

I could already imagine myself, newly released, harder and sadder, slinking from one playground and elementary school to the next, looking for a baby I might not even recognize as a five- or six-year-old.

And then? More of the same. Forever. I already knew the ache would never go away. Some part of me would always be yearning for him.

With Ben, the pain would eventually fade. But that made it no less poignant in the present. It was a mix of missing him — his touch, his companionship, the way he always made things seem better — and being truly angry with him. Just because I had given him permission to leave, it didn't mean he was supposed to take me up on the offer.

Twice, I actually did hear from him. Sort of. One time, he called. I nearly answered, then decided I really didn't want to talk to him. When I listened to the message, it was this nonsensical rambling, delivered at a volume that was barely audible.

"I just wanted to hear your voice. I'm just . . . I'm so lonely right now. I hope . . . I hope you get this someday and . . . because if you do, it means . . . it means it's a happier time. But I can't think about that too much right now. It'll make me . . . Anyhow, I miss you. I miss you so much. I love you, and I guess I just wanted you to know that."

This prompted me to swear at the phone. Then at Ben. I finished my little tirade with: "If you miss me so much, why'd you leave, you dumbass?"

His other attempt to contact me was via text, which I got when I came out of Waffle House one day.

Hey, I know I won't hear back from you. I just want you to know I'm thinking about you. I'm missing you so much right now. Love you.

It made me feel like I was in college, dating a frat boy who tried to break up, then worm his way back into my bed a week later with insistences that he really loved me all along. I didn't fall for it back then. And I sure wasn't going to now, despite one or two weak moments when I nearly gave into the temptation to call him.

Otherwise, I just hobbled along, all the while keeping track of my various legal entanglements. Mr. Honeywell was still trying to pry the name of the confidential informant in my drug case out of the Sheriff's Office in time for the motion hearing.

The negotiations were contentious. The Sheriff's Office was balking at revealing the identity of its informant — who was, after all, supposed to be confidential. The judge promised he would close the courtroom and seal the transcripts, which satisfied the Sheriff's Office. But it didn't satisfy the Commonwealth's Attorney's Office, which brought up concerns about witness retaliation in drug cases. The prosecutor, Amy Kaye, didn't want to reveal the informant's name until the hearing itself.

But Mr. Honeywell won that issue too.

There was apparently a case involving a man named Keener a bunch of years back where an appeals court had ruled the Commonwealth had to both reveal the name of its witness and do so in a reasonable time period to allow the defense time to prepare.

This was all being haggled over on Tuesday, while I was dishing out hash browns — scattered, smothered, and covered — at Waffle House. So I wasn't privy to the details.

I just know that by the time my shift ended, I had an urgent voicemail from Mr. Honeywell. The judge had finally come up with a plan that satisfied all sides.

And it involved a face-to-face meeting with the defendant.

First thing Wednesday morning, I met Mr. Honeywell in the lobby of the courthouse.

He had asked me to wear something nice, so I picked out a light-blue sleeveless knit dress that I had acquired during one of my thrift-store dives. He was back to his gray suit. I was beginning to think it was the only one he owned.

As soon as I was through the metal detector, he rose from a bench and limped toward me.

"Good morning, Ms. Barrick," he said.

"You're looking lovely today."

"Thanks," I said, shaking his hand. "What's this all about anyway?"

"Search me," he said with a little shrug. "Judge Robbins used to be the commonwealth's attorney in Waynesboro. We've had our battles. He's not one to do the defense any favors, believe me. And he can be a little . . . well, unconventional, put it that way. He said he wanted to meet with you before he revealed the identity of the confidential informant. And if you ask me, it's best to give a judge what he wants. So here we are."

I followed Mr. Honeywell at his slow pace up to the second floor. We sat in Judge Robbins's reception area for a while, waiting for the judge to do whatever it is judges do when they're not on the bench. Then we were summoned into a room lined by bookshelves, with a stately oak desk in the middle of the room. Behind it was a white-haired white man in a dark-blue suit. He had two chins. A light dusting of goatee did little to help define the first.

There were three chairs in front of the judge's desk. One was filled by Amy Kaye.

"Good morning, Judge," Mr. Honeywell said, then nodded toward the prosecutor. "Ms. Kaye."

"Come in, come in," the judge said. He had a high-pitched, somewhat pinched voice. He struggled to get his gut out from under the desk as he stood up to greet us.

"Judge, I'd like you to meet Melanie Barrick."

"Good God, Bill, *this* is your client?" Judge Robbins said.

I suppose he had been expecting the Melanie Barrick he had seen in my mug shot — a woman in an orange jumpsuit with tousled hair. His gaze traveled up and down my body at least three times. I was starting to appreciate Mr. Honeywell's sartorial wisdom, to say nothing of his legal mind. Now I fully understood why he talked about "the visuals" when he told me he was opting for a bench trial.

In my college feminist days, I might have been offended about the objectification of women, the tyranny of the patriarchy, and all those other things that had been so important back then. They still were. But not as important as my son.

"Yes, sir," Mr. Honeywell said evenly.

"Nice to meet you, Judge," I said, without any hint I knew he was screwing me with his eyes.

The judge attempted to recover himself. "Have a seat, please."

Mr. Honeywell and I took the chairs on the left side, just like this was a courtroom. Kaye sat in the one on the right.

"Ms. Barrick, I —" Judge Robbins began, then stopped himself. He still seemed a little rattled. Finally, he settled on: "As you're aware, Ms. Barrick, the Commonwealth's Attorney's Office has some issues with revealing to you and your attorney the identity of the confidential informant," he said, tipping his head toward Kaye. "I assume your attorney has explained this to you?"

"Yes, sir," I said.

"I understand her concerns, of course. At the same time, you have your constitutional rights, and I can't deny them to you. Ultimately, the Commonwealth has to produce this witness so we can have what's known as a Franks hearing. But before I tell you and your attorney who this witness is, I want you and I to have an understanding about something."

"Yes, sir," I said again.

He pointed a fat finger at me. "We don't have problems with witness intimidation here in the valley, and we're going to keep it that way. Do you understand? Killing a witness is a capital offense in Virginia. Do you know what that means?"

427

I glanced at Mr. Honeywell, whose eyes were even more bugged out than usual.

"It means you'd get the death penalty," the judge continued.

Mr. Honeywell gripped his chair. Even Amy Kaye seemed unsettled.

"Judge," she began, "I don't think this is really —"

"I'm not talking to you, Ms. Kaye. I'm talking to Ms. Barrick here. I know there are some liberal judges up north who get squeamish about the death penalty. I'm not one of those judges. Now, you don't seem like the type to make any trouble. But I don't want to judge a book by its cover. If anything happens to this witness, I will hold you personally accountable. I don't want him threatened, I don't want him harassed, I don't want anyone you're associated with to approach him in any way. And by God, if he disappears, I will see to it you get the needle if it's the last thing I do. Are we clear?"

"Judge," Mr. Honeywell said, no longer able to hide his outrage. "This is highly inappropriate and incredibly prejudicial. I don't —"

"Shut it, Billy. I ain't talking to you either," Robbins said, then returned his attention to me. "Are we clear, miss?"

"Yes, sir," I said, a third time. What else was there to say?

"Good. Now," he said, then started hunting for something on his desk. "Ah, yes. Here we go. This is the confidential informant. Ms. Kaye was good enough to print out his rap sheet for us all. He's no choirboy, of course. They never are. But this hearing will be about his actions in regards to this case. It will not be an airing of his criminal history. Got it?"

Mr. Honeywell glared at him for a moment before allowing a terse "Yes, sir."

Judge Robbins slid a folder across the desk at Mr. Honeywell, who picked it up. He leaned toward me a little so I could see it. The first page was a mug shot, and it nearly caused me to fall out of my chair.

The confidential informant was Slash, aka Richard Coduri, aka the mystery plumber.

So not only had he planted the drugs in my house, he had also called the Sheriff's Office to tell them the drugs were there, then lied about making a buy from me.

He then told the Sheriff's Office — and, after that, Social Services — that I had inquired about selling my baby.

This, for $5,000 and a pile of cocaine.

All I could think about was the trouble I would be in if Richard Coduri died of an overdose; or if he accidentally got hit by a car, or found early death any of the other number of ways an addict can wind up killing himself; or if Teddy and Wendy decided the next act of their romantic play would be to go after the man.

Mr. Honeywell made a strange noise in his throat. I didn't need to tell him this was the same man I had photographed in Hardee's. He had already figured it out and was now trying to reconcile it with known facts, just like I was.

"Thank you, Judge," is all he said.

"I'm serious, Ms. Barrick. You are not to have any contact with this witness, are we clear?"

"Yes, Judge," I said.

"All right. I'm glad we understand each other," he said, standing up. "Thank you all for coming."

The three of us stood up. Amy Kaye said farewell. Mr. Honeywell didn't say a word. He was still clearly furious, and he was limping toward the door before he uttered something he'd later regret. I followed him out.

Once we were back in the judge's waiting room, I thought that was the end of things. But Amy Kaye surprised me by calling out, "Ms. Barrick, do you have a moment?"

I turned to face her. She was older than me by about a decade, solidly built, with a no-nonsense cut to her short, dark hair. The first time we had met, a year before, we had been on the same side of the law. Now we were adversaries.

Curiously, there was something about her demeanor toward me that hadn't changed. I couldn't say exactly what. I just knew she still passed the five-second test.

"Yes?" I said.

Mr. Honeywell had stopped and turned.

"I haven't forgotten what happened to you last March," she said.

"Oh," was all I could think to say in reply.

"March eighth," she said, looking me straight in the eyes, holding her gaze there so I'd know she was serious. Then she reiterated, "I haven't forgotten."

"Thank you," I said.

She nodded, then exited.

FORTY-ONE

The comment had surprised Amy probably even more than it had Melanie Barrick.

I haven't forgotten what happened to you.

Amy hadn't gone into Judge Robbins's chambers for that meeting thinking she'd say a thing. Melanie Barrick was the defendant in a major drug case. Yes, it sometimes happened that perpetrators of one crime had been victims of another. But Amy was usually quite clear about separating the two.

Really, where had those words come from? Was it just because she felt bad for this woman after Robbins — loose cannon and noted law-and-order lunatic — had threatened her?

Or was it guilt about having struck out with Warren Plotz?

Or was it because she had spent so much time after work staring at that pinned-up map in her home office?

She still hadn't decided what to make of

that. Maybe nothing. It was entirely possible the rapist was simply being cautious. Staunton was a city — not a big city, but a city nevertheless. It was more densely populated than the county, and that meant more neighbors to see things, more cops per square mile, more chances to be caught. There were very practical reasons to steer clear of it.

Or did the fact that the man had seemingly focused so narrowly on Augusta County really mean something?

The human brain is hardwired with a fervent desire to make sense of the world, to create connections between events whether they exist or not. From a rationalist's standpoint, it's something of a design flaw. It's what led ancient people to believe if they danced a certain way, the rain would fall. It's what led modern people to believe vaccines caused autism.

Amy was trying to guard against that kind of thinking now. Especially when there were two recent developments her brain was craving to link up. The first was the missing drugs, which had been taken from a (supposedly) secure lockup in the Augusta County Sheriff's Office. Second was her map, with all its pins, every last one of them within the jurisdiction of . . . the Augusta

County Sheriff's Office.

It was leading her to a conclusion she absolutely did not want to draw. She thought of Skip Kempe, of Jason Powers. Physically, both fit the incredibly broad description of an average-size white male under the age of fifty.

But she knew these men, didn't she? They were decent to the core, dedicated lawmen. She remembered Powers's voice when he told her about Lilly Pritchett and his excitement when he found the prints at the scene. She considered Kempe, the Aldous Huxley reader, and the way he patiently testified at trials.

No way were those two responsible. It had to be someone else from their office.

But now, as she walked back to her office from the judge's chambers, there was one more event she found herself attempting to lasso in with the others: the Melanie Barrick drug bust.

Truly, Barrick was an outlier in the drug world, an educated, married mother with no record, suddenly turning to dealing at age thirty-one. Amy had dismissed any thought of how unlikely that was, simply because there was no question the drugs had been discovered in the woman's house.

Except who made the discovery? Deputies

from the Augusta County Sheriff's Office. With Kempe as lead investigator. And Powers as the boss of it all.

Ridiculous. Totally. Correlation is not causation. Dances don't make the rain fall. There were probably attacks — in Staunton and in nearby counties — she simply didn't know about. She just had to keep plugging away until she got some kind of break.

Check that. She had gotten a break: She had the fingerprint now. She'd send that off to the lab in Roanoke and wait patiently for any results. If she kept following the process — like she *hadn't* done with Plotz — she'd eventually get this guy.

As for Melanie Barrick? Yes, she remained an unlikely drug dealer. But Amy had to chase all the conspiracy theories from her mind. It was her job as a prosecutor to present enough evidence to overcome reasonable doubt, not to definitively disprove every possibility that a wildly inventive mind could create.

And there was no question what a reasonable person would conclude given the facts of the case.

Amy arrived back at her office to find a note on her desk from Aaron Dansby, requesting an audience.

She had already ignored one such note on Tuesday afternoon, so she decided to get it over with. She made the short stroll down the hallway and into the pages of *Southern Living*.

Dansby was wearing one of his good suits and a bow tie. Claire had struck again.

"Hey," he said when he saw her in the doorway. "Grab a chair. I just wanted an update. What's new with my man Mookie's appeal? Powers find those drugs yet?"

"Nope, sorry," Amy said, taking a seat. "And we might as well start facing the fact that they probably never will."

Dansby drummed a pen on his desk. "So break this down for me. When is this all going to come out?"

"After mid-April if that's what you're worried about," Amy said. "I haven't even filed our response yet. I've got a few weeks to do that. Then the Appellate Court will schedule oral arguments. That won't happen for a few months. Then they'll issue a ruling, which will take another little while. Then, if the ruling goes against us, it gets tossed back to Circuit Court, at which point the trial gets scheduled. I'm sure we're looking at after November."

"Really?" he said, brightening more. "You think you could delay it that long?"

"It's not me delaying it. That's just how long it takes."

"Well, that's great news," he said.

Amy might have been angry except she was so unsurprised. Dansby didn't care about losing the conviction as long as he had already won the election.

"Anyhow," he continued, "I'm speaking to Rotary in a few minutes and I want to give them something good. What's up with Coke Mom?"

Amy didn't need to be told there was a large overlap between Rotary and the crowd that would determine Dansby's political future.

"We've got a motion hearing a week from Friday," she said.

"A motion hearing. What motion?"

"The defense is challenging the warrant. They're trying to say the CI the Sheriff's Office used made everything up."

"What?" Dansby said, sitting up, alarmed. "Did he?"

"I doubt it. Kempe said the guy is solid."

Dansby nodded, but Amy could tell from his face he was still working something out.

"So the motion hearing consists of Kempe testifying?" he asked.

"Him and the CI, yeah."

"The CI testifies?"

"Yeah."

"So the confidential informant doesn't get to stay confidential? That doesn't seem right. Can't we fight that?"

"We already tried," Amy said. "Ultimately, if the defense makes an issue out of it, the Sheriff's Office eventually has to show its hand. Melanie Barrick has a right to face her accuser."

"You're going to put the CI on the stand?"

"Well, technically, the defense has to put him on the stand. For purposes of this hearing, the CI is actually their witness. So is Kempe, for that matter. It makes things a little tougher on the defense, because it means it can't just sit back and potshot like it normally does. It has to actually build an argument."

"Yeah, but what happens if the CI cracks under the pressure or gets tripped up? I mean, a good lawyer can turn anyone in circles."

"Then it's up to me to rehabilitate him on cross," Amy said.

"But if it's really bad, I mean . . . These CIs, they're mostly druggies and losers, right? If this guy was a real mess on the stand, what happens then?"

"Theoretically? We could lose the search warrant. And if we lost the warrant, we'd

438

lose the case. But that's not going to happen. Not with Robbins hearing this. You
should have heard him earlier today. I was
in his office when he told Melanie Barrick
that if anything untoward happened to the
CI before he had a chance to testify, he'd
personally see to it she got the needle."

Amy was shaking her head.

Dansby smiled. "I always did like that
guy."

"Point is, he's not going to let us lose this
warrant," Amy said.

"All right. So I can tell Rotary everything
is on track for a conviction?"

Amy thought about reasonable doubt.
And rain dances.

"Absolutely," she said. "It's as good as
done."

FORTY-TWO

Wednesday night was another torture session disguised as slumber, with my thoughts jumping from one awful subject to the next.

Alex — and who had him, and what they were doing with him, and whether he was being loved and cared for — was, as usual, first and foremost.

But what Judge Robbins had threatened me with was certainly in there as well.

Barely sleeping Wednesday night made the swelling in my ankles worse all day Thursday. By the time I made the drive home from Waffle House that evening, it had moved up to my knees.

For my pain and suffering, I had made $81.77, thanks to a tour bus full of unusually heavy tippers that came through around lunchtime.

Before turning up my driveway, I checked my mailbox and, once again, did not find any note from my parents; just a credit-card bill and some junk mail.

I was inside the house when I opened the bill. Then I gasped. I don't put much on the card under normal circumstances, and had been especially careful lately, given my dire financial situation.

That's why I immediately knew the number was all wrong. It was at least $700 more than I expected, which was $700 I couldn't afford if I was going to succeed in scraping together a mortgage payment for April.

With a spurt of panic, I delved into the statement itself. The first charge I didn't recognize was from a gas station in Pennsylvania. Then there were more charges from hotels, fast food restaurants, and gas stations in New Jersey, a state I had most certainly not been in.

But obviously, Ben had been.

From March 10 through 12, my estranged husband had stayed at a hotel in Camden. On March 13 and 14, he moved up to Elizabeth. From there, I couldn't say. March 14 was the last day of the billing cycle.

Camden made sense, being that it was just across the river from Philadelphia. He might have just been looking for a cheaper place while he made arrangements to begin at Temple with Professor Kremer.

But if that was true, what was he doing in

Elizabeth? I pulled out my phone to check and, sure enough, it was an hour-and-a-half drive north of the Philadelphia area. Was there another college or university in that area?

There were actually several. Within a short drive, there was Kean University, Seton Hall, Rutgers-Newark, and many others. I could have called him to find out, except I really didn't want to talk to the man. All I would have ended up doing was screaming at him.

So I did the next best thing: I called the credit-card company, explained the situation, and got them to shut down the account. Passive-aggressive? Sure. Satisfying? Absolutely.

When I was done, I went up to the nursery. It was time to pump. Mr. Snuggs was there, waiting for me. I looked into his glassy little eyes.

"You would never run up a credit card bill on me, would you?" I asked him.

Mr. Snuggs had no response.

"So where am I going to get seven hundred freaking dollars?"

Mr. Snuggs said nothing.

Then my phone rang. It was Marcus.

"Hey," I said.

"Hey, what are you up to?"

"Talking to a teddy bear, wondering if I'm losing my mind."

"You want me to come over? Maybe bring some Thai? Kelly has to work late again so it'd just be us."

"That sounds so good but . . . Honestly, I'm just completely wiped out. I barely slept at all last night."

"I understand," he said. "Is everything okay? You sound down. Did something happen today?"

The bill I had tossed aside was at my feet. I looked down at it. I'm sure Marcus had $700. If I asked him for a loan, he'd say yes. He wouldn't hesitate.

But I couldn't. I already owed him too much.

"No, just tired," I said.

"Okay," he said. "You know if you need anything, all you have to do is ask, right?"

It was like he could read my mind. But I guess that's what best friends do.

"Yeah, I know. Thanks, Marcus. You're awesome."

"All right," he said. "Well, I guess I'll talk to you later."

"Have a good night."

"You too."

I looked at Mr. Snuggs one last time. He had fallen on his side, so I righted him, then

443

gave him an affectionate pat before hooking myself to the machine and letting it go to work.

FORTY-THREE

Richard Coduri's money was getting low. So was his coke stash.

He had abandoned all attempts at rationing himself. The only thing that slowed him down at all was a persistent nosebleed. He was now snorting as much blood as he was cocaine.

The party was coming to an end.

Unless he could find a way to keep it going.

With that in mind, he had called the man again, saying he wanted more money. The man refused. Coduri was pissed, but what could he do?

Then he got that subpoena, which had been served on him at Room 307 at the Howard Johnson. How the cops even knew he was there, he didn't know.

That prompted another phone call to the man. He left a message this time. And maybe there had been more of a threat involved. He hadn't quite said, *Hey, it's Slash. I've been subpoenaed. Give me more money, or else I'll tell everyone what I did for you.*

Well, maybe he had said something like that.

The man had called back, furious, saying that wasn't the deal, saying Coduri had been compensated lavishly for what he had done. The man reminded Coduri he would go to jail if everything came out. He also reminded Coduri that he didn't actually know the man's name, so what was he going to tell the authorities? That *some guy* had paid him to plant drugs in the woman's house? What would that accomplish?

Coduri said he didn't care. He said he liked prison.

That was a bluff, of course. No way Coduri was going back behind bars.

But the man didn't know that. He had made all kinds of angry noises, told Coduri never to call him again, all that. Whatever. Coduri knew the guy would fold. In a game of chicken, the winner is always the person with less to lose.

So Coduri smiled when he saw the number pop up on his phone. It was late Thursday night, maybe early Friday morning, and Coduri was impossibly high.

"I'll show you. Come on."

Coduri fell in behind the guy, who moved at a quick pace, his head down. They passed by dark houses and closed storefronts. Every time Coduri tried to ask a question, the man told him to shut up and keep walking.

Eventually, they reached the iron gates at the corner of Thornrose Cemetery. The man continued past them, then hopped over the low stone wall just beyond.

Coduri came to a stop.

"Where are you going?" he asked.

"It's just up this way."

"I ain't going in there."

"You are if you want to get paid."

"What are you talking about?" Coduri said.

"I hid everything in my family's crypt. It was the only place I knew it would be safe. I've got the key."

Coduri didn't move. He knew there was nothing inherently dangerous about a cemetery, but it was still creepy.

"What are you? Afraid of some old tombstones?" the man goaded him. "You want the stuff or not?"

"Yeah. Whatever," Coduri said, and fell in behind the man as they walked at an angle up the hill.

"It's just over that way," the man said.

They walked deeper into the cemetery. There wasn't much more than a sliver of a moon. They were now away from the glow of the streetlights. The man had removed his sunglasses.

Coduri didn't like the feeling of any of this. He might have turned around, but he knew he'd like the feeling of cocaine withdrawal even less.

The party *had* to keep going.

"Here we are," the man said at last.

He had stopped beneath a large limestone mausoleum with a monument out front. Coduri could make out the name ECHOLS etched onto it.

So that was this guy's name? Echols?

The man had scaled up some steps, then bent down to pick something up.

"Just getting my flashlight," he said. "This key is really finicky. You mind holding this for me?"

"Yeah, whatever."

The man turned the flashlight toward him, shining it in Coduri's face, momentarily blinding him. Coduri winced at the light, squinting and shielding his eyes.

Which is why he never saw the baseball bat coming. Not even when it connected with a sickening crack on the side of his head.

Coduri staggered but did not fall. With all the cocaine in his system, it would take a lot more than a one-handed swing to stop him.

He lunged at the man, still blind from the light. Coduri was aiming for eyeballs, hoping to gouge them out. He missed, landing nothing more than a superficial scratch on the man's neck.

By then, the man had put down the flashlight. He was using both hands now.

The next swing put Coduri down. The swing after that put him out.

FORTY-FOUR

I slept like a corpse that night.

The morning was another story. When I first rolled over and saw the clock — 6:28 — I told myself I should get out of bed and start being productive, maybe do some yoga before work.

Then I fell right back to sleep.

During that second stint, I had a recurrence of the dream that had become the ugly weed of my subconscious. No matter how many times I thought I had pulled it out by the root, it always came back, usually twice as large.

It was the dream where I heard the whisper of the man who raped me. As it had been in real life, I never actually saw the man's features. He was only a shape, looming over me in the dark, talking to me in that whisper that seemed to come out of the ether — like it was everywhere and nowhere, all at the same time.

There were parts of the dream that changed, like where it happened. Sometimes it would be my parents' house in Northumberland; or at one of the foster homes where I had spent time; or, more rarely, at the ground-floor apartment where the attack had taken place.

But the whisper. That was always the same. I would never forget it.

As was typical, the entirety of the dream took place in the moments right before he attacked me. He was crossing the room, clamping his hand on my mouth, the leather of his glove against my lips. The dream never progressed to the actual rape. It was all about the anticipation of the horrible event.

By the time I opened my eyes, it was 10:47 and I was drenched in sweat. My shift started at eleven. Waffle House was only five minutes away, so I could still make it. There just wouldn't be time for a shower. I hoped the customers didn't notice I still smelled like fear.

As I drove to work, I tried to think about Alex. Sometimes it hurt too much to do that, but this time I was able to settle on a pleasant memory, one from when I was still pregnant with him.

It was during my second trimester. I had

been experiencing the miracle that was Alex squirming and moving for some time, of course. But his little flutters — which to me seemed big enough for the whole world to feel — were too faint for Ben to detect. Every time I forced him to put his hand on my belly, he would give me this forbearing smile, then eventually admit he wasn't getting anything.

Then one Sunday morning when neither of us had to be anywhere, we were enjoying lying in bed. Alex was being particularly active and he was finally growing big enough to really pack a wallop. So I made Ben put his hand on my stomach.

Not three seconds later, Alex shifted positions. Ben actually yelped and pulled away, he was so startled. He said it felt like a snake had slithered along his hand. For a while after that, we called Alex "the snake," one of at least a half dozen nicknames we had for him.

From then on, Ben was constantly asking me if Alex was awake and moving. If I said yes, Ben would talk to Alex, telling him he wanted a high-five.

Sometimes I pretended like I was losing patience and asked him if bro time could wait until after I showered or went to the bathroom or whatever. But mostly I loved it. For the entire final trimester, I finally felt like we were actually sharing a pregnancy that up until then had been mine alone.

As I pulled into Waffle House, I was enjoying the memory so much I didn't particularly pay attention to the three Augusta County Sheriff's cars in the parking lot. It wasn't unusual to see them there. We were right by the highway that served as the main artery for the county, one exit away from their headquarters.

Then I got out of my car, and the next thing I knew there were six guys, dressed in black tactical gear, approaching me from all angles. Several of them had their hands on their gun belts.

"Melanie Barrick, put your hands on your vehicle," one of them barked.

I was so confused, I didn't immediately do anything. I just stood there in my greasy uniform, wondering what it was now. The guy in the lead closed the gap between us so quickly I couldn't back up fast enough to get away from him. He grabbed me by the wrists and slammed my hands against the hood of my car, then mashed the rest of me so I bent at the waist.

"Don't move," he ordered.

He ran his hands quickly down my torso, then up my legs, giving me a sickened shiver. Then he straightened me, pinned my arms behind me, and fastened them there.

As he shoved me toward the car, I finally got enough sense about me to ask, "What's going on? Why are you doing this?"

He didn't reply.

"Would you stop?" I pleaded pointlessly. "Can you at least tell me what's going on?"

That's when he finally said: "You are under arrest for the murder of Richard Coduri."

FORTY-FIVE

Minutes before she had to go into District Court Friday morning, one of the deputies at the courthouse had told Amy Kaye the news.

A body — with its skull bashed to pieces — had been found in Thornrose Cemetery, a few feet from the monument to Confederate general John Echols.

The deputy didn't know anything else. But midway through the morning session, when the judge recessed for a break, Amy checked her messages. That's when she learned the victim had been identified as Richard Coduri.

Amy had tried to call Jason Powers at that point. He would know that Coduri had been the Coke Mom informant. But he might not know Melanie Barrick had been given Coduri's name just two days earlier.

There was no answer on Powers's cell, so Amy took the unusual step of calling his home. His wife said he had been out late patrolling — like usual — and was sleeping in, but that he would call as soon as he awoke.

Amy went back into court, worried that this important time, those precious first hours after the commission of a crime, were slipping away without anyone realizing what was going on.

She needn't have. The Staunton City Police had used Coduri as an informant too. Once the police department and the Sheriff's Office discovered their common interest in Coduri, they decided to join forces in the investigation of his death. While Amy was in front of a judge, bringing to justice people who had failed to get their cars inspected in a timely manner, the combined resources of those two agencies were being put to work.

By the time Amy broke for lunch, there was another update: Melanie Barrick was in custody.

Still, it wasn't until close to four o'clock Friday afternoon, when she was back in her office, that she managed to get Powers on the phone.

"Heya," he said.

"Hey, sounds like you guys have been busy today."

"Yep. But it seems like everyone's favorite drug dealer had an even busier night."

"Yeah, yeah," Amy said. "Now, look, I've been in court all day, which means you haven't gotten your dose of prosecutorial precaution yet today. So I'm going to give it to you now: Are you sure it's her? I mean, don't get me wrong, I get why she has to be the lead suspect. But I was in Judge Robbins's office on Wednesday when he told her that if anything happened to Coduri, he'd hold her personally accountable."

"Yeah, I already heard from the good judge three times today. I think if he had an electric chair in his office, he'd be ready to spark it up right now for her."

"Okay, so you know where his head is. But Melanie Barrick did too. Doesn't that seem a little, I don't know, brazen? To go killing a guy after a judge has laid down the law like that?"

"Yeah, but criminals don't respect the law. That's why they're criminals."

"I hear that," Amy said. "And I know at the end of the day it's probably her. I just want to make sure we're at least looking at other suspects? Guys like Richard Coduri aren't known to have great life expectancies. There are probably other people who would love to bash his head in. Could it have been someone else he informed on? I don't want us to get tunnel vision here."

"Oh. You ain't heard yet."

"Heard what?"

"The ME called us a little while ago. Coduri had Melanie Barrick's name and phone number on a piece of paper in his pocket, along with the words 'midnight' and 'Thornrose.' "

Amy digested this for a moment. It was the kind of evidence juries ate up with a knife and fork: The victim was practically reaching out from the grave to testify.

"So what are we thinking?" she said. "Coduri gets a phone call from Melanie Barrick, a woman he's informed on, to meet her in a cemetery at midnight, and he just goes out to see if she wants to swap recipes? Would he really be that dumb?"

"You didn't know Rick Coduri," Powers said, chuckling. "Bless his heart, he was dumber than a bag o' hammers."

"I'm being serious."

"So am I. It's entirely possible he didn't know it was Melanie Barrick he informed on. She probably used an alias when she was selling to him. Her real name wouldn't mean anything to him."

"How could it not? She's been all over the paper since then."

"Rick Coduri ain't exactly a newspaper-reading type," Powers said. "He probably thought it was some kind of business deal, and he couldn't help himself. A guy like Coduri would sell out his mother for a hundred bucks. If he thought going out to a cemetery at night would get him a payday, he wouldn't be too concerned for his personal safety. Especially if he was meeting with a woman. He'd think he could overpower her. He didn't know she'd have a baseball bat."

"Was the murder weapon definitely a baseball bat? I hadn't heard that yet."

"Oh, I'm just making that up. ME said blunt-force trauma — like we couldn't have figured that out. He said if there were just one or two impact sites, he might be able to give us a guess on what did it. But Coduri's skull was so busted up, we probably won't be able to tell. Coke Mom sure got her licks in."

"If it was her," Amy felt like she had to interject.

"Well, come on, who else could it be?"

"That's the point. We have to not only prove it's her, we have to jump through the hoops of proving it couldn't have been anyone else — that we considered every possibility. If this really becomes a capital case, she'll get two attorneys. And then as soon as she's convicted, she gets an auto-matic appeal before the Supreme Court. From there, Virginia is full of clever anti–death penalty lawyers. One of them will find a way to make the thing federal, and then it'll be more appeals. Our actions over the next two weeks are going to be scrutinized for the next ten years by people we can't even dream of. We have to make sure we're doing everything right."

"I know, I know. And I've got a whole lot of people doing the wild-goose-chase thing for just that reason. We went through the cameras at the cemetery, not that they showed us anything. We got our detectives and some city guys at the Howard Johnson, where Coduri was staying. They're dusting his room for prints and everything. Plus we're canvassing all around the cemetery, trying to find a murder weapon but also talking to folks who might have seen any-thing last night. If any other possibility comes up, I promise we won't look the other way."

"Thank you," Amy said. "Keep me in the loop, okay?"

"You got it."

As she hung up, she still didn't like what she was hearing from the Augusta County Sheriff. This had nothing to do with whatever suspicions about Powers and his office she had (mostly) rid from her mind. This was hard-won experience talking:

Few things led to mistakes more than an investigation that was too sure of itself or an investigator who was acting like he already had all the answers.

FORTY-SIX

I was still in some kind of denial throughout the afternoon as a series of hard-eyed sheriff's deputies shunted me from one place to the next.

Even as someone who had been wrongly accused of a crime before, I retained this trust that something would soon emerge to clear me. They would find some physical evidence that pointed them to the real killer. A witness would step forward. Some smart person — like maybe Amy Kaye — would figure out what was really going on.

Something.

While I was still at Sheriff's Office headquarters, I was allowed a brief meeting with Mr. Honeywell. I told him I knew nothing about how Richard Coduri met his end. I had been at home, alone and asleep, from about nine o'clock onward, which didn't help my situation at all. I wished I had taken Marcus up on his offer for Thai food.

I asked Mr. Honeywell if he could check with Bobby Ray Walters and secure the video of me driving up my driveway and then not leaving all night. Wouldn't that confirm my story?

No. Mr. Honeywell pointed out that a video capturing only a narrow slice of my driveway couldn't confirm that I hadn't left my house on foot or by some other means. Bobby Ray's paranoia wouldn't help me this time.

Then Mr. Honeywell explained that even an iron-clad alibi would have its limitations in a case like this. The prosecution would simply argue that I was a drug dealer with an extensive criminal network, the kind of person who could easily order a killing to be carried out by someone else. The law would treat me the same whether I pulled the trigger or paid someone else to do it.

The prosecution's whole case would rest on motive: That I had such a compelling reason to kill Richard Coduri, I had to be guilty.

I was soon swept off to the magistrate, who forwarded me without much delay onto the Middle River Regional Jail. It was a sad testimony to my state of affairs that I was starting to know their intake procedures so well: the surrendering of my personal ef-

465

fects, the signing of documents that I had no choice but to sign, the shuffling from one station to the next.

Even the humiliation of the cavity search was starting to feel routine.

When it was all done, when I was back in jailhouse orange, I was preparing to be packed off to the general population for more taunts from my fellow inmates, who would already probably know more about the circumstances of Richard Coduri's death than I did.

I was being herded around in handcuffs by a corrections officer, and we had reached the point in the labyrinth of hallways where I knew we were supposed to turn right.

Instead, he shoved me to the left.

"Where are we going?" I asked.

"Ad seg," he said coolly.

Administrative segregation. Also known as solitary confinement. I had already heard it being hung over inmates' heads as their punishment for misbehaving. It involved being in a room by yourself for twenty-three hours a day, not seeing or talking to anyone else most of the time, not being allowed trips to the library or other liberties that made incarceration a little less intolerable.

"Ad seg? Why? I didn't even do anything,"

I said, already feeling the panic rising in me.

The guy chortled. "That's not what I heard."

"No, no, wait," I said. "That's just an accusation. They haven't proven anything. I didn't do it."

The CO was still shoving me down this strange hallway.

"Yeah, I'm sure," he said. "Look, all I know is, the warden said to put you in ad seg for protection."

"Protection? Who do I need to be protected from?"

The guy laughed some more. "Not for your protection, sweetheart. For the protection of everyone else in here. You might as well get used to it. Once you're convicted, they'll put you in ad seg too. That's what death row is."

That moment — when he said the words "death row" — was when the denial faded away. The blood seemed to leave my head all at once, and my legs went out from underneath me. The next thing I felt was the floor. Dimly, I could hear the corrections officer call for medical assistance.

I was not "merely" a drug dealer anymore. I was something far worse: a violent murderer whose flagrant disregard for the law had put me on a straight-and-narrow path to the death penalty.

This was no five-year sentence. This was spending the rest of my life — whatever remained of it — being treated like a feedlot cow on my way to slaughter.

It would take a few years for me to exhaust my appeals. But not too many. I had read a story once about how Texas kills more people, but Virginia kills them quicker. It streamlines the appeals process, making it possible to go from crime to punishment faster than anywhere else in the country. I could suddenly see the time stretching out in front of me. It would be both incredibly long and all too short.

The whole time, I would be Melanie Barrick, Notorious Murderer. If Alex learned anything about his mother, it would only be that I was such an awful person, a series of virtuous citizens — judges and prosecutors and jury members alike — determined the world would be a better place if I were exterminated.

There would be no chance to reunite with him, even in some limited fashion as the biological mother whose rights to him had been terminated. Social Services would not permit a child to visit death row; and the Department of Corrections would not allow me to go anywhere else.

I would go to my grave without ever getting the chance to hold Alex again.

FORTY-SEVEN

The ruling came down from Judge Robbins's office first thing Monday morning.

The motion to suppress the search warrant in *Commonwealth v. Barrick* had been summarily rejected. The judge had decided that, as a matter of law, it wasn't of consequence whether the confidential informant was lying or, for that matter, whether he was still breathing. The warrant was based on sworn statements from the sheriff's deputy. As long as the deputy was being truthful — and there was no allegation to the contrary — there was not sufficient grounds to overturn the warrant.

There was no need for a hearing. The testimony of the late Richard Coduri had been deemed legally insignificant.

Moments after Amy Kaye received the electronic notification of the filing, she also got an email from the judge's clerk, reminding her that the trial was still scheduled for

470

April 9. In case anyone didn't get the message already, the judge was determined the case would proceed with or without Coduri.

Amy was just digesting the implications of the ruling — and whether, in fact, it constituted reversible error that might later be appealed — when Aaron Dansby appeared in her office doorway, looking positively chipper.

"Hey!" he said brightly.

"Hi," Amy said, shocked to see him on a Monday morning for the second time in a month.

"Did you see the ruling in the Coke Mom case?"

"Of course. Did you?" she said incredulously. She couldn't remember the last time Dansby had even been aware of a ruling on a defense motion.

"Yeah. I kind of knew it was coming," he said.

"How?"

He closed the door to her office behind her.

"I was at the club over the weekend, and I bumped into Robbins," he said in a conspiratorial tone.

"Bumped into him?"

"Maybe I should say he bumped into me. Claire and I were there for dinner and he

471

came over and said hi. He brought up Coke Mom. Everyone at the club was buzzing about it."

Dansby invited himself to sit down. Amy sometimes wondered if he really should have been a tabloid newspaper reporter. Gossip and intrigue seemed to excite him more than the law.

"He might have had a few — you know how he loves his scotch," Dansby continued. "He sat down with us and was just going on about how we had to make sure Coke Mom didn't get away with this and how we needed to send a message that we weren't going to let the criminals run things and all that. Then he told me he had already written up the ruling rejecting Coke Mom's motion, and that he was just waiting for Monday morning to file it."

"Did anyone hear you guys talking?"

"I don't know. Why?"

"Because what you're describing is an ex parte communication between a judge and a commonwealth's attorney, and it's highly improper."

"Yeah, yeah, whatever. I haven't even told you the best part."

Yes. Because there was always a "best part" about ethics violations.

"After he tells me he's rejecting the motion, he starts giving me advice about what we ought to do," Dansby said. "He was going on about how, 'When I was sitting in your chair, I would have blah, blah, blah.' Anyway, he was saying we should keep on schedule and prosecute the drug thing first. That way, when Coke Mom comes up for trial for the Coduri thing, she's already a convicted felon. He said that would make it more likely she gets the needle. What do you think? Can we do it that way?"

"Uh, yeah, sure," Amy said. She didn't like how any of this felt: a judge and a commonwealth's attorney colluding at a country club. Especially when the defendant had already asked for a bench trial.

"Good. We're still solid on the drug thing, right?" Dansby asked. "I mean, now that he's rejected the motion, it's full speed ahead, right?"

"Yeah, sure. The warrant is lawful, so all the evidence gathered as a result is admissible. It makes things pretty straightforward."

"Good, good. What do you think? Should I send Robbins a bottle of Glenlivet for the free legal advice?"

"Don't you *dare*," Amy spat.

"Kidding," he said, then he winked at her. "By the way, I'm thinking about doing this trial. When is it again?"

"April ninth," she said, trying not to show any reaction.

"Okay. Got it. Keep up the good work."

He rapped her desk twice with his knuckles as he stood up, then left her office.

Amy waited until he was gone to frown at him. When he said he was "doing" this trial, he meant he planned to sit first chair — which was his prerogative, as commonwealth's attorney.

For Amy, it would just mean more work. Getting Aaron Dansby ready for trial took, on average, about three times longer than if she had to prepare only herself.

Amy settled back into her work, still pondering the strangeness of a judge telling a prosecutor how to do his job.

Not twenty minutes later, her phone rang. It was Sheriff Powers.

"Hey, it's Amy."

"Hey," he said. "You got court or anything this morning?"

"No. Not till this afternoon."

"Good. You're gonna want to come up here."

"What's going on?"

"We got a guy who just walked in here and confessed to killing Richard Coduri."

■ ■ ■ ■

As fast as her car and legs could get her there, Amy was seated in the conference room at the Augusta County Sheriff's Office. Lieutenant Peter Kempe was there. So was Sheriff Jason Powers.

Amy smiled awkwardly at them. They didn't know about her pin map; or that, as she sat there, she still couldn't completely rid from her mind the possibility — however slim — that one of them was the man she had been hunting for three years.

Then her focus changed to the man being brought into the room. He was tall, somewhat gaunt in the face, with broad shoulders. Amy pegged him as being mid-fifties. He looked like he worked outside.

She stood up, but the man wasn't going to make it over to her side of the room to shake hands. Powers pointed to the nearest chair, across the long table from Amy.

"Sit here," Powers said, and the man lowered himself into a chair.

The sheriff looked at Kempe. "You got the recorder?"

Kempe waved a small silver digital recorder in the air, then set it in front of the man and pressed a button.

475

"All right," Powers said. "You sure it's going?"

Kempe gave the thumbs-up.

"Good. Then let's get on with it," Powers said. "Sir, can you please state your name?"

"William Theodore Curran, sir. But people call me Billy. Billy Curran."

"Thank you, Mr. Curran. You're here freely and voluntarily, is that right?"

"Yes, sir."

"And you've been advised of your right to counsel."

"What do you mean?"

"That you can have a lawyer if you want one," Powers said.

"Oh, yeah," Curran said.

"And you've waived that right?"

"Yes, sir."

"Okay. Now. What is it you'd like to say to us?"

"Just that, you know, I did it," Curran said.

"You did what?"

"I killed that guy in the cemetery. Melanie Barrick had nothing to do with it."

The way he had said "Melanie" caught Amy's attention. It wasn't like he was talking about a stranger. There was a warmth underlying it. Then Amy made a connection. Curran. A common enough name, sure. But it was also Melanie Barrick's

476

maiden name, the name she had been using at the time of her attack. Was this guy related?

Powers was continuing with his questions: "Why did you kill him?"

"Do I need a reason? I just killed him."

"But did you . . . know the victim somehow? Did you have dealings with him?"

"No. Nothing like that. My wife and I were walking through that cemetery on Thursday night. We like cemeteries. We were minding our own business, looking at the dates on the graves. Then this guy started hassling us. I'm pretty sure he was doped up on something and I . . . I got worried he was going to hurt me or my wife. So I killed him. It was self-defense."

"Your wife was a witness to this?"

"Yes, sir," Curran said. "I'll have her come here and she'll tell you the same thing if you want. But she didn't have anything to do with it either. It was all me."

"But when you say he was 'hassling' you, what do you mean, exactly?"

"Oh, you know. He started by asking us for money and I told him no. I thought he was going to try to rob us. Then he started making threats about how he was going to take me out."

"Did he have a weapon?"

"I don't know. Probably."

"But did you see a weapon?"

"Yeah. I think he had a knife," Curran said. "But I could be wrong about that. It was pretty dark."

"So did he . . . try to stab you or something?"

"I don't know. It happened pretty fast. I just . . . I was just really scared and he was making threats, so I killed him before he could do anything to me or my wife."

"And why are you confessing to this?"

"Because I saw in the paper that some young woman had been arrested and I didn't want someone else to have to pay the penalty for something I did."

"But if it was self-defense, why didn't you just call the police after the incident?"

Curran shifted in his seat. "Because I'm a registered sex offender. I'm supposed to stay out of trouble."

"Oh," Powers said, as if that cleared up everything.

"I didn't think anyone would care that some scuzzball had been killed," Curran said. "And then I saw that young woman in the paper, so I thought I should come forward and clear the air."

Powers looked over at Kempe. Neither of them was likely aware of the Melanie

Curran/Melanie Barrick connection. Still, this had to be one of the flimsier confessions ever recorded in the Augusta County Sheriff's Office. Amy expected this would be the point in the interrogation where the sheriff would delve further into the details of this story and expose its fraudulence.

Instead, Powers said, "Okay. Well, I appreciate you coming forward, sir. You understand we're going to have to arrest you and process you?"

"Yes, sir. You do what you have to do."

"Do you have a lawyer?"

"No, sir."

"Well, then the judge'll probably assign you one —"

Amy stopped paying attention to the back-and-forth. She had shifted her focus to Powers. Why was the sheriff letting this continue? Hadn't he been sure on Friday that Melanie Barrick was the murderer? Was he really that eager to clear a murder from his books that he didn't care he was obviously getting the wrong person?

The pin map. The missing drugs. The Barrick raid. And now the eager acceptance of an obviously false confession. There wasn't exactly a straight line between all four of those things, nor was there any obvious benefit. How would punching this guy's ticket for a murder committed by someone else be of any aid to the sheriff?

Amy couldn't figure it out. She just had to put a stop to it. A false confession would only muddy the prosecution of Melanie Barrick.

"Hang on a moment," she said, forcefully enough that the heads of all three men turned her way. "Mr. Curran, I'm Amy Kaye, I'm with the Commonwealth's Attorney's Office. Do you mind if I ask a few questions?"

Curran looked at the sheriff, who didn't give any response.

"I guess not," Curran said.

"Thank you. You said you were walking through the cemetery. Thornrose Cemetery is a big place. Roughly where within the cemetery did this altercation take place?"

"I don't know. I guess you could say the middle."

"After you killed the victim, did you move the body?"

"No, ma'am."

Amy glanced over at Powers for a moment. They both knew the monument to Gen. John Echols was closer to the western entrance of the cemetery than the middle. But that was splitting hairs. Really, Amy was only trying to get a rhythm going.

"Did you touch the victim?"

"No, ma'am."

"But you knew he was dead?"

"Yes, ma'am."

"And about what time did this occur?"

"Middle of the night sometime. I don't know. I wasn't wearing a watch."

"So call it midnight, then?"

"Yeah, about that."

"Well, that roughly matches our time of death," Amy said. "But maybe you can clear something up for us. The victim was such a mess, the medical examiner couldn't tell if he had been struck by two bullets or three. How many times did you shoot him?"

Curran didn't hesitate: "Three," he said.

Amy looked at Powers, who rolled his eyes and muttered a curse.

"Well, now that I think about it, it *might* have been two," Curran said. "I don't know. I was pretty worked up, you know? And —"

"Mr. Curran, Richard Coduri wasn't shot," Amy said. "And you should know making a false confession is a crime."

Curran brought his head down to the table. When he finally looked away, he was blinking back tears.

"Sorry, Melanie," he said. "I tried."

It took another hour to clean up the mess

that was Billy Curran.

The sheriff was hopeful they could pretend Curran had never happened, but Amy wasn't hearing it. Failure to disclose exculpatory evidence — even a blatantly false confession from a relative — was a sure way for the prosecution to lose a conviction. They had to document this properly, then make the defense aware of it. Such was the burden of being the good guys.

Amy was coming out of Powers's office, heading down the hallway toward the exit, when she heard a man calling her name. She turned to see the relentlessly close-cropped hair of Deputy Justin Herzog.

"Hey, I was just about to call you," he said.

"Oh, yeah? What about?"

"Got something to show you if you have a moment."

"Sure," Amy said, and followed him into a cramped office.

Herzog sat down and was already urging the cranky computer there back to life. Amy wondered if he already felt the desire to high-kick it.

"Don't know if Sheriff told you, but you know that guy they found in the cemetery?"

"Richard Coduri."

"Yeah, him. Sheriff must have thought I was bored or something, but you know we checked for prints in the hotel room where he had been staying, right?"

"Powers mentioned something about that."

"Did he tell you I spent my whole weekend on it?"

"No, he didn't mention that."

"Believe me, I'll remind him of it if he gives me trouble for the overtime. Anyhow, as you might imagine, there were a lot of prints in that room. A lot were partials that were pretty useless. Some of them were unsubs," he said, using the slang for unknown subjects. "And of course, some of them were the victim, whose prints were already in the system. But there was one unsub that caught my eye. It was a pretty good one, too. Lotta oil on this guy's fingers. They pulled it off the dresser, which is a nice, shiny surface. I'd say it was fresh, because the rest of the dresser didn't have any prints on it, which probably means someone cleaned it not too long ago."

Herzog was working the mouse. The computer's hard drive was clicking and clacking so much Amy worried it was going to overheat.

"Okay, here we go," he said, having pulled up two prints onto the screen. "Now, you do this as much as I do, you actually start to recognize fingerprints. I knew I had seen this one before. It's like . . . Well, it's almost like going through a crowd of people and seeing a familiar face. It jumps out at you."

"Sure," Amy said.

"You see this print?" he said, pointing to the one on the left side of the screen.

"Yeah," she said.

"This is the one they pulled off the dresser from Room 307 at the Howard Johnson."

"Got it."

"And I started thinking, Where have I seen that before?" Herzog said. "I began running through recent cases in my mind. Then I remember the one from the Pritchett sexual assault, the guy we referred to as Person B."

"The one I thought was Warren Plotz but wasn't?"

"That's right. But guess who it is?"

"Who?"

"The guy from the dresser. I've already found sixteen points of similarities. It's a dead-on match."

Amy Kaye just stared at the screen.

"In other words . . . ," Amy began, but was too stunned to complete the sentence.

Justin Herzog did it for her: "In other words, the man who raped Lilly Pritchett was a recent visitor to Richard Coduri's hotel room."

FORTY-EIGHT

My new home was exactly eight feet wide by ten feet long. I know because I had nothing better to do than measure it, using an eleven-inch sheet of paper as a ruler.

Other than the heavy steel door, the only opening in the concrete walls was an eighteen-inch-high slit of a window. That it existed, I had learned, was because the Supreme Court had ruled that all inmates, even those in administrative segregation, were required to have a source of natural light — the absence of it being considered cruel and unusual punishment.

Mind you, the glass in my window was frosted, so I couldn't actually see anything outside. In that way, it was like the Middle River Regional Jail extending an eighteen-inch middle finger at both me and the Supreme Court.

There were two sources of artificial light. One was the fluorescent bulb recessed into the ceiling and protected by a metal grate. The other was the one-foot-square, two-inch-thick piece of safety glass in the door, which let in light from the hallway.

I had no control over either. The light above me came on automatically every day at six a.m. and stayed on until ten p.m. The light in the hallway never shut off. It blazed at all hours, forcing me to sleep with my back to the door if I wanted any relief from the glare.

Breakfast came at seven each morning. Lunch was around noon. Dinner was five thirtyish.

All meals were delivered through the narrow slot in the door just below the window. There was a small ledge on my side of the door where the tray just barely fit, but the inmate who delivered it had to insert it gently or the food ended up on the floor. Some inmates waited for me to be by the door to receive the tray. Others just flung it in without caring.

The only furnishings, if you could call them that, were the bed, the sink, and the toilet. The bed had a three-inch mattress that did little to cushion my back from the hard surface underneath. The sink had only cold water. The toilet was a chunk of forged stainless steel with no seat and no way to flush. My excrement either slid down or did not. Sometimes, when it got stuck, I splashed water at it until it disappeared.

Despite these grim conditions, I continued my attempts to keep my milk supply going. Doing my best to block out all the distractions, I would think of Alex, imagining his blue-gray eyes staring up at me, thinking about the moment when he latched on.

It still felt like it took forever for the flow to start. And once it did, I was no longer drawing as much out. It certainly didn't help there was a camera box in the corner of the room, so I knew the guards — some of them male — could watch me. It was nearly impossible to be discreet.

Stubbornly, I kept at it. I told myself Alex would be thankful.

I also exercised, doing push-ups, sit-ups, wall squats, burpees, whatever I could manage in that small space. It was more about mental preservation than it was about the physical benefits.

The other highlight of my existence was when one of the guards remembered to grab a book for me on their way into work. The Middle River Regional Jail's collection consisted almost entirely of genre fiction, mostly romances and mysteries. There was one I enjoyed enough to read five times. It featured a wisecracking investigative reporter named Carter Ross, and I was grateful for the temporary respite it gave me from reality.

For one hour each day — and this, again, was thanks to the Supreme Court — I was invited to stick my hands through the meal slot and be handcuffed. I was then led to an outdoor cage that was wedged between two concrete walls. I didn't have a piece of paper with me, so I couldn't give exact dimensions. My best guess was that it was fifteen feet square.

Every few days, on a schedule I had yet to be able discern, my hour in the cage was cut short by a shower, which I took under the watchful gaze of a female guard.

This was my life, day after day. Recovering addicts talk about hitting bottom, about reaching that moment when they knew they could sink no lower, when they simply had to get sober or they would cease being recognizable to themselves as a human being.

In a strange way, I envied them. At least they eventually found that lowest point. Not so in ad seg.

It was like hitting a new bottom every day.

FORTY-NINE

Amy Kaye's favorite class in law school had been a criminal law clinic she attended during her third year.

The professor began the first day by writing FOLLOW THE EVIDENCE on a whiteboard in the room where they convened. The admonishment remained there the rest of the semester, set off in its own box, with DO NOT ERASE: THIS IS THE MOST IMPORTANT THING TO REMEMBER FROM THIS EXPERIENCE written in smaller letters next to it.

Amy was now tempted to call that professor and ask what she was supposed to do if the evidence she was following didn't make a shred of sense.

The man who raped Lilly Pritchett — and dozens of other women over the course of nearly two decades — had visited Richard Coduri's hotel room.

Richard Coduri, who had been, up until

his untimely demise, the star witness against Melanie Barrick.

Melanie Barrick, who was one of the rapist's victims.

Was there a world where a drug snitch and a rapist just happened to associate with each other? It didn't fit any profile Amy had ever seen.

And the murder had happened squarely within Staunton city limits. Did that mean her pin map was actually misleading evidence? Yes, this was a murder, not a rape. But had the rapist been operating in Staunton as well — perhaps just in a way that didn't show up in the files? Raping, but not whispering?

Amy had turned it every which way she could think. She had created flow charts, timelines, and Venn diagrams, drawing lines and circles in a desperate attempt to make the patterns clearer.

All it did was waste paper.

After a few days of fretting over it, Amy decided it was either a wild coincidence, or it was a puzzle that would go unsolved for the time being.

Meanwhile, the chief deputy commonwealth's attorney had other things to keep herself busy. The medical examiner's report had come back on Coduri, confirming the cause of death was blunt-force trauma and the manner of death was a homicide. It opined the victim had briefly tried to defend himself, enough that he might have left some superficial wounds on the perpetrator. But they were still waiting on toxicology reports and other physical evidence found on the body, all of which had to come from the state lab in Roanoke.

Other avenues of investigation — the sheriff's canvass, the attempts to find the murder weapon — had led nowhere.

Amy had also been tutoring Aaron Dansby, making sure he would be ready to prove beyond a reasonable doubt that Melanie Barrick had possessed drugs with the intent to distribute them. On Dansby's calendar, these appeared as "strategy sessions." In Amy's mind, they were more like exercises in disaster mitigation.

They involved trying to anticipate where her boss might screw up this time. During the Mookie Myers trial, Dansby had nearly forgotten to ask Detective Kempe an entire page's worth of the questions Amy had prepared. At a murder trial two years before that, Dansby told their smoking-gun witness she could wait to testify in the courtroom — as opposed to outside of it. If Amy hadn't seen the woman sitting there moments before opening statements began, the witness would have been disqualified.

The man just had an endless capacity for procedural incompetence. For as good as he could be on his feet — and Amy reluctantly admitted the man had some skills as an orator — he couldn't be trusted with the details. Throughout this coming trial, Melanie Barrick would be one Aaron Dansby blunder away from acquittal.

Amy had scheduled the first "strategy session" for Friday morning at 9:30 a.m.

"Here's the list of questions for Kempe," Amy began, pulling a stapled piece of paper from a folder she was carrying and handing it to Dansby. "You want to start by going over them?"

Dansby scanned it for a moment. "Not really," he said.

Amy huffed at him melodramatically. "Aaron, we really have to —"

"Look, Kempe's going to be solid. He always is. Let's not waste our time with that," Dansby said. "What I want to know is: What's Coke Mom's lawyer going to do? Her whole thing is that the drugs aren't really hers, right?"

"Yeah."

"Okay. How's she going to convince the judge of that? That's what I was trying to think about while I was coming in this morning: If I were her attorney, what would I be doing?"

Amy sat up a little straighter. Maybe the last three-plus years hadn't been completely lost on Dansby after all.

"Well, that's a great question," she said. "I actually haven't checked if there are any subpoenas yet. Hang on."

In Virginia, neither side was required to submit a witness list as part of discovery. The only way the defense tipped its hand as to who it might call is if it has to ask the court to issue a subpoena, which it often did if it was afraid a witness wouldn't show up. Any requests for subpoenas had to be issued within ten days of trial — and trial was now exactly ten days away.

Amy picked up the phone on Dansby's desk and dialed the extension for Judge Robbins's clerk. After the woman answered, Amy bantered with her for a moment or two, then moved to the reason for her call: "Has the defense asked for any subpoenas in C-R-1800015700?" she asked, referencing *Commonwealth v. Barrick* by its case number.

"Hang on," the clerk said.

She clacked her keyboard for a little bit. Then the woman came back with: "Yeah, a

493

request came in yesterday. Let's see . . .
They asked us to serve Bobby Ray Walters
of 102 Desper Hollow Road in Staunton."

Amy recognized the address from having
recently pinned it on her map. It made him
Melanie Barrick's neighbor. He was probably being called to testify that he had never
seen any undue amount of traffic in and out
of the neighborhood.

Which was fine. The commonwealth
didn't have to prove where Barrick did her
selling, just that she possessed more drugs
than any one human being needed for
personal consumption.

There was more keyboard clacking. Then
the clerk said, "Oh, and you're going to love
this. They asked us to serve Demetrius
Myers at the Haynesville Correctional Center."

"Mookie Myers!" Amy blurted, causing
Dansby's face to furrow.

"To know him is to love him," the clerk
said.

"Okay," Amy said. "Anyone else?"

"Nope. But I'll give you a call if anything
else comes in."

"Thanks," Amy said.

Dansby had his arms crossed. "Did I hear
that right? The defense is subpoenaing
Mookie Myers?"

"Yep."

"Why would they do that?"

"No idea. The sheriff's theory was that Barrick had taken over Myers's operation. She was selling the same brand and had the same customers. But whether that's true or not, it really doesn't have a lot of bearing on the case."

Dansby drummed his fingers for a moment.

"What if Mookie comes in and says, 'No way I let this cracker lady take over my turf,' " Dansby asked, making Amy cringe with his attempted imitation of Myers's voice.

"First, I doubt he would do that. He'd be screwing up his own appeal. Second, so what? She was caught with the drugs. That's the only thing that counts."

"I realize that, but . . . I'm worried this means there's something going on we haven't thought of."

"Yeah," Amy said. "Me too."

"So what do we do about it?" Dansby asked, already sounding a little panicky about it.

Amy stared at the desk for a moment. "We just have to make sure we don't open the door."

"What do you mean?"

"I mean under no circumstances do we mention the name Mookie Myers when we present our case. We don't talk about him during our opening. We don't ask Kempe about him. Then if the defense tries to start talking about Mookie Myers, we object and say it's not relevant. Normally, it's the prosecution that has to work to build a foundation for certain evidence and it's the defense that's trying to tear it down. We'll just turn the tables on them."

"Think that'll work?"

"Maybe," Amy said. "I guess we'll find out."

FIFTY

Roughly a week and a half into my stay — and it was getting hard to keep track of the days when every one of them was the same — I was doing the important work that was lying on my bed, staring up at the ceiling. Then my meal slot opened.

It was after lunch and not quite time for dinner, so I knew what that meant. I was already swinging my feet onto the floor.

"Come on, Barrick. Yard time," I heard.

Through the door's square window, I saw the tightly wound braids and ample body of Officer Brown, my perhaps-acquaintance from some time I couldn't remember.

I got myself to my feet and, like the obedient chattel I was, shoved my hands through the slot.

"Are you going to give me any trouble, Barrick?" she asked.

"No, Officer Brown. Of course not."

"Then I think we can skip this step," she said.

It had been so long since anyone had shown me even minimal kindness, I was actually suspicious. Was this some kind of a trick? Was I being set up for something? She had been nice to me before, but that was just softening me up for . . . what?

I felt a little unsteady as she opened the door for me and led me down the hallway. I had already become so habituated to slinking along with my wrists bound, I actually put my hands in front of me as I walked. It felt more natural that way.

Officer Brown loomed behind me until we made it outside. When we reached the cage where I would spend the next hour, she unlocked it for me, swinging open the chain-link door.

The cage was wedged in the gap between two buildings that were several stories high, so it only received direct sunlight during a few hours in the middle of the day. It was now so late I had already missed my chance. The last rays were at least ten feet over my head, reflecting off the wall nearest the cage.

It was — unless I was mistaken — April 2. My trial was exactly a week away. The day was warm, and I suppose I was cognizant that the seasons were changing, or had already changed. It would be another lovely spring in the Shenandoah valley, even if that sort of thing was mostly an abstract concept for someone who spent twenty-three hours a day inside.

Officer Brown still hadn't locked my cage, which increased my unease. First no handcuffs, now this. Was she trying to make this look like an escape attempt? What was the penalty for that? Was there something worse than ad seg?

Then Officer Brown asked, "You still don't remember me, do you?"

I looked up at her, this imposing woman, and searched my brain one more time. The same nothing came back at me, just like the other few times I had seen her.

"Sorry," I said. Then I added: "I wish I did."

"I'm Tracee. Tracee Brown. We were together at Miss Agnes."

The Miss Agnes Home for Girls was one of the group homes where I had spent time. It had been a stopping-off point for a few months when I was maybe fourteen or fifteen.

"You used to help me with my math homework," Officer Brown continued. "You remember that? I was terrible with fractions. No one had ever really taught them to me right. You were the first one to make me cut out a whole circle and say that was one over one. And then you had me cut it in half and say one piece of it was one over two. Everything made sense after that. I know it was a long time ago."

A dim memory of a chubby black girl with cornrows came into my head, freed from whatever deep cranial fold it had been hiding in.

"Oh, right. Tracee Brown!" I said, the recollection growing a bit stronger. "You used to eat Corn Flakes for dinner. We couldn't get you to even try anything else."

"Yeah, and wouldn't you know I can't even look at a box of Corn Flakes now," she said with a little chortle.

"I have that same thing with Spaghetti-O's," I said. "I had this one foster mom that fed them to us, no lie, six days a week. I get chills when I even pass them in a grocery store."

She laughed again. It was nice to feel human for the first time in weeks.

Then the smile went away. "You also told me one time that I had to keep the most important part of myself locked away in here," she said, tapping her heart, "and to make sure I never let anyone get at that. And to remember it was good, no matter what. You told me that's how you survived. And that . . . that really helped me get through some tough times."

I nodded.

"That's pretty good advice for in here too," she said quietly.

"Yeah," I said, looking down at the concrete under my feet. She still hadn't closed or locked the cage.

I wanted to ask her a thousand questions. About how long she stayed at Miss Agnes. About whether she had been adopted. About how she had survived and, apparently, thrived well enough to land a good job like this one.

But she beat me to the next thought: "I hope you don't mind, but I've been keeping track of your case ever since you first came in here. I have a cousin who works in the Sheriff's Office. Have you . . . have you talked to your lawyer lately?"

"No, why?"

"Well, I don't know if this will help you, but a man came in and tried to confess to killing that guy in the cemetery."

For a very brief moment, hope surged in me, until I ran through the sentence in my head again. "What do you mean, 'tried to'?" I asked.

"It turned out he was lying. He said he

shot the guy. But the guy in the cemetery wasn't shot."

"Who . . . who would do something like that?"

"My cousin said the guy's name was Curran. Somethingorother Curran."

I slumped against one of the poles that supported the cage, then slid down it until I was sitting in a small ball with my legs pulled up against my chest.

"You know him?" she asked.

"He's my biological father. Estranged, obviously."

Tracee brought her hand to her mouth. I didn't need to fill in any more blanks for a fellow Miss Agnes alumna.

"Oh, wow," she said.

Which nicely summarized my immediate thoughts on the matter.

"Well," she said apologetically. "I have to close this now."

"I understand."

And then, to make sure she knew I was absolving her totally, I smiled. And I meant it.

I stayed in my little ball on the concrete for a while after she left. Then, eventually, I stood and looked up at the atmosphere, into the high reaches where the air was thin and the clouds wispy.

Somewhere underneath that same sky was my father. And for perhaps the first time in my whole life, I felt myself wishing I could talk to him.

In some ways this was a fitting continuation to our entire relationship, because I never had understood the man. As a little girl I was constantly confused as to why he was so angry all the time. What had I done to displease him? Was I not a good enough little girl? If I cleaned my room or did a better job brushing my teeth, would he finally start loving me?

Now he was even more of an enigma to me. The Billy Curran I had known — the wife beater and child abuser who thought nothing of fondling his stepdaughter — was a total stranger to altruism. He was, in fact, the living embodiment of the opposite of it.

Was there some angle to this I wasn't seeing? Was he getting something out of this?

But for however much I flipped it around in my mind, I couldn't see how he could turn this into an advantage for himself. He had tried to take my place in prison, perhaps even on death row. He had failed, yes; but it was the epitome of an unselfish act.

Especially from a man who knew exactly what he was getting into. Some people, those who have never been incarcerated, have this deluded belief prison is not all that bad — three hots and a cot for free, all this time to do whatever you want, nonsense like that.

My father would have had no such illusions. He had spent five years being subjected to its horrors, serving time as a convicted child sex offender, the lowest of the low in the prison pecking order. He knew what it meant to suffer the loss of one's liberty.

And he was willing to go back, to take all of it on. For me.

Had he really changed? Had prison and sobriety and Jesus and twenty years of reflecting on all his mistakes turned him into something other than the abomination I had known as a girl?

Maybe my mother was right. Maybe there always had been something good in him.

And maybe, just maybe — and this was quite a thing to consider after twenty-nine years of having every reason to doubt it — he loved me after all.

FIFTY-ONE

The call came just before lunchtime on Friday. Not that Amy Kaye was planning to take lunch that day.

She was still only midway through all she needed to get done by the end of the week — a list that was particularly pressing, given that Monday would be consumed by the Melanie Barrick drug trial.

Amy frowned at the caller ID. If it was Aaron Dansby, calling from his back porch, having already started his weekend, she was going to let it slip through to voicemail. Then she recognized the main number for the state lab in Roanoke and quickly grabbed at the phone.

"Amy Kaye."

"Chap Burleson," came the response.

Hearing his name brought back the lingering embarrassment she still felt about Warren Plotz. She was glad the man couldn't see the slight flush in her face.

"Hello," she said.

"Thought you'd appreciate an update on Richard Coduri," he said. "We're not ready with our full report yet, but there are a couple things we can tell you right now. Got a minute?"

"Absolutely. Thank you," Amy said, pulling out the legal pad where she was keeping her notes on that case.

"The first part won't surprise you. Coduri was lit up on cocaine when he was killed. There was enough of it in his blood to make an elephant high."

"Not surprising. What's the second part?"

"Well, that's the real reason I'm calling. I read in the paper your sheriff arrested a woman for this crime, right?"

"Yes. Melanie Barrick."

"Well, I don't know who your perpetrator is, but it's sure not a woman."

"What do you mean?"

"The victim's right forefinger had a fair amount of someone else's skin cells under it. The medical examiner concluded Coduri had scratched the perpetrator. We got a nice sample of it. Being a murder case, we prioritized it, so one of our guys just started testing it today. He told me it clearly belonged to a man."

"Are you sure?"

"That Y chromosome is pretty hard to miss."

"Got it. So if it's not Melanie Barrick, who is it?"

"Haven't gotten that far," Burleson said. "We probably won't be able to run it through for matches for another week or two. But if you have a woman in jail for this, you might want to consider a different theory of the crime."

"Like murder-for-hire," Amy said.

"Like that," Burleson said. "But that's your department, not mine. I just do the science."

They soon ended the call. As she settled the phone back into the cradle, Amy let out a long breath. Murder-for-hire was a trickier thing to prosecute. The first component was proving some kind of consideration had been exchanged, most likely monetary — though a drug dealer could also pay in product.

Amy hadn't yet bothered prying into Melanie Barrick's financial situation. All she knew was that the Sheriff's Office had seized nearly $4,000 in cash during its raid.

There had to be more. It was just a question of where Barrick kept it. The Sheriff's Office was generally pretty thorough when it executed a warrant, so Amy didn't think

Barrick had more cash lying around.

But a bank was always a possibility. A clever dealer could easily find ways to make ill-gotten gains look legitimate.

Amy looked down at the list of to-dos she had been steadily working through. She already knew she wasn't going to get it done before the weekend after all.

In the cop shows, someone barks out "pull her financials" and, within minutes, a detective has a full list of every banking transaction the defendant has made since childhood, including the large cash withdrawal the day before the crime in question was committed.

Reality wasn't quite as easy. Amy could issue a subpoena that would give her access to Melanie Barrick's banking records, yes. But first, Amy had to figure out where Melanie Barrick banked. And she couldn't just subpoena every bank in the area and hope to get lucky. That would be considered fishing, and judges didn't like it. She had to know for sure where Barrick had accounts.

There were two ways to go about that. Subpoenaing the IRS would allow Amy to see if Barrick reported interest income from any financial institutions in her most recent tax return. It would also take a minimum of ten weeks to get a result.

Or . . .

Amy was soon lifting herself from behind her desk and moving toward the parking lot. Desper Hollow Road was less than ten minutes away. She didn't even need to look up the address.

Before long, Amy was driving under the railroad tracks, past a trailer belonging to a Confederate history enthusiast, and to the driveway for 104 Desper Hollow Road.

The best-case scenario would have been a nice, full garbage can — brimming with discarded bank and credit-card statements — that had been put out on the curb. Courts had ruled that defendants had no reasonable expectation of privacy when it came to their garbage, which was considered abandoned property. And if it was on the curb, that meant Amy wouldn't be trespassing when she accessed it. She'd be completely in the clear.

Except, of course, Melanie Barrick had been in jail for the past two weeks. So Amy didn't think she'd find any garbage.

There was, however, the second-best-case scenario.

A mailbox.

Tampering with a person's mail was a federal crime. Likewise, removing the contents of a defendant's mailbox was a clear violation of the Fourth Amendment.

But if the mailbox happened to be open? Well. Accidents happen.

And if Amy happened to be walking by, on a public street, and be able to see a bank statement lying there in plain sight? Well. That would just make her observant.

Amy stopped the car and got out. With her toes still firmly planted on Augusta County–owned Desper Hollow Road, she pulled a pen out of her pocket, inserted it into the hooked handle for the mailbox, and pulled.

"Oops," she said as the lid opened.

She peered inside. The box was stuffed almost to the top. Again using the pen — so, if it came up, she could truthfully testify she had touched nothing — she started sifting through the pile. A lot of it was junk. Or bills.

But about midway through, she came across a half-letter-size envelope from Shenandoah Community Credit Union, addressed to Melanie A. Barrick. Amy recognized a monthly statement when she saw one.

She kept going, all the way to the bottom of the pile. But that was it.

It was entirely possible there were other accounts, of course — a bank that didn't mail monthly statements, or an account whose statements had yet to mail out this month. But this was a start.

Amy drove back to the office and was soon typing up a subpoena duces tecum to Shenandoah Community Credit Union, whose corporate offices were in Staunton — and whose in-house counsel Amy knew.

By two o'clock, she was hitting Send on the email. At precisely 3:17, her phone rang. It was the Shenandoah Community Credit Union lawyer, ribbing Amy about dumping this on him on a Friday afternoon.

By 4:36, Amy was looking at four months' worth of bank statements for the account belonging to Melanie A. Barrick.

There was currently $733.28 in her account. The last transaction was a deposit for $278.17 the previous Thursday, from Hokie Associates. Amy Googled the name. It was the local Waffle House franchisee.

Waffle House? The Shenandoah valley's most notorious cocaine dealer had been working at Waffle House? That was a twist.

There were no substantial withdrawals or transfers. The largest deposits were a series of weekly additions from Diamond Trucking, Inc., but those were below $600, and they had stopped in early March. The largest withdrawals were the monthly mortgage payment and a weekly check for $250 to an Ida Ferncliff, but that also stopped a month ago. Childcare, Amy could guess.

Otherwise? Electric company. Phone company. Insurance company. The usual suspects in what appeared to be a paycheck-to-paycheck existence.

Barrick used her debit card to buy groceries. But from the amounts, it didn't seem like she had been eating much lately. The largest cash withdrawal was $20, from a local ATM.

If Barrick was leading the life of a freewheeling, free-spending drug kingpin, she wasn't doing it through this bank account. Based on the evidence here, she was somewhere between living frugally and flat broke.

There was obviously more to Melanie Barrick than Amy had yet discovered. She'd just have to keep looking.

Fifty-Two

I couldn't say the previous week had flown by, because time in ad seg drags along in the most tedious way possible.

Mr. Honeywell had gone disturbingly quiet, not visiting or calling. He had sent one note, saying preparations for the trial were going well, and that he had been in touch with Ben. About what, it didn't say. I couldn't think of what Ben could do to help my cause. Especially from New Jersey, or wherever he was now.

The note ended with instructions to keep my spirits up.

Right. Because that was so easy.

With nothing better to do than play and replay past events, I thought back to my last interaction with Mr. Honeywell. The way he had looked at me in the Sheriff's Office was different. Like I was now a lost cause. Like I was no longer the innocent he thought I was. Like I was back among that population of clients whose fate didn't cause him to lose sleep at night.

And there wasn't much I could do about it. I couldn't even write back to tell him that, for the sake of my mental health, I could really use a fuller update on my defense. I didn't have a stamp. Again, no commissary. The guards weren't allowed to loan me one either — it was against jail policy for guards to give inmates gifts of any kind.

Sunday, April 8, the day before my trial, was like most others, except that it rained. Late in the afternoon, a guard asked me if I still wanted to exploit my constitutional rights by going outside. I surprised him by saying yes.

We went through the whole routine with the cuffs and the cage. Once I was locked inside, I was uncuffed and left free — funny word, that: free — to explore my fifteen-by-fifteen confinement.

The rain was warm, the kind that nourished crops and flowers and life, and it came down steadily. Not quite a torrent, but close. The water pooled on top of the concrete, forming puddles that danced with every drop that fell on them.

Within a few minutes, I was drenched. It wasn't all that uncomfortable, once there was no more dry on me to get wet. If anything, the rain felt glorious.

My primary reason for going outside was that I wanted to sleep well that night. Fresh air, I thought, would help. So would exercise. I started by running little laps around my cage, then ripped off a set of push-ups.

I was strong. Powerful, even. Now five pounds below my regular weight, my ribs were tight against my skin. When I moved, there was less of me for my muscles to push around. I could do anything. I leapt onto the chain-link fence, almost like I was flying.

Then I dropped back to the ground. My feet hit with a satisfying splash. I did some planks, just because I could. Then some squats. Same reason.

It was strangely exhilarating, working myself this way. Maybe because it reminded me that my body — which was denied to me in so many ways while I was incarcerated — was still mine.

The air was pungent, earthy and alive despite all the concrete around me. The rain began falling harder. I increased my exertion accordingly, springing with manic ferocity from one movement to the next, sprinting and lunging and hurtling myself all over until my chest actually ached from sucking in so much oxygen.

But that was what I wanted, of course.

To feel alive.

When I was done — when I had pushed myself beyond exhaustion — I lay in the middle of the cage, spread-eagle, and let the rain pound me while I thought about Alex.

I didn't go with one of my usual memories of him from the past. For the first time since this ordeal began, I permitted myself to think of the future. I visualized, of all places, Shenandoah Valley Social Services, and the day when Alex would be returned to me. I thought of the family services specialist, Tina Anderson, lowering my baby into my arms. I thought of his joy, of my relief, of seeing those beautiful eyes and the bright smile that beamed out from under them.

It was dangerous, thinking this way.

I clung to it all the same.

FIFTY-THREE

Rain always made for a tough day.

Rain meant she couldn't take the baby outside. Rain meant being cooped up in the house, trying to come up with new ways to entertain the child.

And that wasn't as easy as it used to be. When they first got the baby, he didn't stay awake for more than an hour or two at a time. He was in that phase the books referred to as the "fourth trimester," where he acted like he was still in the womb. When he wasn't eating or pooping, he was sleeping.

Not so anymore. The naps were fewer and further between. The child was waking up, wanting to explore the world.

The woman was fine with that. During the day, anyway. She had gotten a Baby Bumbo, a marvelous foamy little chair that allowed him to sit up; a Johnny Jump-Up, which attached to a doorframe and let him work his little legs; an exercise mat with little animals dangling from a padded bar that looped overhead. He generally didn't last more than about fifteen minutes with each activity, but she could keep him busy, because she had the energy to move him from thing to thing.

Not so at night. By then, she was just done. Because unlike a biological mother, who had all sorts of hormones coursing through her body preparing her for just this purpose, her body had nothing extra in it. Just fatigue.

It didn't seem to matter to the baby. There were times at night — especially when he hadn't been able to go outside during the day — when he woke up for a feeding, and then was just *awake*.

This was one of those nights. A rainy day had led to a restless evening. The boy had woken up at eleven p.m. and stayed awake until one a.m., wanting to play and be entertained the whole time. Then it took the woman — who was so tired she couldn't fall back to sleep right away — another hour to drift off.

Now it was four a.m. and he was up again. The woman rolled over when she heard him. She thought about nudging her husband awake and saying, "Your turn." But he was sleeping soundly, and she wasn't, so . . .

Off to the baby's room she went. She would just feed him quickly and put him back down.

Or so she thought. The baby was having none of it. He wanted more playtime. Thus began the battle of wills, a battle she wasn't going to win. The more the woman tried to settle him and get him to sleep, the more revved up he became.

Somewhere in the middle of this, as the woman's frustration mounted, the man came into the nursery.

"Hey, what's going on?" he asked stupidly.

"What does it look like?" she snapped, holding up a very wide-eyed baby for him to see.

"Okay, okay. Why don't you go back to sleep and I'll take over?" he said, trying to take the child from her.

"No," she said, turning so he couldn't get the baby. "I'm fine. Just go to bed."

"You're not fine. You're exhausted. It's all right. Let me take him."

"I told you, I'm *fine!*" she yelled.

That set the baby to wailing. The woman looked down at what she'd done. Then she started crying too.

The man stepped in, gently wresting the baby from her, then giving his sleep-deprived wife a hug.

"Shh. It's going to be okay."

His comforting words came out in a whisper.

FIFTY-FOUR

The night passed slowly. Despite my best effort to tire my body, my mind was still a boiling pot of anxiety. It made sleep nearly impossible.

The drug trial was really just the first legal hurdle I had to clear, with a murder trial still to come — and a Social Services case peppered in between.

But the fact was, if I couldn't get over that first one, the rest of it became moot. Losing the drug case meant losing Alex. Whoever had taken him would have effectively won.

At that point, what did anything else matter? What did I really have to live for? They might as well execute me.

Maybe that sounds bleak. But at two o'clock in the morning, when you're in administrative segregation, when your milk is failing and the whole world thinks you're guilty, optimism is in pretty short supply.

I had just barely nodded off when the

overhead light came on. Six o'clock had arrived. I was up immediately, like a firecracker had gone off in my cell, my heartbeat already reverberating against my sternum. I went to the door and waited for a guard to pass by, which they were required to do every so often.

"Hey, you guys know I have my trial today, right?" I asked.

"We know, Barrick," the guy said. "We'll come get you later."

I was too nervous to eat breakfast, which was pretty grim anyway. Not long after the tray was cleared away, two corrections officers came and got me, eventually handing me off to two sheriff's deputies, who drove me to the courthouse.

When I reached the holding cell behind the courtroom, I was surprised to find a dress hanging for me from the bunk — courtesy of Mr. Honeywell, I assumed. It was my Kate Middleton dress, which he obviously liked. The heels I always wore with it were attached in a plastic bag. I wondered how he had gotten into my house to retrieve it.

Pinned to the hanger was an envelope with my name on it. Inside I found a copy of an old picture. It showed a dashing young couple, a man and a woman who were clearly in love. From their hair and clothes — to say nothing of how faded the colors were — I'd say it was about 1975 when the photo was snapped. I could practically hear the soundtrack to *Saturday Night Fever* playing in the background.

Then I did a double-take. The striking young man in the photo was Mr. Honeywell: a much younger, much slimmer, much less stooped, much more hirsute Mr. Honeywell. He was wearing a wide-collar shirt and a plaid suit that looked positively debonair on him. His eyes weren't buggy or baggy. They were, if anything, striking.

He was handsome. And more than that, he was happy.

And I could immediately see why. It was all about how the woman looked at him. She adored him. You could tell immediately. Any man who had a woman look at him like that — even once — could surely not have turned out like Mr. Honeywell.

Was she a girlfriend or . . . ?

No, a wife. They both had wedding bands on.

Then I looked more carefully at her. Dark hair, cut almost exactly like mine. Dark eyes, set sort of like mine. Slender build, just like me. She was wearing a belted dress that was the forty-years-ago version of the one hanging in front of me.

She looked like she could be my sister or my mother. I knew she wasn't, of course. But the resemblance was uncanny enough that I held the photo and stared at her for a while longer.

Then Mr. Honeywell's voice came from the far end of the holding area.

"Darn near knocked the wind out of me the first time I saw you," he said. "Felt like I was seeing a ghost."

He had been sitting quietly on a bench, watching me study his past.

"So she was . . . this is your wife?" I said, holding up the picture.

"Her name was Barbara."

"If you don't mind my asking: What happened?"

He took a moment.

"Bad luck, I guess you could say. Bad luck and bad driving. We had been married about a year. She was pregnant. Pretty far along too. We were happy as could be, just a couple kids launching their lives together. We were out for a drive in the country one night. Not going anywhere, just driving. I had a Pontiac GTO, a real muscle car. I was taking the turns pretty tight, gunning the engine. She was just laughing. She had a great laugh, Barbara did. Clear as a bell."

He reflected on that for a beat, then continued.

"We went around this one corner and there was a farmer on a tractor, right in the middle of the damn road, going about five miles an hour, no lights on, nothing. What the hell was he doing out there after dark? I have no idea. I jerked the wheel to avoid hitting him and lost control of the car. We broadsided a tree. Passenger side. We weren't wearing seat belts. No one really did back then."

He stopped.

"Is that where you got your limp?" I asked.

He nodded.

"Busted up my insides a lot worse than it busted up my outsides."

"And Barbara?" I asked.

He just shook his head.

"You never remarried?"

"Never even dated again. Spent too many years either hating myself or feeling sorry for myself to be much good to anyone."

He rose from the bench and walked over to my cell. Those sad, protuberant eyes locked on mine.

"I let her down," he said. "I'm not going to let you down."

I nodded solemnly. "Thank you," I said.

"Okay, then," he said. "Get dressed. I'll

see you in there."

Once he was gone, I set down the photo and changed into my dress. The belt cinched two holes tighter than the last time I had worn it.

Maybe ten or fifteen minutes later, a sheriff's deputy came to retrieve me. He shackled my ankles — though not my wrists — then led me down the hallway, toward a door labeled COURTROOM NO. 2.

The walking was difficult, between my too-short strides and my heels, and it took all my concentration not to trip. As such, I was still looking mostly downward as I entered the courtroom.

In my peripheral vision, I could see Mr. Honeywell's rounded form at the defense table. It wasn't until I reached the table and was able to steady myself a little that I was able to lift my head.

The first thing my eyes fell on was the prosecution table. Amy Kaye was on the far side of it, sitting ramrod straight. A man I didn't recognize was talking to her, though I couldn't hear what he was saying. There was something about him that filled me with an immediate and visceral dislike for him. It must have been the bow tie.

I moved on, scanning the gallery. Sitting

in back were a man and a woman who looked bored and clutched notepads. Reporters, obviously.

A little farther up, sitting in the third row, was Teddy, with Wendy faithfully by his side.

My parents were in the second row. I was still shocked by how old they looked. My mother smiled nervously at me. My father lowered his head, then brought it back up. I brought my hand up to wave at them, almost despite myself.

But I didn't have time to consider their presence for very long. The deputy who had brought me in gently grabbed my elbow.

"Ma'am," he said. "Judge is about to come in. It's best if you're facing forward."

That finally unrooted me. I shuffled into place next to Mr. Honeywell.

I looked toward the judge's desk. It was still empty, but it towered over all other furniture, leaving little doubt about who was the most important person in the room. All my focus — every bit of karma I might have ever accrued in this life — was now aimed at that desk, and the man who would soon be sitting in it.

Commonwealth v. Barrick, a one-day trial that would determine the trajectory of the remainder of my life, was about to be under way.

FIFTY-FIVE

Amy Kaye had been studying Aaron Dansby in her peripheral vision and didn't like what she was seeing.

His hands shook as he shuffled papers and files around on the table in front of him. He maniacally sipped from his water glass, a sure sign of a dry mouth. He kept tapping his foot. And Aaron Dansby wasn't a foot tapper.

He also kept craning his neck toward the back of the courtroom, sneaking glances at the gallery. He seemed okay — if barely — when his only audience was Melanie Barrick's friends and family.

Then a man and a woman entered the room. The man was a reporter from *The News Leader* whom Amy knew well. She didn't know the woman, but she also appeared to be a journalist of some sort, perhaps from *The Daily Progress* out of Charlottesville. Or the *Times-Dispatch* in

Richmond. Or, who knew, maybe *The Washington Post*?

Whatever the case, it was apparently too much for Dansby. As soon as the reporters were settled in their seats, he turned toward Amy.

"You know what?" he said. "I think I'm going to let you handle this."

"What are you talking about?" Amy said.

"The trial. You're more ready for it than I am, anyway. And I just think . . . Well, it'll be better if you do it. Is that okay?"

"Uh, yeah, fine," Amy said.

More than fine, actually. Her only real worry about this trial — the only way the commonwealth could have snatched defeat from the jaws of victory — was if Dansby screwed up something. Melanie Barrick's last best chance for an acquittal had just recused himself from the case.

"Great," Dansby said. "I'm going to go back and tell the press that I'll be available for comment afterward, but I'm letting my deputy handle the proceeding. It's good for them to see me able to delegate important matters. It shows leadership."

Amy was bemused but didn't show it. *Leadership?* she wanted to say. *You're chickening out three minutes before a trial begins and you're calling that leadership?*

But she just said, "Okay. Sounds like a plan."

He rose and went toward the back of the courtroom and briefly spoke to the reporters. Then he took a seat by himself two rows in front of them. Amy quietly added this to the list of stories she'd tell in private someday when Aaron Dansby was in the US Senate.

Then her focus shifted back to the front of the room. A deputy was entering. Judge Henry Robbins was behind him.

"All rise!" the deputy said, then called the proceeding to order, finishing by asking God to save the commonwealth and this honorable courtroom.

"Good morning, everyone," Robbins said. "Have a seat, please. Do we have any last-minute issues we need to take care of before we get going?"

"No, Your Honor," Amy said.

Honeywell just shook his head.

The judge nodded toward Amy. "Okay, then. Is the commonwealth ready to open?"

"Yes, Your Honor," Amy said, buttoning her jacket as she stood up.

She had not planned on giving this opening. But she was prepared all the same. She had written it, word for word, for Dansby to deliver; and she had gone over it with him enough times that she could do it without notes.

"Four hundred eighty-seven grams, Your Honor," she said. "It's an incredible amount of cocaine. In a relatively small county like ours, it's practically an epidemic, all by itself. Four hundred eighty-seven grams is . . . well, it's enough to destroy families. It's enough to cause crime to rise. It's enough to stoke the fires of domestic violence. It's enough to seep into every crevice of our sleepy little valley, to flow from the hardcore addicts all the way down to the high school student who just might be curious to know what cocaine tastes like. And I think we both know how disastrous that first taste can be in a young person's life."

She bowed her head, taking a moment of silence for that unknown teenager whose life was now hurtling out of control. Then she looked back up.

"Yet four hundred eighty-seven grams is exactly how much cocaine the Augusta County Sheriff's Office found hidden in the defendant's house, tucked in the air-conditioning duct just above her child's crib. Now, we don't know exactly how much cocaine the defendant might have had before the Sheriff's Office came and raided her house. Did she start with six hundred grams? Eight hundred? A whole kilo? There's no telling. But we do know what she had been doing with it, and what she planned to do with the rest of that four hundred eighty-seven grams. She was going to sell it, Your Honor. According to the statute, we don't even need to prove that to you. But the evidence is still very clear on this point. We found all the paraphernalia needed for distribution — scales and razors and plastic bags. We found a list of phone numbers that correspond to known drug users.

"But that's not all, Your Honor," Amy continued. "You're surely going to hear the defendant testify that this cocaine we found in her house wasn't hers. Even though it was above where her child slept, in a place where no mother would let any stranger go, she's going to ask you to believe the fiction that this cocaine belonged to someone else, that she had no idea how it just happened to arrive in that place. But when she testifies to that, the thing I'd like you to remember is that we also found her personal cell phone — complete with pictures of herself, her husband, and her child — alongside the drug paraphernalia."

Amy paused to let the judge absorb this critical piece of information.

"So that's dominion and control, right there. The defense will surely try to confuse things, Your Honor. As you are perhaps aware, Mr. Honeywell has subpoenaed a convicted drug dealer to testify about who-knows-what. You're also going to hear from a neighbor, maybe some other folks, who will likely tell you they have no personal knowledge of Ms. Barrick selling drugs. But none of that is going to matter. What matters is four hundred eighty-seven grams of cocaine, found in the defendant's house. Drug paraphernalia, found in the defendant's house. The defendant's cell phone, found with the drug paraphernalia. It's as clear-cut a case of possession with intent to distribute as you'll ever see. Thank you."

She sat down, pleased with her delivery.

"Thank you, Ms. Kaye," the judge said, then turned back to the defense table. "Mr. Honeywell, would you like to open now?"

Honeywell barely bothered standing. "I'll open after the commonwealth has put on its case."

"Which is your right. Very well. Ms. Kaye, would you like to call your first witness?"

Amy nodded at the bailiff, who was already on his way to the back of the courtroom to fetch Peter Kempe. Amy had kept an eye on the detective — and all his colleagues, really — throughout the past week. He had done nothing to further raise her suspicion.

Kempe entered the courtroom wearing a nice-but-not-too-nice suit and a sloppily knotted tie. He nodded as he passed by the judge, took an oath, then settled into the witness stand.

With the sheet of questions she had written out for Dansby as a guide, Amy put the witness through his paces, starting with Kempe's credentials and moving from there. Kempe testified about how he was approached by one of his regular informants, who then made a small buy for the Sheriff's Office. That led to the warrant, which led to the raid, which led to the evidence.

Amy then guided the detective through how the cell phone they discovered did not have a password, enabling the deputies to quickly ascertain it belonged to the defendant; how the state lab certified that the powder they found was, in fact, cocaine, a Schedule II drug; how the phone numbers they found matched known offenders; and so on.

Kempe was brick-wall solid, as Amy knew he would be. This was the government at its best: two seasoned professionals staying on

534

script, presenting their evidence in a nice rhythm, no surprises.

Then Amy announced she was done with Kempe, and Judge Robbins invited Honeywell to cross-examine the witness.

The script was now at its end. Honeywell was standing up, getting ready to remove some bricks from the wall they had built.

This, Amy knew from long experience, was where the trial really began.

Honeywell started slowly, taking his little shots where he could. Did Kempe ever see Ms. Barrick handle the drugs? No. Did he see Ms. Barrick make a sale? No. Did he ever investigate whether someone might have stolen Ms. Barrick's cell phone and placed it with the drug paraphernalia? No.

It was all harmless to the prosecution, and Kempe was a seasoned master of the one-word answer.

Then Honeywell launched on a new angle of attack.

"Now, the names and numbers you found in the box," he said. "You said you had seen those before?"

"Yes," Kempe said.

"Where?"

"As I said, they were known to us as drug users," Kempe said.

"Yes, but where specifically had you seen them before?" Honeywell asked.

Amy recognized a line of questioning that would lead straight to Mookie Myers. This was the door that had to stay closed. She leapt to her feet.

"Objection," she said. "It's outside the scope of his original testimony."

"Your Honor, Detective Kempe has said twice now they're known drug users," Honeywell said. "We have a right to explore how it is he knows that."

"I agree. Objection overruled," Robbins said. "Continue, counselor."

"Thank you, Your Honor. So, again, Detective Kempe, was there a recent case where you saw those same names and phone numbers?"

"Yes."

"And what was that case?"

Kempe bent toward the microphone and said the words Amy had been hoping to prevent.

"The Mookie Myers case."

"Thank you, Detective. And in case the court isn't familiar with that case, can you please enlighten it: Who is Mookie Myers?"

"He was a drug dealer who was convicted of possession with intent to distribute and is now incarcerated."

"And what drug was Mr. Myers convicted of possessing and distributing?"

"Cocaine," Kempe said.

"As you know, and as I'm sure the court knows, drug dealers often will brand their product, using a stamp to give it a kind of identity. What was the name of the brand Mr. Myers sold?"

"It was called Dragon King."

"Thank you. And can you tell me: Do you know where Mr. Myers's cocaine is at the moment?"

Amy felt a sinking in her stomach even as she bolted to her feet. How did Honeywell know about that? But, of course, she could already guess. Sheriff Powers had questioned a number of deputies about the missing drugs. Nothing like that stays quiet very long. Honeywell had lived here his whole life and knew just about everyone. Eventually, the talk was bound to reach his ears.

So this was the defense's plan: Embarrass the hell out of the Augusta County Sheriff's Office, confuse the issue, and hope it would lead to an acquittal. Amy had to begin damage control immediately.

"Objection," she said. "These are two separate cases. There is no relevance here whatsoever. It doesn't matter whether the drugs found in Ms. Barrick's house once belonged to Mookie Myers or to the Easter Bunny. All that matters is that she possessed them."

"On the contrary, Your Honor, this is very relevant," Honeywell said. "This goes to the heart of this case and to the heart of our defense, which is to question how it was possible a woman with no criminal record and no history of drug use could have possibly come into possession of this amount of cocaine. As you know, we have broad latitude to explore alternate theories of this crime, and we will be bringing witnesses who will do just that. That includes Mr. Myers, who has been subpoenaed and is in this courthouse, waiting to testify."

"Sorry, Ms. Kaye," Robbins said. "He's right. I have to allow this. Objection overruled. Go on, Mr. Honeywell."

"Thank you, Your Honor. As I was saying, Mr. Kempe, do you know where the cocaine from the Mookie Myers case is at this moment?"

Kempe shot a glance over at the prosecution table, but there was nothing more Amy could do for him. He was trapped. To say the truth was to jeopardize this case and bring humiliation to his department. To say otherwise was to perjure himself.

Finally, he said, "No."

"Did you destroy it?" Honeywell asked.

"No."

"Is it in the evidence locker?"

"No."

"So where is it?" Honeywell pressed.

"I don't know," Kempe admitted.

"Is it in the possession of the Augusta County Sheriff's Office?"

"I don't know."

"You don't know," Honeywell said, really twisting the knife. "Is it the normal policy of the Augusta County Sheriff's Office to let cocaine go unaccounted for?"

"No."

"Did you perform an investigation when you discovered it missing?"

"Yes."

"And what did you find?"

Kempe screwed up his face as he searched for the shortest answer possible. He finally came up with: "We were unable to reach a conclusion."

"So that cocaine could be anywhere, right?"

"I guess so."

"It could even have been planted in my client's house, yes?"

"Objection," Amy said. "The word 'planted' is very charged in a drug case, and there's no foundation for it here."

539

"I'll restate the question," Honeywell said. "Is it possible that the cocaine from the Myers case is the same cocaine that was found in Ms. Barrick's house?"

"I don't know."

"Well, come on now. You've said you have no idea where the Myers cocaine is and that it could be anywhere. Could it, in fact, have found its way into Ms. Barrick's house?"

"Yes, I suppose so," Kempe said.

"Could, in fact, someone in law enforcement, maybe even one of the officers who helped you execute the warrant on my client, have been the person who took it out of the evidence lockup?"

"Objection. Calls for speculation," Amy said.

"All I'm asking is if it's a *possibility*," Honeywell said. "That's not speculation. That's just connecting the dots."

"Objection overruled," Robbins said. "Answer the question."

"I don't know," Kempe said.

"But again, if you don't know where that cocaine is or who took it, you have to admit that's a possibility."

Kempe, looking utterly miserable, said, "Yes."

"Thank you, Detective," Honeywell said. "Nothing further."

"Ms. Kaye," the judge said. "Would you like to redirect?"

Desperately.

"Yes, Your Honor," Amy said, standing and facing Kempe, who was now sitting in a slumped position.

"Detective Kempe, is there any evidence whatsoever that the cocaine missing from the lockup is the same cocaine you found in Melanie Barrick's house?"

"No, ma'am," he said, his back getting straighter.

"In fact, new cocaine flows into this country all the time, from all over the world. Is that right?"

"Yes."

"So if cocaine goes missing from one place in Augusta County and shows up in another place in Augusta County, that's little more than a coincidence, yes?"

"That's right."

"And no matter where this cocaine originated, you still found it in the defendant's house, correct?"

"Yes."

Which was what counted, as far as the statute was concerned.

So, yes, a door that Amy had wanted to stay closed had been flung open. And it would undoubtedly result in some unfortunate headlines for the Augusta County Sheriff's Office, thanks to two astute scribes in the back of the room.

But as she rested the commonwealth's case, she remained convinced it would only matter so much. The law, the evidence, and — most important — the judge were still on their side.

FIFTY-SIX

Had I never seen that picture of Mr. Honeywell — the young, dashing Mr. Honeywell — I might not have recognized it.

But there was something about watching him flay that sheriff's detective that was almost like seeing the years peel off him. He had an energy to him, a vitality that managed to come through even though he was still as superficially wrinkled and frumpled as ever.

By the time he was done, my eyes were probably bulging just as much as his. He little resembled the attorney who had seemed like such a disappointment all those weeks ago, when I first saw him on the video screen from the Middle River Regional Jail. This was no easily cowed ham-and-egger. This was a fearsome advocate.

And it turned out those surprises were just starting. Mr. Honeywell made a brief opening, saying he intended to sow significant doubt in Judge Robbins's mind about my guilt.

Then he announced his first witness.

"Your Honor, I'd like to call Ben Barrick to the stand."

Of all the names I might have been expecting to come out of Mr. Honeywell's mouth, Ben's was near the last. Mr. Honeywell had mentioned in that note to me that he had been in communication with Ben, but it had never occurred to me that meant he was coming back to Staunton.

Ben appeared in the back of the courtroom, escorted by the deputy who had gone to fetch him. Why wasn't he in Philadelphia or Elizabeth or wherever it was he was making his new life? And what did he possibly have to say to the court that would matter?

My feelings toward him were in a tangle. He had run out on me. His only communications since then had been that lame text and that cryptic voicemail. Our marriage was clearly over.

And yet.

Here he was. Testifying on my behalf. And he was still my Ben, the sexy guy with the V-shaped torso who flirted with me in Starbucks, the man who had laughed with me during some of the best times of my life and held me during some of the worst. I couldn't turn off those memories.

As he approached the witness stand, he looked like the same old Ben, wearing his professor clothes and Malcolm X glasses. I thought maybe some spell would have been broken by his betrayal. But no. I still missed him terribly and was just happy to have him there.

In his left hand, he carried a leather folder. He raised his right hand, swore to tell the truth and nothing but, then had a seat in the witness box.

"Mr. Barrick, what is your relationship to the defendant?"

"We've been married for nine months."

"Before you married, how long were you in a relationship with her?"

"Four years."

"And you live with her?"

"Until she was incarcerated, yes."

"In all that time together, and now living with her, have you ever known the defendant to use or sell drugs?"

"No, sir. Absolutely not. When she was pregnant with our son, she didn't even use aspirin."

Our son.

"So when the Sheriff's Office went into your house and brought nearly half a kilo of cocaine out of your house, you were . . .

Well, tell the court, what was your reaction?"

"I was dumbfounded, thunderstruck, pick whatever word you like. I knew those drugs weren't hers. It simply wasn't possible."

"Were they yours?"

"No, sir. Absolutely not."

"Do you have a criminal record or any history of drug use?"

"No, sir."

"So, given your certainty the drugs didn't belong to your wife, what was your next step?"

"I tried to be logical about it. If they didn't belong to Melanie, whose were they? And how did they get there? I guess you could say I was compelled to find out."

"So you performed your own investigation, is that right?"

"Yes, sir."

"Are you trained as an investigator?"

"In a manner of speaking, yes. Up until recently, I was a PhD candidate in history. While my inquiries tended to be more focused on the past than the present, the skills overlap."

"I see," Mr. Honeywell said. "Can you please tell the court about your investigation into the cocaine that was found in your house?"

"It focused on finding the source of the drugs. I believed that if I could trace the drugs back to the source, I could learn how they had ended up taped in our air-conditioning duct. I couldn't get my hands on the drugs themselves, of course. But I did have a picture of them, thanks to the commonwealth's attorney, Mr. Dansby. He posed in front of them for the newspaper. I was able to purchase a digital copy of that photo from *The News Leader* and enlarge it."

He withdrew a few copies of a photo from his leather folder.

"This is Defense Exhibit One, Your Honor," Mr. Honeywell said. "We've got copies for everyone."

The bailiff shared the photos with the judge and Amy Kaye.

"As you can see, some of the cocaine has been bagged for individual sale and comes with a stamp marking its brand," Ben said. "This particular mark is a dragon with a crown on its head, and the words 'DRAGON KING' are emblazoned underneath."

"Why is this significant?"

"That was my first avenue of investigation. I was able to talk to some local cocaine users. They were people who naturally wouldn't give me their names, but they told me Dragon King was the brand sold by Mookie Myers. They said it was an excellent brand, one they enjoyed very much and missed now that it was no longer available."

"No longer available? For how long?"

"Since Mr. Myers was sent away, apparently," Ben said. "I asked if they knew where Mr. Myers had gotten it from. Most did not. But one person I was able to get friendly with, and who took pity on me because he knew my wife had been locked up, told me Mr. Myers had intimated it came from a dealer who went by the name of Gotham, and that Gotham was based somewhere in New Jersey, perhaps Camden."

Camden. The first hotel in that credit card bill that so enraged me had been in Camden.

"I see," Mr. Honeywell said. "And what did you do with this information?"

"I traveled to New Jersey. I went undercover and assumed the lifestyle of a would-be drug dealer and I inquired about Gotham. I spent several days in Camden, New Jersey, until I was able to ascertain that Gotham was based in Elizabeth, New Jersey. I then traveled to Elizabeth, where I succeeded in making contact with a man who identified himself as Gotham."

"And how did you do this?" Mr. Honeywell asked.

"Again, by posing as a person who was interested in becoming a business associate of Gotham. I had a certain amount of money I was able to show around. That helped."

I thought of Ben, his jazz records, our Vitamix. He had obviously liquidated every possession he had of value and emptied his bank account. That was yet another reason he used the credit card. He was trying to preserve as much cash as he could.

Another thing also made sense: why he had left his professor clothing behind in Staunton. He knew he wouldn't be needing it, with what he had to do. Slightly aged hip-hop clothing would have served him well.

"So you were able to convince people in New Jersey you were the real thing?"

"I did. I realize this is a delicate subject, Mr. Honeywell, but race is a very powerful thing in this country. I have no doubt I was able to gain entree into this world because of my skin color, because I claimed to know Mr. Myers, and mostly because I know how to talk the language."

"Talk the language?"

"Yes. My appearance and speech patterns in this courtroom notwithstanding, I grew up poor and black in Alabama, and I certainly know how to speak that way. I also know how to present myself in a courtroom. My people call what I'm doing right now 'talking white.' I believe psychologists call it 'code switching.'

"The point of all this is that I had no trouble passing myself off as a country boy from Virginia who was coming to the big city to get hooked up. I found the drug dealers I interacted with to be less sophisticated and, I suppose you could say, more guileless than what you might be led to believe from television. It took a week or so of hanging around, but I had a relatively easy time infiltrating its ranks and convincing its leadership I was legitimate."

"I see. So you succeeded in making contact with Gotham?"

"I did," Ben said, adjusting his glasses.

By this point, I was deeply engrossed in the story. Just the picture of my academic husband acting like some wannabe drug kingpin was almost too incredible to believe. And yet I knew he possessed both the intelligence and, obviously, the will.

The will to clear his wife. The woman he loved.

I had already silently forgiven him for leaving me. He thought I was in jail this whole time. That's why he didn't leave a note for me. It was why the voicemail had included the line "I hope you get this someday." It was why the text had begun with "I know I won't hear back from you."

He wasn't aware Marcus had bailed me out and therefore didn't think he could contact me. And, of course, I had been too angry — and hurt — to reach out to him. By the time he reported what he had discovered to Mr. Honeywell, who could have told him I made bail, I had already been put back in jail for Coduri's murder.

"And what happened when you met with Gotham?" Mr. Honeywell continued.

"He confirmed for me that Mookie Myers was one of his associates. He said Mr. Myers used to drive up to Elizabeth to purchase product from him, and he expressed remorse that Mr. Myers was now incarcerated. He asked me if I wanted to take over for Mr. Myers. I asked Gotham about Dragon King, because I assumed Dragon King had been his invention. But he said he knew nothing about that. He said that must have been Mr. Myers's doing. I used that as an excuse to leave Gotham's company without buying any drugs. I told him I was only interested in Dragon King."

"What did you do next?"

"I returned to Virginia, where I visited Mr. Myers at the Haynesville Correctional Center. I told him that I believed someone was framing my wife for drug possession and he told me he was sorry to hear that, but that he had his own problems. Then I told him she was alleged to be selling the Dragon King brand."

"How did Mr. Myers react to that?"

"He became very animated and upset. I think he took a lot of pride in Dragon King. He told me he designed the stamp himself, and that there was only one of them in existence. Back when he had been in business, he guarded it very fiercely. He knew his customers had come to value the brand and that other dealers might try to imitate it. I showed him the picture that we now refer to as Defense Exhibit One. He was very agitated that someone else would be, in effect, taking credit for his work."

"Did Mr. Myers tell you anything else?"

"Not really. He was too angry and our discussion basically ended on that note. Then I came back home and was able to talk to you, and you were able to tell me about how the Mookie Myers drugs were discovered to have gone missing from the evidence lockup."

"And what conclusion did we reach at that point?"

"Well, it seemed pretty obvious that the drugs from the lockup with the one-of-a-kind stamp were the same drugs and stamp that showed up in my house. Someone must have taken them from the evidence lockup."

"And who might have done that?"

Ben maintained his fair, even tone. "I don't know."

FIFTY-SEVEN

Amy Kaye didn't know either.

But as Ben Barrick's direct testimony neared its end, she realized she had a way to find out.

Start with what now seemed clear: The missing drugs from the evidence lockup really were the same drugs that had been found at Melanie Barrick's house. What had seemed like nothing more than a wild, shot-in-the-dark defense theory now appeared to have the imprimatur of truth. Ben Barrick's testimony had been unimpeachable enough to convince her of that.

Not that it meant his wife was innocent. It merely meant there was someone else involved. And — shockingly, Amy realized — it was the same man she had been stalking for three years now.

It fit the facts as she understood them: A member of the Augusta County Sheriff's Office who raped women in Augusta County

— and *only* Augusta County — found a way to steal drugs from the evidence lockup.

The defense was trying to convince the judge that the deputy had planted the drugs in Melanie Barrick's home, then walked away from them. But that simply didn't jibe with Amy. What would the deputy have to gain from that? Nothing.

No, the deputy was looking to cash out on what he had stolen. Knowing he couldn't sell the drugs himself, wasn't it possible he looked for someone else to do the selling? He was well acquainted with Melanie Barrick, having stalked her for weeks before he raped her. He would know she was the least likely person to come to law enforcement's attention. An educated white woman. A mom.

And — he had probably figured this out already, as Amy had when she subpoenaed Barrick's bank records — she was flat broke. And therefore desperate.

She also had no apparent connection to the deputy. It made her the perfect accomplice.

And why would Melanie Barrick cooperate with the man who raped her?

Simple. She didn't know it was him.

Spin it forward from there. Melanie Barrick was happily selling drugs, giving a cut to the deputy. Everyone was making money. Then along came Richard Coduri, seasoned drug snitch, informing Skip Kempe — whom Coduri had previously worked with — what was happening. Kempe investigated dutifully and found all the evidence needed to indict Melanie Barrick.

Which would seem to indicate Kempe wasn't the guy. Just as Melanie thought.

Keep spinning. Now in deep trouble, Barrick asked her partner for help. He would know that if the whole thing unraveled, it would be worse for him than for Barrick. A drug-dealing sheriff's deputy would also face a charge of official misconduct, which could put him away for an additional eight years, if the judge decided to make the sentences consecutive.

So the deputy — a man with that Y chromosome that appeared so vividly under the state lab's microscope — killed Coduri. Which explained the seemingly unlikely fact that the fingerprint found in Room 307 of the Howard Johnson matched the one left by the man who raped Lilly Pritchett.

And that, of course, was his most critical error: the fingerprint. Every deputy who checked in at a crime scene — and she had to imagine that was every deputy on duty — had their fingerprints on file, in case they left prints by accident. Why hadn't Justin Herzog gotten a match when he first ran the print? Because he kept deputies' fingerprints in a separate database.

So all she had to do to find the rapist, Coduri's killer, and Melanie Barrick's accomplice was to have Herzog search that database.

She was tempted to pull her phone out of her bag and send Herzog an email, but there was no way she could get away with it. Judge Robbins would lose his mind. And he was the kind of judge who just might have been curmudgeonly enough to hold her in contempt over lunch break to teach her a lesson.

So she forced herself to wait.

Meanwhile, she had a trial to continue. In some ways, her job here didn't change. If anything, getting a conviction was now more important than ever. She could use it to leverage Melanie Barrick into testifying against her partner at the next trial.

She treaded carefully in her cross-examination of Ben Barrick. He was excellent on the stand — intelligent, authoritative, articulate. She tried once or twice to trip him up, but she could tell it was backfiring. Every question she asked just gave him an opportunity to flesh out his narrative.

But what did it add up to? Again, very little. Nothing the husband said changed the amount of cocaine that had been found in their house next to his wife's cell phone. She knew Judge Robbins, the former prosecutor, wouldn't forget that.

After she wrapped up with Ben Barrick, the defense put Mookie Myers on the stand. Myers quite obviously didn't want to be there, and Honeywell was trying to worm under the convict's skin, perhaps get him angry enough to start talking.

Myers was no dummy. He may have blabbed in prison to Ben Barrick, but he was too cagey to do so on the record in a courtroom. Anytime Honeywell got anywhere close to a matter that might hurt the prosecution — or confirm Barrick's testimony — Myers responded with, "On the advice of my attorney, I am invoking my Fifth Amendment right against self-incrimination."

Good little criminal that he was, he was keeping his mouth shut.

When offered the opportunity to cross-examine the witness, Amy declined. There was no need. Myers hadn't helped the defense one bit. She wanted to keep it that way.

Honeywell's next move was to call Bobby

Ray Walters, Barrick's neighbor. He introduced a low-quality video, showing Richard Coduri driving up Melanie Barrick's driveway at 1:01 p.m. on Monday, March 5, the day before the Sheriff's Office raid. Then it showed him leaving sixteen minutes later.

The defense was clearly trying to intimate that Coduri was the one who planted the drugs. All it really did was further confirm Kempe's testimony. On cross-examination, it wasn't hard to introduce the idea that neither Walters nor anyone else knew what Coduri had done during those sixteen minutes. It was, in fact, very possible he had gone to Barrick's house to buy drugs, just like he had told Detective Kempe.

Beyond that, Amy thought it was a huge mistake to bring Coduri anywhere near this proceeding. All it did was inflame an already fired-up judge.

Perhaps for that reason, Robbins announced a lunch break once Walters was dismissed. Amy couldn't have asked for better timing. The whole time Robbins was chewing his tuna sandwich, he'd be thinking about poor, dead Richard Coduri.

But that, of course, was only a small part of why Amy had been eagerly anticipating a break. The moment the last wisps of Robbins's robe disappeared from view, she pulled out her phone and tapped a message to Justin Herzog. Exhorting him to treat the matter with the caution it was due, she asked him to run Person B from the Pritchett case — and the unsub from Room 307 — against employees of the Augusta County Sheriff's Office.

She marked it urgent, then hit Send.

FIFTY-EIGHT

When they brought me back out into the courtroom for the afternoon session, Ben, Teddy, and Wendy were clumped together in the third row. Ben gave me a thumbs-up. Teddy waved. Wendy smiled awkwardly.

My parents were now sitting with them. They must have been able to take a long look at my brother and make an educated guess. I could only imagine what kind of family reunion that was shaping up to be.

I turned and took my seat next to Mr. Honeywell.

"Things are going well, right?" I said softly.

"We'll find out," is all he said.

Court was soon back in session. I was now expecting such legal sorcery from my attorney, I was actually a little disappointed when he declared, "I'd like to call Marcus Peterson."

I didn't know what good Marcus would

do. Sure, he was a fine character witness. He could testify I wasn't the drug-dealing type. But how much would that really help?

The back doors opened, and in walked Marcus. He didn't look at me as he passed the defense table. He seemed extra boyish, wearing a suit jacket that was just a little too big for him. As he was sworn in and pointed toward the witness box, I got the distinct sense he was uncomfortable being there.

"Thank you for joining us, Mr. Peterson," Mr. Honeywell said. "I know this takes a lot of courage on your part."

Courage? To say I was a nice person who didn't sell cocaine?

"Thank you," he said in that soft voice of his.

"When did you meet the defendant, Ms. Barrick?"

"Two thousand eleven. I was the manager at the Starbucks in Staunton, and I hired her as a barista."

"How would you describe your relationship with her?"

"To her and to others or to myself?" he asked cryptically.

"Both, if you would."

"Well, to her and to others I would say we were good friends, nothing more."

"But that's not the whole truth, is it?" Mr. Honeywell said.

"No, not exactly."

"Could you please tell the court what you mean?"

"It's fair to say I've been in love with Melanie Barrick since I first laid eyes on her."

Oh.

My cheeks grew hot. Ben had told me this many times. I was just embarrassed to have it coming out in court — for Marcus and for myself.

And I still didn't know what it had to do with a drug case.

"Did you ever share your feelings with her?"

"No," he said. "I was close to doing it many, many times. I fantasized about revealing my feelings to her, to be honest. I would play it out in my head when I couldn't sleep at night or when I first woke up in the morning."

"You never did it, though?"

"No. At first I think it was because I was her manager and it wouldn't have been appropriate. After that, well, she was already dating Ben Barrick and . . . I guess I always knew she didn't feel quite the same way about me. For her, it was friendship and nothing more."

"So you pursued that friendship?"

"Yes. I thought a small piece of Melanie, whatever I could get of her, was better than no Melanie at all."

"You're also married, are you not?"

"Yes, but to be honest, that wasn't as much of a factor. I would have left my wife in a heartbeat for even a chance at a relationship with Melanie."

"Does your wife know this?"

"Probably. I always denied it, but she'd have to be pretty stupid not to know I was lying to her."

He was saying these things in a straightforward, matter-of-fact way. I could only imagine the anguish that was behind the words.

"When Ms. Barrick got pregnant and then got married, did that have any impact on your feelings?"

"No. Or, actually, I should say yes. I was more in love with her than ever. Seeing her pregnant was . . . It was very bittersweet. I knew the circumstances under which she had gotten pregnant, of course, so that was part of it. But I also knew how much joy it brought her. I could see that becoming a mother fulfilled her in a way she had never been fulfilled before.

"But more than that, I . . . I just loved the way she looked pregnant, the way it gave her this glow. I dreamed about what it would be like if . . . if I were the father of her child. I wanted to raise a child with Melanie more than anything. I guess I've just . . . I've always just wanted to be around her, no matter what she's doing. She's just so pure and . . . and perfect."

This was strangely brutal, hearing him confess these things. Even without meaning to be, I had been a source of incredible grief in a friend's life. I was just glad Kelly wasn't in the courtroom. I would have been mortified for her.

Mr. Honeywell, who didn't have such an avalanche of feelings to dig through as he heard all this, just kept moving ahead.

"But after she became pregnant and got married, you couldn't be around her as much as you wanted, is that right?"

"That's right."

"So what did you do?"

"I spied on her."

My stomach dropped.

"What do you mean?" Mr. Honeywell asked.

"I gave her a teddy bear that had a camera installed in it. I set it up on the shelf in the nursery."

Oh God. I was now gripping the table in front of me as I replayed all the things I had done in that nursery over the past three months; all the times I had walked in there and casually exposed myself, completely unconcerned that Mr. Snuggs was perched up on that shelf with a perfect view of the chair; all the intimate moments Alex and I had shared that I thought were between only the two of us.

Had Marcus been watching every time? Was he getting off on glimpses of me bare-breasted? It was all making me too nauseated to even think about.

"And how did you monitor this camera?" Mr. Honeywell asked.

"I had an iPad I kept hidden away from my wife, from everyone. The camera fed into that. When my wife was out of the house, I would pull it out and watch Melanie."

"The iPad saved everything, is that right?"

"Yes."

"Is that how you came to possess the footage you're about to show the court?"

"Yes," Marcus said.

"Your Honor, this is Defense Exhibit Number Two," Mr. Honeywell said, extracting three DVD jewel cases from his briefcase. "It comes from Mr. Peterson's iPad. I only became aware of this myself on Friday. It is unedited. I'd like to play it on your television over there, if I could."

"Go ahead," Judge Robbins said.

I was so stunned by everything, I had to concentrate on my breathing, just to make sure I was still doing it. Marcus had turned to face the television, so his side was to me. I was experiencing this odd contradiction: I could barely look at him, but I also couldn't stop myself from staring.

All these years, I had no idea. I thought of the hundreds of times we had been alone together, or drunk together, or watching a movie, or whatever. He had never allowed so much as a single wandering hand to stray somewhere it shouldn't have.

He apparently preferred to violate me from afar.

The television screen in the corner blinked on, then went from dark to light. Then my nursery appeared.

"When was this video taken?"

"March the fifth at 1:07 in the afternoon," Marcus said.

"How do you know?"

"The file is time-stamped," Marcus said.

Nothing happened for about twenty seconds. The shot came from up high on the shelf, where Mr. Snuggs the teddy bear had lived. Then Richard Coduri — halo scar and all — entered the room and set down a duffel bag.

He unzipped it, then produced a cardboard box, which he quickly stashed in the closet.

"Judge, I'm sure you recognize Richard Coduri, the commonwealth's informant in this case," Mr. Honeywell said. "And that box is Commonwealth Exhibit Number Seven."

"Yes, Mr. Honeywell, thank you."

Coduri pulled a small stepladder out of the bag and set it up in the middle of the room. He fished out a screwdriver and, in very workmanlike fashion, unscrewed the air-conditioning vent. Then he set it on the floor.

"Okay," Mr. Honeywell said, continuing his commentary. "Now Commonwealth's Exhibit Numbers One through Six are about to make their appearance."

Coduri went back into the bag and produced six plastic packages of white powder and some duct tape. He climbed the ladder and stuffed powder bags inside the vent one at a time, tearing off the lengths of duct tape he needed to secure them there.

The courtroom had gone completely silent. I glanced over at Amy Kaye. She was as white as the cocaine.

Once Coduri was done with the large bags, he replaced the vent. His final act was to tear open a small package of cocaine. He sprinkled some of it in Alex's crib, then carefully poured the rest on the webbing between his thumb and forefinger.

He snorted it, then stood in the middle of the room and savored the high as the drug entered his bloodstream.

I already couldn't wait to show this video to Social Services.

Coduri left the room, with a now mostly empty duffel bag over his shoulder. Then the screen went black.

No one in the courtroom moved. No one spoke. Mr. Honeywell was giving us all a moment to reflect that *Commonwealth v. Barrick* had just been turned on its head.

Finally, he resumed with, "For the record, Mr. Peterson, what was the time the video ended?"

"One fourteen," he said.

"Thank you. Now, when did you become aware of this video?"

"The day it was shot."

"Did you tell Ms. Barrick?"

"No," Marcus said through a constricted throat.

"Why not?"

Marcus was breaking down now. "I knew it would destroy our friendship if she learned about the camera."

"Did you tell her about it after she was arrested?"

"No."

"Why not?"

"Same reason."

"Even though she was in jail?"

"I thought . . . I thought something would . . . I thought she would be cleared. I didn't think anyone could believe for one second that Melanie was a drug dealer. I kept expecting the sheriff or the prosecution would come to their senses and drop the charges. Then I wouldn't have to tell her about . . . about any of this. And we could go back to being . . . Whatever we were."

"What made you change your mind?"

"When that didn't happen, I . . . I just knew I had to . . . That's why I came to you Friday afternoon. The thought of . . ."

He couldn't keep going. He was crying too hard. The last words he choked out before Judge Robbins called for a recess were, "I love you, Melanie. I still love you. I always have. I always will."

Maybe it was cruel of me. But I turned away as he spoke.

FIFTY-NINE

In eighteen years as a prosecutor, Amy Kaye had been surprised by defense testimony before. She had even been caught outright flat-footed a few times.

But never like this. Not even close.

Ordinarily, evidence like this never made it to trial. The defense showed it to the prosecution, which then dropped the charges.

Then again, thinking like a defense attorney, she could understand why Honeywell had played it the way he did. He had been handed a gift late on a Friday afternoon before a Monday-morning trial. Chances were he wasn't going to be able to get his client out of jail before the weekend anyway, so why give the prosecution a chance to counter the video?

Drop your stun bomb at trial. Get your acquittal. Limp off as the hero.

Amy was glad Robbins had called for a

break. Ostensibly, it was to give the witness time to compose himself. Amy needed a moment or three herself. She was too shocked to fully process what was happening.

Then she checked her phone for messages and her astonishment only amplified. Justin Herzog had written back.

Amy,
Don't know where you're going with this, but Person B and the Howard Johnson unsub isn't one of ours. I ran that print against our crime scene database. Anyone who has logged in at a crime scene in Augusta County is in there. No hit.

Good luck,
Justin

Amy stared at the phone, now totally demoralized. She had again allowed herself to believe she was close — so close — to finding this rapist. She had again been wrong. About everything.

Melanie Barrick was no drug dealer. She had clearly been framed. And the man who planted the drugs was now dead — more than likely killed by his accomplice, whose identity remained every bit as much of a mystery as it had been for three years.

All Amy knew for sure was that she couldn't continue prosecuting Barrick. Not for this crime. Not for the murder either. Trying to go forward with some kind of murder-for-hire scenario would be both unjust and patently absurd, a terrible example of the government being unable to give up the ghost.

As the bailiff brought the court back to order and a red-faced Marcus Peterson resumed the stand, Amy knew what she needed to do.

End this farce.

"Okay, welcome back, everyone," Judge Robbins said. "Your witness, Ms. Kaye."

"Actually, Your Honor, in light of the evidence that has just been presented by the defense, I don't believe there's any reason to continue this prosecution," she said. "The commonwealth would like to ask you to dismiss all charges."

There was a minor eruption from the back of the courtroom, where Melanie Barrick's family began clapping and cheering.

The judge held a hand in the air. "Order. Order, please."

He waited until they quieted, before continuing. "Is the commonwealth sure about that?"

"Yes, Your Honor."

"Mr. Honeywell, I assume that would be satisfactory to your client?"

Honeywell struggled to his feet. "Your Honor, given what my client has been put through, I would ask that the charges be dismissed with prejudice."

"I think we can all agree to that. Ms. Kaye?"

"Absolutely, Your Honor."

"Very well," Robbins said. "Then unless anyone has any more business with —"

"Actually, Your Honor, there is one more thing," Amy said. "And as long as we're all here, I might as well put it on the record."

"Okay, go ahead."

"As you're aware, the commonwealth also has a homicide charge pending against Ms. Barrick," Amy said. "Given the video and some physical evidence the state lab has made me aware of, the commonwealth will not be going forward with that charge against Ms. Barrick at this time. As long as the folks at Middle River don't have any lingering issues with Ms. Barrick, there's no reason why she should remain in detention."

"Very well," Robbins said, then gamely banged his gavel. "This court is adjourned."

"All rise," the bailiff said.

Amy turned to see Melanie Barrick's family rushing toward the divider. There was also someone else coming toward the front of the courtroom.

Aaron Dansby, the duly elected commonwealth's attorney.

"What the hell was that?" Dansby demanded. "Why did you dismiss the murder charge?"

"Are you dead from the neck up?" Amy said. "Did you see that video? There's not a shred of evidence against that woman. Keeping her in jail would be a travesty."

"But she killed Richard Coduri. She shouldn't be going free. She should be on her way to the damn needle."

Dansby was seething, though none of his words were coming out in a normal voice.

It was more of a whisper.

SIXTY

My arms were wrapped around Ben, who had practically leapt over the divider to get at me. Teddy and Wendy weren't far behind him. My parents lingered farther back.

As Ben hugged me, I melted into him. It was a lovely feeling. A safe feeling. It had been so long since I experienced anything like it.

"I missed you so much," he murmured.

Then I was jolted by a sound I never wanted to hear again.

That horrible, horrible whisper.

I had heard it so many times — not just on that awful night but in my head ten thousand times after, whether awake or dreaming. I'd know it anywhere. As much as I wished I could, I would never forget that whisper.

And the thing about this particular whisper was that it wasn't in the ether, like usual. It was here. In the courtroom. Coming from a man who was maybe ten feet from where I stood.

My body stiffened. Ben half pulled away. "What is it?" he asked.

I couldn't answer him. It was like my mouth was paralyzed. The man was quietly berating Amy Kaye. I stared at him, gripping Ben even tighter.

Then I saw the man's eyes and I knew beyond the slightest doubt. They were eyes I had seen many, many times; eyes I could never forget.

Blue-gray. Enchanting. The kind of eyes you could get lost in.

My son's eyes.

Suddenly, I had the answer to the one question that had so bewildered me from the start: Why Alex? Why go through all this trouble to steal this particular baby when there were so many other babies who could be had for far less trouble?

Who would value Alex over every other child?

The answer was now obvious:

The man who raped me.

Alex's biological father.

"Hey, you okay?" Ben was asking. I was lucky he was still holding me. Otherwise, I might have fallen over.

The man was already on his way out of

the courtroom. Amy Kaye was following after him. They seemed to be having some kind of disagreement. Or rather, I should say he seemed to be irate about something.

Before it was too late, I willed myself to move. I reached over to Mr. Honeywell, who was quietly packing his things into a battered briefcase, and tugged his sleeve.

"That man," I said. "The one leaving the courtroom right now. Who is that?"

Mr. Honeywell turned in his unhurried way and studied the man, who was now disappearing out through the swinging doors at the back of the courtroom.

"Oh, him?" he said, like it was an afterthought. "That's Aaron Dansby. He's the commonwealth's attorney. I actually thought he was going to try this case. He usually does when there are reporters around."

Of course. I knew the name, from having read the paper. I just didn't know the face.

Didn't it all make even more sense now? I had always assumed the man who attacked me was some kind of degenerate or drifter, some antisocial misfit who lived on society's outer fringes.

Aaron Dansby was none of those things. He came from a prominent family whose members had been among Augusta County's leading citizens for generations. And he wasn't just a lawyer, but the lawyer responsible for prosecuting all the crimes in the county.

Was that how he had gotten away with it for so long? He had practically been born into the seat of power, raised with intimate access to the inner workings of law and government. And then he actually assumed the seat, and it enabled him to guide investigative priorities, manipulate evidence, and stay one step ahead of anyone who might figure him out.

Or maybe he was just that good at not getting caught in the first place. That's part of what the whispering accomplished, wasn't it? None of his victims would be able to recognize his voice from, say, a political advertisement.

And there were victims. Plural. Even though Amy Kaye had never confirmed it, I had seen it in her eyes when I asked, *I'm not the only one, am I?*

There were probably scores of us. I wondered if they were all like me. Young. Confused. Clueless. Powerless.

Had any of us ever lobbed an accusation his way? Or would it not have mattered? Would he — with his influence and family connections — have been able to swat it out of the sky before it had a chance to take flight?

I could now see everything. Dansby had probably been keeping an eye on me. He had seen my belly swell throughout the summer and fall and had known there was a reasonably good chance the child I carried was his.

My move to a single-family house had been easy enough to track — home sales were public record. If anything, it made his life simpler. There were fewer potential witnesses to his stalking out on Despcr Hollow Road.

Once the baby came out, healthy and desirable and half his, he made his move. I could only imagine what Social Services thought of Aaron Dansby and his wife — this young, wealthy, connected couple — when they first expressed an interest in adopting a baby. None of the foster families I had ever come across would have come close to comparing. Social Services probably couldn't wait to give Dansby a child.

Then the challenge became how to separate me from Alex. But really, how difficult was it for a commonwealth's attorney to frame someone for drug possession?

He obviously had unfettered access to the evidence room. He could have come and gone from that room without arousing suspicion. What's more, he would know the security procedures at the Sheriff's Office and would therefore be able find a way to circumvent them.

And then, in Richard Coduri, Dansby had found a willing accomplice: a seasoned drug snitch, and the kind of opportunist who would love an easy payday. Dansby hired Coduri to plant drugs in my house, reveal to the Sheriff's Office I was a dealer, and tell Social Services I planned to sell my baby.

Dansby thought Coduri would remain anonymous. When Mr. Honeywell jeopardized that, Dansby eliminated Coduri, knowing everyone would think I had done it. That put me on the road to prison — and to the permanent loss of my child — in two ways.

"Hello?" Ben said. "You with me?"

Again, I didn't have words for him. It was all so disorienting, I had entered a kind of trance. I couldn't summon anger, or relief, or satisfaction, or whatever combination of emotions I once imagined I would have in the unlikely event I ever learned my rapist's identity.

All I wanted was my son back.

I looked at Mr. Honeywell. If I blurted

out, "Aaron Dansby was the man who raped me," even the lawyer who had just helped save my life would look at me like I was drunk or high or both. Aaron Dansby was political royalty, not to mention the chief law enforcement officer of Augusta County.

No. I needed evidence first.

And it was already occurring to me there was a very simple way to get it. All I had to do was go to Dansby's house. If he had Alex, it was all the confirmation I needed.

One picture of Dansby or his wife holding Alex would prove everything.

SIXTY-ONE

I waited until I had processed out of Middle River Regional Jail before telling Ben what I now knew, explaining it to him as we made the drive back home.

Even unflappable Ben was shocked. But once he got over that — and digested the implications of what I was saying — he agreed with my logic.

It was the logistics he was stumbling over.

How, he asked, were we going to get this picture? The sum total of our photographic equipment consisted of the cameras on our phones, neither of which had a very powerful zoom function.

I didn't have an answer for him until we passed Bobby Ray's house, with its SMILE! YOUR ON CAMERA! sign out front.

"You think Bobby Ray can help?" I asked.

"That's not a bad idea," he said.

Teddy and Wendy were waiting for us at the top of the driveway, having already decorated my front door with a sign that read WELCOME HOME MELANIE!

I thanked them for the sentiment, then told them about the work we had to do. Neither of them had a decent camera either, so I set them on the task of getting on the Internet and learning where Dansby lived. Ben and I trooped down the driveway to Bobby Ray's trailer and knocked on the front door.

"Hey," he said when he saw me. "You won?"

"I sure did. Thanks for your help. I'd be in jail for a long time if it weren't for you."

"No sweat, man. As far as I'm concerned, it's like this shirt I got: 'You mess with me, you mess with the whole trailer park,' " Bobby Ray said, grinning. "I'd let you borrow it sometime, except it's got one of them flags on it you don't like."

"Thanks," I said. "But I'm actually looking for another favor, if you don't mind."

I described what I needed to accomplish. When I was done, he said, "Oh, yeah, sure. I got a camera that can zoom in real nice for you. It'll take me a little while to unhook it. But then I can be ready to rock and roll."

"Great," Ben said. "And there's one more thing, if you don't mind."

"Sure. Shoot."

"Do you have a gun we can borrow?"

I could barely believe the words had come from my pacifist husband's mouth. Ben despised guns. He was constantly railing about the need for more gun control, particularly as young African American men used them to slaughter one another across American cities.

Bobby Ray shoved his hands in his pockets.

"Uh, actually, I don't."

"You don't?" Ben asked.

"Look, don't tell no one," he said. "But I'm a convicted felon. I could get in a lot of trouble, getting caught with a gun. I just make people think I got a lot of them so they don't fool with me none."

Two hours later, the five of us — Ben, Teddy, Wendy, Bobby Ray, and me — were crammed into Ben's car, cruising through Staunton's nicest neighborhood.

We had decided to wait until after the sun was down, relying on darkness to conceal our movements. We were armed with a camera but not a firearm. I didn't want to know how Dansby might respond if he found us skulking around outside his house.

The address Teddy found was on Dogwood Road, which was lined with spacious houses set well back from the road. The Dansby residence was a Greek revival, done in red brick, complete with towering white columns. It was perched on top of a small hill.

"Keep driving," I told Ben. "Park down the street. I don't want anyone inside to see us."

Ben did as instructed.

"Okay, so what's the plan?" Bobby Ray asked me when we stopped. The camera was on his lap.

"Get as close as you can with that thing and then zoom in. If you get a shot of a baby, your job is done."

"So you want me to go up to the house and shoot in the windows?"

"Yeah, if you can."

"Sorry, I ain't trespassing for you. I'm still on probation."

I looked to Teddy. I would have done it myself, but Teddy was taller, in case there were high windows; and he was faster, in case a quick getaway was needed. He was also a lot less likely to scream the moment he saw Alex.

"I got it," he said.

"You'll be careful, right? Don't take any chances. If you think you've been seen, you'll take off running?"

"Yeah, sure. It's not like they know we're coming."

Bobby Ray gave Teddy a brief lesson on how to work the camera's functions. Then my brother left the car, loped up the street, and crossed into a neighbor's yard.

There was silence in the car once he left. No one had anything worth saying.

I was in another body, or another mind, or something. I had woken up that morning in administrative segregation, with nothing more than a toothbrush at my disposal, and was now perhaps moments away from having the evidence I needed to end this awful conspiracy.

Ben was clutching my hand. It was so strange to have him back. I didn't know what our life together would be like, exactly. There was the matter of all the lies he had told me, to say nothing of his shattered career.

But we could figure that all out. He still wanted to be my husband. I knew that now. And I wanted to be his wife.

Maybe that would be enough to give us a new start.

We had rolled down the windows, allowing the sounds of the night to enter the car. There were not many of them. A lone car, somewhere else in the neighborhood. A few crickets chirping. That was really it.

The quiet didn't last long.

Maybe three minutes had passed when we heard automobile engines, lots of them, coming fast.

Three Staunton City police cars ripped past us. Then a Staunton City police van. They were followed by two Virginia state police vehicles; and several more from the Augusta County Sheriff's Office; and an unmarked car — a Subaru, of all things.

"What the . . . ," Ben began.

"Teddy," I said.

The four of us vaulted out of the car.

The police cars turned into Dansby's place. I broke into a jog toward his driveway.

Then I heard the gunshot.

It came from the direction of Dansby's house.

"Teddy!" I shrieked, and started sprinting.

Why had I let Teddy go into such an obviously dangerous situation? What kind of big sister was I? I had allowed my own zealousness to put him in danger, rather than letting good sense guide my actions.

I reached the Dansby driveway and didn't stop, running up it with my arms pumping, heading toward the house. I could hear yelling coming from inside. The front door was wide open. There were cops crouched just inside with their guns drawn. More cops were outside, hiding behind their cars.

Then I saw a blur, dashing away from the side of the house.

It was Teddy, hurtling away from the house.

There were suddenly a half dozen guns trained on him. In the chaos, the cops didn't know whether he was friend or foe, and they weren't taking any chances.

A chorus of shouts filled the night: "Hands up! Hands up! Stop right there!"

"Don't shoot him!" I tried to bellow over the din. "He's my brother!"

As if they knew who I was.

Teddy thrust his hands up and fell to his knees. He was quickly swarmed by three officers, who grabbed various parts of him and dragged him awkwardly behind one of their cars.

"Teddy," I screamed. "Teddy!"

I ran toward him.

"Oh God. Oh God," he was saying.

He was sobbing. I had seen my brother in all kinds of woeful states — as high and as low as you can ever witness another human being. I had never seen him this distraught.

The words coming from him were so garbled by his hysteria I couldn't even make them out. Finally, between gasps, it became clearer.

"Help her. Please, God. Help her."

"Sir, calm down," said one of the cops, who was kneeling next to him behind the patrol car. "Help who?"

"He shot her," my brother managed. "He shot her."

"Who shot her?" the cop asked.

"Dansby. He shot his wife. I was watching her in the living room. As soon as the patrol cars came up the driveway, he walked into the room and he . . . He shot her in the back of the head."

Teddy brought his hands to his face. He couldn't control himself.

"Her head, it . . ." he said.

And then he collapsed, vomiting on the driveway as he did so. I was now behind the car with him.

"Teddy," I said. "It's me, Teddy."

I put my hand on his back, for what little good that would do.

"Requesting emergency medical services," I heard the radio squawk. "We have a white female with a single GSW to the head. No breathing. No pulse."

"Copy that," the dispatch replied.

Then a new voice burst through the static.

"We're going to need a hostage negotiator

drove the things up to the Sheriff's
, where Justin Herzog was happy to
From his noxious-smelling nerve
, he was able to confirm that the
prints matched Person B and the
307 unsub.

guessed she'd eventually be able to
state crime lab to confirm Dansby's
had also been found under Richard
's fingernails.

rom a legal standpoint, she already
erything she needed. She called Judge
s, who was three scotches into his
but still agreed to sign the arrest
for Aaron Dansby without hesita-

ver liked that li'l sumbitch," he

Amy took this neat package — the
ints, the warrant — to Jason Pow-
was playing the nineteenth hole
found him. A smile spread across
as she explained everything to him.
called Staunton City Police Chief
iams, who mobilized his Critical
Response Team. With assistance
gusta County's CIRT, they quickly
their strike on the Dansby resi-

ce then, Amy had been more of a

in here. The suspect has barricaded himself
in a room upstairs. He's taken an infant
with him. He says he'll shoot the baby if
anyone tries to come in."

Sixty-Two

From the time she left the courtroom, it had taken Amy Kaye about forty minutes to figure it out.

Longer than she might have liked. But still less time than an episode of *Dancing with the Stars.*

She started with Dansby's fury over her decision to drop all charges against Melanie Barrick. He couched it in all the usual ways — it was bad for his reelection chances, what would the party think, they couldn't be soft on crime, et cetera — but it was still notable for its vehemence. She had never seen Dansby care that much about one of their cases.

She thought about the evidence lockup. Who, besides sheriff's deputies, had access to it? Personnel from the Augusta County Commonwealth's Attorney's Office, of course.

Then she thought about the fingerprint.

And the fact that it wasn't
Amy was in the database. S
prosecutors. Everyone co
enforcement eventually w
database.

Except for one man:

Dapper Dansby, the guy
in front of the cameras e
but who never went to
never dirtied his hands
of investigation.

It also explained his
exclusivity. After all,
Aaron as commonwea
father. Had the elder
his son? That remained

The timeline of atta
neatly into Dansby's b
hits in 2002–03? Dan
up high school. The
2004–10? He was of
school. Then in 201
and the rapes came i

It all fit. Still, she
sure this time.

Dansby had not
after the trial, allo
unfettered trip into
Living to grab a few
have his prints on t

She
Offic
help.
cente
finge
Room

Amy
get th
DNA
Codur

But
had ev
Robbi
evenin
warran
tion.

"I ne
slurred.

Then
fingerpr
ers, wh
when sh
his face
He then
Jim Wil
Inciden
from Au
planned
dence.

Ever si

spectator than a participant, driving along and then watching from afar as a salad of badges and uniforms mixed together. Now and then, she received updates — including that Dansby had barricaded himself in the house with an infant, of all things.

She had received her most recent briefing — negotiations had apparently stalled — when she wandered past a patrol car.

Amy had hung back and not gotten involved as they did their jobs. Then she passed a patrol car and recognized Melanie Barrick sitting inside.

"What's *she* doing here?" Amy asked one of the deputies.

"Supposedly, that's her kid inside," he said. "She tried to get into the house. Took four officers to restrain her. We didn't know what else to do with her, so . . ."

He nodded toward the car, where Melanie Barrick was handcuffed to the backseat.

Her kid. Of course it was.

The child who had been removed from his mother's care shortly after the raid. That was Dansby's son. That's why Dansby had Richard Coduri plant those stolen drugs in the first place. He needed Melanie Barrick to be framed with something serious enough she'd never get the boy back.

How had Dansby managed to convince

Social Services to give him the baby? It couldn't have been difficult. The Dogwood Road address and the Dansby pedigree were more than enough.

"How long has she been in there?" Amy asked.

"Uh, don't know. Little while now."

They paused the conversation — out of respect for the dead — as the sheet-draped form of Claire Dansby was carried out to an ambulance. Then Amy asked to be let into the patrol car. At the very least, Melanie Barrick deserved some company.

"Hi there," Amy said softly as she slid into the seat next to Melanie.

"What's happening?" Barrick demanded.

"Aaron has locked himself in the room. He has your son with him. The hostage negotiator is on the other side of the door. Aaron has made it very clear he'll hurt your son if anyone tries to come in."

"But is he making demands, or . . ."

"I don't know. They haven't let me in the house. From what I understand, they're just talking. I don't know if he's asked for anything specific."

"So how does this end?"

"We don't know. We have snipers in place, and the CIRT team is ready to roll. But those are last-resort options. For now, we just have to be patient. Everyone is prioritizing getting your baby out of there alive."

Barrick just looked up toward the house.

"Sorry about the, uhh . . . ," Amy said, nodding at Barrick's tethers.

"Yeah," she said. "Me too."

"And I'm also sorry I didn't figure this out sooner."

"Took me a while too. Can't blame you."

They both stared up at the house for a long moment.

"Has he fathered other children?" Barrick asked.

"Not that I know of in Augusta County," Amy said. "Then again, until a few moments ago, I didn't even know about your son."

That Aaron Dansby might have other children — a strange extended family, united by a father's brutality — was something neither woman could even consider at the moment.

Soon, a mostly bald man wearing dark body armor approached the patrol car.

Amy felt herself recoiling. Had something happened? Was this it? The news that would haunt Amy forever and positively shatter the woman next to her?

The man introduced himself as Staunton City Police Officer Matt Ezzell and ex-

597

plained he was a trained hostage negotiator. Accurately reading the stricken looks on the women's faces, he began with the news they most needed to hear.

"The baby is fine," he said.

"Thank God," Melanie said, putting her hand over her heart.

"We've been talking with Dansby intermittently. Sometimes he answers us, sometimes he doesn't. We're not getting much out of him, to be honest."

"So what does he want?" Amy asked.

"That's why I'm here," Ezzell said, then peered intently at Melanie Barrick. "He wants you. He says he won't talk to anyone else."

SIXTY-THREE

They couldn't guarantee my safety. Ezzell must have told me that at least four times during a monologue about how anything could happen up there, how Dansby had already killed one woman and might be trying to lure me close so he could kill another.

I didn't care. Alex was in danger. That bested any argument he might make.

Once I finally convinced him I wouldn't be deterred, he had me uncuffed and led me up to the house. The officers who had previously prevented my charge inside were now parting for me like the Red Sea, starch-limbed and grim-faced.

As I entered the front door, I looked to my left. The couch and rug, once neutral shades of off-white, were now splattered with blood. The acrid odor of gunpowder hung in the air.

"So what do I do, exactly?" I asked, pausing at the bottom of the stairs.

"Just get him talking," Ezzell said. "Obviously, the end goal is for him to surrender peacefully."

"No," I said. "That's *your* end goal. My goal is to get my son back."

I didn't give a damn about doing it peacefully.

"Call him Aaron," Ezzell continued. "That will make him feel more familiar with you. Once you get him talking, you want to keep him talking. If he's talking, he's not shooting anyone. You're trying to build a rapport with him. You want him to think you're his friend and that you like him. That'll make him more likely to surrender."

Somehow, I didn't think surrender was as much on Dansby's mind as it was on Ezzell's.

Amy Kaye wasn't far behind me. I turned to her before I started climbing the stairs.

"If anything happens to me, please make sure Alex goes to Ben," I said. "Ben is his father. Those are my wishes. Is that clear?"

"Yes," Amy said.

"You promise?"

"I promise."

"Thank you," I said.

Then I started up. The Dansby staircase had a turn in it. I was soon on the second-level hallway. It was lined with men in thick body armor and helmets, crouched behind plastic shields.

"He's straight ahead," Ezzell said.

I walked to the door and knocked.

"Aaron," I said in the calmest tone I could muster, "this is Melanie Barrick."

"Good. Are you alone?"

"No, there are officers up here with me."

"Still? Jesus," he fumed. "Tell them to go the hell away."

"We'll do that if you hand over the baby," Ezzell said.

"Not a chance," Dansby snapped. "And I'm not talking to you anymore. I told you that."

Ezzell and I exchanged glances.

"Ask him what he wants," Ezzell said in a low voice.

"What do you want, Aaron?" I asked.

"I want to talk to you, alone, without those armed goons ready to storm the door the moment I open it for you. I talk to you alone. That's how this goes."

Alex began crying. It was a sound that reached down into that core of me — the piece of me that was Alex Barrick's mother and nothing else — and set a fire going.

"I'll go in," I said to Ezzell. "Please just clear out your men."

He was shaking his head, but I pressed

on: "Look, Alex and I, we're a package deal. If he's got Alex, he might as well have me. I'd rather be in danger but with my baby than safe out here with you."

"Yes, I realize that, but I can't —"

"Please," I said, putting my hand gently on his arm. "Please let me do this."

Then, from inside the room: "Do it, Ezzell. Clear your men out and let her in."

"I can't do that, Aaron!" Ezzell shouted back. "I can't give you another hostage."

"Your job is to save lives," Dansby said back. "You forget: I've seen your training. You have to prioritize lives above everything. And I'm going to make this decision real easy on you. You either clear your men out and let Melanie in here, or I'm shooting this baby. And I'm giving you exactly ten seconds to make up your mind. Ten . . ."

I surged toward the door and threw my weight against it. "No, Aaron, please!" I shrieked.

"Nine," he responded.

I was already crying hysterically as I grabbed the doorknob, trying to shake it loose.

"Eight," he said.

I pounded down on the knob with two fists, using my hands like a fireman's ax. I struck so hard, the pain radiated up my arms, all the way to my shoulders. The knob didn't give. I screamed, banshee-like.

"Seven," he said.

Alex was crying harder. Was Dansby hurting him somehow? It made me even crazier. I kicked the door, but the lock held.

"Please, God. Do something! *Do something!*" I roared at Ezzell.

"Six," Dansby said.

I backed up as many steps as the narrow hallway would allow, then flung myself at the door with everything I had. It didn't budge.

"Five," Dansby said.

Forget the door. I ran up to Ezzell and grabbed him by the shoulders.

"Four."

"Please! Please!" I wailed.

Ezzell's eyes were darting from the door to his men. Was he thinking about ordering them to charge? Wasn't it too late for that? I couldn't tell what was going on in that bald head of his.

"Three."

I started pounding on Ezzell's armored chest, pleading in broken, nonsensical globs of semi-sentences.

"Two."

And then: "Okay, okay, you win, Aaron!" Ezzell shouted. "Stop the count. Stop it right now. We're going. Melanie is coming in. Just give us a moment here."

I stopped pounding Ezzell. My hands were throbbing. I was bawling and hyperventilating simultaneously.

Ezzell was directing his men's retreat down the stairs. I was trying to steady myself. I *had* to keep my senses about me. Alex needed me.

At least he had stopped crying. I'm not sure I could have gathered my wits otherwise.

"They're going," I said in the direction of the door, my voice cracking. "They're going. Just don't hurt him."

My breathing was still too fast. Ezzell came back to my side.

"You all right?" he asked. "God, this is a disaster."

"Disaster," I said between gasps, "is always closer than you know."

He looked at me quizzically, holding the glance long enough that I could see doubt, regret, and a hundred other emotions telling him this was a terrible idea.

"Just get the hell out of here," I said.

"All right," he said, giving my arm one last squeeze. "Good luck."

He walked briskly away, then made the turn down the stairs. Once he was on the first floor, he hollered up, "Okay, Dansby! We've moved out. But if I hear a gunshot, all bets are off. We will come up there and we won't be talking anymore. Is that clear?"

There was no answer from inside the bedroom. I went up to the door and tapped it lightly.

"It's me," I said. "And I'm all alone."

"Are you armed?"

"No."

"You better not be. If anyone comes into this room with a gun, I'm shooting this baby first and asking questions later."

"I swear to you I don't have a gun."

There was a pause.

"Okay," he said. "You can come in. The door is now unlocked."

A large breath leaked out of my lungs. Even my wildest nightmares couldn't have concocted a scenario like this. I was all alone, going back into a room with the man who raped me.

He was armed. And all I had for protection were my own desperate prayers.

Slowly, I turned the knob and pushed through the door into the room.

The bulbs in the ceiling fan were illuminated, casting a harsh white light on everything below.

There was a dresser immediately to my left at an odd angle, like it had been used as a part of Dansby's defensive fortifications but had been shoved out of the way so I could enter. Halfway across the room, an armoire had been moved so it was perpendicular to the entrance of what was either a large walk-in closet or a master bathroom.

A mattress was leaning against one of the windows. A box spring was against the other.

Neither Dansby nor Alex were anywhere within sight.

"Close the door," Dansby said from the other room. "I want to hear it close."

"Okay," I said, shutting the door forcefully enough it made a noise.

"Now, lock it."

I did as instructed. "It's locked."

"Hold your hands out in front of you. I have to be able to see them."

"Okay," I said, palms extended.

For a brief moment, his head flashed from the other side of the armoire, like he was some kind of frightened forest creature. It went back just as quickly. Then he walked out. He had Alex tight against his body, facing outward, and a gun to Alex's tiny temple.

The sight of it — my small, helpless baby

nough. I've never had a problem perform-
ing with any of you. As you know."

He allowed himself a sick smile before
continuing.

"Claire knew I had a . . . a sexual problem,
obviously. She was willing to do anything.
We even tried having her role-play rape
fantasies for me. It didn't work. My equipment always knew the difference."

"So did your wife know about your . . .
about what you did?"

"No," he said, scoffing. "Claire? Oh God,
no. She thought I suffered from frequent
insomnia and that driving to the park and
going for a walk helped me. I quote-unquote
'drove to the park' at least twice a week. All
the while I was looking for my next encoun-
ter. She never had a clue."

"Couldn't you have tried, I don't know,
therapy or something?"

"Are you kidding me?" he snorted. "I'm a
Dansby. You think Senator Dansby ever had
therapy? Or Congressman Dansby? Or
Governor Dansby?"

I couldn't listen to much more of this
nonsense. "Well, you'll get plenty of therapy
now," I said.

"What do you mean?"

"I mean in prison, Aaron. You understand
this is over, right? Those men downstairs,

with that ugly black pistol next to his head
— nearly made me pass out. I had to lean
against the dresser for support.

"Oh God, please, Aaron, no," I said.

"Don't move," he said.

"I'm not going anywhere. Can you please
stop pointing the gun at Alex? He's your
son, for God's sake. Your son."

"I know that," he said. "Keep your hands
up."

I held them a little higher for his inspection.

"Lift your dress," he said.

"What?"

"I want to see if you have a weapon under
there. Do it slow. Real slow."

I reached down for the hem of my dress,
gathered it in both hands, then brought it
up to my waist.

"All the way up," he ordered.

"It's belted, it won't go any further," I
said.

"Fine," he said. "Put it back down, but
keep your hands up."

As I followed my orders, I studied Alex
more closely. It had been a month since I
had seen him. His face had fleshed out. His
head seemed to have become more sym-
metrical. But really, he hadn't changed as
much as I might have thought.

He had the same eyes. His father's eyes. But his eyes too.

He was still my baby. My beautiful, beautiful baby.

"Can I hold him?" I asked.

"No," Dansby said.

He was swaying back and forth to keep Alex soothed, a bizarre gesture considering he had a gun trained on the child. Alex had a slick of drool coming out of his mouth. His hands were perched on Dansby's arm, his tiny fingers splayed out for support. If he knew his mother had just entered the room, he gave no indication of it. Did he remember me? Or was there no place in his still-forming circuitry for someone he hadn't seen in more than a month?

I chased away the thought and focused on Dansby.

"Okay. So I'm here," I said. "You've got a gun. I don't, but a lot of guys downstairs do. What happens now?"

"We talk," he said.

"About what?"

"About whatever," he said. "I always wanted to talk to one of my women. You in particular. I've thought about you a lot. You may find this hard to believe, but I've probably thought about you over the last year more than you've thought about me. I

really . . . I really do care about you.'

I wasn't interested in any of this. I want him caring about me, thinking me, any of it. I didn't want to be in th room as him. I didn't want to be in th universe.

But Ezzell's instructions — *keep h ing . . . build a rapport with him* — can to me.

"If you care about me so much, v you rape me?" I asked. "Why rape us?"

"Good question. Why. I've asked that same question a lot of times."

"So what's the answer?"

"I don't know. I just . . . I had to.'

"That's bullshit," I said. "You choice every time you entered woman's bedroom and forced her sex with you."

"I know, I know. I don't mear compelled by dark voices or ar It's . . . I'm only really alive dui encounters with . . . with women 1 We told people my wife, Claire, have babies. But the fact is, I'm in with her — with every woman I dated, actually. I can only ever perfo a woman if I've broken into her That's the only thing that exc

608
609

they're not going to let you just walk out of here. You might as well surrender. Give me Alex and let's do this without anyone getting hurt."

"No," he said. "No, that's not how this is going to end."

"Yes, it is. Yes, it is, Aaron. Just put down your gun, give Alex to me, and then walk out with your hands up. Let me raise our son the best way possible. He's your flesh and blood. Give him that chance. I bet if you surrender now, they'll send you somewhere around here. Your family could surely arrange that. We'll come visit you, Alex and I."

That was a lie, of course. And it may have been too thick of one, because Dansby's eyes — which had been trained on a piece of the floor — flared up at me, filling with anger.

"You think I believe that?" he said, gripping the gun tighter. "You think I'm that stupid?"

"No," I said weakly. "No . . . I'm . . . I'm serious. Alex is . . . He's going to want to know who his father is. It would be up to him, of course, but we would absolutely visit you if he was interested."

"You're lying to me right now," he said,

his volume growing. "Don't lie to me. Not you."

"Come on, Aaron. You have to think about what's best for Alex."

"I am, I am!" he insisted. "That's what this is all about. That's why I wanted you here. Just . . ."

He was shaking his head. His teeth were grinding together.

"It's just a real shame Alex won't grow up with two parents," he said. "I wanted that for him."

He removed the gun from Alex's head and stretched it out toward me. I was now staring at the black circle of its barrel from perhaps ten feet away. He was breathing hard and his hand was shaking, but I didn't think he could miss from that distance.

I braced myself, keeping my eyes on his trigger finger. I wasn't going to stand there and let him shoot me. I wasn't there to martyr myself. The moment he began squeezing, I would dive behind the dresser. I just couldn't make my move too soon.

"Aaron, please," I said, hoping to at least bargain for time.

"I'm sorry. I'm really, really sorry," he whispered.

And then, in one fluid movement, he tilted

612

his head back, stuck the gun under his chin, and pulled the trigger.

SIXTY-FOUR

The noise was deafening. A bright-red spray burst from the top of his head and onto the wall behind him.

"Alex!" I screamed.

I rushed forward and grabbed him just as he began sliding from his father's dying grasp.

The sound had terrified him, and his mouth opened wide in a cry. From downstairs, men were shouting. I could already hear feet thundering up the stairs.

"We're okay!" I shouted. "The baby and I are okay. He shot himself. Dansby shot himself."

The last thing I wanted was for them to storm in with their fingers restless against their triggers. I opened the door just as they were about to break it down.

"Are you all right, ma'am?" a guy with a shield asked.

"Yes. Yes, I'm fine. I just . . . I have to get

away from *that*," I said.

I jerked my thumb in Dansby's direction but didn't turn. I had no desire to see what he looked like as his life ebbed away. There were already enough horrible images of him in my head.

Maybe this would change, but I felt no immediate satisfaction or closure in his death. There was a hollow place in me where Aaron Dansby was concerned. Revenge wasn't going to fill it. I already knew the emotions, while still too new to figure out precisely, would be more complicated than that.

At that moment, all I really wanted was to take care of my son. Alex was crying. The gunfire had scared him. So had the yelling. I had to get him away from the carnage.

I carried him downstairs, where a multitude of people with badges asked me if I was injured, if I needed assistance, if I had wounds that required treatment.

"I'm fine. I just want to get out of here," I kept saying, cradling Alex protectively in my arms.

Finally, I was out of the house. I didn't see Ben, or Teddy, or really anyone. The night was still being cleaved by flashing lights, blinding me.

"Ms. Barrick, over here, please," I heard a

woman say.

Not knowing who was calling for me or where, exactly, she wanted me to go, I followed the sound of the voice. It led me near an ambulance, where I was greeted by a woman with square-framed glasses and a tight ponytail.

Tina Anderson, the family services specialist.

"Ms. Barrick, are you okay?"

"I'm fine. We're fine," I said, clutching Alex tighter.

"The EMTs need to examine your son."

"No," I said. "No exams. No EMTs. He doesn't have a scratch on him. He never has."

Alex cried harder. His scalp was getting red from the exertion. Anderson reached for him with covetous hands.

"Ms. Barrick, your son is legally in the custody of Shenandoah Valley Social Services," she said. "I'm ordering you to turn him over right now."

"No," I said, shielding Alex with my body. "Leave us alone. Just leave us —"

"Tina, I don't think we need to press the issue," someone said.

It was a woman's voice, deep and commanding.

Nancy Dement, the director.

She emerged from the darkness and slid next to her colleague, gently putting a hand on her back.

"I've been talking with Amy Kaye from the Commonwealth's Attorney's Office. I'll catch you up later," she said, then turned to me. "We're dropping our abuse case against you, Ms. Barrick. Why don't you and your son go home and get a good night's sleep and we'll see you in court tomorrow, when we'll make it official."

My gratitude was so immense, I couldn't even stammer out a full sentence.

"Thank you," I said. "Thank you."

The system had a soul after all.

Alex chose that moment to renew his complaints at an even greater volume.

"I think there's just too much stimulus for him out here. Is there somewhere quiet we can go?" I asked, looking around for a place where it would just be the two of us.

Nancy Dement found one before I did. "There's no one in the ambulance right now," she said.

"Great," I said. "Thank you."

I climbed into the back of the truck, and Dement shut the door behind me. The sensory overload from the street — all that law enforcement light and clatter — faded away. Alex stopped hollering almost instantly.

There was a small jump seat at the front of the cabin. I got us settled into it, nestling Alex in the crook of my arm. I was still shushing him, even though he had quieted. In the dimness, his big, blue-gray eyes were searching around for something to land on. He glanced my way once or twice, but he mostly seemed transfixed by the roof of the ambulance, the walls, anything but the odd person holding him.

I realized I was holding my breath. Here we were, reunited at last. It was the moment I had longed for. Anticipating it had sustained me through the worst of what I had experienced.

But was this reunion meaningful only to me? Was I just another pair of warm arms to this child? Had our time apart made me a stranger to my own son?

Finally, his gaze locked on me. He studied me blankly, with nothing in his stare betraying his thoughts.

Then, slowly, this sly expression began forming around his mouth, like he had already figured things out but didn't want to let on. It spread next to his cheeks. At last, he couldn't hold back any longer. This huge, toothless grin had broken out across his face.

I swear, even if dementia wipes every last memory from my mind many decades from now, I'll never forget that smile. It's because it won't actually be stored in my brain.

It will be in my heart, along with the most important parts of both of us.

"There's my boy," I purred.

He smiled even broader.

"That's right," I said, my eyes blurring with tears. "I'm your mama. You remember me? I'm your mama."

Of course he did.

He was a child forged in a crucible of terror, born under uncertain circumstances to a poor mother whose own parents had abandoned her. But he didn't know anything about that. He didn't need to know. Babies are nothing if not a chance for the world to start over again.

All that really mattered to him was that a connection had formed between us. It began as flesh, at the moment of conception, but had become so much more, growing stronger and more profound — just as he had grown from a tiny seed into the astonishing creature who was now cooing happily in my grasp.

Through everything that had transpired,

that mother-son bond had not been broken.
I knew now it never would be.

ACKNOWLEDGMENTS

A few years back, I began the habit of taking time each day to think about what I'm thankful for. I call this small daily ritual "connecting with my gratitude."

The great privilege of writing novels for a living — really: I have the best job ever — is often in my thoughts during that time. So is being able to publish them with the top-notch team at Dutton.

That begins with my editor, Jessica Renheim, who has been a magnificent shepherd for this novel and its author. It continues with my fabulous publicists, Liza Cassity and Becky Odell; marketing masters Carrie Swetonic and Elina Vaysbeyn (if you ever see me on Facebook Live, it's because of Elina); cover designer Christopher Lin; production editor LeeAnn Pemberton; and Christine Ball and John Parsley, who oversee this dedicated crew with aplomb.

It is a distinct pleasure, both personally

and professionally, to partner with such an exceptional group of people.

The other key editorial eyes on this book belonged to Alice Martell of the Martell Agency, whose counsel has become essential in my life, and Angus Cargill at Faber & Faber, whose insight and perpetually sharp editing pencil are greatly appreciated.

A variety of experts helped inform the procedural aspects of this novel, and I'd like to thank them — even as I absolve them of blame for any mistakes I may have made.

My legal education was aided tremendously by Middlesex County Commonwealth's Attorney Michael Hurd (who is, for the record, a far better lawyer than Aaron Dansby); by the formidable legal team of Shevon Scarafile and Greg Parks; and by Michael Soberick Jr., who is always good for spit-balling ideas.

Juvenile and Domestic Relations Court Judge Sandra Conyers, Middlesex County Social Services Director Rebecca Morgan, and attorney Carla Hook were all kind enough to let me bombard them with questions. Protecting our children is a tough, often thankless job. We're fortunate when such caring people choose to make it their calling.

Chris Anderson of CP Anderson Trucking

helped me create Diamond Trucking. Forensic psychologist Scott A. Johnson filled in where the textbooks left off when it came to criminal profiling.

And I couldn't have written this novel without Nikkita Parrish, whose toughness and courage are an inspiration.

I also need to acknowledge my friends at Hardee's for remaining tolerant of my hours-long occupation of the corner table each morning. In particular, I'd like to thank the real Melanie Barrick, who keeps the morning shift working smoothly; and my teapot buddy, Robin Young.

Of course, none of what I do would matter at all if it weren't for you, gentle reader. I think of the time you chose to spend with this novel as a gift, and I appreciate it more than I can adequately explain. Oh, and Ginnie Edwards Burger? I am hereby putting the following promise in print: One day, I will visit Erie, Pennsylvania.

I'll end by thanking my family. My in-laws, Joan and Allan Blakely, and my parents, Marilyn and Bob Parks, are a nurturing presence.

All that said, my primary source of joy remains my wife and children. When I connect with my gratitude each day, their health, happiness, struggles, and triumphs are the first and last things I think about. They make me lucky and loved beyond any measure one man deserves.

ABOUT THE AUTHOR

Brad Parks is the only author to have won the Shamus, Nero, and Lefty Awards, three of crime fiction's most prestigious prizes. A former reporter with *The Washington Post* and *The Star-Ledger* (Newark), he lives in Virginia with his wife and two children.